FAMILY MATTERS

FAMILY MATTERS

Kitty Burns Florey

Seaview Books
NEW YORK

Any resemblance to persons living or dead is purely accidental. This is a work of fiction.

Manufactured in the United States of America.

FIRST EDITION

Designed by Tere LoPrete

Library of Congress Cataloging in Publication Data

Florey, Kitty Burns.
Family matters.

I. Title.
PZ4.F6329Fam [PS3556.L588] 813'.5'4 79-66076
ISBN 0-87223-558-0

For my mother, and her mother

Amidst our house's ruins I remain
Single, unpropp'd, and nodding to my fall.

—THOMAS EDWARDS,
"Sonnet on a Family Picture," 1748

Many six-year-olds, though they still do not realize that they themselves will one day die, are beginning to get the idea that death is often connected with old age and that the older people often die first. One girl thus remarked to her mother, "You will be an old, old lady. And then you will die. And I will have babies."

—FRANCES ILG and LOUISE BATES AMES,
Child Behavior

FAMILY MATTERS

CHAPTER ONE

Betsy

Betsy Ruscoe was in bed when her mother's summons came. Judd, beside her, stirred in his sleep at the phone's first ring, and Betsy—instantly roused—ran to answer it before it could ring again and wake him. He could be savage when his sleep was disturbed.

"Betsy? It's me, dear. I hope I didn't wake you up."

"Well, you did, Mom, sort of, but—" She squinted at the clock. "Mother, it's four in the morning!"

"Is it? That late? Somehow I thought you'd be up." She gave her worn-out little laugh. "I suppose I thought my *thoughts* would waken you. I was thinking about you, Betsy. There's something we need to talk about."

"What is it, Mom?" Betsy sat down and supported her head with one hand. She was very tired. She had graded a stack of final exams and fallen into bed at midnight. Judd had been asleep already, and Betsy had lain awake: What did it mean, his going to bed and to sleep without her, without lovemaking? No sex in four days! Was it a good sign (we can be natural and comfortable with each other, as if we were married) or a bad one (he's losing interest in me)? The dilemma kept her awake, with all its peripheral anxieties: the analysis of his calm breathing, for example (is it faked? is he lying there wishing I were someone else?), and the cold panic that came rushing to engulf her whenever she thought of sleeping there alone, night after night, without Judd.

"Can it wait till morning?" She had to get up at seven, give an exam to her graduate students at eight, she could be at her mother's shortly after ten. . . .

"I don't think so, Betsy. I'm not at my best in the morning, honey. I don't know what it is, maybe it's having Terry here. That perfume she uses fogs up my brain." The hollow laugh again. Terry was the new day nurse, her mother's special bane: her perfume, her nail polish, her elaborate hairdo. "She looks like a nurse in a *Playboy* cartoon," Betsy's grandfather, Frank, had commented when they hired her. He held his two hands well out from his chest to indicate bosom. "But she's a fine nurse. We have to appreciate that." Frank also, Betsy could see, appreciated the perfume, the hair, the bosom. But Terry was a good nurse—efficient, smart, and kind. The night nurse, Mrs. Foster, was less reliable and not young. She often slept, though not soundly. It was understood she would awaken like magic if Violet needed her.

"Is Mrs. Foster there, Mom?"

Violet laughed. "Sound asleep. Right out. I told her to go take a snooze in the guest room, and she did."

Damn, thought Betsy. She would have to replace Mrs. Foster. At present, there was no need for her services most of the time, but any day, any night, Violet would be needing intensive nursing. She was not in much pain yet, and she still looked on the nurses as jokes—the sexy Terry, the bumbling Mrs. Foster. But the pain was to come, and for sure.

"So this is a good time to talk, honey. Confidentially, I mean."

"Okay, Mom. Shoot. What's up?" Betsy heard her bright, upbeat tone with disgust. This was not the way to talk to a dying woman. But how else to respond to her mother's girlish chatter? Violet seemed at times to be using death as a mode of flirtation, the way a young girl might once have used a fan.

"You'll have to come over, Betsy."

"*Now?*"

"Why—yes. I can't tell you properly over the phone."

"In the morning—"

Violet's voice went petulant—something new for her. "I *told* you, Betsy. I'm not myself in the morning, and that Terry is here butting her nose into everything, and sometimes I feel so *odd,* Betsy, you just don't know! The morning can be so dark, darker than night!"

She took a deep, shaky breath—even over the phone it sounded teary—and Betsy felt tears behind her own tightly shut eyelids. Don't be like this, Mother, don't be dying, don't be sick, don't cry. . . . Betsy opened her eyes and looked around the darkened kitchen, washed here and there with dim light, the dinner dishes still piled in the sink. Damn. She closed her eyes again. Her mother continued to sniffle. "Mom!" She lowered her voice: keep it quiet for Judd, keep it cheerful for Violet. "Mom, is this really urgent? Really, now?"

Her mother caught the bantering tone and giggled. "It really is." She gave one last sniff. Betsy imagined her wiping her eyes with a lace-bordered handkerchief—one of the extravagances she had decided to allow herself in her last days. "I've always hated tissues," she had announced, and Betsy had hunted up, in the attic, a box of the real article, which Terry now faithfully, flawlessly ironed. It was a small task: Violet, once a facile weeper, now didn't often cry. "But who could blame the poor woman if she did?" Terry would say, tenderly ironing lace.

"I know it's late, honey, but—"

"It's all right, Mom. I'll come over."

"Now?"

"Right now. Is Grandpa asleep?"

"I guess. Oh, Betsy—" Violet hesitated, as she always did when the question of Betsy's roommate came up—steeling herself. "Will *he* mind?"—hating his authority over her daughter but nevertheless recognizing it.

"Judd?" Betsy always referred to him with forced casualness. "He won't wake up. I'll sneak over there and back without his even knowing it."

Violet giggled again, but uneasily. She liked the middle-of-the-night conspiracy, but she didn't like Judd.

"Do you need anything, Mom?"

"Not a thing, dear." Neither of them reflected on the irony of the exchange. It was ritual.

Betsy hung up, and, resisting the impulse to lay down her head and groan, she tiptoed back to the bedroom and collected jeans, T-shirt, sandals. Judd lay in darkness; Betsy bent over him and kissed the air an inch above his forehead. "Good-bye, dearest love," she said soundlessly. Even had he been awake, she would not have said those particular words; she uttered them only in her imaginary conversations with him, and he said them back.

She dressed in the living room and, on her way out the door, thought to leave a note. She propped it against the saltshaker on the kitchen table (their place for notes, as it had been her parents'): "Gone to my mother's. A whim of hers. Don't worry." How I love you, how it kills me to leave the bed where you sleep. . . . "Back soon. B."

Barefoot, she let herself out the front door and put her sandals on downstairs, on the porch. They would have clattered dangerously on the steps. She stood a moment, breathing deeply, and looked up for stars. There were none in the pale, predawn sky, but there was a remnant of moon, and Betsy wished on it, childishly, without shame—anything! she would try anything!—before she got in her car and drove through the quiet streets to her grandfather's house.

Another of Violet's terminal luxuries, besides linen handkerchiefs, was candy. There was always candy by her bed, often glossy and expensive chocolates in their fluted nests, but sometimes six-packs of Mars Bars or Almond Joys brought by Terry. The doctors approved of the candy. Anything to keep up her strength and her spirits and her weight. And, of course, as no one said though everyone thought, "What does it matter now?" But it mattered to Betsy, who felt more lost and bereft at her mother's candy eating than at any other aspect of her illness. Her mother, who for years had been a vegetarian, a vitamin freak, a natural-foods fetishist, had taught Betsy that the body was a temple not to be defiled. But when her disease was diagnosed she began to eat candy and to drink coffee again and even bourbon. "My system let me down, Betsy," she had said. The veil of the temple was rent in two.

She was just sinking her teeth into a Mars Bar when Betsy let herself softly into the house and went up to her mother's room. She kissed her, smelling the chocolate. Violet hugged with just her arms, spreading her hands wide. "Careful, I'm sticky." The hug over, she finished the candy bar and reached for another. All the while she was beaming at Betsy.

"You look cheerful," Betsy said, ignoring the candy.

"I love it when everybody's asleep in the house but me. I always have. I used to wake up in the night when I was little and roam around. I didn't care if it was dark, the dark never scared me. Everything looked different—exciting. Once I went into my parents' room, right up to their bed. My dad opened his eyes and looked at me and winked and closed his eyes again." She gave her tired chuckle.

She ate her second Mars Bar, looking at Betsy with twinkling eyes, and then wiped her smudged fingers and lips on a handkerchief.

"Well!"

"You wanted to talk, Mom." Betsy felt more tired than ever now that she was here. Her mother's room made her tired. It was all dark except for the light right over the bed and the dim light out in the hall by which she'd found her way upstairs. And it was warm in there. They still had the heat on, in mid-May—not for her mother, but for Mrs. Foster, who had poor circulation.

"If you're not too tired, honey."

Betsy woke up. "I came all the way over here at four in the morning and tired or not I'm prepared to hear what you have to say if you'll just get on with it."

"Don't get testy. I know I impose on you, but I won't much longer, you know."

Violet could speak matter-of-factly about her situation, but she looked at Betsy fixedly, as if testing her reaction; the grim prognosis was still new to them all.

Betsy took her hot hand. "I'm sorry, Mother. You don't impose on me. I'm glad to do anything I can for you."

"Good." Briskly, Violet withdrew her hand, reached for another Mars Bar, decided against it, and folded her hands in her lap, lacing her fingers together.

"Betsy."

Betsy waited.

"Elizabeth Jane." Her mother smiled. "What an English and literary name. Your father chose it. I made it Betsy."

There was another pause. Betsy waited patiently, observing her mother's flushed cheeks, her brown and white hair cut short now and left straight for convenience, her wide-set brown eyes that gave her the look of a bird, and the slightly beaked nose to match. Violet looked wonderful, everyone said so. She had become plump in middle age, but in spite of the candy bars the disease had begun to whittle her down, and at the moment she was just right. There was always a low fever, and it kept her skin flushed and her eyes bright. She looked impossibly healthy.

"Elizabeth Jane, I want you to find my mama for me."

Betsy went cold and felt the stomach-dropping sensation that means something significant has taken place. Her mother's words were insane, but they came like a pronouncement from on high, a voice from out of the heavens.

"I want you to find my mama," she said again.

Betsy collected herself and adopted a tone of extreme reasonableness. "Mom, Grandma's dead. She's been dead since nineteen fifty-four—"

Violet waved a hand impatiently. "You think I don't know that? I don't remember that? I'm not getting dotty, Betsy. You know what I mean." She waited.

Enlightened, Betsy cried, "You mean your *real* mother?" She felt overpowering relief.

"I do." Violet smiled and pulled a book—a P. D. James murder mystery—from under her pillow and took a clipping from it. "Your Grandpa would never look in here." She held it up for Betsy to see. It was cut from the *Times:* ADOPTEE'S LONG SEARCH ENDS IN JOYFUL REUNION.

"Everybody's doing it," Violet said. "Getting all those records opened up that no one used to be allowed to see. They're passing laws and everything about it." She looked with satisfaction at the *Times* article and tapped it. "This gives a lot of tips—voting lists, old phone books, birth records, newspapers. It would be a nice summer project for you, Betsy. Here, take this. It'll start you off."

She didn't so much hand the clipping to Betsy as confer it on her, as if it were a valuable inheritance. It was fragile, having been unfolded and folded up again many times, and the newsprint was rubbed faint by Violet's eager fingers. Betsy folded it gingerly and held it in her hand.

"But, Mom, she's probably—you know—dead by now." It was a difficult, desperate word to use, in any context. "She'd be a very old woman."

Violet shook her head. "No. I've got it figured out. She

was probably an extremely young girl. Who else would find herself in that predicament but a young, innocent girl?" Violet raised a finger in the air. "I have a picture of her in my mind. A young girl no more than eighteen. She looks very much like you did at eighteen, or like I did. But dressed à la nineteen twenty-two—bobbed hair, dropped waist, trying hard to be sophisticated. But a sad little girl underneath . . ." She laced her fingers together again, neatly. "So—" As if her sentimental vision were conclusive proof. "If she was no more than eighteen when I was born, she'd be no more than seventy-three today, and probably less. I see her as a *very* young girl. She may be barely seventy."

"But I thought there was some story—" Betsy faltered. Her mother had told her the tale of her adoption years ago, when she was in college, and she was embarrassed to find she had forgotten most of it. "Wasn't she married? What was it? She and her husband lived next door to your parents —I mean Grandma and Grandpa—and they couldn't keep the baby—you, I mean—for some reason, and—what was the story?"

Violet dismissed all this with another flutter of her hand. "All nonsense," she said complacently, and went on, "Now, Grandma never spoke a *word* to me about this. It was Aunt Marion who told me—feeling it was her duty before I got married to tell me I was adopted—and it was. A child should always be infomed of such things. Not that I was a child. I was nineteen years old by then, and working. Oh, God, Betsy! The shock!"

She leaned back on her pillow and closed her eyes. She wasn't bothering with her glasses most of the time, and her eyelids looked large and creamy, framed by wrinkles and by the two wings of her eyelashes. "I'll never forget it, to my dying day." Tears had come to her eyes when she shut them, and she dabbed with a clean handkerchief: a theatrical woman.

"But how could you not have known?" Betsy demanded. "For nineteen years! No one let it slip? There were no hints? It seems incredible."

"Betsy, you have no idea what a refined family you come from," Violet said, with a tiny, ironic smile. "How *genteel* everyone could be—especially in those days. Adoption meant there was illegitimacy somewhere, and what could be a worse disgrace than that? That's why I don't believe that story," she continued. "Why would a respectable woman give up her baby? It's just not plausible. No, Marion made that part up, so the story wouldn't seem so—low. But it was that part that got to me, that this woman didn't *have* to give up her baby for adoption. Until I realized, thinking about it while I lie here, that her version was cleaned up for my sake, and I began to see my mother as a young girl, confused, seduced—oh, who knows? But with no alternative but to give me up. And here was this childless couple—your grandma and grandpa—their only child had died at birth, and they wanted a baby more than anything. So you see."

Violet's hand hovered over the last Mars Bar and finally took it. Betsy threw the empty cardboard and cellophane package into the wastebasket. It overflowed with wrappers.

"Will you find her for me? It's important." Violet chewed steadily, but her eyes were troubled, and she kept them eagerly on Betsy's face. "You know how important it is, honey. Everything is important to me now. Before I die. I want her."

The tears came again and were blinked back before she took another bite. Betsy was overcome with sadness and had to blink back her own before she could speak. It was hopeless, of course. It was pathetic, just as the hand embroidery on Violet's bedjacket was pathetic, and the cheery books by her bed, and the damned candy bars. Nothing seemed worth doing, worth anything, just at that moment. There was death all over the room, but she spread her hands and said, trying to dole out equal parts of hope and deflation, "I'll try, Mom. It's all I can do." Was it better that her mother hoped or didn't hope? Did it matter? Did it matter?

"Don't tell your grandfather," Violet said, looking pleased and sitting up straighter. "I don't want to hurt him. He doesn't even know I know. And that article—it says there might be resentment on the part of the adoptive parents."

"But if I should find her—"

Violet considered, carefully. "He may have to know then, but let's wait until it's absolutely necessary." She lowered her voice. "The worst of it is he may even know who she is, where she is. He could give us a good lead. But we can't ask him."

"You're sure? If he knew her name it would save a lot of time."

"Promise me you won't say anything to him, Betsy! Or to Marion! She'd be blabbing it to Grandpa before you could draw breath."

She was agitated, and Betsy soothed her. She patted her hand. Violet finished her candy bar in one bite.

"Just tell me what you know," Betsy said, looking for paper. She had scholarly habits; she would write it all down. She found blue stationery across the room on her mother's dresser.

"There's pens in the top drawer."

Betsy groped and found one. "All right. Now."

"Well, my parents—I mean Grandma and Grandpa—"

"I know what you mean, you don't have to say that every time. If we keep qualifying what we mean we'll never get anywhere."

There was a pause.

"I'm sorry, Mother."

Violet sighed. "Try to be patient with me, Betsy." She leaned forward to Betsy and stretched out a hand, but didn't touch her. "I'm sorry I dragged you out of bed. There are maroon shadows under your eyes."

"It's okay, Mom, honestly it is."

"Are you using that moisturizer, Betsy? It's important that you keep your looks if you want to—to—" Keep your looks and keep your man: the shadow of Judd reduced Violet to incoherence because the last thing she wanted Betsy to do was keep Judd. Betsy, who personally felt she didn't have much worth keeping in the way of looks, saw the problem bogging her mother down. The moisturizers and cold creams and mascara wands and blushers she pressed on her daughter were keeping that man in her bed. Betsy stood up and hugged her mother with an affection that was suddenly exuberant. "I'm using it, don't worry about it. Just tell me what you know about my grandmother."

Violet returned the embrace with surprising strength, but then she lay back, looking drained. She stared at Betsy. "Your grandmother!"

Betsy nodded, pleased with the notion. "My grandmother! Maybe she'll leave me all her money, maybe she's really wealthy, maybe I'm the granddaughter she's been longing for."

Violet giggled weakly. "Oh, Betsy. Do you know, I never thought about her being your grandmother. Isn't that odd? Oh, we do get self-centered when we get old." She smiled happily and settled into the pillows with a contented wiggle. Her bouts of contentment always amazed Betsy. She's *dying,* she thought.

"Well. Anyway." Violet frowned, addressing herself to the paper in Betsy's lap. "My parents and I lived at six sixty-six Spring Street. I'm not sure I'd remember the address if it weren't for those three sixes—we moved from there when I was little. And my real mother—we can call her Emily, by the way—"

"Why Emily?"

"That was her name."

"How do you know?"

"Marion told me."

"You know her *name?*"

"Well, I'm not at all sure of her last name—wait, Betsy, we'll get to that part. I'm ahead of myself. Wait." Violet touched her brow with her long forefinger and closed her eyes. "She must have lived at six sixty-eight, on the right of our house as you went up the hill because—wait, the numbers went down—yes, the Rebhahns lived on the left, and that must have been six sixty-four, in fact I know it was." She opened her eyes, triumphant. "Yes. She lived at six sixty-eight Spring Street—*if* it's true that she lived next door, and I think it was. That has the ring of truth. When you tell a lie, you keep to the truth as much as you can." You should know, Betsy thought. "I suspect Marion only lied about the marriage. Let's accept the rest as true."

"What else can we do? We've got to have something to go on," Betsy said, thinking: hopeless, hopeless.

"Right. So she was a young, unmarried girl living at six sixty-eight Spring Street, and her name was Emily something, like Lofting or Loftig."

"Aunt Marion told you this?"

"She told me the name, but I didn't catch it right. To tell you the truth, I didn't pay that much attention. I was in shock, Betsy. Imagine if you were to find out that *I* wasn't *your* mother? Or that Daddy was never your father?"

Betsy couldn't imagine it. She brushed the attempt away. Besides, anytime she wished she could look in the mirror and see her mother's bird face—eyes and beak, sharpened.

"And, of course, this was thirty-five, thirty-six years ago that she told me. But it was something like that. Lofting. Or Loftig. There were a lot of German families in the neighborhood. Say Loftig. But check Lofting."

"I will." Violet watched anxiously as Betsy wrote them both down. "Anything else?"

"Not really." Violet's eyes became faraway. "Except I saw her once—did I tell you that?"

"Really saw her?" How she dramatizes, Betsy thought. "Really? Or imagined—wished—"

"No, really. I was working at Chappell's, in hats. I made fourteen dollars a week, Betsy. Can you imagine that?" She chuckled, but it was a faraway chuckle. Betsy had heard many times, especially lately, about her mother's brief fourteen-dollar-a-week job, and the lunch she treated herself to every payday: a chicken salad sandwich, iced tea, and a hot-fudge sundae at Schrafft's, all for fifty cents. "So one day your grandpa came in, and there was a woman with him. I was kind of surprised to see him, but I guessed he was going out to lunch, and maybe the woman was a client. He came in the front door with this woman. It was right near the hat department. He didn't come over to me or anything. They just stood there, he and I waved and smiled, but the woman just stood looking at me, and then they left. Then, a couple of months later, when my aunt told me I was adopted, she said remember that woman in the store with Frank? Well, that was her. Emily. She wanted to have a look at me."

"But what was she like?"

"Well—I didn't notice her much, Betsy. Why would I? It was my father I kept looking at, trying to figure out what on earth he was doing there and why he didn't come over. I asked him, by the way, and he said something about this client he took out to lunch and she wanted to stop in and pick up something for somebody, a gift, I don't know, and then changed her mind. I hardly remember. But the woman . . . I know she was tall, like us, and she had a lot of brown hair. I have no idea how old she was. She looked very chic, I think. Most of all I remember she looked *happy*. Now isn't that odd? She looked—joyful. Seeing me, I suppose. Seeing with her own eyes that her daughter was well, was grown-up and healthy, had parents who looked after her, with your grandpa a prosperous lawyer—a pillar of the community and all that. I suppose. But I could tell, even though she did nothing but stand there and look, that she was full of happiness, and then she took my dad's arm and they walked away."

Betsy looked at her piece of blue stationery. It read:

> 1922
> 668 Spring St., Syracuse
> Emily Lofting/Loftig—unmarried?
> 1941, seen Syracuse, Chappell's Dep't. Store, with Grandpa
> tall—brown hair—joyful—chic.

"It's not an awful lot to go on Mother."

"It's enough," Violet said confidently. "The woman in that article had less. What did you do with it? Read it."

"It's right here. I will." Betsy folded the clipping inside the blue stationery.

"Will you get started right away?" Violet was smiling with excitement.

"I give my last exam tomorrow—today. I could start Monday."

"Start with the voting lists. The city directory. Birth records."

"What does your birth certificate say?" Betsy asked suddenly.

Violet looked at her wide-eyed. "I don't know."

"You must know. You had to have it when you got married, didn't you? Where is it?"

Violet was thinking. "Grandma. Grandma. Your grandma. She went down to the county clerk's office . . . " There was a pause while she frowned and tapped her forehead with her finger. "Think. Think." She shook her head. "I can't remember. I will, though, and I'll call you."

"We'll be over for dinner Saturday."

"But not a word in front of your grandpa!"

"No, I know."

"Oh, what was it? My mother *did* something about my birth certificate when I got married. Now what? *What?*"

"It'll come to you. I'll see if I can get a copy of it at the courthouse." Betsy stood up. "Can I go home to bed?" She grinned, lest she be accused of testiness.

Violet stopped frowning and smiled back. "You've been wonderful, honey, coming over here and listening to my ramblings."

"Mother, I'm fascinated!"

"Oh, good, good, good," she said with the gleefulness which, Betsy thought, nothing could ever diminish. "Now just do me one favor. In the kitchen, up in the cupboard over the toaster? There's a big bag of M and M's. Get it for me?"

Betsy got it, in the dark, thinking: A whole package of Mars Bars and God knows what else and now a bag of M & M's. What's it all doing to her? But she gave it to her mother, even ripping off a corner, feeling betrayed, feeling also that she should be amused, but not being. Violet poured herself a handful, greedily. "Melts in your mouth, not in your hand."

When Betsy kissed her, Violet said, "Mmm," with her mouth full.

Judd was up. So much for Betsy's home-going reveries of slipping cozily and silently into bed beside him and snuggling up to his warmth. He was in the living room with the light on, reading the newspaper. He threw it down when Betsy came in.

"It's five-twenty-five in the morning."

He wore a short plaid bathrobe over nothing. His slender, hairy legs were crossed and the dangling foot danced up and down. He looked elegant and angry.

"Didn't you see my note?"

"What note?"

"On the table by the saltshaker. You know."

"Why would I look on the table? Did you think I was going to make myself breakfast?"

She regarded him with sadness. Another failure. To establish shared rituals, patterns, habits, traditions was one of her modest goals—which was, in turn, to lead to the more ambitious ones.

"I *always* leave notes there."

"Well, I'm afraid I don't *always* look there—okay?" He bounced his foot, with its long toes, up and down. His hands were thrust into the pockets of his bathrobe as if there were weapons there. "I'm not a mind reader, sweetiepie." He used the rare nasty tone that made her despair. The whole thing is a house of cards, she thought, and she determined to help him push it over. As always at such moments, she felt very cold and calm.

"And what does this famous note say?"

"You know where it is," she snapped back. "See for yourself. I'm going back to bed."

She turned her back on him and made for the bedroom. She heard him get up, cursing, and stalk into the kitchen.

"God damn it!"

She pulled off her clothes in slow motion, holding her T-shirt daintily by its shoulders before she laid it gently in a drawer. Her jeans she smoothed and draped over a hanger. How neat I am, how complete I am without him; this was what her fastidious movements meant.

He came in, watching her. "Your mother! I might have known. And it was your God damned mother who woke me up at ten minutes after four."

"What do you mean?"

"The phone rings—right? I answer it, there's a little *whoop*—" He demonstrated, in falsetto. "And then *click!* I knew it was your mother."

Betsy pulled her nightgown over her head. So her mother

had called again while she was on her way over. Why? And then, knowing she'd awakened him, saying nothing about it . . . The deviousness of Violet was incredible, but so was her inability to get away with things. The uncontrollable whoop of surprise and dismay was just like her. In spite of herself, Betsy felt a rush of tenderness for her mother.

She got into bed, leaving Judd to turn out the light. She buried her face in the pillow; she didn't want to see him take off his bathrobe and be naked. The bathrobe was flung on a chair, the light switch clicked. After a pause he got in beside her.

I can't keep living like this, she said lucidly to herself. Better to live alone than to put up with this.

His hand was on her thigh. Immediately, her stomach muscles quivered, and she turned to him gasping. They had four or five ways of making love, depending on circumstances. They did it now swiftly and without frills, and by 5:45 they were both comfortably asleep, back to back. In the morning, they discussed who would pick up Sanka and macaroni at the supermarket, whether or not to go to a movie that night, and what a hell of a lot of noise the God damned garbage men were making. It was the way all their quarrels ended—with lovemaking, careful forgetting, and the dawn of a new day.

In the evening, they were both weary, and willing to be nicer than ever. Macaroni and cheese, hamburgers, a green salad, and a bottle of wine—Judd's favorite supper, and he did the dishes. They went to a terrible movie, which they both enjoyed, about a killer whale who gets revenge on the humans who killed his mate. The night was warm, and they took a slow walk home, holding hands. It was very nice, and the niceness of it lulled Betsy, as it always did. She felt plump and ripe with contentment, an earth goddess. She woke up Saturday thinking that if they got married in the summer they could have such a nice vacation—it would be nice, very nice. . . .

She lay sleepily in bed, watching Judd. He had an early assignment to photograph a new shopping mall, and she observed with interest while he got dressed. She loved watching him do things—anything. She liked the economical way he moved, dancerlike. He put on low-slung underpants and tight jeans and a white shirt with the cuffs rolled back precisely twice, and a red and green patterned tie that he knotted loosely, leaving his top button open. He always wore a tie. This delighted Betsy; on Judd, it looked rakish and original. In the summer he wore a straw hat. He also owned a white duck suit and a long woolen cape. A dashing man, she always summed him up—not handsome (hooked nose, small blue eyes, and pitted cheeks), but dashing as the devil. His name was Judd Vandoss, he was thirty-one years old, a successful free-lance photographer. He had moved in with Betsy the preceding winter after deflowering her on New Year's Eve. The bizarreness of the feat appealed to his imagination.

"A thirty-four-year-old virgin! How could it happen? It's like a miracle."

It was, as far as Betsy was concerned. Her other beaux had never achieved it. She could count them on three fingers, starting with Ron, her high school steady, gawky as she but not as bright, who copied her homework and shyly felt her up, but not very far, in the movies. He was a creep (she confessed honestly to herself at age sixteen), but she was lucky to get him. In college there had been Paul: They had done lots of kissing, mostly at Betsy's instigation, but never seemed to get around to anything else. It was all talk and no cigar, and to preserve her self-respect Betsy had had to type him glibly as a latent homosexual. And there was Alan, her linguistics professor in graduate school, who was married; it was sneaking around to her apartment he liked, more than what they did there, and he was afraid to get involved in a real affair.

These were the only men she had ever spent more than a few evenings with. Until Judd, and the miracle, and the continuing series of miracles, not least of which was her feeling for him. She hadn't expected overpowering love to come to her at thirty-four. She'd given up on it.

For almost five months they had lived together in pleased astonishment. All winter they had met chiefly and most intensely in bed. It was only now, with the coming of spring, that they had begun to draw back and look at each other. They were still pleased—the rootless wanderer and the passionate virgin who had been saved for him. But Betsy had to admit, though only to herself, that she was tired. She'd had no idea a love affair would require so much study. She might have been back in graduate school, but it was more complicated than graduate school. She was a student and a spy, engaged in constant, wary espionage, puzzling out how to please him, disguising her own feelings and looking for clues to his. She was aware of it when the obviousness of her devotion began to annoy him—talk of love made him curt and uncomfortable—and she had to teach herself the technique of hiding it. She wanted it to be there for him, as a secure background to his life in case he wanted that security (and she had very little idea of what he did want), but she didn't wish to smother him with it. So, instead of declaring her love, she scrubbed out the tub after him, she let him have the Arts and Leisure section of the Sunday *Times* first, she learned to make omelets and macaroni and cheese, she helped him to quit smoking, and on mornings when he had an assignment and she didn't have a class she got up early with him and made his breakfast.

She did so now while he shaved. She had combed her hair, slapped on a little blusher because she was pale, and put on a silk-embroidered kimono she knew was becoming. She wouldn't see him until dinner, and she wanted him to be left with an attractive image of her to carry through the day. This sort of thing, too, she had taught herself.

She made him a cheese omelet with parsley in the corners, whole wheat toast, fresh orange juice, and coffee. She had coffee and juice. She was going back to bed; it was the first day of her long summer vacation.

"I won't be back for dinner, Bets."

"Oh, no!" Involuntarily, she expressed her dismay, and then checked it at his look of outrage. He loathed nets cast out to snare his freedom. "It's just that Grandpa was really looking forward to having us both."

"So was I, I really was."

Betsy analyzed his regret swiftly: 90 percent genuine, 10 percent appeasement—not a bad mix.

"But when I spoke to Jerry yesterday he said we'd be doing night shots, too. I completely forgot to connect it up with dinner or I would have mentioned it last night. But I just realized—hell, I won't be back till ten at the earliest. More like eleven."

"I won't see you all day!"

Almost a wail—not quite, but he punished it. "Well, I'll have some free time this afternoon between shootings, but I can't see myself coming all the way back here. This place is way out Route 20, almost to Rochester. I thought if I have the time I'd go out and try to get some shots on one of the lakes for that wildlife competition."

"Heavens, no, don't come all the way back."

He inspected her for irony but found only loving tenderness. He sat down to his eggs.

"Tell your grandfather I'm really sorry. And your mother." He raised his head. "How is she, anyway? I haven't seen her for a couple of weeks."

He had had to miss the last two Saturday night dinners—another tradition going down the drain.

"She's just the same," Betsy said.

"She *sounded* just the same on the phone the other night." He grinned. "*Morning*." Ah, that was the official line: no resentment, just that irrepressible Violet. She adjusted herself to it.

"She has a new bee in her bonnet."

"As usual, you'll be the one to get stung."

"Well—yes. She wants me to find her mother, for my summer project."

"Her *what?*"

"Mother. Remember, I told you she's adopted? She wants a family tree. She read an article."

"A bit late . . . "

"That's what I'm afraid of. Among other things."

"But you've got the job. I mean, you took the job."

"Of course." She spoke sharply. "Judd, she's *dying*. You don't say no to a dying woman. You don't tell her *anything* is too late."

"And what happens when you find out? When all your poking around in libraries and courthouses leads to a cemetery? Do you get an old lady from central casting?"

"I'll deal with that when the time comes. Maybe it's not hopeless, Judd."

"Oh, come on." He forked in the last of the omelet, ate the parsley, and gulped coffee. Betsy began to clear the table; it made a pause during which they could both back off.

"I've got to get going. Let's hope my blasted car starts."

"Do you have that map?"

"No! Bless you, Betsy Wetsy." He grabbed her and kissed her forehead. "Where would I be without you? Out in the middle of nowhere looking for a shopping center."

He hunted through his desk, located the map, and said, "You know, you can't be *sure* your mother's adopted."

"What?"

"You know how she makes things up. Nobody else has ever

mentioned it—right? Are you sure she's not just trying to inject a little drama into her situation?"

It was a reasonable question. Even an imaginative one. Nothing to get mad at. Judd's callous, almost flippant attitude toward her mother's state always pained her. Maybe it was healthy? Or a desperate denial of death that was to be pitied? But it pained her.

"Could be. I don't think so, but it's possible. I suppose I'll find out."

"To me, she looks like your grandfather. From certain angles."

He kissed her good-bye with passion, holding her tight. He reached inside her kimono for a piece of breast, and then he pulled her down on the sofa on top of him.

She fitted her body to his.

"This is ridiculous. I'll be late."

"You started it."

He watched her with his pale eyes half-closed while she unbuckled his belt and pulled down his zipper, and then she untied her kimono and awkwardly slipped it off.

"I love it when I'm all dressed and you're all naked," he said lazily, and cupped her breasts in his two hands. She moved so he could close his lips around one while they made love. Almost at once—it was something about the way they fitted each other, they had never been able to analyze it—she began to come. She lay on him with her teeth in his shoulder, tasting shirt. He clutched her buttocks, gasping deeply, and let loose the flood of endearments that came only with orgasm: "Oh, my baby, my love, my little love, oh baby, baby—"

After a minute they looked at each other and laughed.

"Now you can go," she said.

"God, you are terrific. Ah, what an ass—tits—the tightest little cunt—"

"Enough." The words still embarrassed her, and she kissed

him to hide the fact. Then she stood up and put her kimono back on. He lay at ease, unwilling to get up; a shaft of sun across his face made his pale blue eyes look almost sightless, like the eyes of a statue. We are made for each other, she thought.

"You've lost that map again."

They found it on the floor. He adjusted his tie and kissed her again, with no less passion.

"Judd! What's come over you?" Oh, it was good, it was lovely; no house of cards could be this solid, this beautiful.

"You. You came over me." He grinned. "A pun."

"Har har."

She saw him to the door. He kissed her neck. "Give my best to the family. I'll try to be home by eleven."

Back in bed, she hugged his pillow to her breasts, thinking: Judd, Judd, Judd. She felt her vagina contract, sucking in any errant sperm, and then she closed her eyes and, with her arms around the pillow, slept until noon.

In her endless musings on them, her four and a half months with Judd sometimes came to Betsy as a series of photographs —not unlike Judd's southwestern series that lined the walls of the living room. Odd, because she didn't feel comfortable with those photographs. It wasn't just the subject matter—the dead main streets of forlorn Texas towns, garish Mexican roadside shrines commemorating auto accidents, fat women in bars, leathery men with lizard eyes and ten-gallon hats; it was more the way these subjects were presented, in a sunlit, low-contrast style that to Betsy seemed romanticized. The photographs made her uneasy, particularly because Judd was fonder of the series than of anything else he had done. Knowing this, Betsy had studied them intently, wondering what affinity he felt with such bleak memorials, what need to place them in a sunny haze of his own making, but they said nothing to her. They expressed a part of Judd she had no knowledge of and perhaps no liking for, and so to her they were simply false to reality. But her mental photographs had their own falseness.

CLICK! Judd himself, alone, a subject he never would have taken but that she sees clearly. He is doing nothing—at most, half-listening to music he knows every note of by heart, maybe an old Eddie Heywood piano solo or a Billie Holiday record. His ability to do nothing enchants her, he simply sits, the way an animal simply sits, eyes shut, long fingers clasped on chest, where they rise and fall with his breathing. (Her own fingers curl around a book; her mind disciplined to withdrawal by years of drilling, she can concentrate on her reading even in his disturbing presence, but now and then she looks up and takes this photograph.) His hands rest together between his red suspenders, he is wearing a collarless shirt and the wool pants that don't zip but button, and his feet are bare. (Remove him from stereo and Oriental carpet and transport him to a sunny riverbank, and he might be a character out of *Huckleberry Finn*—some drifting ne'er-do-well, maybe a gambling man.) He is barefoot because he believes feet need to breathe. (When she asked him once why feet need to breathe and armpits and crotches and navels do not, he obligingly removed all his clothes.) His closed eyelids are long and narrow—fish-shaped—fringed in stiff black lashes. He has five o'clock shadow all day, and now—at just about five o'clock—he verges on being bearded, the rough skin of his cheeks and chin nearly hidden. He is from the Southwest, and she knows the snow-belt winters make him homesick; behind his closed eyes she imagines he travels into his photographs, down dusty, unimaginably sunburnt roads. She has been west only once, to read a paper at the Modern Language Association convention in Denver; she remembers snow, and awesome blue mountains circling the city. But his West is different from hers, and when he smiles, now while she watches, she worries about his memories: Mexican bars, hot nights, peyote, the Tex-Mex food he misses, and raven-haired women with mysterious sexual arts. She imagines lurid versions of scenes from *Carmen*, and marvels at his tameness, stretched out on her Sarouk listening to piano music, with snow falling outside the window.

He opens his eyes and catches her watching; he grins. "All right, damn it, you win—my feet are cold." She runs for a pair of his wool socks, but that's not part of her photograph, though it may be of his: a tall, serious-faced woman, hippy and busty in blue jeans and a high-necked sweater, who not only brings him the warm socks but kneels and puts them on his feet.

CLICK! Spring comes coyly to upstate New York, with many false promises. On one such deceptive day, Judd and Betsy take a long walk through the city. They leave the Westcott Street apartment and walk down to Genesee Street and out toward the suburbs, exclaiming every time the sun emerges from the clouds. It is a bright gray day, and in an occasional front yard before the shopping centers take over there are crocuses and snowdrops. Betsy's photograph encompasses the crocuses but not the traffic or the stores or the grayness; it is composed of flowers, sunlight, and Judd striding easily along with his hand in hers. But the afternoon extends past the edges of her picture. They stop at a deli for cheese and rolls and fruit, and when they reach their destination—a small park off the road, hemmed in by parking lots and laundromats and restaurant chains—they sit on the greening grass and eat. Perhaps Betsy's photo goes even this far, but there it ends, when the clouds cover the sun for good, and a cold wind comes up, threatening rain. In seconds Judd turns angry and unpleasant, like the weather. They gather up the remains of their lunch, Judd stuffing rolls into a trash container, which he then kicks, while Betsy wraps the uneaten cheese. They stride off toward home, underdressed, walking west into the wind. Betsy carries the bag of cheese and pears. Judd keeps his hands in his pockets and walks slightly ahead of her. He is mad at the weather, mad at her for suggesting a picnic on such a day, mad at the printing problem waiting in his studio that he had taken the day off to escape. They had been discussing, in their oblique and random way, the death of Judd's mother by drowning, and he is also, Betsy knows (trailing along behind him, cold and chagrined), mad at mortality. (The talk had been part of her continuing effort to get him to tell her about himself, but it was like—as Violet might have put it—"pulling him along by his eyeteeth." He had, for example, told her in detail about his brother Derek's reaction, dismissing his own with the observation, "It didn't seem real," his pale blue eyes staring opaquely at her, daring her to probe.) She forces herself to think about Pope's *Essay on Criticism,* which she will be lecturing on the next morning, while the wind blows back to her the curses he mutters at it. In her mind's darkroom, the sunny photo is already formed, and when, a month later, she refers happily to "that nice smelly cheese we took on our picnic," he will look at her in silent amazement.

CLICK! They are in Pennsylvania, on a weekend late in April, visiting Derek, his wife Suzanne, and their three young sons. Betsy and Judd take the two older boys on a hike through a nearby woods to a ravine where Derek says there is a beaver colony; it's the right time of year to see the baby beavers swimming. The boys are very excited; they push gladly into the woods. Hiking makes them thirsty, and there are frequent pauses for cold drinks from the canteen Judd carries in a backpack, but their spirits are high, and Betsy rejoices in their affection for their uncle. Bobby is a cub scout and makes a great show of directing them with his compass; Bertie trips over roots, and picks himself up again and again good-humoredly. But they don't find the ravine, and when the boys finally get tired they all stop for lunch at a spot where two fallen tree trunks provide backrests and seats. They sing, listening for echoes, "John Jacob Jingleheimer Smith," a song Bobby learned in cub scouts, and Betsy and Judd teach them "Kookaburra Sits in the Old Gum Tree." Then Judd decides they must climb the mountain. It's no more than a steep hill, rising ahead of them into the brush, but Judd turns it into the Rockies for his nephews, and the boys rouse themselves eagerly. The hill is muddy, with precarious-looking baby trees scattered sparsely over it. Judd says they'll be able to spot the ravine from the top. He straps on the backpack and off they go. It becomes obvious at the outset that the hill is too much for the children. The steepness and the slippery mud and the lack of good handholds discourage them, and they wish to stop. They look appealingly at Judd, but he keeps his back to them; he ascends steadily, his long legs carrying him easily from tree to tree. Behind him, Betsy and the boys scrabble in the mud, out of breath and enthusiasm. Betsy considers. The climb is not dangerous, merely tedious and dirty and exhausting. The boys are obviously miserable, but they don't complain; they wish this remarkable and elusive uncle, who treats them like grown-ups, to think well of them. If she calls out to Judd, suggesting they give it up, he'll be furious—she can tell by the determined angle of his head, by the way his hiking boots bite purposefully into the mud, leaving deep-set prints behind, which the boys step into. She stays silent. Meanwhile, Bobby and Bert get muddier and more fatigued. They have adopted a four-pointed, reptant climbing style, digging into the mud with their hands and the toes of their boots. They are filthy, and Bert's panting breaths are drawn in almost on a sob. Betsy scrabbles behind them as best she can, until Judd reaches the top—and it is here that her photograph begins to take shape. Smiling, he reaches a muddy hand down to the boys. He helps them up and then Betsy, his gritty fingers clasping hers firmly. "Here we are," he says to them.

"That wasn't so bad, was it?" He grins a wicked grin, and the boys respond to it with exaggerated boasts. "It was just a little old anthill, Uncle Judd," says Bobby, and the boys crack up, while Betsy's heart leaps as it always does when they call him Uncle Judd. They have a drink and walk to the other side of the hilltop. Sure enough, they glimpse water down below, and the boys lead the way, laughing, down the gentler slope. It is Judd at the top, tall and strong, connected to her and the boys by their linked muddy hands, that Betsy preserves in her mental photograph album.

In the evening, the weather was so fine Frank barbecued a steak in the backyard, and they ate on the flagged patio. Violet had the chaise longue, with three pillows and a tray. Betsy cut Violet's meat up small for her because it tired her mother to chew.

"It looks like something for the cat," Violet said.

"Eat. Keep up your strength," urged her aunt. Aunt Marion was Frank's sister-in-law, a spinster of seventy-six who had once written a historical novel called *The Pride of Passion*. It was her *chef d'oeuvre;* since then she had written nothing she considered important, boasting of her forty-five-year writer's block and keeping her hand in with an occasional letter to the editor of the *Herald-Journal*.

"Frank, shoot Violet over another hunk of meat," she said.

"No no no no no, I have enough here to last me two hours, Marion."

"Potato salad, then. Garlic bread, Violet."

"Don't force her, Aunt Marion," Betsy said. "She gets plenty to eat."

Frank was silent, chewing. He was still getting used to his new bridge, and he had a way of scrutinizing each forkful before he put it in his mouth, checking it out for potential problems.

"My Betsy doesn't approve of some of my eating habits," said Violet, spearing a tiny chunk. "Betsy thinks *she's* the mother, *I'm* the child, and *she* knows best."

"Oh, cut it out, Mother. I don't care what you eat." She was missing Judd. His absence embarrassed her. She had no appetite.

Violet discarded the tiny piece of meat and speared an even tinier one. It was a rebuke. Her petty petulance was something new, and uncharacteristic. It was as if she learned it from Betsy, or from Marion, both of whom were good at querulousness. Violet, the middle generation, was famed for her calm and amiability. Betsy watched, sorrowfully, as her mother fussed over her food.

"Where's Judd, exactly, Betsy?" her grandfather asked. They had all sensed the source of her snappishness and were looking at her.

"On an assignment near Rochester."

Aunt Marion sniffed. "I can just imagine what kind of assignment he's on."

"You don't have to imagine, Aunt Marion," Betsy said coolly, "because I'll tell you. He's photographing a new shopping mall that was designed by a famous architect you've never heard of for an article in *Architecture Today,* which he's been commissioned to do because he's the best architectural photographer around, and I'm tired of listening to your snide remarks about Judd. He's a finer person than you'll ever be, with more talent than you'll ever have, and how you can sit there week after week in your polyester pants suits and ridicule him and my relationship with him is beyond me when you know nothing about it or about anything else."

Betsy pushed back her chair and went into the house, heading for the bathroom on the first floor. She locked the door and looked at her face in the mirror. It was perfectly calm, even amused. She felt better after the outburst. She hadn't taken it seriously, not after the first few words, but it pleased her that her great-aunt had. Her worn, rouged, stunned face had gaped popeyed at Betsy's diatribe, not because diatribes from Betsy were new to her but because the subject was Judd. Betsy never talked about Judd. Beyond introducing him to the family and bringing him around periodically, she had done nothing to put Judd over. She had never before reacted to one of Marion's innuendos, and had never volunteered much information. Her relatives discovered he lived with her only when he kept answering the phone, and they had no idea how he, or she, felt about their relationship. Her grandfather got on warily but well with him, her mother disliked him, her great-aunt was fascinated by him and the whole situation.

Betsy smiled at her face in the mirror. It looked radiantly confident, and the sight pleased her. She examined her coming frown lines—they seemed fainter.

"Betsy." Her grandfather knocked on the door. "Are you all right?"

Betsy opened up. There he was—tall, straight, stern, kind, old—and she put her arms around him.

"She has no right to make those nasty remarks," she said, but she was cheerful and he knew it.

He hugged her, and they walked arm in arm toward the back door. "She's looking out for your welfare, Betsy. That's all."

"No, she isn't. If Judd walked out on me tomorrow she'd be delighted. She'd relish it."

He smiled at her. "Only because she'd think it was for the best."

"Well, she'd be wrong. I think Judd and I are a permanent thing, Grandpa, and I wish everyone would get used to it."

"*You* think, but what about him?"

Betsy flushed. "We love each other."

Her grandfather took her free hand, so that they stood linked, as if for a dance. "Then get married, Betsy."

Get married: only because it's not proper for the granddaughter of Frank Robinson to live in sin. She checked her exasperation because—honesty with herself being an intermittent compulsion—she wished it, too. "I imagine we probably will, before long," she said lightly.

She disengaged her arm, but kept his hand. "Come on, I'll go out and apologize to Aunt Marion and finish my dinner. I'm very starving."

It was a childhood expression of hers, and they grinned at each other.

"You're a good girl, Betsy," her grandfather said, and she made a face at him—only partly ironic, because she knew she was.

She crept up behind her great-aunt, who pretended not to hear her coming, and planted a kiss on her gray, dated upsweep.

Aunt Marion turned to her with troubled eyes. "What did I say, honey? I never meant anything by it."

"All is forgiven, all is forgotten," Betsy said, sitting down and slicing into her meat. "And I'm sorry I said such an awful lot of crap. I didn't mean half of it."

"Which half?" Violet inquired slyly.

"I knew you didn't like my suit," Aunt Marion said, restored. "In fact, I said to myself when I bought it, Betsy'll hate this."

"Then why did you buy it?"

Aunt Marion drew back in mock hauteur. "As if I dress for my thirty-five-year-old great-niece!"

"Thirty-four."

"As if I care what you think of my clothes!"

"Well, it's not dignified. Why don't you wear good cotton and linen? At least a skirt?"

"Listen to this!" The hauteur was less mock. "You've got to *iron* cotton and linen. When was the last time you had an iron in your hand, miss? Or put on a skirt?"

"I don't have to be dignified yet. I've got years."

"Oh, shut up, both of you. How can I eat anything when you're squabbling like this?" Violet spoke with her hand on her heart. She had finished all her meat and salad, but Betsy forebore to point this out.

"Truce, Aunt Marion," she said. "What's for dessert, Grandpa? M and M's?"

"Now don't start in on your mother," he warned.

"I must say, you're in top form, dear," said Violet. "You're on vacation now, aren't you?" She spoke with emphasis.

"Yes, but I have a project or two to keep me busy," Betsy said, with equal emphasis, and Violet smiled.

"That's good," said Frank. "I hate to think of all these college professors wandering around all summer, out on the streets, with nothing to do. It's a national scandal."

"What about all these retired septuagenarians?"

"We're busy keeping an eye on our families," he said.

"A full-time job!" put in Aunt Marion, not kidding.

"For them what likes it." Betsy stood up and began stacking plates. "I'll load the dishwasher and make coffee. Coffee, everyone?"

"Bourbon for me," said Violet. "Plenty of ice."

Betsy caught her grandfather's eye; he nodded.

"One bourbon, three coffees."

From the kitchen, Betsy heard her great-aunt's voice: "I don't care, I still think he has the look of a philanderer."

"You can't be a philanderer if you're not married," said Frank.

"That's exactly what I mean!" Aunt Marion replied triumphantly.

"You should be grateful they love you so much."

"Oh, I am, I am." They were in bed, drowsy. She listened attentively to the echo of the word"love" before she went on. "But what is it about old people? I don't pry into *their* lives.

I hope I'm not like that at their age, living through my descendants. If any." She didn't mean all that she said, nor was her dismissive tone completely sincere; she spoke the words for Judd's benefit.

"You won't be."

"Feeding on them, drinking them up."

"You exaggerate. What was this big stink about, anyway?"

"Well—um—er—*you*!" said Betsy, parodying extreme embarrassment and feeling it at the same time.

"Me? Where do I come into it?"

Her heart sank; what a thing to say.

"They were miffed that you didn't come with me." It was the most she could manage. She had meant to say a good deal more—everything. She was beginning to despair of its ever being said.

"And you defended me."

"Of course! I said you were much too busy and important to bother with the likes of them."

"You didn't."

"Right. I didn't."

"Is that what you think?"

"No. I guess I was a little hurt, though. Just nicked. For their sake."

"Next week I'll go. It's just been a series of—you know? It's not that I don't like your family. And you—I like to see you with them, playing the little girl."

She was startled. "Do I do that?"

"Often."

They were nose to nose. In the dark she saw his teeth and eyes, smiling.

She sighed and turned over, and he folded his body against hers.

"Good night, kiddo," she said, but after a few minutes: "Do you really think those killer whales like the ones in the movie are capable of lifelong fidelity to a mate?" It was a loaded question, though she was no longer sure what the ammo was.

"I can't answer. I'm asleep."

"Really—do you?"

"Nope. Now go to sleep."

"I guess that was a preposterous movie."

"Ridiculous. Go to sleep."

"It's interesting, though, how a trashy film like that carries on the *Moby Dick* tradition. I mean, the epic tradition of doing battle with a monster. How it perverts and exploits it. And how it still appeals."

He didn't answer. She lay awake for a long time after he went to sleep, wondering why she was lying in that particular bed, beside that particular man. After a while she turned, put her arms around him and drew him to her, but he rolled over and buried his face in the pillow, grunting. He was a sound sleeper.

CHAPTER TWO

Violet

Sometimes, when Violet woke up, it was 1941. She was wearing a blue jersey dress with a flared skirt and big, carved ivory buttons down the front. She'd paid for it herself, and she had it on when she met Will Ruscoe.

He was an artist, and a drinker. For a living he did drafting in an architect's office down on Warren Street, and later he had a sign-painting business. Violet didn't care what he did: he was as handsome as God, and a great talker. On their first date he drank whiskey after whiskey, and she watched his face get rosy with it. He spoke to her in a crooning voice that almost made her laugh. "You have a fine medieval face, Violet," he said. Then he ran his thumb down her cheek, and she shivered. He told her she had the look of a saint, but a passionate saint. She hadn't known the saints were passionate. "Those heavy-lidded eyes, meant to see visions . . ." His fingers moved down to her jaw and neck. "Ah, I would paint you if I were only worthy of it, Violet. In ten years, I would be ready to paint you, if you were still speaking to me."

In eight years he was dead, and he never did paint her.

She was left with notebooks full of sketches of her eyes and mouth. "I'm a lazy cuss except when I have a sketch pad in my hands," he told her. It was true. He thought he was preparing himself to paint, but his pen-and-ink sketches were his passion and his forte.

Violet and Will went dancing every night until they got married, and then they stayed home and made love and danced to the radio. They moved to Rochester soon after the wedding. Will didn't give up drinking, but he cut way down. His sign-painting business never prospered; meagerly, it supported them. Betsy's first drawings were made on bits of discarded poster board, and her clearest memories of her father were of fanatical neatness. Even in the shop, there was never a mess—never a brush left uncleaned, never a scrap left on the floor.

He had a congenital heart condition that kept him out of the war. He would have been a good soldier, being neat and brave and likable, and he volunteed in '41 and again in '43, when they were taking anyone. Violet always believed the rejection killed him. He fretted over his 4-F classification, and he knocked himself out working for civil defense, and in 1949 he dropped dead in the shop.

"Do you remember your father?" Violet used to ask Betsy. Her daughter's resilience alarmed her; a week after his death Betsy wanted to be in a first-grade Easter pageant.

"He was tall," Betsy would reply, after thinking for a moment. The only image that came to mind was of her father ruling off spaces for letters. "He could draw good horses," she said.

By the time she was eight she seemed to have forgotten him entirely. "He was nice," she would say to Violet, when pressed. "He was the best father a child could have." She stood there, glibly praising, and her thumb stole slowly to her mouth, a sure sign she wanted to be somewhere else.

"How could she forget him?" Violet wailed to her father.

By this time they were back in Syracuse, living with Frank and Helen on Stiles Street.

"Violet, she's a child," Frank would say. "It wouldn't be healthy for a child to grieve deeply. Do you want to see her moping around, in tears?"

"Yes!" Violet's eyes were permanently red-rimmed. It took two years for the intensity of her grief to die down. She missed Will every minute.

Her mother, who had always been a stern and distant parent, was kind in Violet's bereavement. She accepted Violet's inaction patiently. But she was harsh with Betsy, and the child spent most of her time in the attic, with her dolls, or out in the garden with her grandfather. Helen, all the more ferocious because Violet slept late, dragged Betsy to church every Sunday, taking out Violet's defection on the child.

In 1951 Violet got a job as a secretary-receptionist in a large printing concern. Eventually, she had a listless affair with the boss, and the end of it coincided with Helen's death in 1953. She quit to keep house for Frank and Betsy, who was, by then, twelve. She continued to mourn her husband; she channeled her grief into theosophy and Yoga and vegetarianism, but nothing diminished it. Her dead husband was her true calling, her most passionate enthusiasm, and as Betsy got older Violet talked to her more and more about Will.

"Can't you remember, honey?" she would ask. "That little stuffed dog? And when you had the measles and Daddy made ice cream? Remember when you locked Daddy in the cellar? The suspenders game? Remember?"

She could see Betsy trying and failing. In the end, Violet had to tell her all the stories. It was a great joy to her to make Will real to his daughter. Eventually, Betsy would sometimes fail to distinguish between memory and tale, and this pleased Violet most of all.

Nineteen forty-one was the crucial year in her life. Having a job had been the first big event. She only worked, in fact, for three months, but she always recalled her hat-selling job fondly as the big break for freedom, and she never forgot the feel of her own money, in its little brown envelope, tucked into her lizard purse, greener and more promising than money doled out by her parents. Meeting Will was the second event of significance, totally eclipsing the job. It never occurred to her to continue working after they were married; a pot of stew on the stove at six became the point of her life, and Will coming up from the shop, and their evenings together. Her lizard purse got shabby, and there was never much money in it. But Violet remained not only undaunted, but as happy as a heroine in the magazine stories she read. It was a noble calling, to live for your man.

Her lunch at Tubbert's with Aunt Marion, up from New York for the wedding, also took place in 1941, and also helped set that year apart for Violet forever. Violet (lying in bed listening to her heart beat) recalled it eagerly (though it had hurt her at the time) along with the happier memories.

"There's something I think you ought to know before you're married, Violet," her aunt had begun, after a discussion of bridesmaids' hats.

For one daft moment Violet thought her mother had deputized Aunt Marion to tell her the facts of life. She shoveled in her lobster Newburg, keeping her eyes on it, thinking: This is the most embarrassing moment of my whole life.

"Did you ever think you were adopted?"

Adopted? Violet put down her fork with a clatter and wiped her mouth. She would eat no more lobster Newburg. Adopted? Did I ever think I was adopted? Did I ever think I was Santa Claus, or Mrs. Roosevelt? Did I ever think the earth was flat? Adopted?

"No," she said to her aunt.

Aunt Marion was wearing a rose-colored toque and a two-piece gabardine suit with shoulder pads. She had done her lipstick like Joan Crawford, but it was coming off with lunch, and her mouth looked as small and prim as Helen's. I'm not related to you, Violet thought, in a panic.

"You were adopted when you were a tiny baby."

"That's a lie! Why are you telling me this?"

"It's not a lie, honey," her aunt said patiently. "Your parents don't intend ever to tell you, but I thought you should know, now that you're getting married. It's true. Your mother's name was Emily Loftig. She lived next door to your parents on Spring Street. She had a baby and couldn't keep it. She and her husband moved away, and your parents adopted the baby—you. They'd had a baby of their own and it died."

"I don't believe this," Violet said, but she did. It made absolute sense, and it explained why her mother had never loved her.

"It's true, Violet, and I thought you'd better know it. She came and saw you, not long ago. She was here in town. She came into the store with your dad to get a look at you, and then she left. She won't be back. I'm telling you this for your own good. It's not right that you don't know."

"Why did you have to tell me *here*?" Violet burst out. "Didn't you know I'd cry?" She stood up. "I've got to go. I've got to see Will."

"Wait!" Aunt Marion took her arm and walked her over to the front door. Violet was crying quietly; no one seemed to notice. It was a horrible restaurant, Violet thought. Full of people eating, full of the smell of food, full of mouths opening and shutting . . .

By the time they reached the front door she was sobbing noisily. "Sit here." Her aunt—her former aunt—pushed her into a chair. Violet always remembered the chair; rose and tan brocade, the colors of her aunt's hat and suit. There was a pair of potted palms. Violet stared at them through her tears until Aunt Marion returned, check paid and lipstick repaired.

"Is it really true?"

"Yes, it is, Violet." Aunt Marion squeezed her shoulders with more tenderness than Violet could remember her ever showing. She didn't even know her aunt—her nonaunt—very well. She was the loose-living New York aunt who came to visit them once a year, bringing exotic, indulgent gifts that her sister Helen disapproved of—lace underwear, perfume, fancy fruits bottled in brandy. "I know it's hard, but they're still your parents. They love you so, Violet. You're the light of your father's life, and your mother—"

"My mother! She's never been my mother! She's always hated me!"

A party of people came in, women in hats like Marion's, and looked curiously at Violet (a big, striking girl with long brown hair, standing stiff and unresponsive, holding back tears, while a smartly dressed older woman tried to comfort her). Violet glared at them with loathing. She pulled away from her aunt and went out the door.

"Violet! That's not true!" Marion hissed, following behind. "Violet!" She heard Marion groan, and knew the sound expressed remorse for telling her, for stirring it all up practically on the eve of the wedding. Violet slowed and allowed her to catch up.

"I'm glad you told me," she said coldly. She couldn't call her "aunt." "I'm just upset."

"Come on, we'll go home in a taxi." She took Violet's arm again, but Violet shook it off and then relented and let her take it.

But when they got to Stiles Street, Violet stayed in the cab. "I'm going over to Will's."

"Oh, Violet—"

"It's all right. I'm grateful to you for the news. I'll be home for dinner, but I just don't want to go home right now." She gave the driver Will's address, and though she didn't look back she imagined her aunt staring after the taxi in dismay. Violet huddled on the seat, trembling. She wanted Will. Will would be her home, her real family, from now on.

"Mrs. Ruscoe?"

Violet opened her eyes. Oh, that eye makeup. "Good morning, Terry." Wasn't there some kind of nurses' code that forbade such excesses?

"Here's your breakfast."

Ah. Strawberry preserves for the muffin, and an egg in a cup, and melon, cubed. She ate greedily and didn't care, to fill the emptiness. It worked, too, with certain foods—candy and bread, especially. She had two muffins.

Frank came in, just shaved and smelling good. A handsome old man, and picturesque since his hair had gone on top and left a thick white ruff around the sides. "How's the bridge, Dad?"

"It's going to be all right," he said, moving his jaw left and right to test it. He kissed her head. "Feel up to some reading today? Maybe we could finish *Three Men in a Boat.*"

They had read an article about a famous magazine editor who had cured a serious illness with vitamin C and Marx Brothers movies. Violet rejected the vitamin ("It's all bull," she said, "bull" being her strongest epithet), but she agreed to try the humor, and Frank read aloud to her most mornings after breakfast: P. G. Wodehouse and Mark Twain and Eudora Welty and James Thurber. Now they were in the middle of Jerome K. Jerome, at the part where Harris tries to sing a comic song. They both looked forward to it, as a way of spending time together without talking about what was on their minds. They had, in fact, forgotten the purpose of the readings, but her aunt asked, when she heard about them, "Does it make you feel any better?"

"Not really," said Violet. "But I'll die laughing." Her

rare mortality jokes always embarrassed her aunt, who said, "Now, Violet."

"Anthony Trollope," Betsy had said thoughtfully when Violet repeated the joke to her. "Trollope died laughing."

Violet always fell asleep after a chapter or two, and Frank closed the book and crept downstairs to make his daily call to Dr. Baird. Violet's day sleep was sacred and precious because her nights were becoming so restless. Her illness had taken them all by surprise: it was real, and she didn't complain. All her life she had exaggerated and lied, whined over imaginary illnesses, turned colds into pneumonia, missed school, carefully calculated the number of sick days she was entitled to at work and took them all. But a year ago when she began getting the pains in her joints, and the swellings, and the bouts of fatigue, and all the rest of it, it took her months (valuable months lost) before she told anyone, and another few weeks before she'd consent to see a doctor. She wanted to try dolomite, cranberry juice, deep breathing, until Frank and Betsy stormed at her. When all her ailments were taken seriously, and tests (three days in the hospital, with wires, tubes, and needles) showed advanced lymphogranuloma, a rare form of Hodgkin's disease, and Dr. Baird gently told her there was little hope for a cure (in his eyes, she saw "no hope"), she took it placidly. Her last cold had aroused more passion and resentment than this, her last illness.

"I'll be with Will," she said to her father soon after the diagnosis, and though tears came to his eyes he didn't really believe in her remark, at once so romantic and so stoic. He thought she got it out of a book. Though they all noticed Violet had stopped complaining, no one noticed she had stopped lying.

"If only Betsy was settled," she also said, meaning: Otherwise I die content. Judd's name never came up in the family discussions of settling Betsy. There were sighs all around. "Settled" meant "married," but it wasn't so blunt.

Violet had a fair amount of time to think and she thought about the thing that nagged at her, trying to identify it. It wasn't only Betsy's unsettledness that was bothering her. There was another "*If only. . . .*" It was when she began to mull over the past, the years with Will (boning up before the reunion), the 365 wonderful days of 1941 (minus Pearl Harbor, though she remembered that she and Will were dancing cheek to cheek that morning in the kitchen, and she had new shoes, when they'd heard it on the radio), that she figured it out. Her real mother. Not that she'd forgotten she was adopted. Like her love for Will, it was always at the back of her mind. But she hadn't been aware of the intensity of her curiosity, and then she saw that article in the *Times* and took it as a sign.

Often, when she lay there and seemed asleep, she was going over and over what she knew. Loftig? Was that what Marion had said? Or Lofting? She had asked her aunt once. One Thanksgiving, after dinner, when Frank was snoozing in his chair and Betsy was off wherever Betsy went, she had said to Marion, "Tell me what you know about my adoption."

Marion got sullen and stubborn. "It was a mistake ever to spill the beans to you, Violet," she said in a low voice, glancing over at Frank. "I won't say more than I did then. You know, and that's that. You don't need to know more. My sister Helen was your true mother, the one who raised you and cared for you."

"But my real, actual, biological mother, Marion! How can I help being curious? Did you know her? What was she like?"

"It'll do no good to dredge all that up," Marion whispered fiercely. "It's dishonoring Helen's memory. And Frank! Hasn't he been a good father to you?"

Her father snoring quietly in the corner, full of turkey, full of love. It had been a pleasant family dinner. Betsy had been in a good mood for once, Marion had brought a fruit cake and wine, the turkey had been just right. It was their first Thanksgiving without Helen. It was nicer without her. Violet had repressed that thought, just as, faced with the turkey, she had repressed her vegetarian ideals. And she retreated in shame from the conversation with her aunt. I let her get away with it, she thought now, remembering how easily Marion had cowed her. It's my right to know! It said so in the *Times*.

"And don't you say a word to your father about this, unless you want to break his heart" were her aunt's last words on the subject.

Well, it would be her secret project. Wasn't she entitled to a secret project, now that her days were numbered? She blotted out the Thanksgiving scene and went back to 1941. She concentrated fiercely. She could recall the toque, the suit, the lobster, her blue dress, the chair, the palms. . . . Betsy. Betsy would be her salvation. She would turn it all over to Betsy. She smiled, knowing she'd begun to depend on Betsy lately like a child depends on its mother, and dialed her number, realizing belatedly that it was four in the morning.

Waiting for her daughter, she dozed, and awoke with the empty sensation in her body that wasn't hunger but something worse, something bad. She waited quietly for it to pass. It seemed hours since she had called Betsy. Why didn't she come? She dialed the number again: a man's voice. Him. She hung up. The emptiness ran along her arms into her hands and down her legs to her feet. She couldn't feel her body at all. Maybe that's death, she thought. When I'm all hollow I'll be dead. She would be one of those chocolate Easter rabbits she never used to let Betsy have and Frank used to sneak into her basket. She reached for a candy bar, thinking of her daughter.

Elizabeth Jane. Betsy had always been a good child, she couldn't have asked for a better. If only she got along more easily with people. With her mother and her grandfather, with selected friends, she could be so charming, but Violet knew the charm could desert Betsy, and she got scared and tongue-tied and less pretty when she was flustered. Betsy's diaries, when she was in high school, had been painful to read, full of humiliations and rejections. Life was hard for Betsy as it had never been for Violet. Violet drifted through; Betsy struggled.

The emptiness came and went. She tried to keep it straight, all that she had to tell Betsy, but it drifted away from her. She had read a book about remembering once and used to joke, "I can't recall a word of it!" Her memory was getting worse, but she lay in bed placidly enough, chasing it. There was no hurry.

That paradox pleased Violet. Without much time left, she had all the time in the world. She loved the way time had slowed, loved lying in the bed she'd had for so many years, with all her comforts at hand, thinking. She could lie there in her old maple bed and think forever. Remembering details about Emily was like being in a detective story. There was so little, and so much, to be made out of it. Like Peter Wimsey or Adam Dalgliesh she pondered and worried her clues until they connected and a pattern formed.

The house on Spring Street, number 666. They had moved from there when she was little. She could recall the Rebhahns at 664. She used to play with David and Clara. David used to urinate on the rosebushes in the backyard, Clara used to hang by her knees from a branch of the cherry tree with her dress over her head. The Rebhahns had shocked Helen; she'd never liked them. Violet suspected it was David and Clara, as much as Frank's prosperity, that had driven the Robinsons away from Spring Street. But who lived next door, on the other side? The Loftigs—it didn't sound at all familiar. Had they moved when Emily disgraced herself? What would a family do? Surely not continue to live next door to their illegitimate granddaughter and her adopted family. They would move away, and take Emily so she could start a new life. Maybe just across town; "across town" was further away in those days. But it would be kinder to Emily to move right away from there. Imagine running into Helen somewhere, wheeling her baby. . . . No. They would have left the city, if they were kind, and if it was possible. The whole family would be under a cloud—or could you get away with such a thing, in 1922? Send Emily away . . . ? She'd have to leave school—on what pretext? And once the baby was born and safely adopted, would she come back?

Sometimes the pattern refused to form, and all that was clear to Violet was Emily's intense misery. Her heart overflowed with sorrow, and her head swam. She would leave it to Betsy. Betsy's head never swam when it came to the crunch. That book she had gone to England and Chicago and God knew where else to do the research for. She had brought Violet a Staffordshire dog in her suitcase, picked up cheap in London. Violet thought it was ugly, but she loved it because she liked to think of Betsy out on her own, adventuring in foreign lands: poring over old manuscripts in a library, roaming London, actually going into a musty shop and dickering with the owner. "I got him to come down five pounds solely on the strength of my briefcase," Betsy had laughed. "Women simply don't carry briefcases in London. And it only had my lunch and a murder mystery in it." Betsy could amaze her. Violet had long ago taken as her motto, "You never know!" And it applied better to her daughter than to anyone else, except possibly to her father.

With Helen she had always known. Helen did nothing to make life interesting—Violet's criterion for loved ones—and in fact did her best to make it dull and hemmed in. No, Violet didn't love her, though she didn't comprehend that fully until adolescence, when Helen's gloom and sternness became almost malevolent at times. She had been punished for every minor transgression. For forgetting to set the table, the penance was dinner alone in the kitchen. For coming in late: isolation in her room. For lies: slaps. Once, for saying "damn," Helen had locked her in the cellar.

Violet couldn't remember talking much to her mother. Helen was a woman of harsh silences. Frank had probably talked to her too much, Helen too little. She used to ask him why Helen was so mean to her, just to see the look that came over his face, of despair and boundless love.

"It's not meanness, Violetta," he would say. He called her Violetta when he loved her most. "She's a complicated woman. She does love you, but it's not so simple for her."

To Violet, Helen was—among other things—the Catholic Church, and she disliked the church all the while she was growing up because it belonged to her mother. When she was grown, and Will dead, and she could have profited from religion, it was too late; all it meant was cruelty. For years Helen had taken her to Mass and drilled her in catechism for her first communion and kept a rosary in her apron pocket, and it was Helen who yelled and slapped and came up with cruel deprivations. It was just like her, to worship a man bleeding on a cross. Frank was an Agnostic (to Violet it was some kind of religion, like Catholicism, but infinitely more sensible and kind), and never set foot in a church, and yet was loving.

"Be patient with her, Violetta," he said sadly, but what impressed Violet about such exhortations was their goodwill rather than their content.

She didn't enjoy thinking of Helen, but she didn't try to block her out, either. Everything might help, any little thing. And it was, in fact, with Helen in her mind that she remembered the letters. Of course—she had discovered them as a nosy teenager foraging in the attic. Letters from her aunt to her mother, dated 1922, the year of her birth. She had known instinctively not to ask her mother about them, and somehow she had shrunk from asking her father, though now she couldn't remember or imagine why. But she had asked her aunt Marion about them on her next visit from New York, asked her shyly during one of those excursions when Aunt Marion tried to make friends with her. Were they out for ice cream? She tried to picture it: a lemon soda at Schrafft's, the long spoon, the chunks of ice in the vanilla, and Marion . . . She paused, groping down the years. Marion had told her never to speak of them; she had been harsh with Violet, and Violet had cried.

She could recall the look of them, the creamy paper, the fancy, old-fashioned handwriting (hard to decipher), the red stamps, even the tone of them—reasonable, consoling, unlike Aunt Marion in her seventies, who tended to be unreasonable and irritating. But what they were about eluded her utterly, besides the sense they had imparted of the grown-up world as a yawning pit. She had, instinctively, rejected them, hadn't even plowed through them all. But they had registered in her mind. Why, though? Oh, it wasn't fair, what the years did to your memory.

She thought they must be still in the old cedar chest where she had found them, up in the attic back under the eaves. She had kept them in her own room for a while, but then, nervous about being caught, had restored them to the chest before Helen found out she had them. She'd been—what? fourteen? (She'd had a white angora sweater set that year, and breasts.) She set herself to remembering what was in the letters; they had been strange and shocking, that was all that came back to her. They had puzzled and repelled her. Scared her. But now she had no memory of the contents of those thick, squarish envelopes. She concentrated: creamy paper, black ink, red stamps, "Your loving sister," and the 1922 postmark . . .

Urgently, before she forgot everything, she called Betsy.

CHAPTER THREE

Betsy

At three o'clock Monday morning her mother called again. Betsy awoke just too late.

"Jesus!" Judd was out of bed. "What kind of crackpot—"

The phone was in the kitchen; she raced him for it and won.

"Hello." She motioned Judd back to bed.

"Betsy? It's me again."

"Hello, Mother."

Judd looked murderous and made strangling gestures with his two hands before he marched back down the hall, muttering. The bedroom door slammed behind him.

"I know it's late, Betsy, but this is really important."

Betsy calculated quickly. The call would set a pattern if she took it without protest. She made a decision even before her mother's sentence ended: to endure the nocturnal calls without complaint, even if they became chronic. It's the least I can do for her, she thought. She was responding every bit as much to the curses and the slammed door as she was to her mother's last whims, but a silent and vague "to hell with him" was the closest she came to articulating this.

"It's okay, Mom. I don't mind. What's really important?"

"I just remembered I have a pack of letters of my mother's —Helen, I mean, not my real mother—"

"Yes, yes. What letters?"

"From Aunt Marion, when she was living in New York. I looked at them once, years ago. I suppose, technically, they're my father's, but I remember finding them and appropriating them and reading them—when I was a teenager, poking around one day."

I can imagine, thought Betsy, knowing how her mother could poke around. She had, over the years, gone through Betsy's drawers, read her letters, eavesdropped on her conversations, picked the locks of her diaries.

"I can't remember what's in them; they went on in a sort of religious way, I think, which strikes me as odd, now, since they were from my aunt Marion."

"What do you mean?" There was no sound from the bedroom. Please let him have gone back to sleep. Betsy stretched the phone cord to its limit, to the far side of the kitchen, and spoke as quietly as she could. "What were they about?"

"I can't remember!" said Violet in a restrained wail: she, too, had to keep her voice down. "I don't think I even read them all, Betsy, the handwriting was hard to read. I think if there was anything to understand in them, I wouldn't have understood it. But now they might make more sense. There were a lot of them, and they dated from around the year I was born. *That* I remember very well. I think that's what must have attracted me to them, that and the fact that they were hidden, of course. In my mother's old cedar chest, under a pile of winter underwear. And they were horrifying, Betsy, in some way, though I can't remember why."

Betsy felt her patience going. "Somehow I doubt they'll tell us much, Mom," she said, keeping her voice even and the weariness out of it. "If they were from Grandma to Aunt Marion, we might get something out of them, but not the other way around."

"No no no no no, Betsy," came the confiding, confident voice. "I think you're wrong. My aunt is the blatherer. My mother was very close-mouthed. There may be hints." She told Betsy how Marion had reacted to her questions about the letters, how Marion the blatherer had become a Helen, close-mouthed and secretive and curt.

Betsy looked at her watch. Three-fifteen. He must be asleep—otherwise he'd have the light on to show her he was up and fuming. "I'll come over and check them out before I go to the library. Nothing to lose."

"Come over now, honey."

"Mother!" But she had expected it.

"Please?" Had she not noticed the weakness of her mother's voice until it turned plaintive, or had Violet deliberately faded out? Betsy was well acquainted with her mother's dramatic gifts. "I want so much to see them, Betsy. I'm sure there's something in them, and it's . . ." The voice faded, strengthened, died away again on a sigh. "Oh, I know it sounds selfish, it sounds awful, but—this is my best time, honey, I feel so well and enthusiastic at night, Betsy, you don't know what it does to me to upset your routine like this, to call you over here at this terrible hour, but I want you so much—"

"Mom."

There was a final gathering of strength. "Betsy, I can't *sleep* without those letters. Please, honey, it won't happen again."

"Okay, Mom, I'm coming." She would have answered sooner but for tears. The weakness wasn't faked or exaggerated; if only it was. She could hear the shortness of breath, the pain behind the words. She wiped her nose on a table napkin. "I'll be right over."

"Bless you, honey."

She pussyfooted by the bedroom door. She was wearing a short nightgown, and she grabbed a sweater from the hall closet and keys from the table. Again she carried her sandals and let herself out without a sound. Just before she pulled away from the curb she saw a light go on in the apartment. Hell!

She lived on the other side of town from her grandfather's house, but she could have made the trip with her eyes shut. She drove speedily through the deserted streets, afraid. She had just seen her mother on Saturday night, but she never knew when she would find her weakened, deteriorated beyond recognition. A sudden change was possible, the doctors said. Or she could live for months, hanging on. She hadn't sounded good on the phone. . . .

Betsy took her mother's dying personally; it was simply the latest episode in life's ruthlessly waged war on her. There was no need to pity Violet, whose saintly smiles stirred all of them to admiration. Frank had overheard her snapping her fingers and singing "Stardust" one day as she sat on the bedpan, and had reported it to Betsy sternly, as if to say: At my age I have more respect for death. But it was wonderful, they acknowledged, that Violet would go down singing—like the medieval martyrs who went down praying.

It was the left-behind living, as the funeral directors said, who deserved pity and needed comfort: Frank, helplessly watching Violet sink into death while he remained hale; and Betsy, losing her mother at a time when—she felt—she needed a source from which to draw strength for the living of her own unsettled life.

But Violet greeted her joyfully, arms outstretched, from her oasis of light. "My good daughter! And how pretty you look all tousled!"

There was no trace of candy bars, except for a basket full of wrappers. Nor was the night nurse evident.

"Mrs. Foster asleep again?"

Violet nodded mischievously. "Who needs her?"

"Mother, she's getting paid to be on call here."

"Well, she is on call. Don't be so crabby. She's only in the next room, and I have my little bell." There was a silver dinner bell on the bedside table.

That bell. "Grandma's?" When it rang, everything had to be dropped, you had to run.

Violet nodded, pleased at her daughter remembering. "It's been sitting in the china cupboard all these years. Mrs. Foster feels better about her naps knowing I have it."

Betsy sighed. Let it go for now. "Shall I go up in the attic and look around for those letters?"

Violet smiled radiantly. "I'd be so pleased. Honey, look in your grandma's cedar chest. We hauled it up to the attic when she died. They may still be in there, just where I found them—under a pile of long underwear." She made a face. "That darned underwear. Or try the old rolltop desk; your grandpa may have put them in there. Oh, I hope he didn't destroy them, Betsy."

"Well, I'll look. Do you need anything before I go up?"

"Not a thing."

Her grandfather slept in the ground-floor bedroom; a prowler in the attic wouldn't wake him. Next door, in the guest room, Mrs. Foster lay lumpy and fully clothed on the bed, snoring. Betsy shut the door on her.

The attic was stuffy but cool, with a hint of mice. Was it a smell, or the suggestion of tiny movements in the walls? Betsy stood at the head of the stairs and sniffed in her childhood. She used to escape up here; she remembered the loud rain on the roof. There was her old wicker doll carriage, covered with dusty transparent plastic. There was probably a doll in it—maybe Samantha, that once-loved child. She didn't look. Bad luck if Samantha should be gone.

Her grandmother's cedar chest was pushed under the eaves. It bore her initials, carved within a wreath of leaves—H.P.R. —and it was thick with dust that hadn't been disturbed for years. Gingerly, Betsy lifted the top, expecting mice, and found a pile of salmon-pink girdles. Ah, underwear, at least.

She pawed through the chest. It was full of old clothes, some of them her own—cotton blouses, yellowed nylon slips, a bag of white linen collars, camisoles, baby things, and on the bottom the underwear, well-worn long johns of all sizes. Under that: nothing.

She dumped it all back in haphazardly (the ghost of Helen stood over her, frowning) and went to the desk. It was Frank's as unmistakably as the cedar chest was Helen's: a massive oak piece, handsomely carved. It stood in the middle of the floor near the chimney, with canning jars piled on it. These, too, were Frank's; he used to supervise the hot, August canning sessions, stripped to his undershirt, seeding tomatoes—the produce from his backyard garden—by squashing them in his hands. The canning jars contained dead flies. Betsy rolled back the sloping top of the desk. Inside, it was dustless and full of papers. There were twelve pigeonholes, two small chambers with doors, two secret compartments that she knew of—he'd shared with her one day their secret mechanism, the two pillars that could be pulled forward when a bit of carving was rotated. Patiently, Betsy thumbed through everything. It was mostly old tax records, bank statements, paid bills, correspondence from lawyers and accountants. She checked all twelve cubbyholes and went through all the drawers, perversely saving the secret compartments for last. And, of course, each of the compartments contained a tied-up bundle of letters. Betsy flipped through one of them without untying it; the letters were addressed to her grandfather, and whosever they were, why ever they were saved, they were written in a strong, angular hand, not her great-aunt Marion's wispy, artistic script, with its loops and flourishes.

Betsy picked up the other package. There they were, loops and flourishes all over them. Her first reaction was pleasure in the continued workings of Violet's memory. Her second was disappointment. The very fact of her finding the letters seemed to insure that they were harmless. They weren't even hidden terribly well; the trick pillars were an open secret to all of them. Presumably, Frank had stored them there after Helen's death. If they had told all, surely he would have destroyed them. In fact, if they revealed anything useful, Helen would not have hung on to them. On the other hand . . . the date was there—1922—and "Mrs. Frank Robinson" at the Spring Street address. Violet had it all correct. Heavy in her hand, the letters held some sort of promise, after all. *You never know:* that's what Violet would say.

Betsy hurried downstairs with the package. All was still, and within her circle of light even Violet now slept. Betsy's presence had been enough to make her sleep, and smile in her sleep, her head back and awry. Betsy leaned over her. It's how she'll look dead. But the thought didn't touch her—Violet with her high color looked so remote from death. What did jar her briefly was the sudden bereaving realization that she alone was awake in a house full of old people sleeping. She wished Judd were with her, and then acknowledged the ridiculousness of the idea: Judd coming with her on these nocturnal visits, poring patiently over faded letters for clues to the past! Judd was pastless; the present was his natural element.

Betsy turned on the light by the easy chair and sat down with the letters. She untied the brown twine that bound them and flipped through the envelopes—all alike, each with its flowery script and faded carmine stamp—half-thinking that, in spite of her curiosity, she might doze off herself. She was tired, as much from the tension of leaving Judd as from the hour, and it showed in her face. Even in the flattering lamplight, she wasn't a pretty woman, no matter what her mother said. Her resemblance to Violet was strong but generalized; in details she was sharper and plainer. She had too much nose, and a secretive, scared look that thick, arched brows and wide, hooded eyes—not unattractive in themselves—only accentuated. She could look like a bird at bay, and she had the figure of a bird, too—stout through the middle, bosomy, hippy, with slender legs. At best, she looked interesting, with the paradoxical contrast between bony features and generous body; at worst, she resembled a pigeon.

She dozed briefly, and dreamt the letters were simply tedious, full of shopping lists. She rubbed hard at her eyes and then got up, making no noise, and crept downstairs to get herself a cup of coffee.

She knew every inch of the house, from the missing stair post to the location of the coffee jar. It had been her home from the time she was seven until she went to college, the big brick house with the casement windows and the odd mix of furniture—Helen's mother's late-Victorian relics, pieces from Helen and Frank's early married days, massive mahogany monuments to their later affluence, a few modern things Violet had picked up. In her own old room, there was a white iron bed, an oak washstand complete with towel rack (on which she had hung hair ribbons), a rickety upholstered rocker, a threadbare Oriental rug, two new dressers in heavy maple. There was also a picture of the Virgin Mary crowned with thorns and framed in bamboo; Betsy hated the thorns but loved the pretty, impervious face of the Virgin, which, bedewed with blood drops though it was, gazed upward with a look of unutterable calm and sweetness. Betsy never wished for the picture to be removed, any more than she would have suggested replacing the rocker, on which you couldn't rock without some part of it coming loose and falling off; she merely sat still on the rocker and ignored the thorns and the blood, a stoic and reasonable child who learned early to accommodate herself to inconvenience (as the Virgin, apparently, did). It would have done no good to complain to Helen, anyway, any more than it helped to complain to God. Violet and Frank could usually be won over without trying, but Helen had little indulgence for the whims of childhood, and in the end it was Helen who ruled, in a monarchy that was absolute.

While the water boiled, Betsy ate some cold asparagus out of the refrigerator, and then she made a cup of coffee and carried it upstairs. Violet was still asleep, curled comfortably into her pillow and breathing regularly. Betsy knew her mother could sleep like that for hours once she went off. She settled herself in the chair again and picked up the letters.

The top one was postmarked October 13, 1921, a year and two months before her mother was born. She paused before she removed the letter from its envelope. The handwriting, unmistakably her great-aunt's, had faded with time, and the fading distanced it from the loud woman in the upsweep who disapproved of Betsy's sex life. It seemed wrong to read this woman's letters, as it wouldn't have seemed wrong to read Aunt Marion's.

But she opened it. The paper was expensive and had endured. Was this the time of Marion's prosperity? Her *Pride of Passion* period? No, the triumph of her muse hadn't occurred until 1927. The paper was either an extravagance or a gift; both had figured largely in her early, unfettered life.

> Dear Helen, I will come to you at Thanksgiving. You must stop giving way to these morbid streaks, and to call it the unspeakable thing is no way to begin to cope with it and accept it. Helen, your religion should teach you this. Have you talked to anyone? (I mean clergy.) You worry me, that you don't get over this sorrow, when you were, I always believed, the strong sister, and the churchgoer. Dear, don't speak of punishment, not for you or for him. Leave it to God. I must see you, just carry on til I come. Your loving sister, Mamie.

Betsy looked up blankly. Across the room her mother slept and smiled, oblivious. Betsy glanced at the envelope again. Sure enough, her grandmother's name and address and, inside, the signature was the nickname no one had used in years but that she still identified as her great-aunt's. And yet it all seemed to concern strangers. What sorrow? Was it the death of Helen's baby? And why punishment?

She flipped through the letters. There were eight of them, the envelopes all alike, and the stamps. The dates ranged from October 1921 to March 1923. Betsy began slowly to read them. It took some time to decipher the florid, faded script. She could understand why the young Violet, inquisitive though she was, had given up on them, and the more she read the more she thought it was a good thing she hadn't gotten all the way through. What would an impressionable teenager have made of them?

By the third letter Betsy was fully awake and relishing the slow pace. It was four-thirty, and she didn't want to go home. The curses, the slammed door, the light going on like a slap in the face awaited her there. It was another world from the world of her grandfather's house, a world of quiet, peace, safety, with her mother deep in calm and blessed sleep. Even the letters: Odd and wretched though they might be, the love between the sisters was unmistakable, like something in a book—but her great-aunt was real, her grandmother had been real, and the love was real, too. It was what was missing back at her apartment, that kind of secure and comfortable love. But she needn't go home while the letters lasted. She finished her coffee and read.

They continued to make no sense, or, rather, they had their own logic but it bore no relation to anything else, so far as Betsy could see. The first four letters were similar: attempts by Marion to calm Helen in her sorrow. They were all from late 1921 and early 1922. Betsy frowned over the inspirational tone. This was Aunt Marion, then, back when she was Mamie, and wasn't so far removed from the prose of her family's religion, and wasn't so outspoken that she couldn't adjust her responses to the feelings of her audience. An ardent young woman full of affection for her grieving sister. But why grieving? Nothing specific was said about the baby. And though it was never mentioned, Betsy sensed that Helen might have been suicidal—certainly badly depressed. But why?

Betsy thought about her grandmother. Helen had been old even when Frank still seemed young. She was little and hard, with a brown face, and tiny hands with blunt fingers. She was a devout Catholic. She kept a sampler on the kitchen wall on which she had stitched, as a girl, the awesome injunction, "Pray Without Ceasing," and what she prayed for was the conversion of her husband and the reconversion of her daughter, who had bolted the Church after her marriage. She took Betsy to Mass every Sunday while Violet slept late. Helen was not patient with little girls; she seemed to prefer cooking. Once Betsy had surprised her, on her knees and weeping, in her bedroom, and she had turned on Betsy with her hand, tangled in rosary beads, upraised, and unprecedented fury in her old brown face. She was morally incorruptible, with principles of steel, and, never averse to taking Betsy's schoolgirl quarrels in hand, she was a master of the devastating phone call. ("This is Helen Robinson, Betsy Ruscoe's grandmother. I wish to complain about an ethical matter involving your daughter and my granddaughter." And Violet rolling her eyes in the background while Betsy trembled, afraid the fight had been her fault, after all, and she'd catch it. You could count on her grandmother to get the truth.) Betsy had felt an abstract love for her, as for a small god, but it was complicated by humiliating dependence. When Helen died, she felt fear and relief equally: fear that the world would come to an end, relief that her grandmother wouldn't be there to rub it in. And there was sorrow, too, that was partly personal. If Helen could die, anyone could.

Betsy's memories seemed to have no relation to the woman of the letters. Helen weak and morbid and needing the encouragement of Marion? Marion, as she herself righly pointed out, was the weaker sister, the prodigal living a life of shadowy sin in the big city, never holding a decent job or a decent man, getting by (precariously) on her wits. "You know my aunt Marion always has a liaison going," Violet had revealed to Betsy twenty years ago, before Marion had descended to pants suits and the largesse of Frank, on whose bounty she now lived in a suburban condominium. (Her last, chaste liaison.) But Helen . . . was this the same hard, brown grandmother, to whom her sister could write, "Get hold of yourself for the sake of your husband and your future. Good can come out of evil if you refuse to bend before it"? Betsy tried to picture her grandmother without a hold on herself, or bending. These were not Helen's postures. The recollection of her sobbing over her rosary was the only connection Betsy could make. It must have been a family crisis of magnitude for Helen and Marion to change roles.

In the fifth letter, written in the spring of 1922, there was a clue. "You can go on, dear. I see your strength is there. Accept your baby's death, and think of this as another chance. And then you can go on." Betsy sighed with relief; there it was, then, the family tragedy laid out plain: the baby who had died at birth. But then, in the next letter, was the incomprehensible sentence, "Talk of sin and retribution, of the grotesque and the monstrous, that way madness lies," as well as a few brisk lines of sympathy for Frank's cold. A welcome break in the gloom, Betsy thought. A cold was a normal affliction, neither grotesque nor monstrous, and not a sword in the heart but something to dose with honey and lemon (Helen's invariable remedy). It must have helped distract her from her agonies, whatever they were.

The penultimate letter (December 29, 1922—Violet was nine days old) came to the point at last. The prying eyes of young Violet could never have read this far:

> I have seen the child, a lovely little girl. The mother is healthy, the baby is perfect. Let this not be part of your pain, dear, but something fruitful, a chance at life. You

can have her for the new year if your heart inclines to it. The mother is quiet and agreeable, there will be no trouble. *There seems to be no resemblance.* You will warm to this baby, Helen, if you let yourself. I know you have the strength to put aside your sorrow and your anger and open your heart.

Betsy looked up from the letter and tried to order her thoughts. Helen was distraught because her baby was dead. Normal enough, though there seemed to be an intensity to her grief that worried her sister—and a strange duration, too. By this letter, in which Marion still talked of sorrow and anger, Helen's baby had been dead—how long? Well over a year. But all right, the death affected her strongly. Then a baby born out of wedlock to the girl next door must indeed have seemed a gift. . . .

But there was more to it. The letters clouded as much as they revealed. What was the source of Helen's hate? Why all the talk of unspeakable sin? Violet had reminded her of Helen's exaggerated notions of propriety—was it adopting a bastard that bothered her? And why should she hate poor Emily so much that she had to be assured the baby didn't resemble her? And then her own baby—did Helen see its death as a punishment? What on earth for?

Here was the first mention of the mysterious Emily—healthy, quiet, and agreeable. The letter bore out Violet's notion of her as a young and inexperienced girl, but it gave no real information as to age or circumstances or name—as if any mention of these would be too painful for Helen to read. Idly, Betsy inspected the envelope. It was postmarked Haddam, Connecticut. She looked at the others; all were from New York. Another fact: In late December of 1922, Emily was living in Connecticut. Presumably Violet was born there. Interesting, possibly useless. What did one do with a fact like that?

She opened the last letter, hoping for clarification. It was postmarked March 19, 1923. The three-month hiatus might mean Marion went to stay with Helen and Frank when they received the baby, to help out; it was hard to imagine Helen coping on her own. Had Marion, in fact, been the courier who brought the baby to Syracuse from Haddam? The last letter was cryptic, and the sermonizing sounded weary. Helen must have been maddening.

> You're making too much of this. Please, please resign yourself, Helen. It's the way of the world, but it's all over now. You must rejoice in the baby. And as for the other, you must forget at last. You will ruin your life if this goes on, and you now have a responsibility toward the future. Isn't it *just that* that everyone wants? Count your blessings, Helen, for once. Some people would look at your life and, even knowing all, say *she has everything*! I will be with you when I can, possibly early April. Keep writing to me, dear, unburden yourself, I am here to help, but *try*. Love to the pretty little one. Your loving sister, Mamie.

It was almost five-thirty, dawn; Betsy could sense it rather than see it in the lit room with the shades down. The birds were beginning. Betsy reached up and turned out her light. She was inexpressibly weary, and the letters, for all their warm affection, had finally begun to weigh on her like a personal sorrow. What *was* it with Helen? Her strict, upright grandmother was gone forever, and in her place was a grief-mad depressive. She would try later to analyze it. She would spend the day in the library trying to make practical use of her information. All this so that an old woman could be brought to this room to gaze on her wasting child, so that Violet could press her mother's hand and die content. Betsy pictured this scene and found it terrifying, like her juvenile visualizations of her parents in bed conceiving her, kissing and moaning or whatever it was. The horror of grown-ups' secret, exclusive lives. She blanked the whole thing out of her mind and discovered Judd there in its place, naked, slamming a door. She would think of him later, too. Schemes to counter his impatience and disapproval were more than she was capable of. A fearful question blazed dramatically through her mind like neon in the dark: Do I want anguish to be my life's work? She slept on it.

Her mother's voice woke her. "I remembered about my birth certificate, Betsy. It came to me in a dream."

Betsy dragged herself back from sleep and looked at her watch. Seven-thirty. Her weariness bewildered her. She thought, I must be ill.

"I never saw it," Violet went on. "My mother couldn't seem to find it—this was when your dad and I got married. She was always going to get a copy, but she never did. We finally used my baptismal certificate. It seemed to do just as well."

Betsy rubbed her eyes. Violet was sitting up in bed, wearing a lacy jacket. There were noises downstairs in the kitchen.

"Terry came on at seven, but I made her be extra quiet. She put that afghan over you. You had quite a little sleep."

Betsy looked down. Lavender shell stitch covered the letters and her bare legs.

"Your grandpa is up," Violet said pointedly. "He tends to pop in."

The noise of his electric razor sounded faintly from the bathroom down the hall.

Betsy started to speak, but she was overcome by nausea. She stood up, scattering letters and afghan, and made it just in time to her mother's metal wastebasket, where she threw up on all the candy wrappers.

"Betsy! Honey!"

"Oh God, oh God, I feel awful!" She sat down on the edge of her mother's bed and rocked her head in her hands. Another bout of retching sent her back to the wastebasket, but it brought up nothing. She sat back down and wiped her lips with a tissue.

"Betsy, we're going to put you right to bed. You must have that flu. Your hand is cold as ice—and *clammy*."

There were firm footsteps on the stairs, the rattle of dishes. Terry the nurse appeared at the door. She was pretty, perky, brunette, unfazed. She smiled at Betsy.

"Boy, do you sleep sound."

She set the tray on the bedside table: buns, bacon, teapot. Betsy raised both hands to her mouth and gagged.

"Terry, Betsy's got something. She's just thrown up, and look at her. Pale as a ghost."

Betsy smiled wanly. "I'll be all right."

"Weak as a kitten."

Terry applied her cool palm to Betsy's brow. Betsy closed her eyes. Put me to bed, bring me ice water and flexi-straws, pills in a paper cup. . . .

"What is it—just nausea?"

"And I'm so *tired*."

"It's my fault, Terry," Violet said, and her eyes actually filled with tears. "Would you believe I called her up in the middle of the night and dragged her over here?"

Betsy squeezed her mother's hand; it was an effort. "That's not it, Mother. How could that make me ill? No, I've caught something, and I think I'd better go home before you come down with it."

She could see that Terry agreed, but Violet protested. "Put her to bed in the guest room, Terry. She shouldn't go home, she needs looking after."

"I'll be looked after well enough at home. Don't worry, Mom. I feel better, anyway." She didn't, though. Standing up, she felt another wave of nausea and almost sat down again.

"I think it's better that you don't stay," Terry said. She

inspected Betsy with an eye that looked practiced. "I don't think it's anything much, but I have to consider Mrs. Ruscoe."

"It's not anything much." Betsy picked up all the letters and stuffed them in her purse. Terry folded the afghan and when they both stood up she felt Betsy's head again. This time Betsy caught the scent of her perfume and held her breath.

"You feel pretty washed out, don't you? It could be something you ate, even. Put yourself to bed, and if you feel hungry, try tea and dry toast. If you keep that down, have something else, very simple. Avoid dairy products. And apple juice is better than citrus."

Betsy looked at her gratefully. "You think it's just one of those twenty-four-hour things?"

"Sure looks like it."

"Betsy, will you call me later if you're better? If you don't, I'll worry. And I want to know about the *you-know-whats*." Violet nodded her head three times, for emphasis.

Of course. The letters. Violet must be mad with curiosity. "Interesting, though not especially illuminating. I guess I won't be able to get started on the project today." Violet smiled and waved a hand: no rush. "And I'm sorry about the—" Betsy indicated the wastebasket.

"I'll take care of that," said Terry, putting Violet's tray in front of her. "You take care of *you*."

"What's wrong with her?" It was her grandfather, smelling of after-shave. Kissing him, Betsy felt sick again.

"She got some kind of bug," Violet said through her sweet bun.

"Well, what'd you bring it over here for at this hour of the morning?" The gruffness was put on, masking worry about germs.

"She's been here all night, Dad," said Violet. "I asked her to come over and she did, in the wee hours."

"What the hell did you make her do that for?"

"I'm a selfish old woman. I just wanted to talk."

"Talk to Mrs. Foster."

"I will." Violet put down her teacup. "Betsy, I'm sorry," she said, and the tears came to her eyes again. Terry handed her a handkerchief, and Betsy could sense her thinking: She doesn't cry for her own illness, just for her daughter's silly indisposition.

"You get home to bed," Violet said. She held out her arms, and Betsy leaned over the tray to be hugged.

"Come on, I'll drive you."

"I'm OK, Grandpa."

"I'm not letting you drive. You leave your car here and I'll run you home in mine. Come on now."

It was a relief. She did feel better, but weak, and she was afraid of being surprised by nausea. "Could I take a bag or a towel or something?"

Terry got both and handed them to her as she went out the door. "Take care. If you're not better tomorrow, call and tell me. I just might be able to arrange a house call." She dimpled.

"Thanks, Terry."

"Take care, now."

Her grandfather ushered her out the back door and into his Cadillac. Betsy put on the seat belt, but its pressure threatened her stomach. She had to unbuckle it, and she kept the towel ready. Frank looked at her dubiously. "What is it—just nausea?" He started the car and backed it down the driveway.

"To tell you the truth, I think it's mostly fatigue. I'm so tired I feel sick. It's not just Mom getting me out of bed. I had a bad case of insomnia the other night and I'm still catching up."

"And what's giving you insomnia?"

Who, he meant.

"Nothing's *giving* it to me. It was only one night. Everybody has a bad night once in a while."

"I don't."

"And never did?" She thought of the letters in her bag.

"Once or twice. Nothing to shake a stick at."

"I'm not shaking any stick. You are."

"Well." They were stopped at a red light, and he patted her knee twice and looked at her with concern. "You take care of yourself, Betsy."

"I do."

"Well, take care of yourself harder."

"I do." Betsy smiled. "As hard as I can. Green light, Grandpa."

For a moment, as he turned his head, he looked to Betsy not like her mother, as Judd had said, but like pictures of Will, her dead father. Will hadn't been the same type; Frank looked like a preacher, Will like a gambler. But there was a resemblance. When Violet became ill, Marion had said, "Thank God Will went first. He worshiped Violet."

"What are you staring at?" her grandfather asked.

Betsy flushed. She had been trying to find a resemblance between her grandfather and Judd. "You, Grandpa. I like that shirt on you." It was a red and blue Rugby shirt. She'd given it to him for his seventy-seventh birthday.

"I feel like a darned college boy."

"You *look* like a college boy."

Betsy arrived home, feeling better, to an empty apartment. Of course: he would be at his studio today. He had work to do, deadlines. She went right to the saltshaker, forgetting the slammed door and the staying power of Judd's anger. Wouldn't it be nice . . .

The kitchen table bore the remains of Judd's breakfast, but no note. She immediately checked the bedroom closet. His clothes were still there. That was her worst fear, worse than airplanes and dentists: that she would come home one day to find drawers gaping, closets empty, his yellow toothbrush gone from the bathroom, his ten-speed from the hall, desolation and despair in residence instead of her lover. But all was well, all was well.

She was suddenly more hungry than tired, and she put

bread in to toast while she made a cup of tea. The sunny kitchen always cheered her. She looked out the window. Down in the yard was her garden, still brown and bare. "Tomato plants" was written on her calendar for next weekend. Planting and harvesting—she loved it as her grandfather did. The start of the new season always excited them. "Aphid remedies and mulch are meat and drink to you two," Violet had once said.

She carried Judd's dishes to the sink, fondly surveying his crumbs. He'd skipped his usual egg and just had toast. This charmed her, for some reason. It looked like a good sign; he'd missed her, had no appetite. She would have finished off the dregs of his orange juice, but remembering Terry's advice she poured it down the sink. She felt fine—a flash of anger at Judd for leaving his dirty dishes perked her up—but she decided to put off the library and the courthouse until tomorrow. Today she would take it easy. Do something domestic: bake bread, she thought, sitting down to toasted store bread.

After the first bite, she was in the bathroom, throwing up.

When Judd got home he found her sitting up in bed watching the evening news. She heard his key in the lock, and the sound of his sneakers being taken off and dropped, and paper ripping as he opened his mail. Betsy fluffed up her hair when she heard him coming down the hall.

"What's with you?" He leaned against the doorway.

"I seem to have some kind of stomach virus."

Thank God for it! It was their peace pipe. He took her hand. "How do you feel, babe?"

"Okay now. I haven't tried to eat since morning. I was just throwing everything up."

"You stayed over there all night?"

She nodded. "And woke up sick. My punishment."

He grinned reluctantly, smoothed her brow, and kissed it.

"OK, OK. I'm sorry I got mad. I've been thinking about it. I'll stop being unreasonable about your mother."

"She is hard to deal with sometimes, Judd, especially if you're not related to her."

"I just hate to see you jump when she commands. You have your life, too, you know."

She squeezed his hand. It was the inconveniencing of his beloved, his darling Betsy, that had angered him, not the interruption of his own sleep. She was in raptures, but she kept her voice properly subdued. "Oh, I don't mind, really. She's always so sweet about everything. I couldn't be, in her condition. And she's lonely, Judd. If she just wouldn't call in the night and wake *you* up."

He shrugged and dropped her hand. "What the hell. Won't hurt me." He divided life into things Simple and things Complex, rejecting the Complex. He rejected Violet's dying. "Want to try dinner?" He got up and stood at attention. "You command and *I'll* jump, for a change."

"Tea and dry toast and an airsick bag."

She was starving, and the tea and toast stayed down. Judd sat beside her and wolfed a cheese sandwich and a glass of milk, his long bony feet propped on Betsy's knees.

"I wonder if I could try a piece of cheese."

He got it for her, but when she had eaten it and asked for more he said, "Hey, get it yourself, Camille. You seem to have recovered." He was watching Walter Cronkite and eating a handful of Chip-a-roos.

She went out to the kitchen and ate a piece of cheese and a couple of cookies. Then she dialed her mother. Frank answered.

"I'm just calling to say I'm completely recovered."

"Good. Your mother's asleep."

"Tell her I called—OK? How is she?"

"Seems OK. Why didn't you tell me she's been calling you in the middle of the night?"

"Only twice. I don't mind."

"Well, I told her not to do it tonight."

"I honestly don't mind."

"You've been sick."

"Not *sick.*"

"Still." He paused. "Betsy—if you're sick again tomorrow, you call and tell me."

"I won't be. It's gone."

"Still."

"Oh, all right. I'll be in the library all day tomorrow. You won't be able to reach me. I have some research to do."

"You're on vacation!"

"I get restless, Grandpa."

"Well, don't overdo."

She exploded. "For heaven's sake, I'm not *sick.* Can't I get an upset stomach without your turning it into an ulcer?"

"It's not an ulcer I'm afraid of."

After the news, she said to Judd, "Sometimes they drive me crazy."

"Hearing you talk about them all the time drives *me* crazy."

She changed the subject.

The next morning, she threw up, as quietly as possible, in the middle of brushing her teeth and then leaned against the sink, looking fearfully into the mirror. Her face was dead white, and when she started to put on blusher she had to vomit into the toilet again. Shaken, she debated what to do. Not mention it to Judd, for one thing. Enough was enough; he would scorn her weakness. It wasn't much of a virus, obviously, but she shouldn't have tempted it with cheese and cookies. Judd would be going out, and she would stay in bed for another hour or so until it passed, then venture out to the library. She tried again, and this time she got some blusher on and her hair combed. She retched once more, but didn't vomit.

After Judd left, she remembered she had no car, and she called her grandfather. "I need my car. Maybe you could drive it over and then I'll take you back on my way to the library."

"How's your flu?"

"I'm okay. I felt great last night, but I guess I celebrated too soon. I ate like a horse, and it all came up again this morning."

"I'll send Terry over with your car."

"Will she mind doing that?"

"She offered." Her grandfather seemed brusque.

"Did I get you in the middle of shaving or something?"

"Nope. I'll send Terry over now. Your mom's having breakfast and I'll go sit with her."

Waiting for Terry, she could hardly stay awake. She stretched out on the sofa and had fallen into a doze when the doorbell rang.

Terry bounded briskly up the steps. She was very young under all the starch and glamour, Betsy realized, yawning—maybe twenty-three or four.

"How are you doing today?"

"I've still got it, but not as bad."

Terry handed Betsy the car keys and settled down on the sofa. "I like those photographs."

"Thanks."

"And your bookcases. I like that natural wood."

"Thanks. They're new."

"It goes away in the evening?"

"What? The flu? It seems to. Actually, I felt OK all day yesterday, but I was afraid to eat and I slept a lot."

"And then this morning?"

"I paid for last night's debauch. I had all the things you told me to avoid."

Terry didn't smile. "Your grandfather asked me to ask

you—" She stopped and looked fixedly at the bookcases. "Maybe you should have a pregnancy test."

Betsy went clammy again and then flushed. Her heart seemed to have stopped. Everything seemed very quiet.

"Have your breasts felt tender?"

She swallowed. "A little. But I'm expecting my period."

"It's late?"

This is an incredible conversation, Betsy thought. "I'm not sure. I'm not very regular."

"Well, you've got the classic symptoms."

Joy rose in her throat like nausea, and she coughed before she laughed. "Do you think so? Do you think so?"—taking Terry's two hands. "It never occurred to me it could be morning sickness, I can't imagine why. Do you really think so?"

Terry frowned. Her hands were unresponsive. "You don't —mind?"

Betsy's laughter bubbled up again. "Mind? Heavens, no. Judd and I both love children. He's the man I live with, you know. I'm sure you know all about it."

"Well—" Terry was embarrassed; her shrug encompassed all the overheard gossip. Or perhaps Frank had told her. He had confided to her his fears about Betsy's nausea, after all. This fact astonished her, and for some reason it delighted her. The idea of her grandfather going to his daughter's nurse with the problem—a young girl of twenty-three advising Frank Robinson!

Betsy laughed again and squeezed Terry's hands. "Judd's a photographer. He's done some fine work with children. He does buildings now, but not exclusively. That's all his work, on the wall. He's marvelous with children. He has a real rapport with them."

"And you think he'd be glad to have one of his own?"

"Glad? Of course!" But as she said it, the certainty left her. Glad? She had no idea. What had she been thinking of when she stopped taking her pills? Of a picture Judd had taken of little Bert hanging upside down from a tree branch. Another of two solemn little girls playing dress-up, for an insurance company ad. One of a Suzuki violin class playing in unison: six bent arms, six bows, six faces fiercely concentrating. Of the afternoon they spent hiking with Judd's brother's kids. Of her last chance. Of Judd, settled. Of joy. Of nothing. She had thought of nothing that could be linked with reality. It was a Norman Rockwell pregnancy. I must be crazy, she said to herself, and imagined a future of empty closets and gaping drawers.

Terry was standing up, looking relieved. "It's a happy occasion, then, after all."

Betsy looked up at her. "I'd better have a test before I celebrate, I suppose."

Terry sensed her deflated mood and said, to cheer her, "I'd put money on it."

"Well, don't be too positive about it to my grandfather, Terry. I mean, if I *am,* I really ought to tell Judd first." Betsy forced a conspiratorial grin.

"You're right, of course." Terry beamed. "He is an awfully inquisitive old man, though. Wonderful for his age."

"He's seventy-seven."

"As old as the century. And you'd think he was no older than Mrs. Ruscoe."

"She's wonderful for her age, too. All things considered."

Terry's face went somber. "It's a privilege to see her through this."

"How long, do you think, Terry?"

"Impossible to tell, it's such an unpredictable thing." She frowned, flattered she was asked. "But I think she's got a way to go."

Involuntarily, Betsy put her hand on her stomach. She felt strong and optimistic again. The nausea had passed, her tiredness had left her. She came, after all, from a stoic family. Though crowned with thorns, her head would not bow.

"Funny, isn't it?" Terry indicated Betsy's stomach.

"Funny? Yes, it is funny," Betsy said. "It is damned funny." She looked approvingly at Terry's white uniform. This would be her world for a while, the world of nurses and urine samples and personal questions. All the special, healthy, feminine world of pregnancy, with its arcane processes and vocabulary, would be hers, like a club. She patted her flat stomach; it felt good and ripe beneath her hand.

Betsy took a bottle of urine downtown to the Planned Parenthood Clinic the next morning as soon as Judd and her nausea were gone. She was assigned a friendly young woman named Peg who took her into a cubicle and dropped a puddle of urine on a test paper with an eyedropper. She explained everything as she went along. Betsy had thought it was rabbits, and her pint jarful embarrassed her. Why hadn't they told her they needed only a drop? Peg explained about the rabbits, and Betsy tried to look intelligent, but she wasn't hearing a word. She was looking at a framed woodcut on the wall of the little room—a mother and child. There was infinite tenderness in the tilt of the mother's head, in the circle of her arm about the infant.

"Positive!"

Peg poured out Betsy's pint and washed her hands. Betsy sat and watched in silence.

"Are you pleased?" Peg had a tiny lisp, and thick red arms like legs.

"Yes," Betsy whispered, and then said more loudly, "Yes, I am. I'm not married, though. But we may decide to, now. We may."

Peg dried her hands on a paper towel and sat down facing Betsy. Her face was full of the desire to help. "Do you have a gynecologist?"

"Yes."

"Better make an appointment right away. Do you want me to sign you up for some counseling?"

"You mean, don't I want a nice abortion?"

Peg's face went even kinder at Betsy's hostility. "I don't mean that at all. It's simply that women in your position can sometimes use advice. Someone to talk to."

"I can talk to the baby's father. That seems the logical choice." It was all bravado, but Peg didn't know that. She shrugged her shoulders and spread her big hands wide. One of them still held the paper towel, wadded up. "Of course," Peg said. It came out, "Of courth." The paper towel fell to the floor and she bent to pick it up. The interview was over.

Why did I get so nasty? Betsy asked herself. What in hell am I doing, anyway? Her condition was incurable, like her mother's; there was no going back on life any more than on death. She saw herself and her baby in a circle of love. She saw the baby as a piece of herself, transmuted, glorious. But she didn't see Judd at all.

CHAPTER FOUR

Violet

Violet lay, or sat propped, in her bed by the window, peacefully thinking. Her placidity was becoming a legend in the family. She could see them look at her with admiration; in turn she looked back at them, amused. Someone—who had it been? Marion? doing her duty by her dead sister?—had asked if she wanted a clergyman, a priest, and Violet's laughter had bubbled over. She had no need of priests, with the image of Will before her. A priest! She pictured a timid and platitudinous man in black, like the one who'd staged her mother's funeral. At least there would be no priests and no lugubrious chanting at hers. She had specified: no music, no flowers, no church. She had toyed with the idea of having them play "Stardust"—their song—and smiled at the picture of Frank and Marion, Betsy and Judd, fox-trotting at her funeral.

Violet kept her mind, when she could, on her death, preparing herself, examining her conscience, as she'd been taught to years ago by Helen. (You ran through the long list of possible sins and kept a scorecard on yourself.) But she didn't think of her transgressions—and they were few enough, it seemed to her—as sins. Mistakes, rather. The only one that mattered was Betsy; somewhere she had steered her daughter wrong. Oh, if Will had only lived things would be different, Betsy would be married years back, and there would be grandchildren to see her casket lowered into the ground.

But if only Betsy was settled. . . . This sorrow drove out the thought of death and narrowed to an irritation: Judd. Betsy's chosen lover. Violet flinched at the word but forced herself to use it. What else to call him? The Ann Landers column in the evening paper was full of facetious suggestions, but when you came right down to it a man and woman living together were lovers, pure and simple. (No, not pure, and probably not simple, either.) Or else they were husband and wife. In this case, better a lover than a husband; lovers by definition were temporary. But you never know. He is unfathomable, Violet thought—a deep one.

She forced on herself the possibility that he might, for whatever unsavory reason of his own, be persuaded to marry her daughter after all—a man with nothing pleasant or engaging or amiable about him, no politesse. Brought up down in Texas someplace by a fat woman with ten children and her front teeth out. He'd told them that: "I was raised in foster homes. I spent six years with a woman named Bobbie-Dora Prince and her husband Ray Prince. Bobbie-Dora was fat and illiterate and just about toothless, but she had a heart of gold. At one time she had ten of us homeless brats. Her mother had her sterilized when she was sixteen because she thought Bobbie-Dora was mentally defective—she'd already had two babies, both dead. But she was just a good, simple woman who loved kids. Ray was all right when he was sober, he used to play the banjo, but it was Bobbie-Dora who took care of us. I sent her Christmas and birthday cards until a couple of years ago when I heard she died. Actually, she was shot to death by a boy she took in."

He told them that when he met the family for the first time. What was anyone to say? Especially the way he told it, so unemotional, and then he changed the subject, anyway. Betsy, sitting beside him with that moonstruck look as if where she really wanted to sit was at his feet.

He was successful enough, made a living—not that his photographs were much to look at. All they did was show what was there and pretty it up a little bit. He specialized in long street vistas, the seedier and the more depressing the better, so he could make them seem quaint and nostalgic, with the sun on them and a hazy look he must get by shooting through gauze or Vaseline, like they did Doris Day in the movies. It wasn't even very effective; there wasn't an awful lot you could do with parking lots and farm shacks and broken-down storefronts, mostly in dusty southern towns best left forgotten. He'd had a book of these published, but Violet couldn't imagine anyone buying it but his friends—if he had any. Who wanted to look at such things, even through gauze?

She supposed his commercial photographs were better, the ones he got paid so handsomely for. Those buildings. And Betsy swore he did beautiful shots of children, though Violet found that hard to imagine, unless he bullied them into cute poses. She pictured him rough and shouting, pushing children around, and charging huge sums for the results. It seemed a shame—that photography could pay so well. She was remembering Will and his sketches—his unsung talent. Now there was a craftsman, she thought (turning uneasily in bed as the pain touched her). Just a man and his pencil, no camera to do the work for him, no darkroom full of expensive gadgets.

She hadn't looked at Will's sketches in years, couldn't bear to, and the years had covered them with their own gauzy haze. Reconstructed in her mind, their bold, honest strokes were softened. She forgot the economy of his lines and the way he drew, obsessively, over and over, her mouth and eyes, mouth and eyes, sometimes a hand or the curve of her cheek. She forgot her impatience with him for never bringing the pieces together. She would have loved that formal portrait of her he had always intended to paint, treasured it as a memorial to him, not to her. It could have hung on the wall, just there, where she could see it and think of his hands holding the brushes, his frowning face bent over the work. She saw the portrait, in oils, finished and pretty, with her hair done, and completely forgot that he drew her only in rough pieces with black ink.

The imaginary portrait was part of her peace. So was Emily the imaginary mother. It pleased her to see Emily as a young girl in white, not yet a mother at all, a girl with Violet's own face, or Betsy's face. She had turned Emily over to Betsy; for her, only the waiting was left, and waiting was her forte. Lying in bed watching the sun patterns move across the wall, slip into corners, and disappear, Violet was all expectancy. Life, death, pain and relief from pain—all of it was beyond her control, and she was glad to let it go. Only Betsy roused her worry. I will die before I've done a mother's duty, Violet thought. If only she was settled: she said it to herself over and over; the phrase came into her mind whenever Betsy did. And not settled with *him*. It always came back to Judd. She had been willing to be won over, to take to Judd as Frank and Helen had finally taken to Will— Ah, but that was different, this Judd was no Will, and there had been the decent church wedding, with stephanotis and white roses and herself in white satin and a big, flat hat.

If only Betsy would settle down with a nice man, a fellow professor, maybe—a man with some charm, who knew how to talk to a prospective mother-in-law, who didn't growl over the phone, who came to dinner when he was invited, who observed amenities. Judd was ruining her last days, she thought sometimes when she felt crabby and unwell. He was an intrusion, like pain. Maybe it was the way Betsy looked at him, maybe it was those pale little eyes, or his shirts unbuttoned too far, or the closed-up look on his face—or the endless camera clicking: endless, and then he never showed them the photographs.

It became easier and easier, though, to put the problem

from her mind. In fact, as the days went on, the present slipped further from her. Company could keep it close. While Frank sat with her, or Terry (the sticky perfumy smell!), or Betsy, Marion, the occasional friend, the past lurked just out of reach like a cat in a tree, waiting. And as soon as she was alone it pounced with its velvet paws.

Sometimes she would nap briefly and awake to find the sun moving across her thin yellow blanket, and the blanket was the yellow mass of roses on Helen's coffin. The roses were from Frank, and he had tears to contribute as well, as if tears and roses could wash death away and mask its smell. Frank's tears had frightened her, and Betsy's, too, because they were not weepers. It was Violet, the weeper, who had no tears for Helen. Any tears she had she was still spending on Will; for Will, they were an endless resource, not to be spent on this imitation mother. Nearly thirty years hadn't dried them up.

Once, with the tears on her cheeks, she had opened her eyes to see the sun gone from her blanket, and Judd standing by her bed.

"I've brought the book," he said. "Betsy got held up at a meeting."

He laid it on the table—some book or other Betsy had dug up for her in the library—and then he took a handkerchief and gently wiped at the tears.

"Don't cry," he whispered, and when she opened her eyes again it was Frank, waiting to read. A dream, it was—or the pills—though there was the book. She never asked.

Her days were full of such puzzlements. She accepted them, and then she forgot them, the things that happened between sleep and waking.

Once there had been her father's voice, loud as thunder, and her mother's had come in, tap-tapping, tap-tapping, a hammer on a nail. The two voices had been woven together, then wrenched apart with a tearing sound. She was a child, alone in her overheated room, in bed at night, and they were fighting, of course, over her. The crashing, tapping, tearing was all her fault. She pulled the covers over her head, so that the stuffy darkness, which she usually loved, scared her, and the sounds muffled that way were dreadful and strange. They were troll sounds, like the trolls in *The Three Billy Goats Gruff* that made her shut her eyes and cover her ears when her father read it, only his arm around her keeping the nasty trolls at bay and the fear delectable. She raised her head free of the blankets, listening, and the noises ceased except for the tap-tapping and she thought: Mother has won, and she's building something with her hammer—which so terrified her she woke with a scream to see Terry, and her high-protein drink, and a thermometer, and to hear the rain dripping from the gutters.

"I think that storm has pushed your fever up, Mrs. Ruscoe."

The days passed in dreams. Pain was still experimental, tentative. Violet could still sit back and look at it, surprised, as if a puppy had nipped her in play. But it made her suspicious and inattentive; she had to stay tuned to the teeth in her flesh.

She didn't really like leaving her bedroom, but the rest of them thought changes of scene were good for her.

"Nothing is good for me," she said to Frank. He was helping her out of bed. "Just as nothing is bad for me."

Her father just set his face and held out her robe to her, but Marion looked shocked and said, "I wish you wouldn't go on like that, Violet." The two of them helped her down the hall and down the stairs and, now that the weather was so good, out to the green backyard. They sat her in the chaise under a shawl, where she could reach up and touch the lilacs. "Their smell is so sweet and cool," she said when they bloomed. "I like it so much better than roses."

"Well, the roses will be out any day, too," Frank said. He looked forward to them, especially now that he'd given up his vegetable patch. She knew he loved the roses; she was glad

Betsy didn't. Betsy grew useful things, like vegetables, with a row of marigolds put in only to keep the bugs off. Last summer she'd sat in Betsy's backyard with her, watching her weed and cultivate, so much like her grandfather. She could remember Frank, before his hair turned white and disappeared entirely on top, so handsome and lean in his old-fashioned undershirt, with a kettle of mashed-up tomatoes in front of him, scooping them into jars. While he worked he sang old songs no one else ever sang anymore: "Courting songs," he said, winking at Helen's turned back.

"Will I live to eat your tomatoes this years, Betsy?" They all pretended she hadn't said it; perhaps she hadn't.

Then the roses came out (first the climbing Peace roses on the trellis, then the floribunda hedges) and spread their sick smell all over the yard when the breeze was right. Excessive, like too much cologne, like hair spray. Then the Japanese beetles on the old, overgrown raspberry canes. A memory crept up and surprised her; for a second, Helen was in the backyard with them—over there, by the old garden patch, in one of her zip-front housedresses, as real as Betsy. Violet grimaced. Anyone watching her would have thought the pain was particularly bad, but it was the memory: Helen squashing the beetles between her fingernails with a crunch, and crushing tomato hornworms with her bare heel. Ugh! Her mother's brash fearlessness was almost inhuman—and Lord, you'd never have guessed it from her mousy face.

Remembering Helen and the insects, Violet developed a fear of the roses and avoided looking into their hearts lest there be a bug there, a worm curled about the stamens. She laughed at herself. It was like something out of a book, some heavy symbolism. But she recoiled from the roses. And though it had been Helen who prompted her horror, Judd took over as the sun unfolded the blossoms. If she were putting that particular symbol in a book or a poem, the worm in the rose would be her daughter's lover.

Once, sitting outside in the sunshine, with the flowers blooming all around her—opening up, turning gross and helpless, and falling—she had said to Betsy, "The roses only make me sad."

Betsy's hopeful smile faded away, and she said, "Oh, I'm sorry, Mother," with her special grieved look, so that Violet knew it was her disease Betsy was thinking of. The worm eating away at her insides. The insect gnawing out her bones. The beetle in the heart of the fruit.

"I didn't mean anything, Betsy," she said, but Betsy took her hand and kissed her knuckles, with the easy affection Violet loved so much in her daughter. "I'd like a little bourbon, honey." Betsy had to get it for her, of course, although it was barely noon. Crazy, how upset they all would get over nothing, Violet thought, breathing deeply. The ice rattled in the glass because her hands were trembling.

The bourbon always made her sharper. Every hot swallow cleared some of the mist off things, and, drinking, she would glance alertly around her, with her old birdy look. She smiled at them all, hearing their thoughts: Well, it's good for her, let her have it, whatever helps let her have, even though nothing helps. They were thinking, too, of Will, she bet—Will's blunt fingers curved around a glass. "Let's have a drink to celebrate," he would say, and with that strange avidity get out the bottle. Oh, the dear man, with his baroque conversation, his lovely strong shoulders, his sketch pad. And that old dog of his he'd loved so . . . She smiled around at them, loving them all, her family. I will have a loving death, she thought, and refused to let the word scare her. She was far beyond fear. Death was a word on a door: open it, and there was Will.

They were all present, gathered in the backyard for the ritual steak. She didn't like meat. She hoped there would be garlic bread, and a nice dessert. There was wine, but she refused it for bourbon. Let's have a drink to celebrate. I am happy, Violet thought. Better than happy, I am amused. The pursing and unpursing of her aunt's little lips amused her, and her father's veiny, ribbed hands messing with the steak. I won't live long enough to get those liver spots, she thought. Betsy making them all laugh with her gossip—where had she got such a sharp-tongued daughter? Violet wondered, laughing hard. How they made her laugh, even that time she opened her eyes to see that man's hairy hand on Betsy's knee, creeping up—they'd thought the bourbon had put her to sleep. Even that amused her, though she had burst out at them querulously; it was the pain that made her. The pain could pounce as swift and sudden as memory, with jaws and claws that bit and scratched.

She sank back into her shawl, drinking. She would try. He was not the man she would have chosen for Betsy, her dear Betsy—so wrong, why couldn't she see it—but she would try to like him. The attempt would be her legacy to her daughter, all she had to give. Narrow-eyed and clearheaded, she watched him from her seat under the rotting lilacs, forcing a smile when he looked her way or pointed his camera at her. But why must he go barefoot? she thought. Like a hippie. And with such hairy toes.

CHAPTER FIVE

Betsy

Telling Judd the news was beyond Betsy's strength. She waited, as she waited with a toothache, hoping it would resolve itself somehow and make a visit to the dentist unnecessary. I'll wait for him to notice, Betsy thought, and imagined Judd's face transfigured by joy when, caressing her, he comprehended the changes in her body. I'll wait until it shows, she thought. Until I'm more used to it. Until it's absolutely necessary.

What she was truly waiting for remained unvoiced: for him to suggest marriage. That the desire should come before the necessity was all she asked—but she didn't ask. She kept silent, waiting.

The baby was thoroughly real to her from the beginning. She felt friendly and at ease with the full-grown person who would sit at a table with her someday drinking coffee, who would drive a car and go to college and have her own babies. She imagined it, always, as a daughter—hoping, in fact, so vehemently for a girl (sensing that she didn't comprehend boys well enough to bring one up) that she was appalled, and wouldn't let herself speculate on the baby's sex at all. But soon she began to believe that such powerful desire was prophetic, that the baby must be a girl, and she stopped worrying.

They went, as promised, to dinner at her grandfather's. Judd brought his camera, further alienating Aunt Marion, who pretended to be flattered but hated having her picture taken.

"Me? You want to take me?" She lifted her head out of its nest of chins and jowls. "I've never yet had a good picture taken of me."

"The camera doesn't lie, Marion," said Violet from the chaise. The glass of bourbon had become a matter of course.

"Oh, but it does," Judd said, squatting low to get the chins in. "It lies all the time, that's what's so maddening about it." Three quick clicks while he talked.

"I always photographed well, I must say." Violet's tone was petulant, and Judd, sensing a summons, abandoned her aunt and pointed his camera at Violet. "Wonderful light on you, Mrs. Ruscoe." He went down on one knee with the bare pink sole of one foot pointing up, while behind him Aunt Marion patted her upsweep and put her glasses back on.

Violet raised her drink and ventured a smile, her head on one side. "How's this? What angle makes me look least like an old bag?"

"You look great," Judd said. It was true, Betsy thought; her mother was still youthful and pretty. But she had seen, in Judd's studio, a stack of rough prints of her family, and she was appalled at the death in them—her mother's face all bones, her grandfather ropy with veins, her aunt a puffed-up cadaver. Judd seemed pleased with the photographs and flipped through them, smiling faintly.

"You really must hate them," she accused him.

He looked at her in surprise and anger. "Betsy, I'm a fucking photographer. These aren't your mother and your grandfather—they're pictures."

"You've made them look so old and ugly, Judd. They're not like your other things." She was afraid he was getting together a new book, of brutally real portraits of the elderly. His first book, with its sunlit evocations of small-town squalor, had been a modest hit; she knew the publisher was agitating for another.

Judd ignored her words and peered closely at a shot of Violet with her head thrown back and her eyes closed. "I must say, though, your mother has gorgeous bones. Look at these shadows."

To Betsy, it was as if her mother was already dead, nothing left of her but the beautiful bones and the shadows they cast. She turned away from the photographs.

Now, on her grandfather's back lawn, she leaned toward her mother with an involuntary protective gesture, and Violet held out her glass to be filled.

Judd began to tell Violet about a cat show he had once photographed. It was one in his stock of funny stories, produced to distract his subjects from the camera, and Betsy listened fondly, laughing to cue Violet in case pain or dislike made her inattentive. She wanted to say, "Isn't he marvelous? Do you see how wonderful he's being, how he wants so much to get along with you all?" She laughed prematurely at a cat story, and her grandfather gave her an odd look, then laughed himself.

"You've certainly had the life, Judd," he said. "When you're my age, you'll certainly have more to look back on than a lot of musty legal cases."

"That's for sure," said Aunt Marion, keeping a wary eye on the camera; it might have been a gun.

Judd looked through the viewfinder at Frank. "I can't think of anything more interesting to look back on than your career," he said, snapping quickly before Frank got up to turn the steak on the grill. The smell of steak had wiped out the smell of roses and rotting lilacs, and when Frank did get up they all watched him hungrily. "I've often wished I'd gone into something more solid, Mr. Robinson—like the law. Something more predictable."

Betsy tried to imagine Judd in a business suit, sitting at a desk behind a telephone with buttons on it, and reading briefs at home in the evening as her grandfather had, instead of listening to records and looking at photographs. It was worse than trying to imagine him a baby, or a little boy playing in a dusty road.

"Wouldn't suit you," Frank said, and flipped the steak onto a platter.

"Maybe not." Judd wound up the film and put his camera back in its case. "Sometimes I wish it would."

Violet's voice came sharply from her corner under the lilacs. "Would you say you're settled for good in the Syracuse area, Judd? Finding plenty of work here?"

"More than I can handle." Judd smiled at Violet and then turned to Betsy. "I like it here," he said, taking her hand to help her up. "Beautiful country."

Betsy tossed the salad, hiding her smile.

"Now if you could just get that blush of hers on your black-and-white film," said Frank, looking approvingly at his granddaughter.

"Under thirty it's a blush; over fifty it's a hot flash," said Aunt Marion.

"Listen to the epigrams," Betsy said.

"What's in between?" asked Violet.

"Just nervousness," her aunt said sourly, getting up and smoothing her pant legs down. "Nervous coloration."

"Whatever it is, it's very becoming on Betsy," said Frank, and set the steak firmly on the picnic table, closing the subject.

When she was with Judd and her family, Betsy saw the group as two teams—herself and her grandfather on one side, her mother and aunt on the other, Judd the ball they tossed around. It was an odd game, in which her side repeatedly passed the ball to the others, who speedily returned it, as if it burned the fingers. The score so far had been decidedly in the other team's favor.

But this evening over the steak and salad Judd devoted himself to charming them. Betsy watched closely: Violet laughed at Judd's anecdotes, even waited expectantly for more, glass raised and lips parted in her flirtatious smile. Aunt Marion's laughter was more reluctant, but it did burst out of her now and then in small explosions that she got tipsy trying to drown in wine.

"That boy has a gift for telling a story," she said to Betsy after coffee, the winy laughter still simmering. "I'll bet he's an entertaining fellow to have around sometimes."

"A laugh a minute," Betsy assured her absentmindedly. She was watching Judd take leave of her mother: not a false step, the right mix of courtly admiration and filial deference. Scoring points right and left. Oh, isn't he wonderful, she thought, taking his arm and beaming around at them all.

Her grandfather walked them to the car. "Can I cut you a few roses to take, Betsy?"

"You know me, Grandpa. I'd just forget them and they'd petal up the whole house."

He chuckled. "You're a vegetable girl, Betsy. Like your grandmother." The word meant Emily to her now; with an effort she applied it to Helen.

"But she liked those roses, too, Grandpa." They paused by the yellow floribunda hedge and impulsively she tore one rose off. "Here, Judd—" She stuck it through his buttonhole. "A boutonniere," she said, and stopped abruptly because it suggested weddings.

Her grandfather talked roses to Judd, Judd listening respectfully, even asking a question or two. It astonished her every time she saw him in one of these commonplace transactions. He was so miraculous, so special. To engage in normal human intercourse seemed delightfully quaint in him, another proof of his powers: that such a magical being could manage it.

"Well done, my lad," she said as they drove home.

"What do you mean—well done? I wasn't performing."

"A little, you were."

"Nonsense! I like your family. I enjoyed myself."

Betsy turned it over in her mind. She had spent the evening in a glow: that he had worked so hard to ingratiate himself with her family was a sign of his love for her. Now it appeared he hadn't been working at it. Was that better or worse? Surely it was better that he could be natural with them. . . . On the other hand, he could be deliberately disclaiming any efforts to get along with them in order to exhibit his indifference to *her*.

She wanted him to like her family, and not only for her own sake, or theirs. He had no relatives except his brother's family. He had been orphaned young; he and Derek had, in fact, witnessed the gruesome death of their father in a hunting accident. A few months later had come the drowning—possibly not accidental—of their mother. The boys had been raised as wards of the state of Texas. Was he then invulnerable to family feeling? Did he grudge her the little circle of doting relatives?

She shut her mind to the endless calculations and sat close to him, with her hand resting on her stomach. "They like you, too, Judd."

"Well, good. I'm glad." He reached an arm around and hugged her.

She moved her fingers lightly over her belly, calculating, always calculating: when to tell him, and how.

She badly needed the child. She had always, it seemed, needed a child, beginning with Samantha, her first baby. She had escaped to the attic—where she had set up for herself a private corner—to change Samantha's diapers, spank her rubber bottom, dress her up for church, sing to her. Sometimes she simply rocked her doll, staring out the dusty attic window at roofs and trees, while in the rooms below her grandmother irritably cooked, her mother went dreamily through her library books, her grandfather worked at his big desk.

She had been a morose, solitary, intelligent, patient child whose best friends were her father's old black dog and her doll. She had played with Samantha long past the age when little girls cease to play with dolls. Her grandmother disapproved, and eventually she had to steal away to Samantha and cuddle her in furtive silence. Then, gradually, this no longer eased her—it seemed silly—and she laid Samantha away forever in her wicker carriage, wrapped in her sprigged blanket and dressed in her Sunday best.

Life overflowed with losses: her father lying red-faced on the floor of the shop, and her mother's terrible, low moaning; the old dog, Poochie, stiff in his dog basket; her grandmother's sharp tongue silenced, lowered into the earth with her worn-out body; and her lovers, that small and far-from-choice collection, and only one of them her lover in the strictest sense of the word. . . .

She thought sometimes—always with resentment—of Alan, who had sneaked away from his frigid wife to see her when she was his student in graduate school. They had met at her apartment, where they lay on the floor and drank wine. He was the only man, before Judd, she had been really intimate with, but he had insisted they stop short of the sexual act itself. "I don't want to get that involved," he said.

"How could you be any more heavily involved, Alan?" Betsy used to ask. "You say you love me—isn't that about as involved as you can get?"

"That's different," he said nervously, and pulled down her underpants. He would never take them completely off, and with their clothes down around their ankles and up around their necks they made love as best they could. Betsy pleaded with him and nagged him, and when he objected, "You're satisfied, aren't you?", after bringing her to climax with tongue and fingers, she had to admit—though not to Alan—that what she wanted was the thrill of possibility, the knowledge that a baby could be made. Horrified at her motives, she threw herself so passionately into the contrivances of their lovemaking that when Alan left for a new position in Wisconsin he had the vague notion of divorce. But he never called or wrote; he disappeared into the Midwest as if he had died there, and Betsy didn't allow herself to grieve. When a year later she heard that he and his wife had had a baby, she went home and wept.

And now she had done it. She couldn't help viewing her pregnancy as a triumph, something she had pulled off. As she sat with Judd in the evenings, reading and listening to records, her hooded eyes would crinkle into the start of a smile and she would feel her stomach lurch with excitement, and wonder if the baby could feel it. At such moments Judd ceased to exist—just for a second, two seconds—and when they were over she would look at him tenderly, apologetically, and jump up to make coffee or bring him a bedtime snack.

In the patchwork of memories Violet had made for her of Will, her father, Betsy had stitched one of her own. She is very young, she seems to recall a tricycle in the picture, and she and her father are sitting on the front steps with Poochie. Behind them is the magical sign-painting shop where she loves to go with him, but it's a hot afternoon and they sit outside. There is some vague tension. Have her parents had a fight? Or is it the heat? If she concentrates, Betsy imagines she can recall the sunsuit she had on—pink and blue check, with ruffled straps that cross in back. Her father is talking to her, and out of the silken web of words he used to spin comes this, in a fierce whisper, "It's you and me against the world, kiddo," as he picks her up and hugs her. It's hot to be held so close, but she hugs back, sniffing in his nice, fruity whiskey smell.

Thirty years later, with her palm pressed to her belly

where Will's grandchild hurries toward birth, she thinks, smiling, "It's you and me against the world, kiddo," while her lover lies at her feet drinking coffee.

It was still early when they returned from her grandfather's. They went outside to sit on the back steps. In the dying light the backyard—so bland and sunny in the daytime, with its squared-off garden plot and long border of berry plants—looked mysterious and inviting. Betsy had a fleeting vision of herself and Judd lying together on the soft grass under the maple. They had never made love outside, hadn't been together long enough—only since January. But we have years, years, she thought, and turned her head slightly to see his long-nosed profile. He looked sleepy and content—domesticated. It will never be the same between us, Betsy thought. Look your last at that particular face. After tonight it will change forever.

Behind them, in the first-floor apartment, they heard the Brodskys' television. Music, then voices, then music and voices together. Betsy sweated with nervousness; she knew it was time she spoke. Talking wasn't what they were good at. They sat mostly in silence while she rehearsed: Judd, I'm pregnant. No. Judd, I'm going to have a baby. No. Judd, we're going to have a baby.

They watched the sunset colors wash out of the sky, and then everything go dark except the sky, which was pale and then smoky-gray against the precise silhouettes of trees. When the stars came out, Betsy said, "I once spent a summer in the country. There were millions more stars out there than in the city. And the sky was much blacker."

He didn't answer. The perfume from the wilting rose in his buttonhole came faintly to them. She touched his arm with hers. It scared her about him, the worlds he had traveled without her. There were times he traveled them still.

Betsy moved her aching shoulders to relax them and felt sweat run down her sides from her armpits. Her chest hurt with the tension. She took a deep breath. "Judd, we're going to have a baby."

It was a mistake to tell him in the dark; she needed to see his face. He said nothing. He seemed not to breathe.

"Judd?"

"You mean you are," he said at last.

Her heart began to pound, her ears hurt, her teeth hurt. All right. All right, then.

"Yes. I mean I am."

"That's why you've been throwing up."

"I'm afraid so."

"You were on the pill."

"I went off it."

Further silence. Love which does not prosper dies: Betsy firmly believed this, in spite of the example of Eloise and Abelard, about whom she lectured passionately to her students each spring in her Pope seminar. Under the stars, she said it over to herself (love which does not prosper dies), expecting it to give her comfort. But she felt as cold and hard and comfortless as a stone.

"Judd?"

"What about an abortion?"

"I want this baby." Her heart leapt; they could discuss it.

"You see my position, Betsy." He lifted his arm to run his hand through his hair, and when he put it down it was no longer touching hers. "I'm not the marrying kind. As they say."

"I'm not asking marriage," she said, chucking it then and there.

"Or the settling-down kind."

"Ah. Well."

"I don't want to be anybody's father."

But you love children! You'd be a good father! She

wouldn't let these cries escape her. She felt their falseness. The world had turned around in five minutes. The stars should be under their feet, the Brodskys' TV the roar of the apocalypse.

"So you see my position."

"Yes, of course."

They sat awhile longer, and then she said, "I suppose we might as well go up."

At the door she saw his face in the light from the back hall. It was sorrowful. "I wanted us to be together, Betsy."

He followed her upstairs. In bed she wept in his arms, and then they made love. He thrust furiously into her, as if to rip from her womb whatever of himself was there. It was the first time their lovemaking had failed to move her, but she pretended it did, as a bon voyage present.

But nothing happened. In the morning, while she retched in the bathroom, she fancied she heard him dragging out his suitcases and throwing clothes into them. When she emerged, he was scrambling eggs, whistling, wearing a red tie.

"Feel better?"

"I think so," she said, and breathed deeply to calm herself. Her heartbeat was audible. She was afraid to speak: there was a spell, and if she broke it he would walk out the door forever.

She made tea while he bolted his eggs. "I'm late—got to get this printing done by noon."

"You'll be in your studio?"

"Till noon."

And then? and then? She lifted the hot tea to her lips; it warmed her but she couldn't yet drink. "And then?"

"Lunch with Kramer, appointment with Jerry at two, and then—" He drained his coffee cup, clattered it down, and grinned. "Home early, I guess."

The steam from the tea brought tears to her eyes, quickly blinked away. This was the way it would be—panic and relief, panic and relief, like a deathwatch. We must talk it out, she thought, get it straight. If you're going, go, leave me in peace. "Then I'll see you later," she said, smiling radiantly and lifting her face to be kissed.

The late spring was full of rain. At the end of May Betsy planted her garden and watched the rain darken the brown soil. It washed up her lettuce plants, and she replanted, patting the damp earth around the roots and thinking of Judd, Judd, Judd. Before she met him, in her virginal spinster days, she had prided herself on keeping her solitary life turned outward, toward the world; now, with a man in captivity, her life had shrunk to a cage. Betsy pondered the irony of this fact, but she was helpless to fight it. There was even a sick happiness in bowing before it.

The days passed. He was kind to her—too kind, she thought when panic took her over. He wooed her as he had wooed Violet and Marion and her grandfather, but to what purpose she could not tell. Her head ached from the strain of figuring. Her back ached from bending over the garden plot. Every morning she retched, silently, invariably, and every evening she fought sleep, struggling to stay awake with Judd. Laughing, he would send her to bed and stay up alone, reading or watching television or listening to records while she lay awake long enough to wonder: what is he thinking? will he go out? what must I do?—before she fell into a thick, flannelly sleep from which she had trouble waking in the mornings.

They never spoke of her pregnancy. One night they went to the movies and saw *Three Women.* Judd left during the childbirth scene. He was waiting for her outside. "I just couldn't stand seeing you so excited," he said. He had taken up smoking again.

"If it'll make you feel any better, the baby was born dead."

"Oh, great."

When she was with him she tried to read his face, and when he was away she analyzed it. She could think of nothing but Judd, Judd. Even the quest she'd set herself on her mother's behalf blurred before his name, and whenever a vague guilt or an equally vague sense of purpose came to her, the question of Judd sharpened into focus and drove everything else out. The quest for Emily had lost its immediacy; nor had she told her grandfather about her pregnancy. She must wait and see what Judd would do. She felt herself to be under siege, and she waited, as if for the decisive battle, gardening in the mornings and spending the afternoons in a daze with a book called *Your Guide to Pregnancy and Birth,* which she kept hidden.

They went regularly to the Saturday night dinners, but things did not go well. Judd was polite, but he was preoccupied and distant, with little appetite for Frank's steaks or for photographing Violet. She could see he disappointed them. The old team spirit returned, and Betsy sat helplessly in the lush garden, watching the people she loved best feint awkwardly at each other. She talked and talked—she became feverish with talking—to cover up Judd's silences, and her mother's.

Violet was changing, quieting, becoming absorbed in her illness, although Terry insisted there was no difference in her. The end could come suddenly, or it could creep up. . . . Betsy saw death creeping up on Violet like a predatory animal that stalked with incredible subtlety, whose cunning exceeded the human imagination—and Violet was falling into its clutches without a fight.

She had stopped calling in the night—she was on a new kind of sleeping pill—but when one night she finally did call, Betsy slept through the ringing and Judd answered. He shook her urgently.

"It's three o'clock in the morning and your mother's on the phone. She doesn't sound good."

Violet was whispering. "Betsy? Oh, I had the worst dream,

honey. Mrs. Foster is in the john. Have you found my mama?"

The next day Violet had no memory of the phone call, and on the morning after that Betsy forced herself to drive down to the library.

She hadn't been inside the public library in years, not since she'd been teaching at the university. But she remembered it well—the worn-down marble steps, the locked cabinet of biology texts, the odd characters reading newspapers, the grimy oak. She and Violet used to go there on Saturdays and pick out books, a volume or two of Mazo de la Roche for Violet, *Betsy-Tacy* or *Freddy the Detective* for Betsy. It was something private she and her mother did; Helen never read a book (barring the Bible and her Sunday missal), and Frank read chiefly newspapers and briefs. The library was hers and Violet's.

She found a book called *Digging Out Your Past.* It was illustrated with line drawings of a happy family searching busily through libraries and newspaper files and old photograph albums. They looked like people in *New Yorker* cartoons except that they weren't doing anything funny. In the end, they found great-great-great-aunt Louisa and great-great-great-uncle Frederick, who were represented in oval tintypes, looking just like Mom and Pop. On the last page, the happy family lined up, proudly rooted beneath their family tree.

It wasn't very helpful. Genealogical research wasn't what she was engaged in. It was more like a search for a missing person. . . . Should she go to the police? Hire a detective? Put notices in newspapers?

She couldn't rise to such melodrama. She looked in the card catalog again; not surprisingly, there were no books about finding missing persons. She was baffled—she was used to turning to books for what she needed—and she was also, unexpectedly, personally let down. Looking at the happy cartoon people, with their children and their ancestors all around them, she understood that the search for Emily was as much hers as Violet's. It was a search for her baby's family. An only child, fatherless, her mother dying, Betsy was without relatives. She hadn't properly taken it in before, but in the library she did. She saw herself telling her child, someday, about Emily. Her child would tell her grandchildren: "Once upon a time, my mother set out to find her mother's mother, whose name was Emily. . . ."

She put the book back on the shelf, feeling urgency. She must find Emily before Emily died, too, and took all the secrets with her. She got out her notes. On Violet's blue stationery she had added the facts gleaned from the letters, a sorry and tenuous few:

hated by Helen (why?)
healthy and cooperative at time of birth
gave birth Dec. 1922, Haddam, Ct. (probably)
Aunt M. brought baby to Syracuse? Jan. 1923?

(She had taken great pleasure in writing "gave birth" and "time of birth" and "baby.") She read the notes through again, mulling over possible unravelings. There wasn't much to go on. What she needed was Emily's last name, and all she had was a hint and an address. Was there some kind of directory? She thought of city directories—the *Times* article mentioned them—and walked over to the courthouse from the library.

I should be good at this kind of detective work, she told herself. She had been promoted to associate professor on the strength of her annotated edition of a diary kept by Rose Deasy, the literate wife of a Grub Street hack who had known Samuel Johnson and other members of the Ivy Lane Club in 1749. The work had required a six-month sabbatical, a small grant from the Johnson Society, and painstaking research, over the course of two years, in the British Museum and the libraries of three American universities. It had brought her a paradoxical reward: great fame in circles no one had ever heard of (including, as an offshoot, a review in a feminist journal that tried unpersuasively to turn Rose Deasy into an inspirational, emancipated heroine). Almost as much as on the obscure fame, Betsy had thrived on the task.

But this one, considerably less complex (though also less clear-cut) and with considerably more at stake (the peace of mind of her dying mother, whom she loved), was making her weary before she'd even begun it. *Your Guide to Pregnancy and Birth* put it succinctly: "Many pregnant women find it difficult to wrench their minds away from what's happening to their bodies long enough to cope with the practical world. You may find yourself in a perpetually dreamy state during part or all of the nine months." That was it exactly, and ever since she'd read the passage it was doubly true. Walking to the courthouse, she wasn't planning strategy; she was looking at the petunias in the park, and thinking, Next year at petunia time I'll be wheeling my baby. She went slowly, already adopting the pregnant woman's back-tipped goose walk, engrossed by passing mothers and children. Her breasts were swollen and tender, and she fancied her waist had thickened. She thought pregnancy would look good on her, regretting that she'd have no man to appreciate it. Somewhere in the back of her head a voice said, He's not gone yet, he's still hanging around, he may decide to stay—but Betsy tried not to hear. She would ignore all the inner voices and concentrate on her task. But the mysterious Emily Lofting, or Loftig, at times so real to her, had a way of receding and giving way to the greater reality, the half-inch fetus in her womb.

At the county clerk's office she was sent back to the library for the city directories. Damn. Trudging down the hall again, she stopped on an impulse at a door labeled "Family Court: Adoptions." Inside, she was told by a young man in a bow tie that all adoption records were sealed, unavailable.

"Even from that far back?" The *Times* article had said that barriers could be breached with charm and *chutzpah.*

"I mean, the people involved are all dead. What harm would there be?"

The young man in the bow tie didn't seem charmed. "You can try to get a court order to have the papers released," he said. "But there would have to be a good reason." He was chewing gum, and he gave it a snap.

Defeated, she went back to the library, and there, in the Local History and Genealogy room on the second floor, Emily leapt into existence.

There was half a wall of city directories, and in the volume labeled 1922 there was a listing for 668 Spring Street that read: "Harold Loftus (Cora), motorman." Betsy stared in disbelief at the page. There they were, documented, Emily's parents, Violet's maternal grandparents, her own great-grandparents, her baby's great-great . . . Her mind whirled. She couldn't get over it. Harold and Cora Loftus. They sounded like real people. She could even see them: Harold with a paunch, Cora in a bun. Good, conventional people, the motorman and his wife. Motorman? She asked the man behind the desk: "What was a motorman?"

"Probably a streetcar driver or conductor," he said, peering at the book with her.

"It's my great-grandfather!" she said happily, and he smiled at her, but it wasn't an enthusiastic smile. He was used to discoveries.

Betsy sat down at a table with the directory. She liked looking at the words: "Harold Loftus (Cora), motorman." And there, at 666, was her grandfather—or, rather, not her grandfather, but: "Francis Robinson (Helen), lawyer." It was inexpressibly exciting. What a pity they didn't include the names of children: Emily, the Loftus girl. . . . Betsy saw her in the spring, in a dress with a dropped waist, sitting on the front porch of a little frame house trimmed with fish scaling and a trellis, wishing for her real life to begin. . . . It was Violet's vision; now she would accept it as truth.

Betsy bloomed with excitement. She strode back to her

car, briskly plotting. The petunias might have been parking meters. She knew Emily's name. It wasn't a lot to know, but it was more than she'd known an hour ago. She felt, somehow, that she would find Emily; for the first time she believed in her. Every year, she read to her students Boswell's "Inviolable Plan," part of which read, "Be firm, and persist like a philosopher." Boswell didn't often follow his own advice, but it was good advice all the same. She would be firm, she would persist like a philosopher, and she would find Emily.

Where to go next? She would check the Haddam, Connecticut, records in the county courthouse—what county? She'd look it up. She could picture that, too: a pretty little Greek Revival or Victorian Gothic building on a square of green, and inside it somewhere the birth record of a baby girl born to Emily Loftus in December 1922. She would write and ask for a copy. Or would she have to make a trip up there?—to one of those marzipan New England towns, all clapboards and historical markers. She and Judd could go, perhaps. They would walk hand in hand down the narrow streets. . . .

She pictured Violet's transfigured face: a name, a birth certificate, a mama . . . perhaps not least, a daughter who delivered the goods.

Feeling righteous, she drove home to find Judd at the kitchen table drinking beer, wearing the kind of fixed smile he discouraged on the faces of photographic subjects.

"You look weary," she said, flopping into a chair. But it was she who was weary. It was coming, she knew, and she was tired, all her exhilaration gone, as if she had already gone through the ordeal ahead.

"I don't like confrontations, Betsy," he said. "I spend my life avoiding them. But it's time you and I talked."

He spoke awkwardly, shy with her, and she responded with silence.

"Why did you do this to us?" he asked, and when she saw the effort it cost him she had to answer.

"It was my turn," she said without thinking, and looked quickly at him, surprised at herself.

Curiously, he understood. "Because of your mother?"

She knew he didn't like to speak of it—Violet's dying, or anyone's—and she nodded at his oblique reference. They faced each other across the table, drinking cold beer. She was pleased, and then stricken with remorse, to see how unhappy he looked—unhappy and too young to be a father, Betsy thought, wondering if he felt the same way. He was barely thirty, four years younger than she; and yet she always thought of him as far, far older, though this never kept her from feeling maternal not only toward his child but toward him.

He took her hand and said, "It could wait, Betsy. I understand how you feel, but it could wait. We could, someday." She remained silent, trying to fill in the gaps, and they sat like that, hand in hand, with the conditional tense between them until he spoke again: "It's not fair to me this way, Betsy. To go ahead without consulting me. It's not my mother that's dying, my mother's been dead twenty years. What about me, Betsy?" His voice had lost its diffidence, and was harsh and passionate. She listened in amazement, almost missing his words—he had never spoken to her so personally, in such a voice. "There are things I need, too. I never bargained for this. I need time, I don't leap into things, I need to get my breath. I need *you* while I'm getting it."

"Are you saying you'd stay with me if I had an abortion?"

"I don't know. I'd certainly planned to stay with you, if you wanted me to."

"You're getting back at me for it!" she burst out, her voice as harsh and alien as his had been. "I know you're going to leave me, why not do it? Get out, leave me in peace, don't torture me." She laughed a little at the melodrama, but he dropped her hand and turned his face impassively toward the window.

"Betsy, this is your doing. I thought you were on the God damned pill. You tricked me into this."

"I know that. Haven't I said I'm willing to take the consequences?"

"I don't want us to split up!" he said, and she knew he meant it. "We were just beginning to work everything out—didn't you see that? Everything was fine."

It's true, she thought, but it struck her in a detached way, like old history. What a nice country this was before the revolution, the coup, the assassination. "I suppose I've been stupid," she whispered. She spread her fingers across her belly, not really believing what she said. A drizzling rain had begun, washing down the window. She watched its senseless pattern. "I suppose I've been stupid."

Judd sat hunched, with his head in his hands. "You look weary," she said again, gently, and reached out to stroke his hair.

He looked up. "I hope we can part friends, at least."

It was what she had waited for, it was what she had been marshaling her strength for all these weeks for, but it caught her unawares.

"What difference does it make?" she asked him, immediately in tears.

When she was a little girl she used to fear that Poochie, the old dog she'd inherited from her father, would be killed by one of the cars he chased down Stiles Street. Instead Poochie died peacefully in his basket. To Betsy it was all the same: she had no dog.

"Why do we have to part at all, Judd? It'll be my baby, I won't let it bother you. We could work this out." She had come up with that idea last night, while he slept beside her. It was what people did, they worked things out.

"Come on, Betsy." His face was stone. She could see it was an effort for him not to shout at her. "Try to face life for once like a big girl. Spare me the crap. You choose. Me or it."

She comprehended him briefly as a heartless and brutal man, with the face of a monument—very briefly, before her love came flowing back, but it helped.

"Me or it."

"Doesn't it mean anything to you?"

"It's something I wasn't ready for. It's all *you,* Betsy."

"I know, Judd. I'm sorry." She gave one sob and swallowed sourness. It was late afternoon, but nausea threatened her. "I wanted to keep you, Judd," she said with effort.

"Then get rid of it!" he shouted, not taking in her past tense. He gripped her arm. "Betsy, I don't want to leave you, damn it. Get rid of it!"

"I can't." She broke away from him and ran to the bathroom, slamming the door.

She stayed there. She heard him make coffee. He could never remember not to fill the teakettle all the way up. It took forever to boil, and she heard him sigh through his teeth with impatience. Finally he poured a cup and sat down with it. A newspaper rattled; the evening paper had come.

After a while he came to the door. "Betsy?"

"I'm all right." She had the crack in the tile floor memorized; it looked like the southern boundary of New York State.

"I've got to go out. Are you sure you're okay?"

"Sure." Where are you going? Where? She sat with her head on her knees. The nausea had passed, leaving her empty. Her bare knees were cold, her wet forehead colder.

"I was thinking, Betsy."

Silence.

"I'd like to pay for this. The hospital and all that. You have the bills sent to me."

"No, thanks."

"Well, I offered." He seemed to be searching for something else to say. "The offer stands."

"Okay." Where? Where?

"I won't be long. I can't miss this appointment."

She racked her brain automatically: What appointment? What had he said that morning? "No, I know. I'm okay."

"We'll go out for dinner later."

"Yes, okay, fine."

He left, and she continued to sit on the bathroom floor, crying weakly. Then she scrambled to her feet and looked in the mirror. You don't go crazy, she said to her face. You pull yourself together. The words came to her involuntarily. She wondered if Emily had said them to herself fifty-five years ago, and if she'd inherited them. *You don't go crazy*: a family maxim.

She thought her face looked very ugly. She was so pale her freckles stood out like blemishes. I look different, she thought. Already, I look different. She rubbed Violet's moisturizer into her skin and put on some makeup. Like somebody's mother, she thought. Judd's mother. She turned from the mirror in disgust.

She needed a friend, but she didn't have a friend. Her best friend, Caroline DeVoto, who taught Romance languages at the university, was in Paris on sabbatical. She wrote Betsy letters about the food. Her other friend was Julia Cameron, and Julia had recently married and moved to Maine. She could call her up. It was Julia Betsy had once shared a summer cottage with in the country. But ever since the night, toward the end of their stay, when Julia had climbed in bed with her and embraced her, Betsy had found it hard to talk to her. Julia laughed at everything. She had laughed at what she called Betsy's prudery. She would laugh at this. She could call Caroline in Paris, but such grand and expensive gestures were beyond her—and what good would it do? "Life is the great adventure," her mother always said, "but you're in it alone."

Betsy tried to imagine herself with a baby. She couldn't, except in terms of Norman Rockwell covers, Ivory Soap ads: rocking it in sunlight, singing to it, planting a garden while it babbled in its playpen, the two of them making a circle of love. . . .

No. She made herself switch gears: exhaustion, boredom, resentment, badly prepared classes, childhood diseases, soggy diapers, a circle of drudgery. Contemplating these, Betsy was bucked up. There was a set of problems to be solved. All right, she thought, making toast. All right. I'll have this baby next winter. I'll need to take the semester off, a medical leave. I'll have to write a letter. The awkwardness at school. All right, I can cope with that. Then I'll have this little baby. Little babies need diapers and rattles and blankets and—what? Mobiles over their cribs and teething biscuits. And I'll need help at first, I'll need a Terry. All right.

She ate her toast, talking to herself, and then she made a list. She worked out her finances. She'd be paying all the rent herself now, but it would be, barely, all right. She would get along. She moved through the apartment with her hand on her stomach, figuring. The back bedroom for a nursery, and there the playpen, and she could keep the carriage in the downstairs hall, where Judd's bike was. She stepped over some of his scattered records, a slide box on the living room floor. It would not be long—how long would it take him to leave her? for her worst nightmares to come true? He'd be gone, records and toothbrush and all.

She stood in the middle of the living room, holding her stomach with both hands as if it pained her. She was understanding how true it is, that love which does not prosper dies; but it dies slow.

They did go out to dinner, at a bar with a television set, where they watched a baseball game. They hardly spoke, but there was no hostility between them.

"When will you go, Judd?" was all she said.

His answer was oblique. "It's not easy, Betsy."

The next morning they avoided each other and went their separate ways, he to his studio, Betsy to her obstetrician. When she returned, the worst had happened. Bike, slides, records—he had taken all his things, in the space of just a couple of hours. He had sneaked away from her.

It was harder than she'd expected. The apartment didn't exactly echo—nearly everything was hers, after all—but it looked bleak, with disconcerting bare spots. Betsy walked from room to room. It was the absence of the photographs that made it so bare, she realized. He had left only one: a framed photograph on the bedroom wall of the two of them, arms linked, beaming. It was a nice photograph; their heads were touching, they looked happy and fond of each other. Had he forgotten it? or left it behind as a gesture of kindness? or cruelty? Betsy dusted it with her sleeve. What did it matter? Such speculations were unnecessary now. She remembered when Alan had moved to Wisconsin with his wife. This desertion felt something like that one had, and she'd gotten over her love for Alan with dispatch when it hadn't prospered.

Later, vacuuming, she found an old sock of Judd's under the bed. She tossed it into the wastebasket, quickly, before she could do anything so silly as press the smelly thing to her lips, and finished the vacuuming. She cleaned the apartment thoroughly, and changed the sheets on the bed, with the strange feeling that she was cleaning up after a crime.

She didn't see the note on the kitchen table until evening. She was throwing together her dinner—unwanted, but a duty to the fetus—when she spotted a piece of Judd's expensive, recycled light-brown professional stationery on the table. She unfolded it gingerly.

> Dear Betsy, It's been a great five months. Why did you have to fuck it up? Love, J.

It wasn't the contents of the note that got her crying; it was the way it had been propped against the saltshaker.

The next day, Saturday, she went as usual to her grandfather's for dinner. She parked her car in the driveway, behind his Cadillac, and surveyed with affection the big brick house that for years had been her refuge. It was the house her grandparents had bought at the beginning of Frank's success—from Spring Street to Stiles Street was a significant leap, not merely across town. It was the house both she and her mother had grown up in, and Betsy's fondness for the place was ungrudging.

The cold tyranny of her grandmother, all her growing-up years, had been offset by the love of her mother and her grandfather, their love like a pair of warm boots—occasionally too tight, but mostly comfortable. She used to write her address: 217 Stiles Street, Syracuse, New York, U.S.A., North America, Western Hemisphere, Earth, Milky Way, Universe. What kid didn't? But Betsy, dearly though she loved the details of that address, had always imagined another little girl, with the same brown braids and yellow pencil, writing something similar from her home (also red brick) on another street and planet—a comforting little alter ego, almost an imaginary friend, extending life's boundaries.

Betsy urgently needed the extension. Her life had been bounded closely by grown-ups. A fatherless child, she felt no need of a father, closely surrounded as she was by mother, grandfather, grandmother. Her family seemed large, endless, and like no one else's; it wasn't until she was grown that she noticed what a small family it was, how knotted together. And the knots held. This was why Violet and Betsy had moved back home after Will died, and why Betsy at thirty-four still lived in her hometown. But who knew what that other little girl was up to, on her faraway planet? What sublime, mysterious future was in store for her?

She walked up the driveway. They were all in the backyard, having drinks. Betsy kissed each of them—Frank, Violet, even her great-aunt—with particular tenderness. Her pregnancy, the finding of Emily, the loss of Judd, all gave family a particular value. It seemed odd to look at her grandfather and think: no relation. But it didn't matter. It wasn't the tie of blood relationship that she sought in him. They were bound by love, with all its subsidiaries. Like—she remembered this from time to time—a look they had once shared behind Helen's back, a mutually checked grimace in response to a bit of her moralizing when Betsy was eleven. (It was winter, Betsy could have elaborated. In the kitchen, late afternoon. Sweet potatoes. Red gingham curtains. Helen's text: gratitude for small blessings in the face of large disappointments. The disappointment: Betsy's not having been invited to Mary Kay Brophy's birthday party. The small blessing, could Helen but know it: Frank's moment of disloyalty to his wife shared with his granddaughter. It had been one of the milestones in her growing up.)

Frank had been the center of everything for all of them. He had always been there before Betsy—busy, involved, important, catered to—as the image of a great man, as what a man should be. A great lawyer, who fought for the underdog but made money at it. An enormous man whose greatness shaded them all. His greatness was different from her father's; Will Ruscoe's value lay in his being dead. He seemed never to have really lived, but existed only in her mother's mind, built out of her mother's desires. Betsy suspected he hadn't been great, alive. But her grandfather's greatness increased continually. Even as an old man, retired, past his prime, he was sought out as a sage. Life in upstate New York couldn't function properly without Frank. He had a hand in everything—law and politics and real estate and the new arts center and the workings of the university law school. "When he dies, it's the end of an era," Aunt Marion sometimes said. (It was the prose of *The Pride of Passion*; it may have been true, nevertheless.)

They ate dinner, as usual, in the flowering backyard, and Betsy told them right away about Judd's leaving. She was too tired to fudge. (Beat, *I'm beat*—an old expression of Violet's, one she used to employ on hot afternoons when she came home from work wilting and dropped into a chair with her high-heeled shoes kicked off.) They took it without gloating. Even Aunt Marion didn't say, "I told you so," though she practically did.

"He seemed pretty distant last week," Frank said. "Things didn't seem right between you."

"It was inevitable," said Aunt Marion, tearing a roll in two and smearing butter on it for Violet.

"*Why* was it inevitable?" Betsy asked in an attempt at indignation.

"Don't jump on me! I only meant it's always inevitable. Isn't it?" She looked around the table. "Isn't it?"

On her chaise longue, Violet, who had known true love, looked as if she might disagree, but she only smiled to herself. Frank said nothing.

"Well, it is," Marion concluded. "Take it from me."

"I'm not devastated by it," Betsy said. "For the record." She didn't know yet if this was true or not, and was not sure how devastation was measured. Her tears had had a limit, the empty feeling seemed limitless. But the brave front was vital; of that she was sure. "I think I'm taking it rather well," she said, with a smile she took pains to make genuine and unforced.

Violet squeezed her hand. The relief on her face was astonishing. Betsy hadn't understood the extent of her mother's hatred for a hippie photographer with love-'em-and-leave-'em written all over his face: thus, in better days, had Violet expressed it to Frank and Marion.

"A woman is better off alone," Aunt Marion said with firmness.

"Bull," said Violet, her eyes bright. "You'll find someone

else, Betsy. Someone fine and good." Her voice drifted off, and she crumbled a bit of roll between her fingers.

Betsy said nothing about the baby. Her grandfather didn't mention it; she wondered what Terry had told him. He had taken to watching her quietly, sizing things up as if she were an accused criminal on the witness stand, waiting for her to make a slip so he could pounce on her. At the news of her breakup with Judd, he sat up and sent her a knowledgeable, grieved look. He accurately guessed it all. But still she didn't confide. It was hard, with the family, not to be a child again, and pure—the real Betsy, who'd been lost somewhere and had her place usurped by this fallen adult, this criminal. Loving them though she did, she'd never been much of a confider, anyway. Having secrets held them off—not far, but enough to get a little stretching room. The emptiness she would keep to herself. The fullness that both sustained her and contributed to the emptiness—the child she carried—that would be found out soon enough. It wasn't a secret that could be kept long.

There was a change in Violet that was absorbing all of them; even Betsy's news didn't entirely break their concentration. Part of her light was extinguished. She seemed to be permanently turned inward, listening to her disease. Her private voices made her inattentive. Aunt Marion had to tell her twice about Louise Rallender's sister's new house before she understood, and then she forgot and asked about it. She ate several bits of meat with her fingers before she caught herself and picked up a fork. She spilled bourbon. She seemed as dreamy as a pregnant woman—"with death" the way Betsy was with child. She didn't take Betsy aside to ask about Emily, and Betsy said nothing yet about the Loftuses on Spring Street. She'd wait until she had Emily a little more firmly within her grasp.

She went home to her empty apartment. She lived on the middle floor of a three-family house. Upstairs lived a nurse who was hardly ever home. Downstairs were Mr. and Mrs. Brodsky, the landlords, who watched television in the evenings and would have been friendlier to Betsy if they'd dared. They had been gathering courage for a day and a half. Now, when she came up the front steps of the house, they both appeared at their door.

"How's your mother, Betsy?" Mr. Brodsky asked. It was rehearsed: he'd ask after her mother, and then his wife would pop the question.

"Not very good tonight."

"You tell her we were asking. She's in our prayers."

"Thank you. I will."

There was a pause during which Betsy almost eluded them. Mr. Brodsky nudged his wife, who said, "Was your young man moving out, then, yesterday?" She was born in Ireland; Mr. Brodsky met her in New York when he was just starting out in the fruit business. Her voice had kept its lilt, especially when she asked a question.

"Yes." It was shyness that kept her from being chattier with the Brodskys.

"You've come to a parting of the ways," Mrs. Brodsky helped out. Her husband nudged her again, harder. This was too much, and not in the script. He had a horror of seeming to pry.

Betsy didn't mind. It was a relief to tell people, and the Brodskys were always nice to her. (Mr. Brodsky, who ought to know, praised the strawberries she grew out back.) Also, she had drunk two gin and tonics and two glasses of wine at her grandfather's.

"It just didn't work out," she elaborated.

"Well, we're sorry," Mrs. Brodsky said. "You two seemed to have such fun." She was referring to the bed squeaking all the time.

"It was a mutual decision," Betsy said, adding, inspired, "Our careers conflicted." The Brodskys were relieved. Of course. Conflicting careers. They nodded through the screen. "I may as well tell you," Betsy went on, "I'll be having a baby in January or February."

They were at a loss, but not for long. Mrs. Brodsky unlatched the screen door and came out to her. She had raised three children, but she had plenty of motherliness left over and no grandchildren yet. She put her arm around Betsy. "You're a brave girl," she said.

"We'll stick by you," her husband said awkwardly, taking his turn.

"Do all we can," said his wife.

"Anything you need."

"Just come and ask."

Betsy nodded, grateful.

"How do you feel, then?" Mrs. Brodsky lilted. She stepped back to look at her. "You don't show yet, not a bit."

"I feel fine. I get sick in the mornings."

"Didn't I, too, Nick? Do you remember my morning sickness? It was something ferocious."

He shook his head from side to side, in the way that signified assent.

"It'll pass," she said soothingly. "You've got the build for babies, like me." She patted her thick middle approvingly. "Hippy!"

Mr. Brodsky was frowning. He had to ask. "And the little baby, Betsy? You're planning to—to—" He made a gesture that encompassed all possibilities, but Betsy understood it.

"To bring it up myself? Yes. I am." She smiled in the porch light. "I'm looking forward to it." She moved toward her own entrance. "I hope you won't mind there being a child here. I'd like to stay on, if I could."

"Mind? Oh, my God, no!" They followed her to her doorway, protesting.

She thanked them, suddenly overcome with weariness; it was the relief, she thought—a hurdle crossed. "Forgive me, I've got to go to bed."

Mrs. Brodsky nodded with understanding and got in one last pat, on the arm. "You get tired."

"Yes," said Betsy feelingly.

"Go on up to bed, then. Anything you need, now."

"Don't hesitate to ask."

"Please start picking the berries as soon as they're ripe," she urged.

"Looks like a fine crop this year, Betsy." They were both behind the screen; she heard the lock click into place. "Get a good sleep for yourself."

In the huge, barren, forsaken, cavernous bed, Betsy went immediately to sleep, and dreamed of Emily. She was very old, sinking fast. Betsy stood at her bedside and said, "I'm your granddaughter." Emily took one look at her and died.

She wrote to the Middlesex County Courthouse in Connecticut, asking for a copy of a birth certificate for a child (possibly called Violet) born December 20, 1922, to Emily Loftus, in Haddam. It was a month before she got a reply. During that time she haunted the local courthouse, looking for death certificates for Harold and Cora and Emily Loftus, for property or mortgage deeds, for wills, for tax records. Nothing. The family must have moved out of the area. The 1923 city directory didn't list them. Betsy asked Violet, "Where would your parents have kept the records of your adoption?"

"You don't think they'd be *around,* do you?" Violet asked, with a touch of asperity that Betsy recognized was directed not at her but at the secretive Helen and Frank.

"They'd be in Grandpa's safe deposit box, I suppose."

Violet shrugged. The effect of the new medication had worn off, and she had begun to call Betsy regularly in the night, whispering piteously, but in the daytime the question of Emily didn't interest her much. She was simply confident, waiting. She left it to Betsy, she had her own concerns.

Betsy searched the rolltop desk in the attic again. Nothing. In a pile of papers, she came across a yellow newspaper clipping, her father's obituary. "William Ruscoe, of 737 Garden Street, died suddenly yesterday . . ." She was startled to see her name: "He is survived by his wife, Violetta M. Robinson Ruscoe, and a daughter, Elizabeth Jane Ruscoe." She was surprised, too, to discover her mother's name listed as Violetta. She'd thought that was just a pet name.

She asked her grandfather about it, out of her mother's hearing; such a question would have made Violet nervous.

"Why did you name Mom Violetta?"

They were in the kitchen, and he was opening a bottle of wine for one of the Saturday dinners. He believed in the old-fashioned corkscrew method. It made him red in the face.

"Why do you ask?"

"It's not a name I would have expected Grandma to pick."

"The opera. *La Traviata.* She loved it."

"Grandma?"

He turned away from her to get wineglasses out of the cupboard. "Why not?"

Betsy made a snorting noise, deliberately offensive. The only music she had ever known her grandmother to love was "Holy God, We Praise Thy Name," which she sang every Sunday at the end of Mass in a loud, creaky soprano that made Betsy want to crawl under the pew.

"I wouldn't think *La Traviata* was exactly Grandma's thing."

He looked straight at her, loyalty to Helen's memory written all over his face. "Your grandmother was charming and sweet as a young woman. She had a hard life and it soured her. You never knew her at her best."

"What hard life?" Betsy asked. She had been hearing for years about Helen's hard life without ever believing in it. "It seemed to me she had a pretty easy time of it, and if it was hard she made it that way."

Her grandfather snapped at her, "Don't talk about things you have no knowledge of."

She snapped back, "Well, she sure made it hard for *me*. And for Mom, too."

All the fight went out of him. "And for me, too, Betsy. But I deserved it all. There were times I made her life a hell. I'm sorry she took it out on you and Violet. You can blame me for that, not her."

She was already beside him, with an arm across his shoulders, apologizing. He stood with his head bowed. "We loved her, anyway, Grandpa," she said. "In spite of everything. I know she meant well. It's just that we always loved you more."

It amazed her sometimes that she could say such tender things, with such ease, to her grandfather; she always had. I will love my baby, she thought suddenly; it was a thing she'd been wondering about, the continuity of the circle of love. "You were right, by the way," she decided it was time to say. "I am pregnant."

"Oh, Betsy." He groaned it out, and groaned again when he saw her shining face. He aged before her eyes, he sank and weakened until he looked like Judd's photographs of him. "Where do you get that?" he asked her, with a bitterness in his voice that went with his new wasted, defeated face. "That bed-of-roses look? I sometimes wonder, Betsy, when you're going to grow up."

Judd had said the same thing. Betsy caught her grandfather's arm. "This is it, Grandpa," she said urgently. "This is where I grow up. I think having this baby may be my first adult act."

She thought he would smile, but he straightened up and shook her hand off. "You're going to *have* it?"

"The baby? Of course! I never even considered an abortion." His question stunned her. She knew he supported federal abortion funding, and would have fought to the death for some poor woman's right to terminate her pregnancy. But this would be Frank Robinson's great-grandchild; there were conditions under which he would consider abortion unthinkable. "I wouldn't have expected you to suggest it," she said. She saw the problem reflected in his face and decided to rub it in. "This may be your only great-grandchild, you know. I'm almost thirty-five, Grandpa."

It seemed suitable to get back at him, mildly. The indignation—worse, the shocked recoil—she felt when anyone mentioned abortion astonished her. Playing mother to a doll was all very well, and so were vague longings for a baby. Becoming a solitary parent was something else again, and her calm acceptance of that state as a natural and inevitable one was the strangest thing of all. She had not expected, at her advanced age, to learn anything new about herself.

Her grandfather regarded her sternly, masking his pain and bewilderment with a look of plain disapproval. But she had seen it, and would respect it. He was generations away from her, after all; he would have to adjust. It would take a while.

"People do this sort of thing all the time now," she said more gently. "It's no big deal, really."

"No big deal—and you claim to be an adult!" He turned away from her in scorn and embarrassment. "Movie stars do it—not English professors. How could such a thing happen? At your age?"

"I thought he'd marry me," she said simply.

"God damn the man!"

Betsy caught his arm again, having visions of shotguns and vendettas, her grandfather dragging Judd to some altar and flinging them together. "No—it's all right. Honestly it is. It's not his fault. I deceived him."

"He didn't deserve you."

She looked at him gratefully. She was still his Betsy, then. But she must put him right. "It's not that simple, Grandpa.

He just wasn't ready. It didn't work out the way I thought it would."

"He's a scoundrel!"

"He's not!"

He held up his hand like a traffic cop: enough of Judd. There was a pause before he spoke again, and Betsy steeled herself. This would be his official, patriarchal last word on the subject. He would not refer to it, willingly, again. But he would expect her to abide by what he said. The act of stiffening herself against him made her miserable. She was used to bending, to melting, to merging with her grandfather's superior mind and its superior wisdom. Even Judd, a potential discord, had not challenged its hold on her. Her grandfather, she realized, had sensed Judd's impermanence—as she should have sensed it herself. But a baby—an illegitimate baby, she amended, thinking of Emily—that could not be harmonized, not yet, anyway. (Oh, wait until he held the little thing, wait until it called him Grandpa!) She waited, ready to defend the baby in her womb with her last breath.

"Betsy," her grandfather said finally. "I think you are foolhardy and headstrong." There was another pause, during which she contemplated, half-amused, the old-fashioned words: Judd was a scoundrel, she was foolhardy and headstrong. He went on more angrily, sensing her detachment. "I disapprove of this whole thing. I think you're crazy to go through with it. It could ruin your career. It could ruin *you*. You don't know what you're doing. It's not easy to bring up a child, even with two parents. You're not considering the reality of it, the day-to-day reality—and the humiliation."

"I don't feel any humiliation. I've told the Brodskys, and they rallied round beautifully, Grandpa."

He brushed it aside. "And then the baby, growing up without a father—under that cloud."

"Oh, for heaven's sake! What cloud?" She was furious with him—she could not recall ever having been so furious. "It's all in your mind—*your* mind, your generation. None of my own friends will think twice about it. There are plenty of kids growing up with only one parent—and who's to say I won't get married someday?"

"Who would have you, after this?"

They stood glaring at each other, and then she started for the kitchen door. He called out, "I'm sorry, Betsy. Come back here. Let me finish."

She came back and sat down at the table, fiddling with the saltshaker. Eternally, a saltshaker would remind her of Judd; she put it down. Outside, in the yard, she could hear Marion's loud voice, talking grocery prices, and the softer, vague tones of Violet.

"All right," Frank said, keeping his voice low. He sat down across from her. "All right. Certainly you may marry someday, and certainly the child may not suffer from its situation if you don't. I know things are different. But don't take those chances, Betsy. You're right—it's my great-grandchild and I want what's best for it. But I want what's best for you most of all. Have the baby. I can see you're determined, and I think you're right to be. I admire you for it. But then give it up, Betsy." He covered her hand with his; it felt old and dry and cold. "Let it be adopted. The world is full of nice people who want babies. I know—I've worked with plenty of them over the years. Give the baby up for adoption, Betsy."

She waited for more, but he was through. He's not going to tell me, Betsy thought. Even in a moment like this, he's not going to tell me my mother is adopted. She looked sadly at him, overcome for an instant with pity and affection, and turned her hand up to grip his.

"No, Grandpa," she said. "I want the baby. I'll be a good mother. I'll be just as good alone as any two nice people would be together. You wait and see."

"You'll smother it!"

She suppressed her anger. "I know that's a danger," she said. "I have thought about it. But I'll try hard."

Her hand left his and stole to her belly, resting there below her belt. His gaze followed it. "I'll love it," she said.

He turned away. "You know my feelings."

She sat bemused. The important thing was under her hand, under her skin, swimming through its dark world toward life. She cradled it. Was this what Emily had felt? And yet she had given it up, surrendered it to two nice people. Helen! Imagine giving this baby up to a Helen! Betsy stood suddenly and got the wine bottle and two glasses.

"Come on, Grandpa. Toast me." She clanked her glass against his and he drank grimly, as if he needed it.

Before they left the kitchen, she said, "I still don't understand why Grandma would want 'Violetta.' It's a fallen woman's name, not a saint's."

Tell me, she pleaded silently. Tell me about Emily. It's wrong not to tell me.

But he only looked exasperated. "Your grandmother insisted on Mary for a middle name. Violetta Mary. All right?"

"It's really a weird name," she said, but what was really weird was the way he put it: "Helen *insisted*." . . . I'll bet Emily named her, Betsy thought triumphantly. We'll find her in spite of you.

"Drop it, Betsy. Okay?"

"Okay, Gramps." She grinned at him and put her arm through his. "Cheer up. You'll get used to it. I want you to be happy, for my sake."

"You always were a doozie," he said, shaking his head from side to side like an old man.

Her intuitions, while interesting, weren't useful. Emily might well have given Violet her outlandish name, but Betsy's inquiry progressed no further. She waited impatiently for information from the Middlesex County Courthouse. When it came, it was a mimeographed letter that said: "Thank you for your inquiry. We regret we cannot process it without your remitting the sum of ($2.50)." There was a form enclosed for her to fill out; she had to give her relationship to Violet Loftus and her reasons for wanting the birth certificate. "Daughter," she wrote. "Family records."

She mailed it with a check and continued to wait, cursing her own inefficiency. I should go to Connecticut, she thought. But she hated to leave Violet. Her mother's condition seemed to have stabilized again, but she was decidedly weaker, and her placidity was simple loss of energy. There were certain things she refused to do, like be helped down the stairs for dinner. "No more," she said irritably, clinging to her bedcovers. A table was set up in her room, and Frank ate his meals up there with her while she had a tray in bed. The Saturday dinners were held there, too, with everyone crowded around the table and Violet on the bed as if on a throne.

Betsy saw her almost every day. "I feel so weak and empty," she confided once, but she got no worse, and the pain wasn't bad yet, though sometimes she said her legs hurt so, she felt she'd just taken a long hike. Once a week, Frank still drove her to the hospital for treatment; her kind of cancer was supposed to respond well to therapy, but the doctors were discouraged: it didn't. Violet opposed the hospital visits.

"They tire me so," she complained. "I'd feel better without them."

"They might help, Violet," Frank said to her.

"They won't," said Violet calmly. She seemed truly to know. "They just make me sicker. It's not dying I mind, Dad. It's being disturbed."

Nor would she go into the hospital. "I'll die at home, thanks," she said, and when for a while there was talk of radiation therapy, surgery, she wouldn't even discuss it. But that was given up, finally, as futile by the doctors.

Betsy agreed with her mother. If her disease was incurable, why did they persist in trying to cure it, or in trying to prolong what was to become an agony? To tame the wild beast inside her? But, for the moment, at least, the visits to the hospital continued. Sometimes Betsy took her, and once while Violet was with the doctor she took the elevator down to the maternity floor.

"Can we help you?" asked a nurse at the desk.

"I'm expecting a baby," Betsy said. "I just wanted to look around."

The nurse was interested and helpful; they were both members of the Pregnancy Club, though in different capacities. "You can arrange to have a tour of the whole thing—labor and delivery rooms, and the nursery. Through your doctor."

Her doctor hadn't suggested it. Betsy was still trying to persuade him that she wasn't a special case, that she was looking forward to her baby as much as any respectably married woman. From down the hall came a baby's cry, and she caught herself exchanging smiles with the nurse.

"It won't be long," the nurse said encouragingly: one of the Club mottoes.

Betsy paid close attention to the changes in her body, charmed by them. She loved the round, smooth belly she was getting, and the way her breasts had firmed into globes. She felt as luscious and desirable as a basket of ripe fruit; at times she was moved to tears by her unplucked beauty, and her loneliness.

She tried not to think of Judd—as an ex-smoker tries not to dwell on thoughts of lighting up, and inhaling, and sitting back, relaxed, with a cigarette to tap on the edge of an ashtray. She tried not to adjust her route so that she drove by his studio. She only did it once; seeing his bicycle chained in front, she was sick with longing. She tried not to miss him, but she did. She didn't miss the vigilant, submissive lover she had had to be; that role she was glad to reject, and she promised herself she would never dwindle to it again. But she missed *him,* the excitement of his rough edges.

Already, though, the baby was company. She perceived it as a real individual to be reckoned with. It had a heart that beat, fingernails, a sex (female, she prayed confidently), knees, brain, eyes. It got bigger, and she obligingly got bigger to accommodate it, and she walked naked around her apartment the better to admire the hospitable architecture of her body.

In August, she had to buy a pair of maternity jeans. She stopped tucking in her blouses. "You look sloppy," Violet said to her, but she noticed nothing else. Betsy wanted to keep it from her as long as possible.

"She'll worry," she and Frank said to each other, but there was something else as well, which neither of them voiced. She might not live long enough to see her grandchild.

"I wish she didn't have to know at all," said Betsy.

"It might do her good," said Aunt Marion, who had been told before she guessed, which miffed her. "In the midst of death we are in life."

"No," Betsy and Frank said together, and Marion shrugged. "You know best," she said skeptically.

Violet called Betsy perhaps once a week in the middle of the night, while Mrs. Foster—who had been lectured and no longer napped, but sat alertly in the easy chair, knitting—was out of the room.

"I can't sleep, Betsy," she would whisper. "Have you found my mama?" Sometimes she had a dream. "I'm so lost, honey. Where's my mama?"

Betsy was keeping her posted. She confided her suspicion that Emily had chosen her name herself. "She was an opera lover, Mom. Isn't that exciting? It's the first real thing we know about her."

"We don't know, Betsy." Violet was unwilling to speculate; she wanted facts, progress, an old woman at her bedside.

"Well, I think it's an excellent deduction. I'm quite proud of it."

Violet stuck out her lower lip and shook her head. Slowly, she reached for a chocolate, took a bite, and put it back. "Not very useful, though."

A letter finally came from Connecticut. It was, indeed,

Violet's birth certificate, xeroxed. It revealed that Violetta Loftus had been born to Emily Loftus in the town of East Haddam on December 20, 1922. The spaces for the father's vital statistics were blank, as expected. Betsy wondered for the first time who he'd been, and wasn't surprised that Violet didn't seem to care. "Female adoptees," the *Times* article had stated, "almost invariably concentrate on finding their mothers." And then, Violet had no need of a father; Frank had been a "real" father to her as Helen hadn't been a mother.

She waited until privacy was absolute, and then she showed the document to Violet. "It's you, Mom! You were born!"

Violet smiled. "It's Emily." She rubbed her finger over the name.

"Our first real proof of her existence. And look—it gives her date of birth; she was born in 1905. She was only seventeen when she had you."

Violet smiled. "April 9, 1905. She's younger than Grandpa."

"She's only seventy-two."

"Can you find her, Betsy?" Violet clutched Betsy's hand in both of hers.

"I'll try, Mother."

"Find her for me, honey."

"I will." But Betsy's heart was sinking. She had to admit (though not to her mother) that she'd come to a dead end. Emily existed, she might even be alive still, she'd given birth to Violet fifty-five years ago in a Connecticut River town. And except for a brief return appearance in 1941, she'd vanished from the face of the earth.

Betsy tried to think it through. Where would she go? What would she do, bereft of her baby, in disgrace? Presumably she'd returned to Harold and Cora, and moved away with them—but where? And she had probably married at some point. The possibilities were appalling. She could be any Emily, anywhere.

For the moment, Betsy was stymied, and there was another problem occupying her. It was already August, she had a potbelly that wouldn't be able much longer to pass for overweight, and school would be starting early in September.

She called Crawford Divine, the chairman of the English department, and requested a meeting. He had a presumptuous way of sounding immensely flattered when he was asked anything, as if he believed that people simply wanted his attention or his company, which was sometimes not the case.

"Why, I'd love to see you, Betsy," he said over the phone. "How's your summer? You caught me between Italy and the Cape. Come over for a drink."

Crawford's wife, Thisbe, had died a year ago when a toilet had overflowed and she had tried to vacuum up the water, electrocuting herself. Crawford's grief had been real, his embarrassment greater. He had two teenage children, both difficult. Since he'd become a widower, relations had been strained between him and Betsy. She was one of three women in the department; the other two were married and past fifty. Betsy thought Crawford seemed always to be expecting something from her, she had no idea what; she didn't think it was encouragement he wanted, though she didn't like the way he eyed her legs. She was always very brisk and impersonal with him, but it wouldn't be easy to keep it up in her present situation.

He took it in instantly, ogling her smock-top dress and whistling. "I *see*."

They sat in the living room of his house. His son was out; his daughter had kept to her room since the death of Elvis Presley. The hum of an air-conditioner shut out all other sounds and made it seem a tête-à-tête, intimate.

"I'm expecting at the end of January and what I wanted to talk about was a medical leave for the spring semester."

He looked disappointed, as she'd expected him to. She hadn't come to gossip or weep on his shoulder. He supposed it was that photographer she'd taken up with. Where was *he* in this picture? My God, Betsy Ruscoe was the last person you'd expect it of! He said all this, and more, on the phone to various people as soon as she left.

"No marriage plans, Betsy?"

"Nope," she answered cheerfully.

"Well . . ." He spread his hands, which were pink and freckled. He had gained weight since Thisbe died. "You're going to raise this child, I assume? Hence the semester off?" He lit a cigarette and let the match fall to the rug.

"Of course I am. What else would I do with it?"

"I really can't imagine. Don't be so antagonistic, Betsy. It's only natural that I should ask a few questions."

"Sorry, Crawford. I suppose I've become a bit prickly."

"*Become,* Betsy?" he asked, blowing out a cloud of smoke and imitating a smiling, twinkly-eyed man. Then he got down to business. "Well. As I see it, your only problem is the scandal. I don't see anything to prevent a medical leave. John Alderman will be delighted to take your Pope seminar—good opportunity for him—and as for the rest of your courses—"

"What scandal?"

He gave a sour smile. "You do have a way of zeroing in, Betsy. Well, the *scandal,* of course. You don't think there will be one?"

"Why should there be?"

"The students, Betsy. They'll just eat this up."

"Oh, come on, Crawford. Half the women students have probably had abortions."

"That's just it! They haven't gone through with it. You must admit there's a certain ostentatious visibleness to your condition."

"What's *visibleness* got to do with it, Crawford? If I were married, no one would think twice."

"Ah, but you're not. That's where the canker gnaws." He couldn't get through the simplest conversation without some trite quote.

"Crawford, you're out of touch with reality," she said

blithely. "Times have changed since you were in short pants."

"I'm not sure they've changed enough to encompass babies born out of wedlock to university professors. Essentially, Syracuse is a very small town."

He flicked cigarette ashes on the rug and leaned back, watching her through narrowed eyes like someone in the movies. But Betsy saw that he was serious. She didn't let herself get irritated because she knew Crawford, for all his absurdity, could be a formidable enemy. She remembered when Roger Blake had called Crawford a pompous, sniveling asshole at a party once, and how Crawford had persecuted Roger with everything from eight o'clock classes to a cramped and airless office to unannounced classroom visitations. She really wanted the leave.

"I'm not exactly going to flaunt it, Crawford," she said evenly. "I don't think ostentatious is a very good word."

"Well—" He shrugged, not retracting it. "Be discreet. And be prepared for a certain amount of talk. I'll deal with any unpleasantness. I'll stick by you." Why did the phrase sound different coming from him than it had from the Brodskys?

"I honestly don't think there will be any, Crawford. I think you're overestimating my importance—my 'visibility' around this place—and underestimating the sophistication of our students."

"Nevertheless, should anything come up, refer it to me."

Betsy tried to imagine herself weeping on her knees to Crawford, and failed, but she promised. She supposed she ought to be grateful. She noticed, though, that he didn't offer her a second drink.

" 'She's somebody's mother, boys, you know,' " Crawford said as he was seeing her out. " 'For all she's aged and poor and slow.' " He held the door for her, smirking, with a cigarette between his teeth dribbling ash. From somewhere in the house came faintly the mournful twang of "Heartbreak Hotel."

"Come off it, Crawford. It's not a joke."

He sobered. "No, I know it's not. I'll see to it that it's treated with proper gravity."

"Just forget it, Crawford. Don't see to anything but my leave. Please."

He leaned forward. He had a thin moustache, like an eyebrow. For a dreadful moment she thought he was going to kiss her, but he merely looked deeply into her eyes. "Trust the old Crawford," he said, puffing smoke out of the sides of his mouth. She fancied as she drove away that she could hear him dialing the phone.

She had never not looked forward to getting back to school after the summer vacation, but this year she was indifferent. She was having trouble concentrating on reading Boswell for her Johnson-Boswell course; it occurred to her for the first time that Boswell could be a very dull dog. And she was unsure, now, of what her reception would be. Crawford's warning of a scandal didn't worry her, but his attitude did. She had a horror of being laughed at: would her students think this was *funny?* That Betsy Ruscoe, aging and unbeautiful spinster, whom they'd probably thought was destined to remain a virgin, whose chief passion was Alexander Pope, had been—knocked up? Why had she assumed they'd hardly notice? Of course they would. She didn't mind astonishing them, but she didn't want to amuse them. It was a hitch even her grandfather hadn't mentioned.

She looked at herself in the mirror. Never petite, she was filling out like a pear—a busty pear. She tried to imagine how she would look by Christmas—more like a butternut squash. She smiled at her reflection; she was thrilled by it. Let them laugh. She was happy.

One night soon after, Violet called, weeping softly. Her mother's voice on the phone, hushed and plaintive, was the voice of a ghost. "Betsy, it's taking so *long.*"

What did she mean? Her dying? Or Emily? "I'm trying,

Mother," Betsy ventured. "I just can't think. Listen—don't cry, Mom—can't we ask Aunt Marion? I know you don't want her to know, but she could probably give me a lead. I just don't know, really, where to go from here."

"No!" Violet's voice rose, then quickly sank; she believed her nocturnal phone calls were a secret from Mrs. Foster. "No, honey, I can't let your grandpa find out. Especially now, he's so good to me, it would be so ungrateful."

"I could ask her not to say anything."

"Honey, you know my aunt! No! Please! I never would have mentioned this if I thought you'd tell her. Promise me, Betsy." She was agitated, her voice strong and rising. Betsy promised, and Violet quieted down, placated, and sniffed back her tears.

When she hung up, Betsy wept for a minute or two herself, out of frustration. She had tried; she had gone through old records and newspapers and deeds and documents until her fingers were gray with dust. But her research had come to nothing. The Loftus family had vanished from Spring Street into oblivion. She could think of only two possible courses of action: to ask Aunt Marion without Violet's knowledge or to travel up to East Haddam and see if she could find any record of Emily there.

She shrank from asking her great-aunt. It was true that Marion was a blatherer, and that she and Frank were very close. Violet's illness and Betsy's maverick pregnancy had, in fact, united them more than ever. Betsy knew they hashed her over thoroughly, and while she didn't begrudge them the hashing she knew her mother was right. Secrets weren't safe with Marion. It was she, after all, who'd spilled the forbidden beans to Violet about her adoption.

But—what if Marion *did* tell Frank? Would it be so awful? Betsy didn't know. She doubted it. Though she was past middle age, and dying, Violet was still (everyone knew) his darling, his little girl, the apple of his old and tired eyes. Surely he would understand and sympathize with her natural curiosity about her mother, her dying whim. And it was, after all, her mother she sought—not her father.

But Betsy knew she couldn't ask. It wasn't only that she had promised; the most stringent ethical code wouldn't hold her to such a promise if breaking it would help her mother. But the tone of Marion's old letters held her back; the aura of strangeness, almost of horror, that surrounded Violet's birth and adoption. Frank had had the opportunity to confide, and had deliberately let it go by. There was more to it than she or Violet was aware of, and it was that part of it that she hesitated to recall to her grandfather.

She made preparations for a trip to Connecticut. She told Violet her destination, and Violet smiled happily. She was having a weak day, but Dr. Baird had assured Betsy there was a long way to go. Don't die while I'm gone, Betsy begged silently, and pressed her mother's hand. Violet understood. "I'll be all right," she whispered. "Stay as long as you need to." Her cheeks were flushed. She was thinner, and her nose had sharpened. Now and then her eyes closed briefly as if in utter weariness or in pain. But she seemed more contented than ever, and her bouts of petulance had gone. "You'll find her, honey. I know you will." And she closed her large, calm eyes as if she really did have a secret source of knowledge.

Betsy told her grandfather she was going to New Haven to do a job of research in the rare-book library at Yale.

"In your condition!" he protested, looking at her sharply, and she blushed for her lie.

She wouldn't have put it past him to know all, to have listened in on all her midnight talks with Violet, to have spied on her visits to the attic, to have dogged her to the courthouse. When she was a child, he had, during their long talks out in the garden, been able to cut through her chatter to the heart of things and reveal it to her before she grasped it herself. He always *knew*. He had infinite wisdom, like God. He could probably look into her eyes and see the whole thing:

Harold and Cora, her letter to the Middlesex County Courthouse, her canceled check for $2.50, her Connecticut map with the route to Haddam traced over in red. . . .

"I've got another week before school starts, Grandpa, and I'm working on something important. Don't you want me to be a full professor someday?"

He smiled, disarmed. He was proud of her career, delighted in her modest fame, her publications, her elevation to associate professor so young, and now the possibility of a full professorship.

"Well, take care of yourself." He had his wallet out. "Here. Stay at a good hotel in a safe neighborhood and get yourself some protein to eat."

She tried to wave the money away, but he insisted. "You don't have money to throw around anymore. Consider it as my investment in your future career. Come on. Take it." He pressed the little wad of bills into her hand.

Betsy took it, not without guilt. What would he say if she told him he had just made a contribution to the Emily Loftus Research Fund?

She headed east on a hot morning at the end of August. She had her strategy all planned. She would go to the courthouse in Haddam, the county seat, and tell them her plight. She pictured a nice gray-haired old gent, a New England Frank, who'd lived there all his life and would be a fountain of information. Emily Loftus, aged seventeen: surely there would be a way of finding out where she had lived. Maybe with a Loftus relative? in a rooming house? in a home for wayward girls? Maybe whoever had given her refuge lived there still. "Ah, yes, Great-aunt Emily. Her name is Bainbridge now. She lives in Springfield, here's her address. . . ."

But though her brain moved in these directions, and though she traveled steadily east, Betsy knew it was all moonshine. Why should there be a record in Haddam, or East Haddam, or any Haddam? It was absurd. The idea would have been to keep the girl under wraps—and surely fifty-five years would be enough to turn any trail cold. But she had to look somewhere.

She turned south on Route 91 and got on Route 9 past Hartford. With a pang, she saw the signs for New Haven; she couldn't recall ever having lied to her grandfather before. She had kept things from him often enough, as a matter of survival, but though she could fool herself she was compulsively honest with others, particularly since she had learned, early on, what a liar Violet was—poor Violet, the dramatizer, doing her best with the colorless life that had been thrust upon her, that she didn't deserve. But Betsy was a literalist, lacking the imagination and confidence for whoppers. Heading down Route 9, she thought she might better stop off in New Haven on her way home and inspect the Boswell papers at Yale.

She pulled into Haddam (pop. 5,000) late in the afternoon, hot and tired and hungry. She felt that her waist had expanded several inches on the trip, and her back ached. The only motel in town seemed to be one on the outskirts—cabins backed by woods, called the Traveller's Rest. It didn't look promising, but it was nearly full, and the woman at the desk told her she was lucky to get a room anywhere in August without a reservation.

"If this was the weekend, you'd be sleeping in your car," she told Betsy with satisfaction. She was elderly and wore an askew blonde wig and pancake makeup the shade of a tan. Betsy wondered about Emily. She kept imagining her in black lace to the floor, with her honest gray hair in braids around her head. She would probably be loud and pants-suited like Aunt Marion, with a red wig and blue eye shadow, Betsy told herself, bracing for the worst. But the revised image refused to take over; if Emily was imaginary, she might as well be ideal.

"What's the attraction around here?" Betsy inquired. It seemed godforsaken enough; on the map the insignificant little towns were spaced far apart. In the *Connecticut AAA*

Guide her grandfather had given her, Haddam had rated one attraction: a nine-hour boat ride down the Connecticut River to Greenport, Long Island.

The woman shrugged. "The river. The scenery." She waved one hand toward the window, which looked out on a Mobil station.

An old man behind her, seated on a folding lawn chair, said, "Nature," and added helpfully, "You may not know that Connecticut is two thirds forest."

"Then there's the opera house over in East Haddam."

"We got a state park right here," said the old man.

"Don't forget Gillette Castle. Take a trip up there." The woman pushed a folder at Betsy. "And go over to Essex on Sunday for the brunch at the inn."

Betsy left, armed with folders. The old couple were natives of the area and old enough to have known Emily. Maybe that should be her method—go around and ask, "Do you remember a young pregnant girl named Emily who was here back in nineteen twenty-two? She had a baby around Christmas—do you know where she went after that?"

The cabin was just big enough for bed, desk with phone, and huge television. Betsy lay down with her hands folded on her belly. The bedspread smelled musty; there was mildew up in the corners of the room, around the ceiling. Outside, a pigeon bubbled, the sound of contentment. Somewhere in the world, Emily Somebody, née Loftus, was sitting down to afternoon tea, or being fed an early supper in a nursing home, or dandling a great-grandchild, or sitting in a motel on her summer vacation, or moldering in her grave.

Betsy looked over her notes. Her new information, still scanty enough to fit on the piece of blue stationery, with room to spare, read:

> named baby Violetta—probably opera fan?
> Harold and Cora Loftus left Syracuse late 1922(?)
> Emily aged 17 at baby's birth.

The whole thing was riddled with question marks and vague suppositions. It was hopeless. But she would go to the courthouse next day and see what there was to see. What else could she do? She had never once, she believed, failed to do her duty.

She had dinner at a locally famous restaurant, where she let the friendly waitress talk her into Indian pudding for dessert. It sat heavily inside her like a bag of sand.

The waitress refilled her coffee cup, smiling broadly. "I can't help but notice," she said, indicating Betsy's maternity dress with a nod. "I just had one in April. A girl, my first. When are you due?"

"January or February," she said meekly enough.

"Oh wow! You're lucky it isn't in leap year—right?" The waitress's face was genuinely relieved. "You could have it on the twenty-ninth, the poor thing." She brightened up. "Mine was a real pain, no pun intended. I was in labor twenty-two hours."

"My goodness!"

"Well, my husband was there the whole time. Believe me, it helped. He was great. Do they let the fathers in where you're having it?"

"I believe they do."

"It makes all the difference, take it from me. I mean, it's scary if you're by yourself. I don't care how nice the nurses are." She set down a tiny tray with the check on it. "This isn't your first, though, is it?"

"It is, as a matter of fact."

The waitress pursed her lips as if to whistle. *At your age,* the whistle would have marveled. "Well, good luck," she said, touching Betsy on the shoulder. She began to pick up Betsy's dishes. "Hey! You didn't finish your pudding. You're eating for two, you know."

Betsy gave an apologetic smile. The cheery waitress, with her trim figure (in a brown uniform with a long, squared-off white collar as if she were a waitress at the first Thanksgiving), her supportive husband, her long, proud labor—the woman depressed her utterly. Betsy compared herself and longed for such normalcy. She wondered for the first time who would be with her when she gave birth. No one, of course. Nurses. Her subtly disapproving obstetrician. Not her grandfather (obscene!), not her great-aunt (God, no!) . . . Crawford Divine? John Alderman, in gratitude for having her Pope seminar for a semester? Mrs. Brodsky? Violet, miraculously cured?

She paid her check and left. *Star Wars* was playing at a theater she passed on the highway, and she bought a ticket. She and Judd had meant to go, but never did. The theater was full of teenagers who seemed to know the plot by heart. Betsy had come in in the middle, but she caught on quickly that the nice, human-looking people were the good guys, and the ones who looked like Nazis were the bad guys. The teenagers applauded whenever a bad guy was zapped; they cheered the pair of heroes and the princess. Betsy relaxed and began to cheer up, and by the time the bad guys' space station was blown to bits she had begun to believe that, in her researches on the morrow, she'd unearth a whole clan of Loftuses, who would rally round her and her baby. She left the theater in a warm glow, borne along by a horde of teenagers.

But the courthouse yielded nothing. The clerk wasn't the old man she'd pictured, but a youngish one, dark and skinny like Judd. She kept looking at him, at the strong, graceful way he moved, and his long legs. There were times when she missed Judd desperately. Inspired by the paired-off teenagers at the movie, she had halfheartedly masturbated the night before in her little cabin, and awakened that morning from an indefinably gruesome dream, wanting a man worse than ever.

The clerk, whose name was Dave, had a beard and gentle brown eyes. He seemed much nicer than Judd. He dragged old records off shelves and out of filing cabinets until he sweated, but there was nothing beyond the birth certificate. He and Betsy gazed at it earnestly, their arms almost touching on the counter top, and then exchanged a hopeless look. He seemed as let down as she. He called the library and had them check the town directories for 1922 and 1923. No Emily Loftus. He made two more phone calls, checked another file, shrugged, and sent her over to the Historical Society. She left reluctantly. She'd half-hoped he'd ask her to lunch, they were getting along so well. But he only wrote down the address for her and wished her luck, that was all. Why should she expect more, pregnant and clumsy as she was? She caught sight of her reflection in a window; to herself she looked blooming and beautiful. How did she look to others? The thought frightened her. The old woman at the motel, when she looked into the mirror to put on her wig and her pancake makeup, probably thought she was beautiful, too.

She stayed all afternoon at the Historical Society. There was a clutch of historically minded women there, glad of a customer, who happily racked their brains—going through old photographs, checking cemetery records, recounting tales of luck and skill in their own genealogical researches.

One woman—Mrs. Hall—pointed her forefinger to her temple suddenly like a gun and barked out, "Wait!" She had interrupted a long and rambling account of the finding of a *Mayflower* ancestor, but the rambler was silenced. They all looked tensely at Mrs. Hall, who tapped her temple and pursed her lips. "That—name—is—familiar," she said, nodding on each word. "Emily Loftus. I—have—heard—that—name."

The women relaxed and smiled at each other. They were on familiar ground: on such intuitions whole dynasties were reconstructed. Mrs. Hall went, muttering, into the back room. While the women chattered, Betsy kept her eyes on the door she had disappeared through. She longed to go in after her, but a sign above the door said "Staff Only." Had Mrs. Hall only gone out for tea? But no, she was back with a cardboard folder tied up with tape, looking pleased with herself.

"I knew it!" she said, waving the folder, and the *Mayflower* descendant subsided once more. They watched with respect as Mrs. Hall sat down and opened the folder. Inside was a huge genealogical chart that she spread out on the table. "This is the West family chart; there was a man in here just a few months ago looking at it. That's how I remember the name—Loftus! There!" She jabbed the chart with her gun finger. "Emily Loftus! Married Eliot West of Essex, they had five children: Horace, Arthur, Emily Delight, Jocelyn, and Eliot. See there?"

Betsy looked, and the woman in the hat peered over her shoulder. "But, Nancy, this woman was born in eighteen seventeen."

"Well, of course she was." Mrs. Hall glared at the woman and then smiled at Betsy. "I don't mean this is the gal you want. But it must be the same family. You track down these Loftuses, and mark my words—you'll find your Emily. This woman probably had a brother who moved to Syracuse and started a line. This one will turn out to be a great-aunt. A great-great-aunt. You'll see."

The woman nodded as if this prophecy were conclusive, but Betsy looked dubiously at the chart. There it was, certainly: Emily Loftus. The sight of it made her heart pound. Emily Loftus in a long calico dress, a bonnet, with her five children clinging to her skirts, with Violet's eyes and smile. But gradually the excitement ebbed. This Emily was over a hundred years old when Violet was born. How did you track down the family of the great-great-aunt of your grandmother?

"I don't have any information on these Loftuses," Mrs. Hall was saying. "Best to hire someone for this; you'd have no idea how to go about finding them." Betsy looked at her respectfully: she could read minds, then, as well as prophesy.

"I recommend Henry Bemis, in Hartford," she went on. "I can give you his card, in fact. He's a genealogical researcher, and he's a wonder. Now I'm pretty sure these Loftuses were not from this area, but Henry will go over to the state archives for you in Hartford and dig them out. Let me just—"

She went off in search of the card. The woman with the *Mayflower* ancestor said to Betsy, in a low voice, "It looks kind of tenuous to me, actually," and the other woman nodded. "A long shot."

"But still—" The women looked at each other and shrugged. "You know Nancy. She does have a knack."

Mrs. Hall gave Betsy Henry Bemis's card, and there was a chorus of good wishes. Betsy smiled and took the card, but without hope. There was nothing to link this 1817 Emily with her own Emily but the bare fact that she had married a Connecticut man in 1839. Emily Loftus West shrank and faded until she was just a name on a chart. With a last, skeptical look at it, Betsy left.

She had checked, earlier, to see if *La Traviata* had played at the Goodspeed Opera House in East Haddam in 1922. That would be a nice, neat fact; if it had, Emily had probably seen it and named her daughter after the heroine. Violet would like knowing that. But the Goodspeed had closed in 1920, and remained so for forty-odd years. Emily had fallen for Violetta and Alfredo somewhere else.

On the way back to her motel, Betsy drove by the old opera house. It was freshly painted, flower-decked, and down behind it the river glittered with coins of sunshine. There was a revival of a 1928 Gershwin musical playing. Betsy thought of Judd, who loved such things, and wished he were with her. They could have dinner, go to the theater, return to the motel together. . . . Her trip would be transformed into a joyous quest—what would it matter that it was unsuccessful?

Betsy returned, alone, to her room, more discouraged than she'd expected to be. She'd thought she was prepared for such a failure, and perhaps she was, but not for its aftermath: Violet's disappointment. It was this that haunted her. What if the hope of Emily helped to keep Violet alive? She couldn't shake the idea that the failure was her failure. Somewhere, a stone had been left unturned, and because of it Violet might die without the clasp of her mother's hand.

Emily Loftus West was not that stone. She dropped Henry Bemis's card into the wastebasket. She would have to ask Marion—no: she'd go right to Frank. She'd risk it all—anger, hurt feelings, whole cemeteries of dead ancestors rising up to shake their bony fists at her. . . .

In the musty cabin, she lay down on the bed and let dejection and relief wash over her in equal parts. She hadn't found Emily; she would turn it all over to her grandfather, as she had always turned things over to him. It was a defeat, but her object hadn't been personal triumph. Her object had been the finding of Emily for Violet. Frank would accomplish it more effectively than she ever could—might, in fact, already have the secret in his possession. But as she lay there, the spirit of . . . She wondered afterwards what spirit it could have been. St. Anthony, patron of lost things, Helen would have said. Your own common sense—nothing spiritual about that, Frank would snap. Helen, guiding from the grave, making things right. Her own unborn child, wanting its family tree. The tranquil confidence of Violet, reaching east.

Whatever it was, it impelled her to pick up the phone book and leaf through it. There could be Loftuses in the area. Lobell, Locke, Lockwood Farm, Lodynsky, Loeb, Loeb, Lofting . . . Betsy gave a scream and hugged the phone book to her chest, and then she looked at it again. "Loftus, Emily," it read, "19 River Rd. E. Had." With her face transfigured by joy, she looked (had she but known it) just like her grandmother.

CHAPTER SIX

Emily

Emily was on the phone with Jean Wood when the doorbell rang. Jean was telling her about her annual European vacation—a series of complaints: high prices, red tape, heat, exhaustion. Emily, who had spent the last ten summers in East Haddam, had given up trying to persuade Jean to do likewise. When the doorbell rang, she wasn't entirely sorry. "Damn it, Jean, there's the door. I'll have to call you back."

She smoothed her hair as she hurried to the front of the house; you never knew, it might be someone wanting an interview.

It was a sharp-featured young woman in a maternity dress.

"Yes?" Emily inquired. Definitely not a reporter, more likely an antique nut gaga over the fanlight and wanting a private tour.

"Are you Emily Loftus?"

"I am."

A trembly smile, tears in the eyes. Could it be a fan? Too young, surely.

"I think you may be my grandmother," said the young woman.

Fifty years on the stage had prepared Emily to deal with most shocks, and she dealt with this one. "Come in," she said calmly, "and tell me why you think so." Only her hand on her heart betrayed her. Her heart's flutterings weren't visible. She breathed deeply, to calm herself, and led her visitor into the living room.

The molding, the fire screen, the wide-plank floors—the woman didn't notice any of it. She sat herself down on the sofa, heavily, and applied a handkerchief to her eyes.

Emily didn't help her out. She sat up steely-straight in the wing chair and waited.

"My name is Betsy Ruscoe," the woman said finally. "I've come all the way down here from Syracuse to find you—well, to find my grandmother. I suppose there's always a chance you're not the right Emily, but—" She had the handkerchief ready. "You look so much like my mother!" She pressed it to her mouth, to stifle something between a sob and a giggle.

"And your mother is—"

"Violet—Violetta."

Violetta. She hadn't allowed herself even to think the name in years—thirty years? thirty-five? Hearing it uttered aloud was like the breaking of a spell. She looked helplessly at Betsy Ruscoe. It was a long time since she had given way to the kind of emotion she felt now.

"She's my daughter," Emily said. "She was born right here in East Haddam. And you're my granddaughter." She groped in her pocket for a tissue and found one. "You look just like my brother Henry."

They sat blowing their noses, laughing awkwardly, not knowing, out of the cornucopia of things that must be said, what to say next.

"I suppose we could have tea," Emily said finally and wiped her eyes. She stood up, thinking: Why did she have to catch me in my old gardening dress?

"Is it all right?" Betsy was asking. "I mean, I'd love to stay, but if you're busy—"

"My dear Betsy Ruscoe!" Emily went to her and took her arm. "You're my granddaughter! Do you think I'm going to let you go that easily?"

Her blush and tentative smile—Emily had to press her hands to her heart again—were like those of her Violetta, long ago, that bright-faced girl with the long, soft hair. It was frightening, the way the past could rise up like a club and knock you down.

In the kitchen, the cats lay in a heap in the late afternoon sun. They stirred slightly and stretched, not opening their eyes. Their sweet dopiness soothed Emily; it was why she kept cats. That bland, dumb, graceful acceptance was, she believed, instructive for an old lady.

She took down the big brown teapot and smiled. "I guess I'm the typical little old lady—cats, tea. . . . " She raised one foot. "Even sneakers. I used to be quite glamorous, you know," she added, running water into the kettle. "But it's hard to keep it up at my age. I'm seventy-two." She said it proudly, and added, "A few years ago I wouldn't have admitted it. But I've found that I like having people tell me I don't look my age."

"That's what they always say about my grandfather," Betsy said; she was on the floor with the cats, being shy.

"Your grandfather?" Emily frowned over the tea—she'd lost count of how many spoonsful she'd put in.

"Well—my mother's adopted father. Frank Robinson. He's seventy-seven and absolutely marvelous. "

"Oh, of course. Frank. Yes, I'm sure he is." She threw in another spoonful and turned to Betsy. "You look quite pretty with the sun on you. Not nearly so much like Henry. You know, that dreadful woman stole my baby right from under my nose."

Betsy looked wondering, as well she might.

"That Marion Palmer," Emily explained. "She took her away in the night." She sat down on a chair, shaken. It was something else she hadn't let herself think of in years. Oh, there would be a rough couple of hours ahead if she didn't stay on her guard.

"But she was legally adopted, wasn't she?" Betsy prodded when Emily said no more.

Emily sat looking at the cats. "Oh, yes," she said finally. "In his position, there could be no other way, though in those days people weren't often so scrupulous. But the papers were all signed. And then—she told me, you see, that I could have a few days more—" She broke off, shaking her head. "It was the dead of winter, and we were in the middle of a spell of good weather. They told me it was better for her to leave with the baby right away, before the weather changed. Better for the baby!" she said bitterly, and she leaned forward and put a hand on Betsy's shoulder—an old woman with white hair in a fluff around her face, her skin crisscrossed with fine lines like a map, the tears in her eyes magnified by gold spectacles. "Can you imagine what it's like to wake up in the morning and reach for your baby to feed it and find it gone? It's like an amputation, that's what it's like." She reached for her tissue again, blew her nose, and managed to smile. "Oh, I don't care anymore. It all worked out for the best, I suppose. Maybe it was even the humane way to do it." She could still feel it, that sick emptiness and the horrifying knowledge that it was to be permanent, and to get rid of the feeling she said, "I want to hear about you. Tell me all about yourself. You can tell me about your mother later when I'm a little more used to this." She wiped her nose and aimed her tissue at the wastebasket, resolving not to need it again. "I'm sorry I'm being so emotional." She made a basket and smiled. "Now!" she said, looking expectantly at her granddaughter.

"I never thought what effect this would have on you," Betsy said. "It never occurred to me that—well, that you might not want to be found. Maybe because I never really thought I would find you."

"I was a needle in a haystack, I suppose," Emily said.

"It was sheer luck that I looked you up in the phone book. I spent all day trying to track you down, at the courthouse, at the Historical Society over in Haddam. And you're in *East* Haddam, of course."

"But no one had so much as heard of me?"

"Not a soul. And there was no record of you at all."

The kettle boiled, and Emily got up briskly, thinking: *Sic transit so-called gloria. . . .* "I used to pray for this day to come, Betsy," she said. "And then I stopped letting myself think about it." She poured water into the teapot; the familiar act restored her calm completely, and she said, "I'm glad you found me. Really I am. I'm delighted!" Her face creased into a wide smile. "I now realize a granddaughter is just what I've always wanted. Now tell me all about yourself."

Betsy cuddled one of the cats, looking at a loss. A nice girl, Emily thought. Not used to talking about herself. Not much stage presence!

"Are you musical?" she encouraged her.

Betsy laughed. "Not very. I had the usual piano lessons, but I turned out bookish. I teach English at Syracuse University—eighteenth-century literature, Pope and Johnson chiefly."

"Do you really?" Emily sprang up. "It's in the blood—look!" She left the room and came back with a pillow bearing a needlepoint motto: "It is better to live rich than to die rich."

"Dr. Johnson." Betsy smiled. "Did you do it?"

"Another of my little-old-lady vices—needlepoint. But go on. Do you like teaching English?"

"I suppose I do. I'd rather just read and write about it, but I need to make a living. I'm a good teacher."

"And what does your husband do?"

Betsy flushed. It makes her look prettier, Emily thought. "I don't have a husband."

"But—" Emily's gesture was meant to indicate Betsy's pregnancy; she regretted it as soon as it was made.

"Yes, I'm due at the end of January. I'll be bringing it up myself. Marriage wasn't feasible."

She could see her granddaughter wondering: What about you?

"It's in the blood," Emily said again with an ironic smile, and was relieved to see Betsy smile back. Tactless old bat, she admonished herself. She had to say one more thing. "Don't let anyone take it from you."

"I won't. I'm looking forward to it. I think things must be different now than they were in nineteen twenty-two."

"A damn sight different!" Emily poured tea, wondering what her life would have been had she kept the baby and raised it: God-awful. She could have told Betsy, but didn't, how her family, while not exactly casting her out as a sinner, had cold-shouldered her for years, not only for sowing and reaping her wild oat, but for going on the stage to complete her downfall. Enough was enough! Only her brother Henry had approved, his approval rising out of his own stage fever. (He'd never given in to it, and worked for the railroad all his life, a good son to his parents.) She could have told Betsy how her mother—Cora Ann Smatt Loftus—had held Helen Robinson up to her as an ideal—a role model, as they call it now—and how her father had said, as he put her on the train for Connecticut (alone, with her lunch in a basket and her clothes in a carton): "Em, if you like it up there at Myra's, you stay on." He said it shamefaced (the poor man, he'd been put up to it by her mother), and she had refused to kiss him good-bye. But she'd seen him and Cora in Dayton often enough over the years, and though her mother had never really forgiven her for not leading the kind of normal life people like Helen Robinson led, Emily forgave her mother for her wishes and her father for going along. Nobody ever mentioned the baby to her, never so much as inquired whether it had been a boy or a girl, except Henry, once.

Betsy came to the table, and the cats stretched and re-formed their pile.

"You're a brave young lady to be doing what you're doing," Emily said.

"You mean the baby?" Betsy tossed it off as if it required no more courage than plucking a tomato from a vine. "I got myself into it. I'm not a teenager. I *wanted* a baby."

"They say that every woman who has a baby wants it."

"Not *you!*"

"Well—" She spread her hands, disconcerted as always by their marks of age. Where were they, her beautiful white tapering hands? "I didn't care what happened, I suppose. I was so desperately, desperately in love." Her voice sank to a whisper, and she sat looking at her hands, remembering what it was like to be young and willing on an unseasonably warm night in March.

Betsy put one of her plump, firm hands over Emily's. "Please," she said warmly. "Will you please tell me who you are?"

Emily told. After the baby was born, she had run away from East Haddam, to New York, at the age of eighteen. She liked the thriving river town, but she didn't like being Myra Bell's housemaid. Myra was her father's cousin, and she had a rooming house in town, the kind of place where the maid was run off her legs to maintain the house's reputation as a comfortable place to put up in. Myra sat in the front room entertaining the lodgers, chiefly traveling men; a few years before, when the opera house was open, they were usually actors, but the house had degenerated. While Myra made coffee and listened to men's jokes, Emily beat carpets and polished furniture and changed linen practically up to the day she gave birth. And she'd stayed on there awhile, not knowing what else to do.

Emily's parents had moved back to Ohio, where her mother's people were, and Emily had no wish to go to Ohio. She wanted to be a singer. She used to wander over to the old Goodspeed on her afternoons off and look up wistfully at its faded, lost glamour. It had closed two years ago. If only it were still going, she used to think. She saw herself wandering timidly into a rehearsal, being asked to sing. . . . The more she thought about it, the more plausible it seemed, and finally one spring day she realized that it could happen—it could—though not in East Haddam. She would have to go to New York. New York! Of course! Was there any other way? Any other place?

She boarded the train, taking with her the suitcase she had lifted from Myra's attic, and she went directly from the train to the stage door of the old Music Box Theatre.

"And the rest is history," she said to Betsy, not forgetting her ironic smile. "Well, no, I suppose it isn't. I was never what you'd call famous. But I made it. I was always there. Light opera, musical comedy, occasionally even grand opera, on tour—whatever there was, I was always there. They used to call me the eternal Emily. I didn't play leads, not usually. I played the second leads—the friend of the heroine, the villainess, the comic relief, the suffering sister, the woman of ill repute. I played them all. And touring? I loved to tour! No ties anywhere! I made sure I never got knotted up in any." She paused, sipping her tea, absorbed.

"Wasn't it a lonely life?" Betsy looked ready to pity, and Emily jumped on her. Anything but that.

"Lonely! My goodness, no! I always had friends in the company, and if I was alone I didn't care. I *liked* my solitude. Ah, what a gift for a traveling singer, Betsy."

"For anyone."

Emily nodded, absent again. A solitary life was to her taste, and had been ever since she was willing to remember.

It might sound like bravado, but it wasn't. Even now . . . this interesting granddaughter would be gone, finally, and she would be left to unravel the experience and reweave it into sense, alone with herself.

Someone had once told Emily her life seemed to encompass every interest but human interest, but this was nowhere near true. In addition to her house and her cats, her needlepoint, her collection of opera recordings, her visits to the public library, her morning *Times,* her solitary trips into Hartford for movies and lunches, or to the same English hotel every October—besides all that, there were her friends, and they loomed large in her life, always had.

She was sought after as a confidante, even though she never confided. Her reputation rested not on reciprocity, but on her utter discretion and intense interest and ready sympathy—far more flattering, really, than bartered personal gossip. Emily cultivated her friends as she did all her interests. The lives of other people were like theater—occupation and escape. And the friends who began by finding her mysterious concluded that her mystery—her *oddity*—lay in her absolute simplicity. She confided no secrets because she had none. Not that there weren't men; she drew them. But there were no intrigues. She had a talent for making an affair last just so long and no longer, and for turning her lovers into friends in the end—friends who, needless to say, confided in her.

Emily's attention flickered back to her granddaughter. "You look like a loner yourself." It was in the secretive, timid eyes.

"I suppose I am. Not entirely by choice. But I've always liked being by myself."

"And your mother?"

"No—not my mother," Betsy said slowly. "She needs people, maybe too much. She gets along wonderfully with people, though—I've always envied that. She had a perfect marriage with my father." A tendency to idolize, Emily ticked off in her head. "He died when I was little. Since then she's lived with my grandfather—Frank. My grandmother—I mean Helen—died years ago."

"Helen. Yes."

"You knew her?"

"Oh, yes. I lived next door to the Robinsons, you know. Helen Robinson, with her everlasting headaches and church-going! I've never met anyone with such a knack for turning something small into something big, and vice versa. Like binoculars. Amazing woman." She spoke out suddenly, with vehemence. "It killed me to have her bring up my child!"

"Then why—?"

Emily waved this away, as a digression. She was still angry. Her pale lips turned down and tightened. "And it was her fault, all of it." There was a long pause. "It was," she went on almost in a whisper. "If you were tracing back to final causes."

"I don't know what you mean," Betsy said hesitantly.

"Forgive me," Emily said, and turned her lips up again. "There's a lot you don't know—and perhaps won't," she added with what she knew, from experience, to be a benign twinkle in her eyes.

"I won't ask," Betsy said, pretending to be concentrating on the cats again. "It's your past, and it's not my business. It's your present I'm interested in. I want you to come to Syracuse with me and see my mother. She's not well. She wants very much to see you."

"You'll be a good mother, Betsy," Emily said, as if her granddaughter had said only half what she'd said. "Generous."

"But will you come?" Betsy demanded, looking at her directly.

"We'll talk about that." Emily tried to laugh and pressed her hand to her heart—the old stone heart that blood could occasionally be gotten out of. "You know, I gave up smoking twenty years ago, and there are times I still crave a cigarette." Ah, the poor girl, looking at her so puzzled and hurt. She took a deep breath. "I can't bear it, that my baby is old and sick. An old woman! It's the only thing I fear, Betsy, the only thing in the whole world."

Betsy understood what she meant, Emily could see that. "I'm sorry. I won't ask you to do anything you really don't want to do. I have no claim on you. But I should say I'm here at my mother's request."

"You say she's not well. What, exactly—"

Betsy was silent.

"Is she dying?"

"Yes. Very slowly." Emily closed her eyes. "And very cheerfully, except for this one thing. It would help her so much if you would see her."

"I can't, Betsy, dear." Emily opened her eyes and looked around helplessly. If she didn't watch herself, this sweet, determined young girl would destroy everything. "I can't see her, Betsy. I'm too *old.* I'm seventy-two, I have high blood pressure and a bad heart. And there's so much you don't know—"

Emily closed her eyes again, feeling the tears cling to her lashes. She recalled as if she were still seventeen the pain and heaviness in her breasts as she waited for the baby to wake. A good sleeper, that baby was—too good. She used to fear Violetta would sleep herself to death. She used to hover over her, willing her to wake up. Her time with the baby would be short, as it was. . . .

Betsy, dear girl, cleared her throat and said, "What should I call you? We haven't decided. Not *Grandma!*" She pulled her chair forward with a squeak and poured tea, very efficient, changing the subject.

"You called Helen that, I suppose," Emily said with an effort, grimacing. She blinked the tears from her eyes unobtrusively. "You'd better just call me Emily."

"All right, Emily, I will, Emily."

"That's it. Get used to it."

They smiled brightly at each other. The girl is intelligent, thought Emily. Betsy interested her, in a way, more than Violetta did. She was so young and promising, with an innocence about her, really very like Emily's brother Henry, whom, though he'd been dead for fifteen years, she still saw as a little boy in overalls who cried when she went away.

"What I wanted to say was that I'm glad you don't seem to have changed—since my mother saw you, I mean, back in nineteen forty-one in that store she worked in."

"She knew who I was?"

"Aunt Marion told her who you were. And my mother said you looked joyful, that was the only way she could describe it."

"Oh, I was, I was," Emily said, faintly sarcastic, and cast her mind reluctantly back, letting her memory nibble on the fringes of that day: the lovely morning, and seeing her pretty little girl, all grown, and the theater that night—a successful tour, with her name in the papers, and imagining Helen's pique. But her baby, that was the high point; she could call back the moment, intact, though she hadn't done so in years. The tall, slender girl with the pretty eyes, the happy grace with which she'd waved at them across the hat counter. It was the next day that Emily shrank from remembering.

"You still look that way," Betsy said shyly. "I'm sure she would recognize you."

"Betsy, I'll tell you something." Emily clasped her hands earnestly in front of her on the table. "In spite of everything, in spite of my life's great tragedy—which it was, believe me, the whole thing, ending with that empty cradle on New Year's morning—" She broke off and closed her eyes again briefly, revealing creased eyelids that used to be smooth and pale like Betsy's own, and she thought: No, it didn't end there, of course it didn't. She looked at her granddaughter, who knew nothing. "In spite of everything, I have had a wonderful life, Betsy. And I'm still having it." She unclasped her hands and moved as if to take one of Betsy's, but didn't. "I'll give you one more piece of advice. Don't let anything get in the way of your own wonderful life. You have a right to it. And that's not as selfish as it sounds. I don't need to tell you that a happy life is impossible if it brings grief to someone else." She tightened her lips again. "I'm thinking of your grandmother, of course."

"Grandma wasn't happy."

"Good," Emily said, and smiled apologetically at Betsy as soon as it was said. "I'm a nasty old woman. I've probably been alone too much."

"But you have family now, Emily."

Betsy delighted her—a shy bird, but tame. She did take her hand. "That's true, I do. My old convent has been stormed by a whole horde of relations."

"Not much of a horde." Betsy smiled. "Me and my mother."

"And a great-grandchild on the way. Was ever woman so blest?" She believed she truly was, to have a pregnant granddaughter in her kitchen.

She fed the cats, who had unbraided themselves and were meowing in chorus, and asked Betsy to stay to dinner. When she consented, Emily went further and made her check out of the motel and spend the night. While Betsy was gone, she put clean sheets on the guest-room bed. She would make a good dinner, and then she'd get out her albums and show Betsy all the clippings.

She saw the two of them as characters in a play—one of those predictable ones, all talk, about a person from the past who steps in and changes, irreversibly, the present. Of course this visit from Betsy would change her life, might even change *her* unless she could prevent it. She rather thought she could. She had no intention of traveling to Syracuse, New York, that was for sure. Abominable city, full of wretched memories. She had played the Strand there, the Crescent, the Empire—flitting in and out, keeping the real business that took her there under her own hat, and singing and dancing in spite of it with as much spirit as she could muster so Helen would read about her in the paper and mope. But after 1941 she had never gone back again. She had kept the image of her sweet, happy Violetta in her heart. And she surely wasn't going back now to watch Violetta die. I'm a hardhearted old lady, she thought, but she excused herself: I've worked hard for this life, and I aim to keep it as it is. The play had better not go beyond Scene 1.

Emily realized it might not be possible to achieve what she wished to achieve: intimacy, friendship, family affection between herself and Betsy, but on her own terms and with East Haddam as the locus. She saw Betsy and her little one spending summers with her—a baby on a blanket in the backyard, a toddler running on the grass, a child on the swing they'd hang from the apple tree. She'd buy such lovely presents for it, like the knitted French underwear she'd given the Potter grandchildren, and those life-size dolls that woman in Essex made. She'd take it out to lunch, see to it that the child knew how to behave properly, take it to the opera, start it young. . . . There was no room in the picture for rotten memories, bitter confrontations, a woman wasting away in that awful city. It might be an impossible picture, but she would fight for it with all her strength, which—in view of her age—was, she felt, considerable.

As she worked, readying the guest room and then chopping eggplant in the kitchen, she caught herself humming "Sempre Libera" from *La Traviata,* and stopped short. A bad sign. She never sang; her voice was completely gone in the upper register. And she had kept herself unsullied by that opera for years, refusing to see it or hear it or—she'd had the chance once, on the road—sing it. Why had it come to her just now, when she needed all her armor on? She switched deliberately to a Gilbert and Sullivan tune, humming it a full octave lower than she used to sing it. She would tell Betsy about that Canadian tour and about her great triumph, when Peggy Allard got sick and she took her place as Matilde in *Elisabetta* and the Toronto paper had hailed her as the new Mary Garden—overoptimistically, as it turned out. Ridiculously. But still . . .

She laughed at herself. She often thought—and said so, charmingly, to friends—that her true childhood had come to her in old age. She had always worked hard, gone on the stage at eighteen, and here she was in her seventies with her little house and her pets and her toys, as happy and occupied as a girl of seven. She stood at the stove and looked out over her perfect backyard—the herb garden, the gnarled apple tree full of green fruit, the rare dolphin weather vane on the roof of the barn, the sundial, and her comfortable old wicker chairs—and decided that, absurd though her vanity might be, she was entitled to it. If Betsy was bored by her clippings and her tales of a lifetime in the theater, so be it. Youth must respect the crotchets of age. And when the daughter of your bastard daughter turns up on your doorstep, it's your right to direct the conversation toward safe paths, lest it be too great a shock to your poor old system.

Betsy was either impossible to bore or even more intelligently tactful than Emily had realized. They sat up until midnight with Emily's scrapbook. She had saved every mention of herself. Even the one-liners were clipped neatly and pasted in: "Miss Emily Loftus acquitted herself with grace and talent in the role of the Sybil. . . ." "The sweet lyric soprano of Emily Loftus more than did justice to the librettist's flawed conception of the housemaid. . . ." "There is more beauty and elegance in Miss Emily Loftus as the heroine's sister than in . . ." As her career progressed, the clippings got lengthier. She had been interviewed in dozens of small towns where she'd toured or appeared in summer stock; the interviews almost always commented on her slender figure and marveled at the loveliness of her voice. ("It's not pasta that makes a good singer," she'd been quoted more than once as saying. "It's discipline!") There were notices from papers in England and Canada and Australia. She had played Contrary Mary in *Babes in Toyland* in a Toronto revival when she was fifty-five, and sung Adele in *Die Fledermaus* at the age of fifty-eight to great acclaim in Dallas. She had gotten away with Micaela until she was well into her forties. She had done television commercials and had been written up in the *Times* ("Aging Trouper Finds Success in New Sphere"). It became obvious from the scrapbooks that she had worked without ceasing as Helen had prayed without ceasing, and had for her reward not heaven (as yet) but a wisely invested and tranquil old age.

"My voice went, in the space of a month, when I was sixty. Not that it was as good by then as it had been when I was younger. I had a pretty voice, completely untrained." This too was a mark of pride with her, mentioned in all her interviews: never a lesson, a natural musician. "Do you know, my earliest memory is of myself singing? But, of course, I was losing the lightness, the ease as I got older, and I had a terrible time with the high notes. But the winter of sixty-five—" She stopped, thinking back on it, the second great and terrible tragedy of her life. "I came down with a cold, then the flu, and when I recovered all I could do was croak. I was a contralto all of a sudden, and not a very good one. And I didn't want to retire, Betsy. At sixty! I felt like a girl—but I sang like a witch." She laughed. "That's when I hired myself out for TV. I did a commercial for denture cream—you have to have all your own teeth for denture-cream commercials! And then I did one for Alka-Seltzer, rather an amusing one. And suddenly I was in great demand. But I didn't make that many. No matter what I may have told the *Times*, I felt silly and degraded. Did I show you that Toronto clipping? Another Garden! Selling patent medicines! It would have broken my heart if—" She almost said, if I had a heart to break; it was one of her perennial lines. "If I hadn't had the great resiliency I've been blessed with. So I quit. I rested on my laurels, such as they were, and retired up here, ten years ago. I always loved this town, in spite of its sad memories for me. And this house." She looked around at the lamplight falling on glowing wood and smiled tenderly at it all. "After a life in small-town theaters and music halls, I'm living in a stage set for a drawing room comedy."

"It's a lovely place," Betsy said.

"I'll leave it to you!" Emily exclaimed, for the pleasure of seeing her granddaughter horrified at the idea. She went on quickly, "I never had a home before, after I left my parents' house. Furnished apartments aren't homes. Rooming houses. Hotels. I'd saved my money. I knew what I wanted. I'd admired this house when I was just a girl. I was seventeen when I came to East Haddam. It was spring and the town was so pretty. My favorite buildings were that huge cake of an opera house and this place. I used to take tremendous walks on my time off, all that spring and summer and into the fall, until I got so big Myra wouldn't let me. . . ." She lapsed back into memory, recalling Myra Bell's attempts to humiliate her, and her inability, surprising even to herself, to feel any humiliation at all. She had felt only dreary sorrow—more like disappointment—and even that could lift at the oddest times. On her walks around town, for instance, the lines of this old house had gladdened her heart. But she felt no shame. Hadn't it been a child of love? That thought had warmed her for twenty years, until in the space of a few minutes—that afternoon in 1941, at the Onondaga Hotel, when she had retreated under the bedclothes and refused to come out until he left and took his lies and false promises with him—it had turned chilling. Sometimes she cursed her innocence, and sometimes she thought that without it her life would have been empty.

Betsy did more leafing through the scrapbooks. Admirable girl! She had come dressed for dinner, had put on earrings and stockings and ridiculously high heels, considering her condition. . . . Well brought up, thank God. They looked together at a picture of Emily from 1932—at her height, such as it was, when she was in New York and regularly on Broadway, in small roles or the chorus. Betsy looked fondly at her sculpted curls, her eyelashes, the pretty curve of her lips.

"You were just lovely, Emily," Betsy said sincerely. "My mother was very pretty when she was young, but you were beautiful."

Emily smiled with pleasure. How long since anyone had told her that? To think she had been eager for this agreeable girl to leave. There would be time enough to mull things over in solitude. The thing to do now was to keep her here as long as she could.

Betsy was saying, "I guess the family beauty got watered down a bit as it was passed along." Ruefully, wistfully, she examined the old, yellowed pictures of Emily in the book.

Emily said, firmly, "You are very attractive. You have a nice, fresh bloom about you, Betsy. And when you smile and let your face light up—"

Betsy gave an exaggerated smirk, waving away the compliment, and turned the page. "Somehow I'd expected to see you in the role of Violetta, in *La Traviata*. Isn't that a good lyric soprano part? But you don't seem to have played it at all."

Emily's smile went bitter. "It's not exactly one of my favorites."

"But didn't you name the baby—"

"Ah, I was a pathetic little thing, Betsy. He took me to the opera—it was *La Traviata*—the night your mother was conceived. That's why I say the whole thing was Helen's fault, though I don't mean only the opera ticket. That was just the end of it. It was her coldness, too, and the way she carried on about her baby's death. And something else—there were times I thought she engineered the whole thing for perverse reasons of her own. She practically threw us together, and that's the absolute truth."

Emily frowned peevishly; Helen was probably the only person she had ever hated. "But the opera—she came down with one of her imaginary illnesses and refused to go, so he took me, little Emily the music lover!" Emily gave a harsh agitated bark meant to be taken for a chuckle. "Oh, I can laugh now, but at the time I saw that night as the most important night of my life. And would you believe he kept me dangling for twenty years?" Her guard dropped with a crash, and she raced on. "Until the day I met him in Syracuse, so I could see my daughter. He came right out then and told me—for Violet's sake, was what he said. We were going to leave together at last, after twenty years of promises, but he thought it over, and he couldn't do it. Overnight, it was finished. Oh God, the scene I made, but of course there was nothing left for us. The worst of it was I had to go on stage that night—"

"Emily—who? You can't mean my grandfather?"

"You never knew, did you?" she went on recklessly. Let the girl know. All the old resentment rose up and choked discretion. "He wouldn't have the guts to tell you. And Helen—you'd never get it out of her, that's for sure. She thought it was the end of the world—and then she decided it wasn't and she devoted herself to punishing us both. She'd found her calling in life! She only adopted the baby to spite me." Emily smiled, with her hand pressed hard to her heart. "Oh, yes, Betsy, Frank is your grandfather—yes, indeed!" And her eyes behind her spectacles gleamed with something like glee, like relief, at seeing the skeleton tumble at their feet.

CHAPTER SEVEN

Betsy

Betsy had been back at school for over two months when Crawford Divine's prophecies of scandal came true.

Until then, the semester had gone quietly enough. Betsy had settled into pregnancy as into a comfortable garment, and ever since the baby had begun to kick she had lost that dazed feeling the book had warned her about, of being a cow in a pasture, or a madonna in a frame. It was as if the baby kicked her into alertness. At school she was energetic and even amiable, even in the Johnson-Boswell seminar for which she'd thought she'd lost her enthusiasm. Boswell seemed no longer a dull dog but the delightfully neurotic reporter who always tickled her. "Remember the dignity of human nature," he had written in his youthful enthusiasm for virtue. "Remember everything may be endured."

Betsy wondered what Boswell would have done, if he had been a woman and in her situation? what Johnson would have done? what Rose Deasy would have done, pregnant out of wedlock and forced to face the world with the wages of her sin? Thrown herself into the Thames, probably. Boswell and Johnson would have gotten out of it, somehow; Rose Deasy would have perished of it. Betsy thought of all the women in literature who had been in the predicament, the Hetties and Effies and Hesters and Carries. She thought of Emily and her lasting bitterness and regret, and she patted the growing mound of her belly with affection and with joy. It was good to be no longer childless—to be childful, to know the child was dreaming within her. Her own dreams became gentle and childlike and gay—dreams of small animals, of quiet, enclosed places, of celebrations.

At the university, her usual claque of prize students was on hand, hanging on her words but not afraid to argue. Every professor had them, but hers tended to be female, vocal, and exceptionally bright; there was a shortage of women teachers to rally round. One of her students, an intense girl named Rachel Grace who was actively committed to a staggering variety of causes, was doing her thesis on Boswell under Betsy's direction, and the project had roused again Betsy's interest in an article she was planning when Judd moved in, on Boswell's relationship with Belle de Zuylen. She might even get another book out of it, about Boswell's women and what his relationships with them revealed about him. She began to glow faintly with the ambition she had burned with before her life split into pieces; the pieces were reassembling in (she felt) a neater, more interesting pattern. Something was tightening up inside her that had snapped and gone loose.

Violet continued to sink, but so slowly, so imperceptibly that it seemed years, decades, whole lifetimes must pass before she died. She grew thinner and had given up candy bars. She slept a lot, with the help of drugs. She was gentle and at peace. Even her demands to see Emily had diminished to mere wistfulness. She seemed satisfied with the account of Emily's unearthing and with the two letters Emily had written her: "My dear, long-lost daughter, What a satisfaction it is to me to have news of you after all these years, and to know that I have a family at last, how I wish I could be with you, I wish it were possible. . . ." Betsy had emphasized Emily's elderliness, her reluctance to travel, her goodwill toward her daughter. She hadn't told Violet of Emily's fear of death—both her own and Violet's—nor about Frank, and she didn't let her know that Emily spent the month of October in England as she always did. (She suppressed the postcard, addressed to Violet at her address as all the letters were, which said: "Having a wonderful time resting up for the hard winter ahead, wish you could all be with me," marveling at Emily's oblivious cruelty.) Nor had she reproached Emily for any of these negligences, now that she officially understood her grandmother's many hesitations about traveling to Violet's bedside. She understood Emily, but she thought she was damned unreasonable all the same.

We found her too late, she thought regretfully in her more indulgent moments. Emily was like a prisoner who had spent her life in jail and who, on release, can't face life on the outside: before long, she's back in. Betsy had watched her grandmother enact this ritual over and over again during their talks—back off and advance and back off again, in the end leaving the biggest barrier intact, her refusal to see Violet. Betsy thought she could wear her down, but Violet's time might be running out.

"What is she like?" Violet asked her many times, waiting with childish impatience for Betsy's answer. It was a fairy story, a bedtime story to be told and told again.

"She's like a grandmother in a book," Betsy said sometimes. "She lives in a narrow brick house with a fanlight over the door and an apple tree in the backyard. She has three cats named Jennie, Nellie, and Geraldine. She's tall and very slender, with fluffy white hair."

"And she wanted to know all about me?"

"Everything," Betsy lied. Emily's indifference to the grown, dying Violet was something else she kept to herself.

"I sent her some pictures of you. She has always had a great love for you, Mom. She calls what happened the greatest tragedy of her life—giving you up." That, at least, was true.

"Then why won't she come to see me?" Violet asked this only once or twice, in the beginning.

"She's old, Mom, and very set in her ways. She's afraid to do something that would upset her too much. She seems to have a bad heart."

Violet accepted this with the same pacific acquiescence with which she accepted everything. Betsy wondered if she sensed it, that Emily couldn't bear to see her die.

When she pondered all the things Emily had told her, Betsy saw them—as she had seen her life with Judd, now so distant—as a series of photographs. Old ones this time, browning and age-speckled: Frank, looking like the Arrow collar man, his hair abundant then and slicked back, his eager eyes bright with passion and ambition; his cold, drab wife, with the maniacal gleam in her eyes and the corners of her mouth just beginning to turn down hard; and Emily dressed for the opera, radiant with the promise of it all. "I was under the spell of the music," Emily had said, her neatly wrinkled face rapt even now. "It seemed heroic to be together."

To Betsy, these portraits were unreal—pictures from a novel, or from someone else's family album. She found it hard to connect young Frank the seducer—the cad who had tormented two women—with old Frank, her sad-eyed grandfather. "He kept me dangling for twenty years," Emily had said. "He was always going to leave that woman. For years, we used to meet, whenever we could. He never loved her. She was his duty—so he said. But his duty was to me, Betsy. I can't get over thinking that."

"So it's because of him that you won't come and see my mother," Betsy had said, meaning only to clarify. But Emily had taken it as attack.

"That's half of it, of course. And why not? He ruined my life, young lady! If it weren't for Frank Robinson, would I be a sour old woman living alone? He's put me where I am, and I'll stay here. Why should I go back now? After thirty-five years? Why should I enter the house that should have been mine? I gave up my life for him, I gave up my baby on the promise that we'd all be together someday—"

The old woman had collapsed in sobs, and Betsy saw that her various griefs had stayed fresh all these years, as perfectly preserved as paintings in a closed cave. Her anger had kept her thin and upright and energetic—even, in a peculiar way, strong and happy. Her grandmother seemed the least theatrical of people—reserved and composed rather than, like Violet, self-dramatizing and volatile—but Betsy received occasional glimpses of the disciplined will that kept the curtain down. These revelations, these tears, were terrible blows to Emily's pride. Betsy almost regretted that she had tracked her to her snug fortress and forced them from her. She put her arms around her grandmother, but the sobbing had already begun to subside, and Emily felt bony and rigid and almost intangibly distanced.

"May I tell my mother I found you, Emily? Even that much would make her happy."

"Tell her, Betsy." Emily had wiped her eyes, but they looked older and reddened. "Make it all right, tell her I'll write her. I *will* write her, that's all I can do. But don't hate me for it. I just haven't got the strength."

Tenderly, Betsy reassured her, wondering how she could make it all right. But she had forgotten Violet's saintly passivity.

Not only did Violet not question Emily's curious reserve, but she hadn't said a word about Betsy's pregnancy. Betsy wondered whether she honestly hadn't noticed, or refused to take it in, or accepted it as a fact to be absorbed but not discussed. It worried Betsy more than any of Violet's symptoms because it made her unlike herself. Violet had always been dreamy and placid and sweet-tempered, but she had never been incurious or unobservant. The draining away of her vigor Betsy could accept; her withdrawal from life was harder.

Betsy wanted to tell her that Frank was her true father, but she couldn't find words. And she had an uneasy feeling that she ought to check with Frank; it was his secret. But she couldn't imagine saying such a thing to him—not any longer. What she had learned about him made him remote from her. All Emily's years of hope and disappointment and sorrow were stacked up behind him when she looked at him now, and she couldn't help but think of Judd. She remembered, with chagrin, the times she had tried to see a resemblance between the two men, grandfather and lover—and there it had been all along, their essential sameness. They were men who deserted their women in a crisis. Even now, Betsy thought wryly, even now he's deserting me—meaning Frank and his silent, ashamed outrage at her condition.

And then there was the fading of his Violet, his adored daughter. Her he didn't desert. He had, in fact, become utterly absorbed in her condition, and he didn't talk about or appear to think about much else. He spent most of his time sitting with Violet, watching her sleep, with a look of sad puzzlement on his face, or reading a P. G. Wodehouse novel aloud. They spent weeks on the same book, a page or two at a time. Betsy became used to the sound of laughter as she went up the stairs to her mother's room, but the laughter was always Violet's. Frank wasn't finding anything funny.

"My heart is breaking, Betsy," he said once after a couple of drinks. "There's nothing worse than watching your child die." It was what Emily had said.

He had nothing to say about Betsy's pregnancy. Betsy

sometimes wondered if what was repugnant to her grandfather was the idea of birth in the presence of Violet's calm drift toward death. She longed for him to be reconciled to her baby. To Betsy, that coming birth bound the three of them more securely than ever—daughter, mother, grandfather—so that she saw them as three persons in one, like the Trinity—that close. But Frank held her off, and for the first time in her life she found she couldn't speak to him of what was on her mind. She wavered between thinking it her duty to inform him that she knew so she could tell Violet, and feeling that it didn't matter. Violet couldn't love her father more for knowing she was his daughter by blood. Betsy saw how it comforted her to have him in the room, how delight spread over her face when he made one of his infrequent jokes, how her eyes rested happily on him when he was reading. What could Betsy's revelation add?

In some ways, despite the rift with her grandfather, Betsy thought she had never been happier, and that she would look back all her life with joy on these few months, when her baby was still a promise, when her mother was alive and not yet suffering, when the excitement of finding her grandmother was still fresh, when she herself seemed to be blossoming mentally and physically. She looked in the mirror and saw herself bright and pleased and healthy, with the "nice fresh bloom" Emily had insisted on, and thought how becoming her life was to her at the moment.

Much of it was a solitary life. Her friends left her alone. They had begun leaving her alone when Judd took possession of her. During his residency they saw *his* friends; Judd jokingly but unmistakably discouraged her from inflicting hers on him: "Spare me the intellectuals," he said, with a groan. Before Judd, she regularly had given elegant, old-fashioned dinner parties for her colleagues, two couples at a time, seating them, in the alcove off the living room, at a table that was just right for five people because one end of it had to fit tight to the wall if they were all to get in. She had liked presiding there, alone, while her married friends talked books and devoured her fussy dinners—pâtés and chickens in aspic and puff-pastry tarts—a fifth wheel so often, for so long, that she didn't notice anymore that others rolled along while she stayed put. She was becoming a fixture in the English department. She would be there forever, competent and just this side of drab, a spinster professor whose work was her life. This was her situation when Judd took her down from the shelf and set her whirling. Now she stood still and looked straight ahead, and tried to see her way.

She had told a select few people of her situation and left them free to spread the news. She found that people avoided her, at a loss. They were furtive with her, and resolutely didn't look at her expanding middle, talking nervously about department business and avoiding the personal, glad to get away. This didn't worry her; she assumed it would pass. Meanwhile, as she had told Emily, she didn't mind being alone, though she hoped her old age wouldn't be as solitary as Emily's. Betsy couldn't see herself living for her peace of mind.

When she was home, she took to sitting naked on her bed, with her spine pressed hard against the headboard for the sake of her backaches, and her hands folded on her stomach. She loved the hard, strong feel of her belly, and the way it bulged when the baby struck out. The kicking, swimming, battering presence was her insurance against an old age like her grandmother's.

She was often with her mother. She had been thinking lately of her childhood, and getting Violet to talk about it. She wanted to know at what age she had crawled, walked, cut teeth. She recalled herself as a solitary child who clung to home. Violet had tried to push her out, Frank had encouraged her to hold back—her grandmother had had no opinion, demanding only that Betsy be quiet and obedient, and eat what was put on her plate.

"You were such a good child it scared me sometimes,"

Violet reminisced one evening over her bourbon. "Sometimes a child can be *too* good." But she smiled up at Betsy.

Her grandfather sat across the room. He had said she would suffocate her baby with love. Betsy frowned silently at him. You were the suffocater, she thought. She made frantic resolutions to herself: play groups, nursery schools, extended family . . .

"Except for the one thing," her grandfather said, suddenly, from his corner.

Violet looked over at him, her face clouded over. "What do you mean, Dad? What one thing?"

"Betsy knows," he said, and left the room.

"What, Betsy?" Her mother clutched her hand. "What one thing?"

Betsy smoothed her dress over her large middle: Violet didn't see, or didn't understand. "I suppose he means Judd, Mom. That whole thing."

"Ah," Violet said, squeezing her hand and releasing it. "Yes, that whole thing. I suppose you're lonely, honey."

"A little."

"But it's for the best. He wasn't the man for you. Don't you think it's for the best?"

Violet so obviously thought it was that Betsy made herself smile. "Yes, I suppose it is, Mom." Her mother smiled sweetly back.

The day came, late in November, when the scandal boiled over, when it became obvious that it had been simmering all autumn. Betsy was in her office on a Monday morning when Roger Blake, whose office was next door, burst in.

"Have you seen this, Betsy? You're being used as a pawn in some sordid campus power struggle." He was holding a copy of the college newspaper, and he put it down on her desk on top of *Boswell in Holland*. "Read this."

The paper was open to the letters to the editor, and Roger had marked one letter in red with an angry circle. The headline was "The Reign of Hypocrisy." Betsy began reading. It was a diatribe against one of the deans, who had publicly advocated the establishment of an abortion referral service on campus and then in his official capacity worked against it.

"What's it got to do with me?"

"Read on," Roger said grimly. He sat down and took a series of impatient puffs on his pipe. He and Betsy were old friends who had agreed to agree on nothing. He was lending her a baby carriage and a changing table, and was one of the few who spoke frankly about her pregnancy.

"Then there's all this stuff about the Board of Directors."

"The last paragraph, Betsy dear. Keep reading."

She read aloud: "Mention might also be made of a touch of related hypocrisy among the ranks of the faculty. One wonders at the mentality of a professor who can reconcile her conscience between, on the one hand, signing a petition favoring the establishment of an abortion referral service and, on the other, publicly flaunting her own visible argument against such a service and the principle behind it, as a mockery (every bit as blatant as the actions of Dean Koch) to those who support it, and as a moral outrage to those students accustomed (at their peril) to look up to their professors as mentors and role models. There may, of course, be circumstances that extenuate, and surely the private lives of the faculty cannot concern us except as they impinge on the life of the university. But in the case at hand it seems especially apt to quote Alexander Pope: 'What can we reason but from what we know?' " It was signed Jonathan Simonson.

Betsy finished reading and looked blankly at Roger.

"Well?" he demanded. "Recognize yourself?"

"I suppose so. . . . I did sign some sort of petition, I think."

"It's libelous! It's actionable!"

"Oh, Roger, it isn't. It's just—" She read the florid prose of the paragraph again. It seemed impossible that anyone could say those things about her. She knew Jonathan Simonson vaguely; he'd been in a class of hers. How dare he drag her into this? She felt a surge of anger to match Roger's. "The pompous young twit!" she said.

"It's an outrage!" Roger insisted.

"Apparently, it's I who am the outrage," Betsy said. Her flaring anger subsided as she read the veiled insults. Crawford had spoken in almost exactly those terms, of her flaunting the visibility of her condition. She wondered sickly if he was behind the letter.

"Do you know this Simonson?"

"He was in one of my classes, the eighteenth-century survey, I think, last fall."

"Look him up. What grade did you give him?"

She consulted an old grade book. "He got a B. He wanted an A." She smiled briefly. "He did a paper on *The Castle of Otranto* that included an adaptation for a movie he wanted to make. Real Vincent Price stuff. He takes himself very seriously, I think."

"He's a fathead with a grudge," Roger said. "It makes me wonder about the wisdom of things like this abortion referral service when you have idiot thugs like this one supporting it. I think you should press charges. He makes you look like a fool."

"Pressing charges would make me look like a fool!"

"There are certain things that have to be fought for," said Roger sententiously, posing with his pipe, "whatever the cost."

"No, there are certain things that have to be ignored, Roger, whatever the cost."

They glared at each other, then laughed, though not without some lingering antagonism. During the late sixties, Roger had been an activist at Columbia. He had been arrested there and his phone had been tapped (he believed, proudly) for two years. Betsy, at Syracuse, had retreated uninvolved from the militant campus life into her dissertation, a humorous study, called *Pigs in the Garden,* of Jane Austen's villains. Now—in what he called "the snug, smug seventies" —she and Roger found it amusing to stereotype each other as, respectively, ivory-tower isolationist and knee-jerk activist, but they were serious, too, and got on each other's nerves from time to time.

"Face it, Roger, you know I'll never sue."

He gave her an exasperated look. "Jesus, Betsy, what does it take to get you worked up? First you let what's-his-name walk off and leave you with this—" He jabbed his pipe in the direction of her belly; he had advocated making Judd pay. "And now you're going to let this little shit of a student get away with calling you a hypocrite and a moral outrage!"

Betsy lost her composure. "Damn it, Roger, I value my privacy, I value my peace of mind. As for *this*—" She put her hands over her stomach protectively, finding the gesture ludicrous but uncontrollable. "I've explained to you, even though it's none of your damned business, that I have no claim on him, that it was my choice and I made it freely and deliberately."

"Under the illusion that—"

"Roger, my humiliating illusions are of my own construction. I've made my bed and I'm lying in it very comfortably. I don't need a lawsuit to make me happy. I *am* happy, I'm a very contented woman. And as for this"—flicking the newspaper with her finger as if it were a dead bug—"of course it gets me worked up! Of course it gets me angry! But dragging this stupid kid into court isn't going to make me feel better. It would blow the attack up out of proportion. As it is, half the campus won't notice it and the other half will forget it in a week."

He puffed away angrily. "It's the principle, Betsy. You let people get away with this sort of thing and you contribute to the breakdown of justice."

"I'm not good at abstractions, Roger, and I don't agree

with you that the principle is more important than I am." She calmed down and looked at him earnestly. "I don't want my child born under a cloud. If illegitimacy is considered a cloud, there's nothing I can do about it. But I refuse to sink to the level of some misguided college student and turn myself and my child into objects of ridicule."

Roger sighed, deflated but unconvinced. "Ah, Betsy, I'd marry you myself if I didn't have a wife."

It was a peace offering, and she accepted it. "I'll bet there are times Karen would be glad to have you run off with someone else and stop haranguing her."

They smiled at each other, and he stood up. "You will dine with us on Friday?"

"I believe that's the arrangement. Here—" She held out the newspaper to him. "Take this filthy rag with you."

"No, thanks. Take it home and wrap your garbage in it."

Betsy tossed the paper into the wastebasket and returned to Boswell and his woman in Holland, the ironic Zélide. Resolutely, she forgot about it, but when her classes were over she drove to her grandfather's to spend the evening grading midterms and listening to snatches of *Right Ho, Jeeves,* fully aware that she was using her family, perhaps not healthily, as an escape.

The scandal's next installment came two days later, in the form of an answering letter in the newspaper. Betsy saw it as she was drinking coffee in the faculty lounge. It was signed by Rachel Grace, her thesis advisee. "I wish to protest the scurrilous charge made by Jonathan Simonson against one of our most respected and accomplished faculty members." Betsy flushed and looked around the room. If anyone caught her reading this! The praise was more unsettling than the attack that had prompted it. The room was nearly empty, and she read on, helpless and shamed. "There are varieties of courage which are always unfairly labeled immoral by foolish and narrow people. History provides us with a wealth of examples—" O God, not Joan of Arc and George Sand. Betsy felt faint with embarrassment. "Students in need of mentors and role models might well look to those who act on the courage of their convictions and yet do not deny freedom of conscience to those whose beliefs run contrary to theirs." There was a good deal more. Betsy was glad to see it was more gracefully written than the Simonson attack and that it didn't veer off toward fanaticism as she had feared it would. The letter ended, "I can only conclude that Mr. Simonson must be among those whom Pope derided in the *Dunciad* as having 'a brain of feathers and a heart of lead'—those to whom a moral inspiration is a moral outrage, who mistake honesty for hypocrisy, and who, lacking consciences of their own, are unfit to pronounce on the consciences of others."

Betsy sat reading it over and over. She felt sick. She would have throttled Rachel if she could.

"Hot stuff, eh?" It was Crawford Divine standing behind her, balancing a cup of coffee and a doughnut on a book. He sat down and picked up the newspaper. " 'A brain of feathers and a heart of lead.' Very good, very good indeed, though she could have put it into context better."

Betsy said nothing, sipping her coffee.

"Cheer up," said Crawford. "You've been vindicated." Adding quickly, "Not that you needed vindicating."

"I just hope this is the end of it," Betsy said finally, watching Crawford devour his doughnut. He spilled sugar all over the table. She felt thoroughly depressed. Crawford Divine with his fat hands and flip remarks was part of her depression, and so was the shabby faculty lounge and the tepid coffee and her backache and the prospect of facing her students in ten minutes.

"You're embarrassed by this eulogy?" Crawford asked archly,

"I'm disgusted by the whole episode, Crawford. I feel like quitting teaching."

"Oh, come on."

"I mean it. I don't like being talked about. It was you who kept nattering on about my visibility, Crawford, but I was practically invisible until this started. Why should I suddenly be everybody's business? I can't tell you how many people have spoken to me about this, including people I don't even know. They stop me in the halls, students come up after class—"

"All in your favor, I assume." He smirked as if he'd scored a point.

"Of course. The ones who think I'm a moral outrage just stare at me. But whether I'm stared at or defended it's an invasion of my privacy." Her eyes filled with tears, making her angrier. This was what Crawford liked, an emotional scene where he could take charge.

"Betsy Betsy Betsy," he crooned, meaning to soothe, and transferring sugar from his hand to hers with a few brief pats.

"Were you behind that letter, Crawford?" she demanded, pulling her hand away. "All that business about flaunting my condition!"

"Me?" He seemed genuinely shocked. "Behind that exercise in illogic and hot air?" He looked at her sadly. " 'Oh, Hamlet, thou hast cleft my heart in twain.' "

"I'm not going to laugh, Crawford. I'm perfectly serious. Did you put the idea in that little bastard's head? He sounded like your echo."

"Your condition has unsettled your brain," he said curtly. "I told you I was on your side. You seem to remember everything I said but that. And if you can't take the heat, you should have kept your knickers on."

He glared at her, picked up his book, and left.

There were no more letters, and the issue seemed to blow over, but it had brought Betsy into prominence and made it possible for people to talk to her frankly about a situation they had pussyfooted around before. She was overwhelmed with offers of secondhand baby necessities, midnight rides to the hospital, baby-sitting, moral support. She received letters of congratulation from both feminist organizations and right-to-lifers. Her seminar students looked pleased and secretive, and she had a horrible feeling they were planning some major gesture of support, like erecting a statue of her, belly and all, in front of the Hall of Languages.

"Why so depressed?" Roger asked her. "You've brought illegitimacy out of the closet and into the classroom." He was buoyed by Rachel Grace's defense and its aftermath; it smacked of underground networks, the solidarity of the people. "You've become a good cause. We need causes. You're a public benefactor."

"Please don't joke, Roger. I don't want to be a good cause. I just want to be left alone."

"Acts of courage never go unsung."

"What act of courage?" she asked desperately. "All I'm doing is having a baby. People do it every day and nobody calls them heroines. Why me? And Roger—" She hesitated. Everything she said lately sounded so dumb-innocent, it seemed either larger than life or calculated. She had never felt so alienated from her own utterances, as if she thought in English and it came out Russian. "Roger, do you think there's any danger of Rachel or any of these young women students glamorizing my situation to the point where they *would* imitate me? You know—go out and get themselves knocked up so they can be heroines? Because it's being made to look like a romantic sort of challenge?"

"How many of Joan of Arc's sympathizers leapt into the flames with her?"

"No, really. Tell me honestly. Am I a bad influence on these kids?"

"Where were you brought up? In a Henry James novel?"

They were sitting in his office, and he leaned forward over his desk and took her shoulders in his two hands—an act of unprecedented intimacy. "Betsy, my dear, what you're doing is, like it or not, an act of character and courage that the average person simply isn't capable of."

"I didn't want you to say that, Roger."

"Of course you didn't!" He let her go and sat back in his chair, looking fed up. "Would I be giving you these fucking compliments if I suspected you of fishing for them?"

Betsy flushed and pressed her hands to her cheeks. "I'm sorry. I don't know how to handle this—being onstage." She thought of Emily.

"What's so funny?"

"I was thinking of my grandmother," she said, and she would have told him about Emily but she was too agitated to tell it coherently. It had been months since a man had touched her. She could still feel the pressure of his fingers on her shoulders.

All the autumn Emily had been calling once a week, except for when she was in England. "How is Violetta?" was always the first thing she asked. Betsy could hear the effort it cost her, the apprehension in her voice. As soon as Betsy answered, without detail, "about the same," the subject was dropped, and Emily relaxed into chat.

She liked to hear about Betsy's life, and when she called on the Friday evening when Betsy was getting ready to go to dinner at the Blakes', Betsy told her about the furor at school.

"Well, maybe furor is too strong a word. Fuss is better. I've caused a bit of a fuss."

"But that's monstrous, that letter!" Over the phone it was hard to remember that Emily was seventy-two. She sounded very much like Violet, or like Betsy herself, both of whom had inherited her clear, pleasing voice, but not the musical gift that went with it.

"Well, it's over now," Betsy said. "I'm passing into oblivion as a rallying point the way the Chicago Seven did. Do you know, I have students who never heard of the Chicago Seven?"

"Who are the Chicago Seven?"

"Oh, Emily!"

"I'm teasing, dear. Those boys from the sixties, is that it? I hope all this nonsense at the university hasn't affected your health. I hope you're eating right. How are your backaches?"

Betsy smiled to hear her. Emily was in the Pregnancy Club: great-grandmothers were members emeritus. "I get them, especially after I've taught all day." It occurred to her that Emily was taking the place of the oblivious Violet.

"Do you need anything? Can I send you a crib? Some sleepers?"

"Nothing, thanks. I have enough stuff here for triplets." It was true. For a heroine to refuse her laurels was unimaginable; she had accepted everything.

"Well, keep me posted," Emily said, and signed off as she usually did, "Please give Violetta my dearest love."

Easy talk, Betsy thought, hanging up. She couldn't help resenting Emily's aloofness, gracious and loving though it was, understandable though it might be. There she was up in East Haddam in her perfect little house, a comfort to her cats instead of to her daughter.

Quickly, Betsy finished dressing, then found herself with time to spare. She walked from room to room straightening things. She was messier alone than she had been with Judd. She had become used to his absence—or, rather, her apartment had reverted to the way it was a year ago, before they met. The bare spots had filled themselves up again. She had put his photo of the two of them in a drawer. It would, she understood, have been pathetic of her to keep it on the wall, even though it was for the baby's sake she wanted it there. She intended to be fair and open, up to a point, with her baby. "That's your daddy," she would instruct it, but she didn't know where to go from there. "He walked out on me when he found out about you"? "He was a gypsy rover"? "He came to me in a dream"? She expected the child to look on its father as a fabulous being, like God or Santa Claus, to be believed in for its mother's sake—a father not unlike Betsy's own.

She put on her cape—a legacy of her days with Judd; he had bought it for her—and went out into the wind. The weather had gone cold. There was frost every morning where her garden used to be, a smell of snow in the air. The bone-chilling, soul-numbing upstate winter was on its way, but for once Betsy didn't mind much. She was six and a half months pregnant, and toting her burden around kept her warm and sweaty. She welcomed the cold. "You got big early, like I did," Emily had said approvingly, ever on the watch for family similarities between herself and her granddaughter. She was perpetually amazed that Betsy had no theatrical ambitions, and neither sang nor danced nor played an instrument. "I do teach a course in Restoration drama," Betsy told her hopefully, making Emily laugh.

Betsy walked to the Blakes' dinner party. Roger and Karen and their four children lived a couple of blocks from her in a ramshackle house with bicycles on the lawn. Betsy almost tripped over one in the near-dark. Their porch light was always burned out. Roger opened the door, and light from within guided her up the steps. "Careful, dearie, you're walking for two," Roger said, putting a hand under her elbow. She laughed and shook his arm away, and then there was what sounded like a tremendous roar of voices shouting, "Surprise!"

The Blakes' house was full of people grinning at her. Faculty from the university, graduate students, a couple of selected undergraduates, some people she didn't recognize. Roger opened champagne and gave Betsy the first glass, and people milled around her, drinking and offering her food.

"I don't understand this," she said, taking a cracker from a basket. "What's the occasion?"

This was passed around as a choice piece of wit, and Rachel Grace, who was standing beside her with a bowl of potato chips, said, "It's a baby shower, of course."

It was the last tattered flag of her invisibility being torn down. Betsy caved in. She drained her glass and filled it again, and let people hug her. The ones she didn't know turned out to be members of the various organizations on campus who were applauding her stand. One of these, a tall girl who seemed alarmingly young but who was the head of Feminists for Free Choice, said as much.

"But I haven't taken any stand!" Betsy protested.

"This is a stand!" said the girl triumphantly, patting Betsy's belly.

"No—no, it isn't," she said, stepping back. "I wish I could make that clear to everyone."

"The fact that you don't see it is part of it!" said the girl, with shining eyes, and Betsy, who had begun to fear that her sense of humor was slipping, felt it coming back. But it did her no good. Earnest, determined faces surrounded her, congratulating her and talking seriously of heroism and progress and blows struck for freedom.

Across the room, Karen Blake was setting out more food on a long table. She was wearing an apron that said, "For this I spent four years in college?" and she looked frazzled from getting the kids out of the way before the party started. Betsy waved to her; Karen waved back with a jar of mustard in her hand and disappeared into the kitchen.

The Blakes were always giving parties, and Karen was always frazzled. Betsy had met Judd at the Blakes' New Year's Eve party. He had been brought by a friend of a friend of Karen's, whom he had deserted. He and Betsy had talked, and he had walked her home. It was freezing out. She invited him in for coffee and within ten minutes they were in bed. He moved in a week later. The Blakes had a stuffed owl named Harold stuck up on a ledge in the study, and it was in front of Harold that Judd had first kissed her. Betsy started to make her way over to Karen, to help with the food, and she wandered into the study en route. The owl stared angrily off into space. She remembered her pleased surprise, at being kissed like that without warning. And later, in her living room, Judd had taken off her clothes, she remembered, starting with her parka and boots. He had kissed her cold red knees. He had buried his face between her breasts and told her she had a body made for loving.

The den was empty except for herself and Harold. Betsy would have liked to sit quietly in the corner, drinking champagne, but she went out to the kitchen. "I hope this party doesn't just make things worse," Karen said nervously. She was slicing bread, and she gave Betsy a jar of pickles to arrange in a dish. Karen had large, benevolent blue eyes that her children had inherited. As a family, they looked perpetually thoughtful and wondering. "Sometimes Roger's ideas are a bit extreme. But I do think it's better to bring it out in the open. I mean, it wasn't long ago when this would have been something shameful, something to be deplored." She widened her wide eyes and said formally, "We want to show you that we rejoice with you."

"I think it's wonderful of you, Karen," Betsy said, making the pickles line up in rows. She had hoped for a lighter touch from Karen.

"Well, we think you're the wondeful one!"

Betsy persisted. "You shouldn't have done it—the champagne!"

Karen put her knife down and poured champagne for both of them from a bottle on the counter. "Everyone chipped in," she said. "Do you know, these students are loaded! When we were in school everyone was so *poor*." She caressed the bottle, with its New York State label.

"Speaking of which, you forgot to take off your apron," said Betsy.

"It's part of my outfit—part of my statement," Karen confided. "Roger and I are in the midst of renegotiating our marriage." She knew such jargon had to appear ironic, and she smiled ruefully at Betsy. "What a load of crap—right?"

"I don't know," Betsy said, with rue of her own. "I've never even negotiated one, much less renegotiated it."

"Good! You're taking this in the right spirit!" cried Karen, drinking off her champagne. "Keep your sense of humor, Betsy, and you can survive anything." She made a sweeping gesture with her glass that took in four children, a husband, and any number of parties, and then asked abruptly, "Do you ever see Judd?"

"Never." Betsy buried her nose in her champagne glass. She had driven by his studio only that one time, when she had wept to see his bicycle chained in front of it.

"He's around, you know."

"I assumed he was."

"I've seen him with Joan Arletta once or twice."

"Ah. Yes." She and Judd had met Joan Arletta at a party once. Joan had played up to Judd, and Betsy had reveled in her rare triumph, that she was the woman other women envied, the one with the desirable man. And now Joan had him.

"I assume *la commedia è finita* with you two?" asked Karen.

Betsy shrugged, and Karen shrugged back. They exchanged an ironically anguished grimace: Men!

Betsy brought the pickles into the dining room and stood in the middle of the floor, thinking: He is truly gone, then. She hadn't known about that scrap of lingering hope until, with Karen's revelation, it left her. He had someone else. Oddly, she had never imagined it, had seen him as a loner, herself as an uncharacteristic interlude in the life of an eremite. But he had had plenty of women before her—she knew that well—and of course he would have women after her. Joan Arletta. He'd probably been seeing her all along; he was with her now, no doubt. Betsy tried to imagine his hands on another woman, but she only succeeded in imagining his hands on her, and his mouth—she remembered how he had turned to her in the dark. . . .

Betsy opened her eyes, still holding the dish of pickles, now precariously tipped. She set it down. The party had become very noisy. There was a strong background smell of marijuana, and there were sandwiches and a sinkful of champagne on ice. Betsy realized she was getting drunk. As guest of honor, she was not allowed to have an empty glass. She set her ham sandwich down somewhere and never found it again.

"Champagne is good for babies," said a young man named Stephen, who was Rachel Grace's date. "Champagne and beer, nothing stronger. Especially when you're nursing. They stimulate the flow of milk."

"Isn't anybody embarrassed by anything anymore?" Betsy asked with despair that was meant to look mock but was at least half real.

"Are you embarrassing this lady?" said Roger, taking her arm. "That is not the point of the evening."

"Stephen is a medical student," said Rachel, pulling him away. "Doctors can say anything."

Stephen grinned and drifted with Rachel toward the dope corner. Roger surveyed the crowd in his living room and looked pleased. "All we need is Errol Flynn swinging from the chandeliers." He moved closer to Betsy and said in her ear, "I've found out something interesting about Jonathan Simonson's poison pen letter." He put his arm around her, letting his hand rest low on her hip, and murmured appreciatively, "Mm, there's nothing sexier than a woman with child." He was an exceptionally handsome man, tall and muscular, with frizzy brown hair and devilish green eyes. Betsy had seen Paul Newman once, on a news program, lamenting the fact that he was nothing but a sex symbol to so many women. "It really bothers you?" the interviewer had asked. "God, yes!" Newman had replied, looking pleadingly into the camera, his blue eyes brilliant and sexy and distressed. Roger reminded Betsy of Paul Newman. She was aroused by his closeness. He knew it and smiled lazily at her—a practiced, movie-star leer. She wanted to say, "It's nothing personal, Roger. It's just that it's been a long time." But she only gave a strained smile and drew away.

Roger sighed elaborately, with mock pain. "Well, I'll tell you my news, anyway, in spite of your superhuman powers of resistance. Your pal Simonson is great chums with John Alderman. John's got your Pope seminar next semester and it's gone to his head."

"What do you mean?"

"I mean that I suspect old John, who is a bit of a shit, wouldn't mind seeing you discredited. This department ain't big enough for two eighteenth-century specialists, says old cowboy John. It's her or me, one of us hombres has gotta go. And since cowboy John has only, to my knowledge, published one article in his lifetime—a lame little effusion on Dryden he probably cribbed from one of his graduate students—" Roger shrugged, waving his pipe. "I leave it to you to guess who'd be canned if any canning were to be done."

"I don't know how my pregnancy could advance John's career. I really don't see the university firing me for it."

"You don't see it, and I don't see it, especially since you have tenure and old John doesn't, but since when is everybody as rational as you and I? And I think that for John your getting caught with something in the oven is only the frosting on the cake—as it were. He's been a-wantin' to ride you out of town on a rail ever since your book came out."

She refused to be ruffled. "My God, Roger, I've got an enemy," she breathed with reverent sarcasm.

"A little one. A mosquito," said Roger, sucking on his pipe.

Betsy wished she had a pipe for a prop. She finished her

champagne instead and asked casually, "You don't really think I'm in any danger, do you? I mean it doesn't say in the contract anywhere, does it, that thou shalt not give birth to a bastard while on the job?"

"Be serious. No court in the country would let you be fired."

"Roger, I don't want to go to court!"

"Don't sweat it. Really. These aren't the Dark Ages, even in Syracuse."

"I thought it was Crawford behind the letter."

"Crawford?" Roger removed his pipe to laugh. "Crawford Divine adores you! He'd be your little lap dog if you'd only let him. Your big, slobbering lap dog. Lucky you."

He filled her glass again and excused himself. "I see my good wife signaling frantically to me for help. She probably can't get the dancing girls to pop out of the cake."

He flashed his smile at her again and disappeared, but his place was taken by other friends. No longer uncertain as to what line to adopt, they treated Betsy with humorous regard. She felt like the erring daughter they were all fond of. It occurred to her that what she knew was termed behind her back "Betsy's escapade" had enlivened a dull department. It had, after all, been a year since Thisbe had electrocuted herself with the vacuum cleaner.

Everyone assembled for cake and coffee. Betsy's heart sank at the pile of presents, but Karen had organized the gift giving, and all the packages contained children's books. Betsy began opening them, ripping off pink-and-blue paper printed with ducks and puppies. *The Wind in the Willows. A Child's Garden of Verses. Mother West Wind. Winnie-the-Pooh. The Story of Doctor Dolittle.*

"All the favorite books of our childhood—I made everyone sign up, so there'd be no duplicates," Karen explained, looking pleased, equally, with her organizational efforts and with Betsy's cries of recognition and delight.

"All the books we wish our own kids would read instead of watching *The Incredible Hulk,*" said Roger. He picked up *Doctor Dolittle* and began to read: "Once upon a time, many years ago—when our grandfathers were little children —there was a doctor, and his name was Dolittle."

Betsy began, to her horror, to cry. "Stop, Roger!" She took the book from him and began leafing through it, head bent to hide the tears. "It was my favorite book when I was a kid," she mumbled in apology. "It sounds so odd, somehow, to hear you read it now." She couldn't have explained the effect those few lines from the book had had on her. It was partly that they brought it all back: the oppressed, long, solitary days of her childhood, and the books that had helped push back their boundaries as nothing, not even imagination, could do so well. But it was more than that—any recollection of her childhood brought with it, now, the melancholy shadow of her mother's dying, and the dread she felt of the darkness that shadow would cast her into.

"Quiet, everyone!" Roger said loudly. "Dr. Ruscoe will now reminisce about her childhood."

Betsy tried to laugh, wiping her eyes on a paper napkin. "I just want to thank you all," she said. She rested her hands on the stack of books on the table before her, and as she touched them a swift, portentous image came to her, of herself reading through them, late one of these nights, wallowing in morbid tears and despair. She rejected the image, she steeled herself against it. "You're all too kind," she said further, when Roger insisted on a speech. "I'm overcome by it. I consider myself very lucky."

There was a fusillade of applause, and Roger embraced her drunkenly, but she turned from him and hugged Karen. "It was all your doing, and I'm grateful," she said.

"Better books than booties," Karen replied. Roger, behind her, with his arms around one of his female graduate students, was reciting from *A Child's Garden of Verses,* and

Karen was averting her eyes so determinedly from the spectacle that it was clear she was wounded—and scarred, too, from old hurts, inflicted perhaps during other futile renegotiations.

Crawford Divine came in while they were packing up the books in a carton. He had been letting his moustache grow all the autumn, so that he looked like a large, addled walrus. He swayed slightly and spilled half the champagne Karen poured for him, and Betsy saw that he was already drunk.

"Better late than never, Crawford," Roger said, smirking at Betsy.

"You may not know that particular cliché is from the Bible," Crawford said. "Matthew twenty-one—I forget the verse."

"I'll look it up."

"You won't, but you should." Even tipsy, Crawford was adept at sailing over sarcasm. "It doesn't hurt to have a bit of fact at your fingertips."

He handed Betsy a package—*Mary Poppins* in stork paper—and when she kissed him a peck on the cheek in thanks he pulled her to him and aimed for her lips. There was more applause. Betsy struggled away, spilling the rest of Crawford's champagne, and, to cover his discomfiture, announced that she was exhausted, she had to leave, it was hours past her bedtime. Crawford stood scowling at the rug.

"Here, Dr. Ruscoe." Rachel stood at her side with a brimming glass. "Just one more so we can toast you."

Betsy took it dutifully.

"Champagne is really an incredible high," Rachel said. "I think it's fantastic when all these academic stuffed shirts let their hair down and really live."

"Like Crawford here," Roger said. "Here you go, Crawford." Roger handed him a glass and Crawford began sipping, not waiting for the toast.

Roger raised his glass. "To Betsy and Betsy Junior," he said in a furred voice. "May they both thrive."

"Amen," Crawford said.

Betsy drained her glass, feeling they expected her to. It was a mistake. When she set it down, she tottered. She looked around for the medical student. "Is it all right for the baby if I'm ever so slightly drunk?"

He smiled woozily. "It's good for the baby," he assured her. "Best thing for babies."

Crawford was at her elbow with a conversation stopper. "When Thisbe was pregnant both times, she gave up the sauce entirely. Of course, she resumed quickly enough afterwards." He filled the pause with a little chuckle and went on, to Betsy, "If I apologize for grabbing you, can I walk you home? It's such a beautiful night—"

His pink, piggy face was amiable again, and Betsy disguised her dismay. She couldn't insult him twice. "Of course, Crawford."

She saw Stephen and Rachel turn away, smiling to each other at the stuffed shirts letting their hair down, and was dimly conscious of the indignity of it all: herself months pregnant, Crawford Divine panting after her, both of them royally drunk.

Roger left his graduate student and went to get Betsy's cape. He draped it, with flourishes, over her shoulders while Karen stood by looking sober and aggrieved. "My wife thinks I have had too much champagne," Roger said to Crawford in a stage whisper. "But the fact that I'm still aware of what she thinks means I haven't had enough."

"I have to agree with Karen," Crawford said in a prim voice.

"Well, fuck you, Crawford," Roger replied genially, and there was uneasy laughter from the students gathered around.

With dignity, Crawford tied a muffler around his neck and took Karen's hand. "A very nifty party, Karen. Admirable. Elegant. First class."

Karen smiled tremulously at his strange adjectives and wished him and Betsy good night. The expression in her large eyes was both weepy and defiant. Betsy wanted, suddenly, to leave. The house was cursed, first by her ill-starred meeting there with Judd, and now by this rotting marriage, and Karen's unhappiness, and the four small children asleep upstairs. It all seemed connected: we also would have come to this, she told herself, and gave Karen a last, impulsive hug.

Crawford insisted on carrying the carton of books. "No problem," he said, brushing away protests. "No problem." He held the carton to his chest and glowered over the top of it.

"Let me drive you," said Roger at the door.

"No *problem,* Roger!"

Roger shrugged and stepped outside with them. "What can you do with these *macho* types?"

Crawford marched warily down the walk with the books. "It was a lovely party, Roger," Betsy said. "Thank you."

Roger kissed her on the lips. Crawford didn't look back; he stood at the end of the walk, stonily waiting.

"Betsy?" he called finally.

She broke away, breathless. "I'm coming, Crawford." She made a face at Roger—wry, deprecating, chagrined—but it was doubtful he saw it in the dark. She went unsteadily down the path.

"Take my arm," Crawford instructed.

Obediently, she did so, looking back at Roger, but he was just going in, outlined in the light from inside and then cutting it off as the door shut.

She took several deep breaths and said to Crawford, "It's cold out."

"I suppose it is." His voice implied that small talk was beneath him. They didn't say anything else until they got to Betsy's front porch. Crawford was breathing heavily, and he leaned the carton of books on the porch railing while she fumbled with her key, her breath visible in the light and her nose numb. Through the Brodskys' front window the television was a pastel square. Betsy wondered if they had waited up for her.

"It was awfully nice of you to carry those for me, Crawford," she said, hoping he would dump the carton and leave.

"I don't mind." He climbed the stairs behind her, grunting, and deposited the carton on the floor of the living room. Relieved of his load, he looked pleased, as if he hadn't known he could do it. "A cup of coffee would be most welcome, however," he said, gazing around the room with interest.

"I was just about to offer you one," Betsy said belatedly. All she could think of was Judd under the same circumstances. She could feel his hands on her still. She shouldn't have kissed Roger. The nippy air had sobered her, and she knew, with a kind of advance disgust, that she'd feel terrible about it in the morning.

Crawford looked through her bookcases while she made coffee in the kitchen. When she came in with two mugs, he turned to her and said, "Why do people always do this? Inspect each other's books?"

"I suppose they tell us a lot about each other."

"It always amazes me"—he sat down on the sofa beside her—"when I catch myself doing something everyone else does. It's reassuring."

Betsy didn't answer. She didn't want to talk about Crawford and what amazed and reassured him. She wanted him to drink his coffee and go so she could fall into bed.

"I'm very drunk, Betsy," he said after he had taken a sip.

"So am I, Crawford." The heat of the apartment had, in fact, restored the champagne's effects. *Muzzy,* she thought: it was one of her mother's words. Violet never got tipsy—only a little muzzy.

"But that doesn't have anything to do with what I'm going to say. Drunk or sober, it wouldn't make any difference." Crawford spoke slowly, emphasizing each word, the way he did at department meetings when he was making an announcement. "It's not the booze talking." He paused portentously. Betsy didn't know what to do. She was sure of one thing. Whatever it was he was going to say, she didn't want to hear it.

"You and I could get married, if you wanted to."

It was worse than she'd expected. It was unimaginably bad.

"I need a wife," he said. "My kids need a mother. And you—" He smiled sidewise at her. "You could use a husband."

"Crawford—"

"Wait." He set his mug down carefully and took her hand. "I know I'm considered a figure of fun by some people. I honestly don't know why. I am, after all, chairman of the English department at a large and respected university. I think of myself as an intelligent, ordinary, hardworking man. That's all I want to be. I don't understand why people think I'm pompous or silly. I hope you don't think it."

"I don't, Crawford," Betsy said, ashamed of herself because she did. She had never heard him speak so simply. It seemed to be from the heart. But she felt hysterical laughter gather in her.

"We could be happy, Betsy. I've put on a little weight, but I think I could get rid of it if I were happier. I'm a good father. Of course, a father can't do everything. Children need a mother. And I think you and I, together—"

She released it, but it wasn't laughter. It was the torrent of tears she had anticipated when she put her hand on the pile of children's books, but it was Crawford who released it, not Winnie-the-Pooh or Doctor Dolittle. She put her hands over her face and wept, rocking forward and back.

Crawford patted her awkwardly and then put his arms around her. "I'm sorry, Betsy, it was just a thought." He cradled her, and she leaned her head on his chest and sobbed harder. She thought she might sit there forever, sobbing, until he started kissing her neck. Then she sat up with a start and moved away from him, but she continued to cry, pressing her two hands to her mouth.

Crawford sat facing her, looking drunk and sorrowful. "I'm really sorry, Betsy. I'm not doing anything right. Maybe I should have said that I'm very, very fond of you, and have been for some time."

She let him hold her again, she felt so sorry for him, but she couldn't stop the tears, and they streamed down her face onto his sweater. He patted her back, but he didn't attempt to kiss her again. She tried to set her mind on something neutral, but every aspect of her life struck her as tragic. She reflected that not long ago she had thought herself happy, and she was appalled. Her mother dying, the gossip about her pregnancy spread all over campus, her bastard baby due in a couple of months, her job in jeopardy, her lover gone off with another woman, and now Crawford wanted to make her Betsy Divine, mother of his children and supervisor of his diets. Everything that came into her mind brought fresh tears. Life held no comforts.

Eventually, she managed to give Crawford his coat and maneuver him toward the door. "I'm sorry, Betsy," he said again. "I still think it might work out."

The tears slipped down her cheeks, and she shook her head back and forth until he turned and went down the stairs. Then she closed the door behind him and sank down on the rug, crying softly. It wasn't fair, she thought to herself, fully conscious of the childish irrationality of the words: *It's not fair, it's not fair*! As if, in the years beyond childhood, fairness ever had anything to do with it. But it's *not,* she thought stubbornly (her tears subsiding, and only the sound of crying left), it's not fair—that the man she wanted languished in the arms of another woman, while the man she didn't want carried her books and proposed marriage.

She would have liked to call Emily and ask her where she'd gotten her strength, but—drunk though she was—she couldn't bring herself to drag an old woman out of a sound sleep at midnight to listen to her angry woes. She took them to bed with her instead and hugged her pillow for comfort—as, back in her *Doctor Dolittle* days, she used to hug her doll.

The semester ended two weeks later—two weeks in which Betsy scurried in and out of the Hall of Languages as if escaping from snipers, arriving as her classes began and disappearing immediately after, avoiding her own office, where Roger could waylay her, and the English department offices, where Crawford lurked. She tried to make herself stop doing it, to face up to life instead of hiding from it, to open herself up to experience for her baby's sake. "You'll smother it!" she told herself in her grandfather's words, but she continued to sneak around, and, at the end of her last exam, she drove to her grandfather's house to curl up in the chair in Violet's room and mark papers while her mother dozed.

As the winter days went by, as the sad Christmas came and went, as the snow piled up like cement along the streets, Betsy spent more and more time in the quiet, dim-lit sickroom. Though Violet's coming death and Frank's hostility lodged there with her, it was the place where she felt safe. "It's ridiculous to drive over here every day on these roads," her grandfather said one January afternoon, and eventually she brought a suitcase and lived there for days at a stretch, sleeping in her old room with the grieving Virgin and the broken rocker, and spending the days with her mother. She worked on her Boswell article, or she read, or she talked to Terry—or she simply sat, watching her mother sleep. Her grandfather often sat there, too, but across the room, and they seldom spoke. She was very pregnant, and very large. In his presence, her big belly embarrassed her, and she could see that the signs of her pregnancy irritated him. If she, on standing, pressed her hand to the pain in the small of her back, if she kicked off her shoes to ease her swollen feet, if she pushed away her dinner uneaten, he would turn away from her with thinly disguised disgust. His protest against her daily drive in the snow hadn't, she suspected, been an invitation to move in, but she had willfully interpreted it as such, and she defied him (sitting across the room, watching him across the sleeping form of Violet) to cast her out. But she sat with the afghan tucked around her, to hide the evidence of her rebellion against his wishes. "Your great-grandchild!" she pleaded silently, and in vain. "Your own flesh and blood!" He kept his eyes turned from her, and Betsy thought she began to see what Emily had been up against.

Meanwhile, the promised pain had invaded Violet, and it was necessary to keep her almost constantly drugged. As they watched her sleep, they could see its approach. She became restless, her thin hands—white and small, and mapped now with blue veins—groped among the blankets as if searching for something lost, and if her eyes opened the look in them would be anguished and bewildered.

"Are you in pain, Mrs. Ruscoe?" Terry would say, and give her an injection in one of the fine blue veins, and Violet would sleep again.

One January day, Betsy rose late and breakfasted alone in the kitchen. Sleep was a struggle. It was hard to settle her heavy body comfortably in the narrow old bed, and she tended to fall asleep toward dawn and wake up with the full snowy light of late morning in her face—greeted by the silent scorn of her grandfather, who had the elderly habit of early rising.

Though it was close to noon, she felt as if she hadn't slept at all, and when Frank came into the kitchen she was yawning over her coffee.

"Takes a lot out of you, does it?"

She smiled at him. "It kicks all night."

"Hmm," he said, and then gave a belated, grudging smile. "You look a lot like your mother, when she was—" He gestured vaguely.

"Pregnant with me?" she finished for him, pleased.

"Mm. She was huge. She and your father were living in Rochester, and your grandmother and I used to go up and see them." He didn't sit down, but he leaned against the counter with his hands in his pockets. Betsy rejoiced. He hadn't talked to her—really talked to her, about anything but her mother's illness—in months. "She was so big we expected twins at least, but she looked so pretty, so young and lighthearted through it all—your mother—"

He had to turn away.

"Grandpa—"

"I'll just go and see if the mail's here."

He wouldn't let her comfort him. He was, solely, the father of his dying girl; grandfatherhood didn't interest him, and great-grandfatherhood repelled him. Betsy sighed and went up to Violet's room. She would never forgive him for not telling her, for not including among his occasional reminiscences the fact that her mother was his and Emily's child. She would not forget his hostility toward her own child—that the public man who cared what people thought had got the better, even briefly, of her loving grandfather. Poor Emily, she said to herself, poor Emily. She would call Emily later when she went over to her apartment to water the plants and pick up her mail.

Terry gave up the chair when she came in and made a whispered inquiry about Betsy's condition. It was her theory that the baby was due any day, though officially there was over a week to go.

"Anything yet? Any pains?"

"No."

"Won't be long, though," she said. She kept her voice soft, knowing instinctively that Frank disapproved. Or did they discuss it? Betsy wondered. Her grandfather had become an enigma to her.

Terry went downstairs in a wave of perfume. Every day at this time she made a high-protein milk shake for Violet to drink on waking—and they would all watch anxiously as Violet, sip by sip, got it down. She had lost all interest in food. "She's trying to starve herself to death," Frank had said once, and they had retreated in shocked silence from the idea, and no one had mentioned it since. But it seemed to Betsy to be true. In the last few weeks, death seemed to have crept perceptibly closer, to have taken part of her already. Her pale skin that had been so firm seemed suddenly slack, with furrows from nose to mouth and between her eyebrows. She was thinning out, looking more like Emily. Ah, if only Emily would come. Betsy sat in her chair, imagining Violet waking to find her mother at her bedside instead of Terry with a milk shake. Her face would get radiant and girlish, all the lines smoothed out, and she would roll out of bed with her old, easy gusto, scrub her face with hot water and soap in the bathroom, and march downstairs barefoot to make a big pot of vegetarian bean soup. "Good for what ails you," Violet would say in her old voice, raising a spoon to her mouth. "This is just what I needed."

Betsy woke with a start. The book she'd been trying to read had fallen from her lap, and Violet was murmuring from the bed. Betsy thought she was asleep, but when she went over to her she saw that her eyes were open.

"I want my mama," Violet whispered once, and then, more loudly, "Betsy, I want my mama! I want Emily! Why won't she come and see me?" As her voice rose to a wail, Frank came upstairs and stood in the doorway, pale as death.

CHAPTER EIGHT

Emily

Emily enjoyed her house in winter as much at she did in summer. Once the snow fell, it stayed—in large, bare tracts across the backyards, crisscrossed with animal tracks, and on the back of the dolphin weather vane like foam, and frozen into brown-sugar ruts on the streets, where the white houses stood stark and clean against it.

Inside, she kept it good and warm. She ate bread and thick soup and rich desserts, and she drank sherry, always putting on a few pounds. She would pat her plumper hips and say, "I'm at my hibernating weight." The word "hibernating" was not lightly chosen; there was truth in it. The winters seemed to her longer and harder, and there were weeks at a time when she didn't venture out. Groceries were delivered. Most of her friends had gone south. There was nothing much to go out and risk a fall on the ice for. So she stayed inside, hugging herself to herself like a small animal in its den.

This winter she had something else to do besides listening to music and reading and eating. She had heard Betsy's silent reproaches, and, trying to nerve herself up for a spring trip to Violet's bedside, she had been forcing out her memories and looking at them hard—the bad memories, the ones she had spent thirty-five years sucessfully repressing, until Betsy found her and brought them all back.

And the snow . . . She looked out at the snow and let her mind go slack, and the snow drew the memories from her. It had been winter the first time she saw Frank Robinson—really *saw* him. Until then, she had considered the young married couple next door to be unutterably boring. So that was marriage! Helen with her dreary pregnancy, Frank with his dull job in a law office. No, thanks! Then, in November, Helen's baby had been born and died, and the Robinsons took on a new interest for her. There were rumors of the ferocity of Helen's grief, tales of madness. Helen's sister Marion (reputedly no better than she should be) came from New York to nurse her. Once Emily heard hysterical sobbing through the windows. Frank Robinson took to walking in his backyard at dusk, smoking cigarettes under the bare trees in the cold. Brooding. That was where she used to watch him, from her bedroom window, and he looked different. He struck Emily as a romantic figure, a man of sorrows. She thought of Mr. Rochester and his mad wife.

Gradually Helen seemed better, and her sister returned to New York. But Frank continued to brood under the cherry trees. Once Emily had seen him out there, bare-headed, in the midst of a snowstorm; whatever his secret sorrow, it must be tragic indeed to drive him out in the snow. The gossip had been that Helen blamed him—his heredity, specifically—for the baby's death and now barred him from her bed. Emily kept her eye on him, inventing twists on the tragedy, and one evening at dusk she put on her boots and went boldly out to talk to him. She had never conversed with a man of sorrows. They talked of music out in the cold. He too was a fan of Victor Herbert. Emily had gone to see *The Red Mill* with her parents, downtown at the Empire; he had been there, too. They talked until her mother called her, and she went to the woodshed for an unnecessary armful of wood before she returned to the house.

She began to seek him out, listening each evening for the dreadful noises of his car coming home, and before long she was officially the Robinsons' little friend—running errands for Helen during the worst of the winter, keeping her company after school, singing for them in the evenings (even as a girl she was renowned in the neighborhood for her voice). Her parents approved of their daughter's friendship with a mature, domestic woman; they believed Emily, who was frivolous, could profit from her association with Helen, who was anything but.

Emily didn't like Helen. She didn't like her looks, for one thing. She looked more like an old maid than the wife of a man like Frank—though she was at her prettiest when she was sick, Emily thought charitably. Against the stark white of nightgown and sheets, she looked colorful by contrast. Her hair wouldn't stay skinned back into its mousy knot, so she wore it in two loose braids along her cheeks, and it softened her features. But she could never be called a pretty woman, Emily used to say to herself with satisfaction—she was too *ovine,* like old pictures of Queen Victoria. And she never had much to say. She couldn't even show her gratitude for Emily's favors; she had an aristocratic way of accepting them as her due, as if she really were Queen Victoria.

But it was Frank Emily was doing the favors for. She began slowly to worship him. She had never seen a man so tall and handsome, and, at twenty-two, he made the raw boys in her high school class look like babies—and act like babies, too, with their stupid jokes, their shallowness. Eddie Mason, who played football and whom Emily used to consider a god, now seemed a silly ape with pimples on his neck. She quit the dramatic club at school (though she stayed in the chorus, where she was principal soloist) and spent her spare time hanging around the Robinsons.

The Robinsons couldn't afford a hired girl. Frank was just a law clerk, and Helen hadn't—as Emily's mother put it—"brought anything" to the marriage. Emily often helped Helen in the kitchen, and if Helen was feeling particularly poorly, Emily read to her after dinner—from the *Catholic Devotional Weekly* or the more chaste popular novels. Sometimes she sang hymns, unaccompanied.

No one knew what was wrong with Helen or in what her delicateness consisted. Months after the birth and death of her baby she was still moping, still tired and apathetic. She had been pronounced well by her doctor, and her sister had felt she was fit enough to cope on her own. There were times when she seemed almost normal. But some days she scarcely left her bed and lay all day with her head turned to the wall. On the wall was a crucifix. In the next room was the bed where (Emily knew) Frank slept; his brushes were on the dresser, his old maroon bathrobe on a hook behind the door. It was supposed to have been the baby's room, but when the baby died Frank moved in. Everything had been taken away except a dresser scarf embroidered with yellow ducks holding umbrellas. No one seemed to notice it, even though Frank set his brushes on it every day, and Helen, on her good days, dusted around it. Frank slept in a white iron bed, little more than a cot. Emily, poking around, used to go in and lay her head on the pillow, smooth the quilt, look at the yellow ducks. She took a couple of hairs from Frank's hairbrush; for years, she kept them in the blue velvet box with her locket.

One day she got Frank to kiss her, by the simple expedient of grabbing him around the neck and pressing her lips to his. She thought she would die from the scary joy of it, but she didn't. I've come alive, she said to herself. She got him to kiss her again, and before long that was her sole purpose in going to the Robinsons'. She helped Helen with the wash and chopped nuts for Christmas cakes, and all the while she was stalking Frank.

It was a profoundly moving experience for Emily to wash up their dinner dishes in the kitchen at night. Usually Frank was in the sitting room reading the paper, Helen was asleep upstairs, but her own parents didn't expect her home for over half an hour. She didn't hurry over the dishes—washed them, in fact, lovingly, being especially tender with the cups and glasses. His lips had rested there! Sometimes she sang to herself the old hymns she'd been singing for Helen, but she kept her voice low. At the first restless squeak from the bed upstairs, she would have been off home; she had had enough of Helen.

But when the dishes were washed and dried and the dish towel hung up, she went into the sitting room, where Frank sat with his newspaper. Invariably he had already laid it aside, hearing her approach; invariably, he rose eagerly when she entered the room and caught her in his arms. "Ah, God, Emily," he would whisper, and kiss her several times before he gripped her shoulders hard, looked sorrowfully at her, and said, "We can't continue like this." This, too, was invariable, and his soft groan when he pulled her to him again. They always continued.

She didn't share his anguish. She felt herself bloom with bliss after these encounters. Sometimes they met in the pantry, quickly, if Helen went upstairs for a minute—sometimes Emily followed him outside—once he stumbled down the cellar after her when she went for potatoes. Always, he clutched her as if she was a part of himself that might get away if he didn't keep it pressed close. She held him and kissed him, gladly, every chance she got. The evenings when Helen took to her bed were the best, those long minutes in the sitting room. One night, without a word, he had turned her around, trembling, his breathing ragged, and undone her buttons. She had let her blouse fall down around her waist, and her camisole with it, and he had closed his eyes and worshiped her breasts with his lips and fingers. She had stroked his soft brown hair, and, looking down at his closed eyes, his rapt, reverent face, she had felt her mind go blank of everything but her love for him. Later, going over the scene in her room, she realized he had banked the fire first—for her, to warm her nakedness.

Sometimes, on evenings when Helen had some energy, the three of them talked. Emily got a queer, special pleasure out of talking to Frank and Helen together about her concerns. She caricatured her classmates and teachers, and was triumphant when she got a chuckle from Helen. Helen, in fact, was the first person ever to say to her, "You should go on the stage." Frank was endlessly amused by her; this seemed to make Helen's laughs all the more rare. Emily was conscious of wanting to be the little ray of sunshine around their house, and Helen's lack of response didn't daunt her. It wasn't Helen's response she wanted, and she knew the contrast of her sparkle with Helen's gloom suited her—although, if she could cheer Helen up a little, so much the better, she thought in her high-minded moments. Helen would need all her strength, she would add when optimism took over from charity. For every tiny pang of guilt she discovered in herself, there was a reasonable argument that said: Helen never discourages my visits, Helen is always kind to me, Helen needs me to help her. . . . And behind all this was her suspicion that Helen had something in mind for her, something else besides hymn singing and washing up. She never for a second doubted Helen's complexity; her bland little face could wear an expression of frightening intensity. Emily would put nothing past her.

She would have liked to discuss Helen's state with her best friend, Virginia Baldwin, but there was something about the Robinsons that she felt herself unable to talk over with Virginia. The something, she vaguely understood, was her feeling for Frank, and though up to that point she and Virginia had told each other everything, she knew she couldn't discuss the fascination Helen had for her without including the fascinations of Frank. It felt odd, having these secrets from her friend, and it wasn't easy. At times, she had to appear almost rude. With a pang, she saw Virginia turn to Betty Schmitt—walk home with her, trade homework, pass her a copy of *Rose in Bloom*. It was the first Christmas since they were eight years old that she and Virginia didn't exchange handkerchief sachets. Proudly, Emily sought out Frank, feeling herself removed from silly high school girls. The Robinsons gave her a copy of *Great Operas of the World* for Christmas.

What Helen liked best was Emily's singing, and she preferred hymns—not necessarily Catholic ones; she liked them all, drinking them in the way an alcoholic will take anything he can get. Frank only tolerated the hymns. He would have preferred some light opera, something from Gilbert and Sullivan or Victor Herbert, but he put up with anything for the sake of hearing Emily. "Whatever I sing is a love song to you," she told him once with deliberate sentimentality—it was one of the ways she made him laugh, her eyes going all fluttery and a simper in her voice—and he caught it and smiled at her, but they both knew she meant it. When she sang, Frank didn't look at her. He sat in his big armchair and looked fixedly at his hands clenched together in his lap.

Once, Emily sang for them a new hymn she had learned, dismal and passionate:

> Flee as a bird to your mountain,
> Thou who art weary of sin,
> Go to the clear-flowing fountain,
> Where you may wash and be clean . . .

When she recovered from the effects of her own singing—a cappella, she was always particularly struck by the clarity and accuracy of her voice—she saw that there were tears running down Helen's face. Frank took his wife up to bed.

"What's wrong with her?" she asked him when he came down.

He had replied with hesitation. "I think she feels guilty about the baby's death."

"But why? It happens to everyone. My mother had two babies die!"

"Helen is very religious, Emily—" Frank looked fierce for a moment and then said, more mildly, "She seems to feel she's being punished, the baby's death was her punishment." He spoke in the detached lawyerlike tone that Emily later learned covered deep feeling when he used it with her. But his detachment seemed cruel to her, and she burst out, "Punishment? But Helen goes to church every Sunday, even when she's sick!" It seemed the height of goodness; her own family slept late on Sundays, and her father read the newspaper in bed. "Punishment for what?"

"For love!" Frank spoke the words much too loudly, and he turned away from her after he said them. "You know what I mean, Emily. For *sex*. For the pleasure of it."

They were in the sitting room. Helen was quiet upstairs. Emily put her hand on his arm. She understood everything; though she was not yet seventeen, she had read hundreds of books. "How terrible for you," she whispered.

He faced her, looking stricken. "I shouldn't tell you these things."

"You should," she assured him gently, leaning against him. He pulled her close and kissed her silently, over and over.

Things went on like this all that winter, until the evening of the opera.

Helen was feeling too ill to go and suggested Frank take Emily, who loved singing and had been so nice. Thus Frank reported his wife's words to Emily's mother when he went next door to invite her. His composure awed her; she hadn't dared look at him. She fled to her room to change into her dark brown lace, and then she was beside him in the car, unable to speak. He chattered to her all the way to the theater, and she sat through the overture in misery. Was this all, then? Was he just taking little Emily to the opera because she loved music and had been so nice?

Then the opera began and she forgot him; Violetta and Alfredo and their friends took over. After the intermission she saw that Frank was watching her and she became self-conscious. It had never occurred to Emily that her passion for music was charming—her own pretty voice, yes, but not her thirst for the voices of others. She saw herself in his eyes, pretty and precocious and flushed with happiness, and her heart beat fast with excitement, as much at what she had learned about herself as anything else. But when the curtain went up again, it was as if he and she were the stage people and Violetta and Alfredo were real life. He held her hand, finally—discreetly, between the seats—and she sat through the end in a daze. Every bliss was hers: music, love, beauty!

Afterward, they drove out to the lake, where he pulled her lace dress up to her waist and gently, gently deflowered her. It was more rapture than she knew existed, to make him so happy, and she wept in his arms, explaining carefully that they were tears of joy, that she felt proud and noble, that she loved him desperately. The music still echoed in her head.

They sat by the lake—it was an unusually warm evening, with a false hint of spring—and he made his first promises and told her explicitly of Helen's rejection of him. The marriage couldn't last, he said. Deeply though he pitied Helen, he couldn't endure such a mockery of all that marriage could be. He kissed Emily as she hadn't dreamed people kissed. Someday, somehow . . .

Soon after that evening Helen got unexpectedly better. She came downstairs in the evenings and sent Emily home early, with an admonishment to do her homework. Emily fancied that Helen looked at her, sometimes, mockingly, and she wondered what Frank's wife knew. She began to avoid the Robinson house; it was a different place with Helen up and around. She and Frank met only twice, briefly, for desperate kisses at night out under the cherry trees.

Then she missed her period, and she told Frank. They waited, anxious and unamorous, for a month. Spring was coming in earnest by then, with so many places to meet, but they hardly noticed. When her period still didn't come, he made her an appointment with a doctor way over on the south side, picked her up after school, and took her there.

"We'll get married, Emily," he said on the way back. He looked dragged out. "We'll get married." The words restored her boundless joy, and she saw that there were tiny pale-green leaves on all the trees.

It didn't work out quite that way. Talk of marrying stopped abruptly. First Frank went home to Helen, and then he was closeted with Emily's parents for an hour. When he left, with a grave look at her, he seemed allied with them against her: grown-ups against children. Her father, silent and sad, beat her, and she was sent to Connecticut the next day. Her mother wouldn't speak to her; she stayed in her room and cried. Her father put her on the train without a word of encouragement, glad to have her gone. She cried all the way to Utica, where the miracle happened: Frank leapt onto the train. But the miracle hadn't quite the depth and breadth she expected of it. They weren't eloping. He was merely, in defiance of Helen and the Loftuses, escorting her to East Haddam. They couldn't marry. Her parents wouldn't allow it; she was underage. And Helen —Helen had lapsed back into her half-mad melancholia. Her sister was with her again. He couldn't leave her yet. Give it a year—when Emily would be eighteen. . . .

They sat with their hands entwined. It was a long trip. As the train steamed along the Connecticut River, Emily conceived a daring plan. They would stay at a hotel together that night. Her father's cousin Myra wasn't expecting her; Emily was simply to appear, with a sealed letter from her father and her tail between her legs. What difference if she got there a day late? And Frank had to stay over, anyway; there was no train back until morning. Why shouldn't she stay with him?

It was nine o'clock when they reached Middletown. They

got off there and checked into the Dart Hotel as husband and wife. Alone with Frank in the hotel room, Emily forgot she was tired after the trip and the sleepless night before: he made her forget. He was infinitely gentle and patient, he kissed the bruises the beating had left on her back and buttocks, and she was thunderstruck to discover that the pleasure could be hers as well as his. They slept at last, and she awoke at noon anxious to try it again.

In the afternoon, they went out for a walk. It was a fine April day. He wanted to buy her a bracelet they saw in a shop, but she wouldn't let him. She'd been in their house often enough to see how little money he had. He bought her a pincushion instead—pink satin, with "I Love You" embroidered on one side and "Souvenir of Middletown, Conn." stamped on the other. It cost a quarter, which seemed reasonable to Emily. (Twenty years later, when she threw it out with the rest, she thought it was cheap and tawdry—typical and symbolic.)

She understood that marriage was not to be discussed. It was a sweet dream for the future. Frank had to "work on" Helen. The original plan was for Emily to keep the baby. As the months went on this was revised. Frank had a new plan, and he took the train to Connecticut to tell her. He and Helen would keep the baby, and someday Frank and Emily and the child would all be together. It would take time. This revision dulled Emily's joy somewhat. She wanted the child she carried, she didn't want promises. The shininess went out of her life. Everything was flat: she was only an unwed mother working, in disgrace, as a maid in a rooming house.

It was that flatness that prompted her to flee to New York the next spring when the baby had been spirited away and Myra was working her harder and harder. She would supply her own future, and if the sweet dream came true as well, then it would. But she had grown up, and the rule for growing up was: Rely on yourself.

Whenever she appeared in Syracuse, Frank came to her. Helen knew it. Emily wanted to see the little girl, her Violetta, but Helen wouldn't allow that. Emily saw her once, when she took a taxi past their house on Stiles Street and Violet was playing in the yard. She was seven or eight then. Emily had the driver go around the block and then cruise slowly by again. The little girl waved and smiled. The third time they went by she was gone. And then there was the time in the department store, when Emily thought that because Violet was engaged to be married, she and Frank would be together at last. But it turned out that it was impossible simply *because* Violet was engaged. "I can't do it to her, Emily," he said miserably. "She has her whole life ahead of her." They were in the Onondaga Hotel, between Emily's matinee and evening performances. Emily sank down in the bed and pulled the covers over her head. In the darkness a great light dawned. It would always be impossible. "Go away, Frank," she said from under the blankets. He pleaded with her and made excuses and promises. He pulled the covers off her but she got back under. "Go away," she said. Finally, he did, and she got up and took a bath and sang Micaela in *Carmen* that evening, and never saw him again, until he rang her doorbell that January , thirty-five years later, in the middle of a snowstorm, just as she had decided to stop thinking about him.

She knew him immediately. The bald head didn't surprise her; he'd begun losing his hair in his thirties. To her, he didn't even look especially old. He just looked sad and worn-out. They stood, measuring each other.

"So it's you," she said, and moved aside so he could come in. She felt perfectly calm—this calm was the only surprise. "In a way, I've been expecting you."

There were snowflakes on his head, melting. She took his coat into the bathroom and let it drip into the tub. When she returned he was still in the hall, looking up the staircase in bewilderment.

"It's not a Bulfinch, of course—just a local imitator," she said.

He hadn't yet spoken; he stared at her. The look on his face she considered pathetic, though it used to melt her: the look he wore when he asked forgiveness. But he was still a handsome man. His wrinkles were fine and neat—they seemed to hold him in like netting. His face hadn't slipped down, as with so many people, the old flesh gathering in jowls and chins. Nor had hers. They were alike. She had thought so in 1922, and she thought so still, in spite of herself.

She felt suddenly afraid of him. There had been a time, best forgotten, when she had been happy just looking at his ears, running her fingers over his hand, observing the length of his spine. . . .

She shivered, and he took her in his arms. "Emily," he whispered, as if it was a precious secret he'd been saving up all these years.

They sat next to each other on the sofa, drinking whiskey and trembling.

"I suppose you've come to take me to her."

"Yes," Frank said, wiping away tears. "She keeps asking for you. Betsy told me where you were. Betsy told me everything."

"I'll come," she said.

For the moment they left it at that.

They exchanged lives. She listened grimly to his tale of successes—she could have predicted it all, it sounded so dull. She'd been better off racketing around in small-time theater than as the wife of a lawyer. But she was gratified when he said, "If I'd only known then what I do now, Emily, I would never have let you go."

She looked away from him, out through the fringed curtains at the snow, but the lamps were lit and all she saw was her reflection, drooping and old. "That you preferred that woman to me!"

"Never!" He turned her around and made her look at him. She could read the chagrin in his face, for the disloyalty she had forced from him so soon; but she saw also that it was true.

"I did nothing for myself," he said.

"Or for me," she said, with scorn.

"Maybe I thought we were the stronger ones, we could take it."

"Rationalization after the fact!" She glared. It was the old stuff again.

"Oh, Emily—" He sighed and moved to put his arm around her.

"Actions speak louder than words," she snapped at him like a schoolmarm, stiffening, and then the whole thing struck her as absurd, and she took his two hands, remorseful because he looked so forlorn. "It doesn't matter now, Frank."

Surprisingly, it didn't. All her bitterness was gone—all of it. She felt as light, as free from the weight of years as she had that day when he jumped on the train. Was that all it required? For him to come to her looking so humble and swearing he'd always loved her? admitting his long mistake? Or was it the thirty-five years—as simple as that, the passing of time? Here they were, two old people who had once been lovers, drinking together.

"Here, Frank," she said, pouring him out another glass. "Put this down where the flies won't get it."

He wanted to take her out, but she insisted on making dinner for them while he sat, watching, in the chair Betsy had sat in. She gave him potatoes to peel, noticing the long, bumpy blue ropes of veins on the backs of his hands, just like her own.

"That Betsy is something," Emily said. "Tracking me down the way she did. And having that baby and hanging on to it."

He didn't answer at first, and then he said, "Things have changed, Emily." His voice was gruff, and she wondered at it. "It's a different world." Did he resent it, then—that the world was so much more hospitable to his granddaughter than it had been to his old love?

Emily thought back to that world of fifty-five years ago. No one had ever suggested she keep her baby and raise it herself.

The idea had been to get her out of sight as quickly as possible, and then to dispose of the baby, and then to pretend it never happened. She had thought one of her parents—her father—might bring it up in old age, not to apologize, not to regret, but just to get it out in the open. To see how she'd felt about it: another subject that had never come up. But they had wasted away quietly out there in Dayton, and when Emily went to see them she talked investments with her father, and Henry's children with her mother. They seemed to have forgotten it. She was with her father when he died; the last thing he said was, "Put the coffeepot on for me, will you, Em?"

"Why did you let her do it, Frank?" She turned to face him.

"Who?"

"Your sister-in-law. Marion Palmer. Why did you let her take the baby like that? Did you think I wouldn't give her up?" They had gone over it all fifty years ago, but both of them had forgotten. "I was no fool," Emily went on. "And I was no Betsy. I was seventeen years old, I'd quit school, my parents were out in Ohio, I had a job as a housemaid in a rooming house—what would I do with a baby? You didn't have to kidnap her."

"I had nothing to do with that, Emily." How blue his eyes were still, how troubled. "It was all Marion's doing."

"That damned woman. I hear she's still alive and kicking."

"She's all right. Reformed in her old age. She's a Gray Panther."

"That's where the men are, I suppose," Emily said sourly.

He hesitated. She could tell he wanted to say something, and she waited, but she was thinking of Marion, that vulgar tart, that kidnapper. She was living with a man in New York in those days—living *off* him, everyone knew that—and she had the nerve to lecture a girl of seventeen, pregnant with a child of love, about morality. "You can still make a life for yourself," she'd said, something like that. "If you stay away from Frank and Helen. It's not right to take a man away from his wife."

When it was common knowledge that *she*—! "You've bewitched him," she'd said. "You took advantage of him when his own marriage was in trouble. You know, it's practically a crime, what you two did." She had said all that, and worse things that Emily had blocked out. Marion Palmer. Large, jeweled, made up—dissipated, though she was still in her early twenties. A crime, to love as she had loved Frank, as he had loved her!

"Violet is dying," Frank said in the silence of the kitchen, and Emily made a move to shush him but checked it. "She's become rapidly worse since around Thanksgiving, faster than the doctors thought. It's cancer, Emily—I suppose Betsy told you—cancer of her lymph system, but it's in her bones now, and she's in terrible pain, she's aged twenty years in two months. . . ."

Emily forced herself to look at him, but he was gazing out the window, out at nothing, as if his daughter were there. "But my God, Emily! The resignation—no, that's not right—" The wrinkles on his forehead deepened as he tried to define it. "The contentment, the peace, the *happiness* about her." He shook his head in such sorrow that she had to turn her back on him. She went to the stove and stirred the onions, remembering the little girl who had smiled and waved. Had she been wearing a white dress, or was she idealizing the scene? Had she really smiled and waved? The radiant young woman in the hat department . . . Briskly, she stirred the onions and almost missed Frank's whisper: "She looks so much like you, Emily."

She heard him set down the potato peeler, and she looked round at him. A cat had jumped into his lap. "I hope I can have that kind of peace when it's my turn," he said. "I don't expect to."

"I can't imagine going *happily*."

Death hung in the air with the smell of onions until he eased the cat to the floor and came up to her. They embraced again, clinging to the life in each other, but she stiffened when he kissed her and pushed him away. "Two old bags of bones!" she said, with a sob at the end of it.

"Don't," he said gently, smoothing her hair. "Emily, my Emily, my dearest Emily . . ." She let him fold her in again, and they kissed until the onions burned.

After dinner, she put on her new recording of *Rigoletto.* "Did you see it on TV?" she asked him.

He had watched it with Violet. "It reminded me of you. All music reminds me of you."

"Remember when I sang Gilda at the old Empire?" She began to hum, but caught herself. "I wasn't really ready for it, but I think I carried it off."

"You could carry anything off."

"Except you," she said with a touch of the caustic.

"But you'll come back with me?"

"I could never refuse you anything," she said, and he went from the sofa to his knees and buried his face in her lap.

"As God is my witness, Emily, you're the only woman I've ever loved."

"Melodrama," she scoffed, but when she saw how it wounded him she took his face between her palms and said tenderly, "I never stopped wanting you, Frank. And now it's as if fifty years have just—gone. We're back where we were." It wasn't quite true—romantic nonsense—but it did no harm, and it wasn't entirely false, either.

"Back in all those hotels," he said. He sat beside her again and held her. "Do you remember that whole week when we were both in New York?"

"Do you remember that time in Buffalo?"

"I remember every time."

"It was always so good, Frank."

It seemed absurd not to sleep in the same bed.

It was still snowing lightly in the morning, but the blizzard seemed to be over.

"We'd better wait, though," said Frank. He looked perfectly at home in his chair by the kitchen window. His shaving things were on the shelf in the bathroom. "We could wait till noon or so."

"Not if she's that ill, Frank, and wants to see me. Every minute counts." Emily spoke from duty, without urgency. They had waited this long; surely, Fate would allow a little more time. She felt she needed a good deal of it.

But Frank looked at her approvingly. "I want you to know I appreciate this, your coming back there with me. I know it's not easy." He finished his coffee in a gulp. "Tell you what—I'll call Betsy and see how things are."

"You forgot to call last night."

They smiled at each other and touched hands across the table. "I forgot everything last night," Frank said.

"Imagine," said Emily. "A couple of old farts like us."

She saw his smile turn sad; he was remembering Violet. In the light of day (she thought to herself, with some bitterness) he was feeling a twinge or two of guilt, for forgetting his daughter in the arms of his old lover. Together they looked out the kitchen window. The air was thick with snow flurries, the fence a vague row of mounds like seals. She thought how she would hate to relinquish him. He would be different back home, in that house of death where Violet waited.

"You'd better call," she said.

While he was at the telephone, she tried to prepare herself. It would be an ordeal, going to Helen's house where Violet now lay dying. Her own mother had died at home. Emily, summoned by her brother, had been there at the end, and she remembered the nurses, the whispering, the dim-lit sick-room with its smells, the atmosphere somehow composed equally of crisis and boredom. And she thought of her Violet, tossing on the pillow asking like a child for her mother. Emily's eyes filled with tears. She was ashamed of not wanting Violet as Violet wanted her. It was before her, the family reunion she had longed for once—herself and Frank and their daughter—but it was all wrong, it was grotesque, too late. Having Frank come to her was enough; the rest was beyond her. And yet she would go through with it, not for the sake of the old sweet dream, but for the sake of Frank, an old man who had driven all the way to her house in a snowstorm to carry her off.

"There's no change," he said, returning. Emily dabbed at the tears under her spectacles with her napkin while he got the coffeepot from the stove. "In fact, she ate a decent breakfast, for once. French toast." He poured out the coffee. "It's funny—Violet used to be a vegetarian, a health freak, until she got sick. Then for a while she was eating the darnedest things—junk food, candy, a lot of that spongy white bread. And drinking! Bourbon, just like her husband. That guy could put it away! But now, of course, she doesn't show much interest in food. Every once in a while she'll surprise us, though, like this morning—French toast!" He laughed without humor. "These meaningless little victories."

Emily's eyes were quite dry. "Whatever made her turn vegetarian?" she asked, to distract him.

"Violet was always susceptible," he said, his smile coming back. "She'd fall for things, and she had a taste for the far-out. She was interested in UFO's, and in vitamin cures. She took yoga for a while. She always liked astrology, in a wishful kind of way. Helen soured her on religion, but she seemed to have a craving for the supernatural." He paused, musing. You could see his daughter had charmed him, whatever she did. "The thing was, Violet wasn't a deep person, you couldn't even say she was especially intelligent. There was never any question of her going to college or having much of a career. But she had a lively mind, within its limits. A great imagination, a lot of curiosity . . ." His voice trailed off; perhaps he had caught his use of the past tense.

"A touch of the theater in her blood," said Emily. She wanted Violet to be more real to her, but she was a ghost. "I wish I'd known her, Frank, long ago." It's too late, she thought. This curious daughter with the lively mind was nothing to her. She even felt a melancholy resentment that Frank should be distracted by her; she wanted him to herself.

"She may hang on awhile yet, Emily," he said. "You two may get to know each other pretty well."

Emily smiled reluctantly. "I'd like that, Frank." But she wouldn't. She wouldn't care if they never reached Violet's bedside. But she would go, she would make one more sacrifice for him. Exactly what the sacrifice was she couldn't have defined clearly—the sacrifice of her comfort, maybe, more than anything.

He leaned over and kissed her cheek. "This is from Betsy," he said, smiling. "She's so grateful to you for changing your mind."

They sat over their coffee all morning. By noon the radio announced that road conditions were still hazardous but that the plows had been out and the roads cleared.

"Listen," Frank said. "I've got brand-new snow tires and a two-year-old Cadillac. I drove here yesterday without any trouble at all, and it was much worse then. We'll keep to the main roads. I'll take Nine up to Ninety-one and then get right on the pike. We'll take it slow, and if it gets bad we'll stop."

"At a motel," Emily said with an extravagant leer. "We may be snowed in for days." She saw with pleasure how his smile hadn't changed—how his lips twitched briefly before first one side, then the other, stretched humorously. A cautious, lawyer's smile, all the more valued. She called Ellen Morris, her neighbor, about feeding the cats. They were really going, then; there was no turning back. If it started snowing again, they would simply wait. If they got stuck on the road, they would stop until things improved and then go on. There was no hurry, Frank said. He would wait, and be cautious, and bring her back alive. She was his prey. He had hunted her down, and he wouldn't let her get away now.

They were merry, though, starting off—as unlike a cat and its mouse as it was possible to be. The day was bleak and sunless, but the roads had been neatly scraped and the snowbanks glittered with their own cold light. Frank's car had been parked outside all night and was covered with soft snow, and she stood on the steps under the fanlight, snow falling lightly on her mink, and admired him cleaning it off. He was quick about it and only slightly short of breath as he stowed their suitcases and helped her in.

"It's like feathers," he said. "Won't amount to much. The worst is over."

The roads were nearly deserted, but one lane was plowed all the way up Route 9, and they could proceed slowly. From time to time they turned on the radio. There were lists of school closings, cancellations, snow statistics. They were calling it the Great Blizzard of '78.

"Nonsense," said Frank. "This is nothing."

"It doesn't seem all that dangerous," Emily said. It was cozy in the car, and she had faith in Frank's driving—steady and sure, but relaxed. He wasn't a bundle of nerves behind the wheel as so many old people were—as she was herself. Snuggling into her furs, she watched his profile.

"Well make it," he said jauntily. "This is a good car, as good as a jeep in weather like this."

"I should have come before, Frank," she said. "I don't know why I didn't want to see you."

"You hated me, didn't you?" He took his eyes quickly off the road for a tragic, braced look at her. "Didn't you?"

It pleased her, how she had become the important thing to him again. "Yes," she said, and then, "No. I tried to, Frank, for years. But I never managed it. I just tried not to think about you. It was bad for me, like smoking."

"I was a fool."

"Did you ever love her?" Oddly, it was something she had never asked.

He considered. "When we were engaged—then I was fond of her. She was such a good, domestic creature. I wanted a home and a family, Emily, and I thought she was cut out to provide them. She was different before the tragedy, no one will believe that."

"Before the baby died?"

"Before the baby died," he said, but his tone was odd. Emily studied him—an unfair advantage, she knew, because he couldn't study her back. "You know . . . " he said, and seemed to be groping for further words.

"Yes?"

"You know, the baby didn't die, not right away."

She blinked, startled. "What baby? Helen's?"

"Mine and Helen's." He turned his face just slightly to her, but kept his eyes on the road. He was smiling slightly.

"What do you mean, it didn't die?"

"She lived two days. She was—horribly deformed, Emily. She had a little flipper instead of a right arm, and her face was all askew."

"Helen's baby," said Emily, and great, shocked satisfaction filled her. "Poor Helen."

"She took it hard, wouldn't have anything to do with her. She just screamed and screamed when the baby was born. We never told anyone what she was like. And Helen never let me in her bed again. But you know that." He reached out and touched her gloved hand with his.

"Because of the child?" He nodded. "Was she like—like a thalidomide baby?"

"I guess so. She was grotesque, I suppose. It wasn't just the deformed arm, the crooked face—there was something about her. The nurse in the delivery room threw up when she saw her, and Helen screamed when she came to until the baby was taken away. They gave Helen something to calm her down. But, you know—" He paused, still smiling. "I went up to the nursery to see the little thing. She was surrounded by nurses—nursing sisters, they were, Helen went to the Catholic hospital. Some of them were crying, they knew the whole story, they didn't know what to do. I don't suppose they'd ever encountered a mother who rejected her baby so violently. But I picked her up. Her little flipper waved around and she made sucking motions with her mouth and then she began to cry, and she sounded just like any other baby, Emily. She was—cute. I began to love her, in spite of the horror of it. I named her Anna, after my mother. But she died in my arms the next evening."

They had reached the Massachusetts Turnpike. Emily looked at her watch; it had taken them over two hours. Outside, it was snowier; the flurries had changed to a swirling mist of snow. The windshield wipers became caked with ice, and Frank got out to clean them off. The snow whipped into the car when he opened the door. Emily took his hat and brushed snow off it onto the floor. She was ashamed of her joy in Helen's suffering; she thought what a fine man Frank was, really—but weak. The thought just tickled her mind that he would have been finer and stronger with her as his wife instead of his bit of fluff. She smiled to herself as he edged the car back onto the highway.

"Why didn't you ever tell me?" she asked. "About Anna."

"It was my secret," he said lightly, but seeing she wanted an answer, he went on, "I don't know, Emily. I suppose it was odd of me not to tell you. But I was so used to keeping it from people, and it made Helen sound so—made her sound unbalanced."

Emily thought about it. "It makes her sound *less* unbalanced, it seems to me," she said. "I mean, a deformed baby is a *reason*. . . ." She remembered the beauty of her own baby, the magical perfection of her. "If I had known about Anna, I would have had a lot more sympathy for Helen."

She meant it and was surprised at herself. It was the first pang of regret she'd ever felt for Frank's wife.

"The poor woman," she said, and another thought struck her. "You really stacked the cards against her, didn't you?"

"Only because I didn't want to lose you," he said placidly.

"Frank!" At her tone he turned and looked at her, then back at the road, frowning. "Frank, love doesn't excuse *everything*."

He put one gloved hand over hers on the seat. "I thought it did. I'm sorry."

Exasperated, she pulled her hand away. "So no one knew but you?" She knew he wanted to drop it, but she persisted. "You and Helen?"

"Marion knew. It's probably the only real bond between us."

"She knew, and I didn't."

She saw that he was undeceived by her forced lightness of tone, as she had meant him to be. "She was *there* at the time, Emily. She was Helen's sister! It wasn't a conspiracy—she was at the hospital."

"The meddling bitch." It was crazy, to be jealous of Marion Palmer, a worn-out old tart, and of course it wasn't Marion—not only Marion—she was lashing out at; it was his whole, full, populated life contrasted with her own. He could even love, all his life, the poor deformed baby he'd held only briefly fifty-odd years ago. Easy enough, to love a memory . . . But, damn it, he'd had a real, actual daughter to bring up, and a granddaughter, too, and she'd had none.

They rode in silence for a long time. The years had been erased last night, but now they came back with all their torments. Emily felt old and creaky and galled.

At random, she asked, "Did you ever go to bed with her? Marion Palmer?"

He didn't answer, and she stared over at him. "You did!"

He made a gesture of impatience. "We had an affair, back in—oh, I don't know—years ago. It was nothing."

"Nothing! My God, Frank!"

"And you never had another man, all those years when you refused to see me?"

"Refused! You make it sound like you were battering down my door. If I recall, there were two letters and one phone call!"

"Answer my question."

"Of course, I had other men. But that was different—you know it was different, Frank. Marion Palmer!" She saw an exaggerated Marion, all corpulence and makeup and flabby thighs spread wide. Her men, at least, had been thin, narrow, neat, sober—like Frank.

"I don't see the difference," he said. "You had a grudge against Marion—I never did. She was handy and, God knows, she was willing. And I owed her a lot."

"I can't believe it. Marion Palmer, of all people."

"Jesus, Emily! It was years ago!"

She would have screamed at him, would have called him some terrible name, but the car swerved just then and skidded across the road, where it plowed into a snowbank. She gave a little cry and pressed her hands to her heart.

"It's all right," he said. "No harm done. Let me just get us out."

He put the car in reverse and they heard the wheels spin when he gave it gas. He shifted to forward, back to reverse. The car rocked, the wheels whined against the snow, but they stayed put.

"I could get out and push," he said dubiously.

"You'll do no such thing!" cried Emily. The feeling in her chest scared her—it was as if a large dog had sat down there, suddenly. Her pills were in her suitcase, her suitcase was in the trunk. He tried the car again, and this time it stalled and wouldn't start again.

Outside, in the swirling snow, there was no ground, no horizon, no perspective. Then the wind stopped and they could see the highway. Two cars crept slowly by at long intervals.

"We'll wait," Frank said decisively. "Somebody'll stop or alert the troopers. Damn these roads! All the plows do is make them slick." She could tell he was embarrassed by his inability to get them out.

"We were crazy to come," Emily said with difficulty.

He moved closer to her and kissed her cheek. The wind blew the loose snow against the car windows and away again. "There'll be a trooper along soon," he said. "Or another snowplow. We could follow the plow right to New York State, maybe. You know, speaking of Marion, she told me I should get a CB radio. Wanted to give me one for Christmas. I should have listened to her, for once."

Emily drew a little away from him. "You do botch things up, don't you?"

He gave a short, mortified laugh. "I don't believe anybody's ever accused me of that but you, Emily."

"Maybe I'm the only one who was in a position to notice."

They were silent for a while. The drifting snow was beautiful to Emily—the whiteness of the earth in its old age seemed appropriate. But the car was cold, and her chest hurt; the heaviness wasn't passing as she'd thought it would.

He drew close to her again and said, "It's never too late, you know, Emily."

"Too late for what?" Her voice frightened her.

"For us. We could get married."

"Why now, Frank? Why all of a sudden—after thirty-five years?"

They sat in silence; Frank smiled out at the snow. Looking at him, Emily felt her heart lurch, as if the big dog had gotten up, shaken himself, and plopped down again.

"Frank?"

"I'm thinking, Emily—trying to sort things out."

"No—it's my pills. I need my pills. I need my pills."

He turned to her. "Oh God, Emily, where in hell are they?" She could see that her appearance frightened him.

"My suitcase—the trunk." She pressed her hands to her

chest, but when he started to get out she stopped him in panic. "No! Don't leave me! Frank—" Her voice dropped to a whisper.

"Emily, for Christ's sake! Let me get them!"

"Please, Frank, I'll die if you leave me!"

They were still at this impasse when the troopers arrived.

CHAPTER NINE

Betsy

In the house on Stiles Street, they waited.

Violet, waiting in the dim-lit sickroom for her reunion with Will, slept and woke, slept and woke, listened to the silence made by the snow and wondered what it was. Betsy and Marion sat in the kitchen waiting for the phone or the doorbell to ring. Marion kept the radio on. The "Storm Watch" with a mixture of pride and horror announced that it was the Northeast's worst since the famous blizzard of '88. Marion listened with the same mixture, in which satisfaction was lightly mingled: she had told him so.

"But I don't worry about Frank," she said, keeping her back resolutely to the window. "Frank can take care of himself."

"Why don't they call?" Betsy asked for the twentieth time. She had heard nothing of Frank and Emily since early that morning, when her grandfather had phoned. "Your grandmother is coming with me," he'd said, and his voice was noncommittal. "Tell Violet her mama is on her way."

Betsy couldn't ask him not to come, to wait out the storm at Emily's house. Violet had been asking for him—but she didn't tell him that, either.

"You could have called us last night," she said. "We've been worried sick." She was stiff with him; they hadn't parted on good terms. She had slept badly, the harsh words they had exchanged tumbling in her mind all night while the blizzard raged outside.

"What was there to worry about? The storm wasn't so bad yesterday."

"It's bad now."

"We'll take it easy."

There was more she would have liked to say, but she couldn't bring herself to it. She could only resurrect the old upbeat voice she used to use with Violet and urge him to drive carefully.

And where was he now? Where was Emily?

"Maybe we should call the state police," she said to her great-aunt.

"What on earth for, honey?" Marion's condescending patience made Betsy want to scream, though she knew it was put on and that Marion was as worried as she was. "It's going to be a long, slow trip, and that's all there is to it. Bothering the troopers in weather like this won't accomplish anything."

She knew that—calling was simply something to do, and she spoke irritably. "Neither will listening to that damned radio!"

Marion tightened her lips, but left the radio on. "I *told* him not to go out in this," she muttered, as if to herself.

Terry came and went, aimlessly moving from sickroom to kitchen to the front window, where she stood for minutes at a time watching for the car before she scurried back to her patient.

Violet had eaten her bits of French toast and then fallen into a long, oblivious doze, but Betsy—though urged by Terry and Marion to nap, to rest—was unable to sleep or even to sit still for long. Aside from her anxieties about Frank and Emily, and about Violet, the baby's activity kept her restless.

"He's tired of being cooped up!" Marion said when Betsy complained. "He's kicking to get out!"—in the unnatural, saccharine tone she had decided was proper for her to adopt.

Betsy sat mesmerized by the raging snow outside, imagining the baby being born on a deserted road in a blizzard, being born on this very kitchen floor, in need of oxygen or blood or rare drugs that no one could get through to the hospital for, the baby born dead, choking, retarded—and her grandfather's Cadillac skidding off an embankment somewhere in Connecticut—and Violet breathing her last in great pain. She sat immobile, chewing the cuticle around her thumbs, drawing blood, until she felt compelled to get up and move about the still house.

She would have liked to be alone. It seemed to her she had a great deal to think about—though, in fact, her mind was dulled and blank. She would have liked to sit by Violet's bedside, without Terry or Marion, wrapped in her mother's silent, painful peace. She didn't want to share her dolors. But Terry hovered, full of lugubrious self-importance, and her great-aunt had settled into the spare room with a small suitcase. She knew Marion had come for her sake, to keep her company while her grandfather was away. Betsy tried to be grateful, but her thoughts were of peace, quiet, space—of these and of the morbid ideas that Frank and Emily had perished on the road somewhere and that her mother's death was imminent.

Violet had become somewhat worse since Frank went off into the blizzard, as if his presence in the house had been a prop that sustained her. For the first time, the injections against her pain seemed ineffective. Violet moaned weakly in her sleep and woke often, asking for the drug.

Dr. Baird had struggled over early that morning. "It won't be much longer," he had said, and, though when she pressed him he wouldn't be more specific, Betsy felt it was only a matter of days, perhaps less. "She's as comfortable as she can be," the doctor said, hinting at his disapproval that Violet was being allowed to die at home. He had given up recommending her removal to a hospital. "As comfortable as she can be, considering . . ." Betsy, looking at her mother's placid sleeping face, watched it crease with pain and then smooth again, and thought ahead, with grief and trepidation, to the day when she would be left alone in the echoing house.

Still she longed, perversely, for solitude. Marion's chatter was driving her crazy, and the staticky drone of the radio was unnerving, but she kept returning to the kitchen where they both were, drinking cup after cup of coffee, not knowing what else to do or where to go. She wandered up to Violet's room, but Terry urged her to stay downstairs. "I'll call you if she wakes," Terry promised. Her tone was possessive.

"*Any* change."

"I'll call you." Terry looked as glamorous and efficient as ever, but her eyes were red, and tears spilled over at odd moments as she sat by Violet—not reading or knitting, just watching.

"How does she stand it?" Betsy said to Marion.

"Who?"

"Terry. To spend her life watching at deathbeds."

"Oh, I doubt it's as bad as all that. Most of her cases recover, I'll bet." Marion cleared her throat. "No one said your mother's on her deathbed yet, anyway."

The false words gleamed in the air, then went out. Betsy had nothing to say; she stared out at the snow.

Irresistibly, she told herself her rosary of troubles, over and over. There was no comfort or happiness for her that she could see. Her mother was at the threshold of death, any day she would—alone and unfriended—give birth to a fatherless babe, and her grandparents were missing in the snow.

The argument with her grandfather oppressed her. "I'll go and get her if I have to drag her," he had said. "I won't have your mother grieving like this."

"Grandpa, Emily's got troubles of her own—let her be."

He was taken aback at Betsy's easy mention of the name. Then he brushed her words aside; he was hearing nothing but Violet's request: *I want my mama.* "That damned woman!" he muttered, and Betsy knew he meant Emily.

"How can you call her that?" she demanded. "After the way you treated her!" She had resented Emily's aloofness; now she defended her to this thick-skinned, predatory male.

He turned on her in a rage. "You two are mighty chummy, aren't you? Got the whole story, didn't you?" They were in Violet's room. He took Betsy's arm and steered her out the door, and they stood in the hall, shouting at each other.

"It's about time I knew—time *someone* knew who my mother's parents were. You kept it from us all these years—it wasn't fair!" There it was again, the childish lament.

"It was my business. Damn the woman! Damn her for telling it to you, for dragging up all these dead issues. What does it matter now? The interfering old bitch!"

"Don't you talk about her that way!"

"You're her granddaughter, all right," he said with a look at Betsy's belly.

She didn't even try to excuse him—to blame his brutal words on grief and outrage, the shock of Betsy's search and Emily's revelations. Pure, cold, limitless anger made her incoherent.

"How can you—how can you! Don't you understand *anything*?"

"I understand that I won't let her do this to my daughter. I'll drag her up here if I die in the attempt. I'm damned if I'll let her get away with this."

Half an hour later he had slammed out the door. And where was he now?

Hours went by. They had all risen early, and the morning was immensely long. They had lunch. Marion made large tuna-salad sandwiches for the three of them and then loudly did the dishes, humming to herself. Betsy retreated from her great-aunt's studied optimism, upstairs—not to Violet's room but to her grandfather's study. They had shouted at each other: had they ever done so before? She couldn't remember, ever, hearing his voice raised to her. Still, she wouldn't take back her words—she wished only that there could be more of them, that he were there, now, at his desk, and that they could talk quietly. There was more to be said.

The storm made the study dark. Snow clung to the two windows and kept out most of the daylight, but Betsy knew the room by heart, and she tried to take comfort from its familiarity. It was dominated by her grandfather's desk—a large, bland office model (the replacement for the quirky old oak piece in the attic)—but it bore his mark upon it, unmistakable. It was very neat, the working space of a man who didn't really have any work to do. In the center were a calculator, the university law review, a mugful of pens, a little pile of letters. But arranged in each corner were more personal things: an old iron bank he'd had since boyhood, a sand dollar, a small marble fish Violet had given him, a wooden egg that had been his mother's. Betsy picked each item up and turned it over in her hand. Each was warm to the touch, as if her grandfather had handled the things just before she came in, but they only made her lonelier. He had stalked off into the snow, leaving her behind in the empty house with nothing to do but wait and brood.

Betsy sat down heavily at the desk. The tuna fish had not agreed with her. Nothing agreed with her. The coming of the child oppressed her; in spite of all her cares, she could think of nothing else. *What am I doing?* she asked herself, and, resting her hands on her huge belly, she asked the child within, *Who are you? What will happen?*

There were no answers; she had expected none. In fact, the questions had become rituals that set up a rhythm in her head whenever she lapsed into the blank, bovine trances that had come back during these last weeks of her pregnancy.

She longed for the birth, even as she dreaded it. She longed for her passivity to come to an end so her life could go forward. Sitting at her grandfather's desk, she felt a dull stupefaction stealing over her, and she blinked and sat up, wincing at the pain in her back. She leafed through the pile of letters on the desk: bills, a renewal letter from *Consumer Reports,* a notice of a board meeting. Pathetic, Betsy thought. The dregs of an active life. What would he do once Violet died? Go back to his board and his consultations and his club lunches with old cronies? His friends were dying off, she knew; this had begun to depress him before Violet's illness absorbed him utterly. What now? And what would he do with his resentment against Emily? Did it even exist anymore? And—the question kept coming back—was he dead with her somewhere in the snow?

The shelf over his desk was crowded with photographs. There was a faded one of Frank himself, in a stiff collar, smiling confidently at her—taken back in the days when he was deceiving Emily, Betsy thought. There was one of herself, with the dog, Poochie, in a stranglehold. A snapshot of Helen, dressed for church, in a hat with a veil. One of her parents, laughing, outside her father's shop.

Emily, it occurred to her, was missing from the shelf. Would her grandfather put up a picture of his old love, now that she'd been brought to light? One of her glamorous portraits? She belonged there, just as she belonged in the family plot. I'll bury the three of them all together, Betsy thought fatalistically, and imagined the three gaping holes in the frozen earth, like the last stanza of a tragic ballad.

And Emily's house in East Haddam—that gem shining now, empty, in the snow. What if Emily, lost in the storm, *had* left it to her? What on earth would she do with it? She fancied Emily would scream from the grave like a soul in torment if she sold it. She wondered about offering it to the state as a landmark: the Emily Loftus House—a museum of theatrical memorabilia? Under that memorial, Emily would surely rest in peace. Betsy smiled to herself. She would go up there in the spring with the baby. The sun would shine on Emily's treasured fanlight, there would be blossoms on the apple tree, the baby would snuggle against her. "This was your great-grandmother Emily's house," she would say, putting the old key in the old lock. Inside, Emily's sturdy spirit would hover around her and the baby, showering blessings. . . .

No. Panic overwhelmed her. She knew she couldn't bear it if they all died, and in her panic she knew they wouldn't. Comfort and confidence came to her from all corners of the room. She was sure of it: Frank and Emily were safe. Her grandfather's room breathed life—it was in the smiling faces of the photographs on the shelf, in the little man on Frank's old mechanical bank who would doff his hat if you put a penny in. . . .

They would be safe. That particular oppression would not fall upon her. The certainty calmed her, until down the hall she thought she heard Violet stir and cry out, and the panic returned. What did anyone else's life matter? Violet would die. Before much longer, she would be motherless and alone. Betsy wanted to whimper—she was always wanting to whimper lately, to go someplace and cry, but where did one go in such pain if not to one's mother? The subtle terror of it possessed her. The terror not of one's own death but of one's last parent's death—the death that confers adulthood, ready or not. I don't want my mother to die, she cried silently. I don't want to be the mother!

As if in protest, the baby began to thrash around inside her, and Betsy calmed again. All right. All right. I didn't mean it. But the calm came with difficulty, the peace was hopelessly shattered, and she got up and walked down the hall to Violet's room.

Terry was crying. She looked up guiltily from her tissue, caught in the act, as if it were a dereliction of duty. Betsy stood in the doorway, and they exchanged sad, silent smiles.

Violet slept, her wasted face calm. As they watched, she twitched and mumbled, but didn't wake.

Betsy went back downstairs. Marion was in the kitchen, with the radio, still drinking coffee. Her pendulous red face was freshly made up, her tiny mouth gleamed with rosy, improbable lipstick, and she looked up eagerly when Betsy came in.

"How is she?"

"The same."

"The snow seems to be letting up."

It was hard to tell. Out the window, all was white, fading to blue-gray. As Betsy looked, a streetlight went on, and against its light she couldn't see any snow falling.

"Look at that," said Marion. "Streetlights on at two-thirty in the afternoon. That's the worst of winter, in my opinion—the dark."

"I think you were right—it *is* stopping."

Her aunt snapped off the radio. "Let's take a break from this, then." Betsy went to the stove for a cup of coffee, thankful for the silence. Without warning, it was broken by a sudden harsh sob from her aunt.

Betsy turned. "Aunt Marion!"

Her great-aunt's face was crumpled, weeping. She sat hunched at the table, one hand over her eyes, the other stretched out blindly.

"Betsy . . ."

Betsy went to her, knelt down, and took her hand. "Aunt Marion, what is it? What is it all of a sudden?"

"I can't stand the waiting anymore, Betsy. Go ahead—call the troopers. I can't take this."

It was Betsy's turn to speak patiently, rationally—out of her own irrational certainty. "He'll be here, don't worry." As she spoke, she wondered at Marion's emotion and then realized how much Frank must mean to his sister-in-law. They were, after all, old friends.

Marion raised her naked red face to Betsy. Her makeup was all rubbed off or collected into furrows. The red lips stood out garishly, and her face was shiny with tears in the light from the window. Betsy remembered Judd's photographs.

"Don't cry, Aunt Marion." She took a table napkin and wiped her face, but the tears started again, and Marion buried her head in her hands and moaned.

"I can't bear it if he goes before me. I can't."

Betsy did her best to provide comfort, wondering. She remembered what Marion had said of Will, her own father: "It's a blessing Will went before Violet. He worshiped her." She put her arm around her and waited for the crying to stop; she didn't know what else to do.

Finally, Marion raised her head and sat up. She took a tissue from her sleeve and blew her nose. "I'm sorry, honey," she said. "I'm upset."

"Well, of course you are—" Betsy started to say, reasonably enough, but Marion forged ahead.

"I always loved your grandfather, you know. I mean, I've been in love with him, for years. You never knew, no one did."

Oh God, the poor woman, here we go. "I knew you two were fond of each other, of course—"

She was cut off again. "Fond! Fond of each other!" She gave her brittle laugh. "He was the great love of my life. There was a time when I was closer to him than anyone. I mean, we'd gone through it all together. I was always there for him. When Helen went off the deep end. And when she kicked him out of bed for good, and then Emily—you see what I'm saying, Betsy?"

"I suppose I do," she replied reluctantly and felt a vague anger rise in her.

Marion went on before she could say more. "I'm sure your mother told you I was a trollop. Did she? A scarlet woman?"

She raised her head and patted her upswept hair with something of her old dignity. "Glamorizing as usual, that's Violet. I was no trollop. I had lovers, of course—not casual affairs, either, like young people today, but real love affairs. And I'm not referring to you and that photographer, either, so don't get huffy."

Betsy wasn't feeling huffy, she was feeling oppressed. Would life ever go forward instead of back? She was caught in a web of other people's memories. She wanted all this to be over. She longed to be home, in her own bright apartment with Dr. Spock and Dr. Johnson, changing her baby's diapers and working on her book.

"I had a special friendship for many years with a man in New York," her great-aunt continued imperturbably. "A married man. He didn't keep me, I always made enough to support myself. Oh, he helped out, but I could have gotten along without him. The bohemian life, you know. The Village in the twenties and thirties. We were going to go to Paris, he and I—"

Betsy listened, amazed in spite of herself, not at the story—which was, generally, what her mother had told her—but at Marion's willful vulnerability. She was letting down her pride, drawing her own sting. Betsy wished she wouldn't do it. She liked their old, distant, abrasive relationship, and she knew the reminiscences would end in more tears.

"He died in nineteen fifty-six, and that's when I decided to move back here to my old hometown. It wasn't easy, to leave the city for this dreary upstate backwater, and I missed Sam—Sam Hemming was his name, no harm in your knowing now. I saw him three times a week for eighteen years. Heart attack, and he wasn't sixty yet! Well then, there we were, your grandfather and I. Helen was dead—not that she was ever a real wife to him, poor woman. And Emily Loftus had given him her final ultimatum years before—he was through with her. So he and I just drifted, quite naturally, into an affair of the heart." Marion pronounced the old-fashioned phrase with a self-conscious, girlish smile. "It would have been odd if we hadn't. I wasn't a young woman, Betsy, but I fell in love with him like a kid, and I thought—right up until the end, I thought—" She paused, took a quavery breath, and went on. "I can't tell you what a shock it was to me when you located Emily Loftus after all these years—and then, when Frank went trotting off after her, just like her little puppy dog again. I mean, I always thought . . ."

"You thought *what*?" Betsy asked when Marion hesitated.

"I thought he might marry me."

It was as if a light went on in the dark kitchen. Betsy looked across the table at Marion and saw herself. She stood up. "I won't have it!" she announced. "I won't put up with this, I won't listen." Marion looked up at her and blinked. Betsy took a step away and then came back. "I'm *glad* I'm not related to you," she said, leaning heavily on the table. "I wish I weren't related to any of you. It's not *good* for me, it's not healthy to be part of a line of—hopers and adapters and waiters. If life doesn't fit right, you twist and turn yourself to fit it until you're deformed, and then you smile so hard no one notices the deformity."

"What *are* you talking about?" Marion asked in her best ironic tone.

Betsy had meant to storm from the room, but her eloquence had worn her out. She was hot, she felt shaky and sweaty, and her head hurt. "You know what I'm talking about. I won't put up with it," she said again, but without intensity. She sat down and drank some coffee, staring down into her cup so she wouldn't have to look at her great-aunt's face. She recognized that her brief glimpse of herself in Marion was a genuine illumination. That was the road she was headed down, and she was rocked by the knowledge. "I won't," she repeated.

Marion waited, as if for a clock to stop striking, and when Betsy was silent, she said, "That was uncalled for, Betsy—

especially under the circumstances." She raised her eyes in the direction of Violet's sickroom, but Betsy didn't look up to see her do it. "And it wasn't true, either. Any of it. I know you think I'm nothing but a silly old woman—"

"No, no," Betsy said more calmly. "I think you're a tragedy." She got hold of herself and raised her head, fearing to see her own face again across the table. But Marion was Marion, and she looked hurt and affronted.

"I'll tell you something, Betsy," she said, raising her voice. "I don't want peace, I don't want my days to be empty and quiet and—nothing. You call me a hoper, a waiter—whatever absurd things you said, I don't remember, thank God. But I need my emotions. I need to be in love. You can laugh, I know it's ridiculous at my age—"

"I'm not laughing."

Her great-aunt did, her quick, harsh bark. "It's what makes the world go round, after all." She sobered quickly, and her face crumpled again. "But if he should go, Betsy—I'd be lost, lost. I mean that seriously, and I don't care what you think of me for it."

Betsy murmured vaguely. She was thinking, thinking, and anger continued to simmer in her. It had been simmering—brewing, germinating, all those metaphors for quiet readiness—a long time, all through her lonely pregnancy, maybe all her lonely life. It was anger against all the men in her life: her father, who died; her grandfather, who ruled; her boyfriends, who failed her. And against the women, too—against Helen's tight-lipped rage, and Emily's twenty duped years, and Violet's saintly passivity, and now Marion's long, fruitless devotion. And—God knew, here's where the anger was concentrated, coiled into a hard, harrowing ball—against her own long-suffering acquiescence to things, her own fatal adaptability. She was like the Virgin, who, when the blood dripped from the thorns down her face to her lips, licked it away, smiling.

Marion honked into a tissue. Betsy picked up her cup and sipped at her coffee. She would deal with the blood and the thorns later. They had nothing, after all, to do with her great-aunt. It was time to change the subject.

"Tell me about Helen and her baby. And how she adopted my mother." They had gone over some of it already, but not this part. "Tell me how it all happened."

Marion seemed glad of the request. She put away her tissue and sat up straight, thinking. "Your grandmother was a complex woman," she said finally, "with exaggerated ideas about sex. We were brought up in fanatical strictness, and it affected both of us badly—though in rather different ways," she added with a short laugh. "She thought her baby's death was her punishment."

"For what?"

"The sins of the flesh—what else? For giving in to—well, I'm sure even my sister Helen had a little niggling bit of lust. I saw how she used to look at Frank in the old days."

"But then adopting my mother, her husband's bastard—"

"As a chastisement to them all, Betsy. She told me that. As a reminder. Rubbing their noses in it."

"My God!" Betsy had a quick recollection of Helen, in tears, on her knees in that dark bedroom, her teeth bared in anger.

Marion looked at Betsy, then away. "You resemble her—Emily Loftus. Both you and your mother do—your mother, especially, but you have more of that *look*—"

"What look?"

"That look she always had." Marion shook her head, disapproving. "I can't describe it. You know what I mean."

"I don't!"

Her great-aunt said triumphantly, "There! You've got it now, that snotty, self-contained look—like a bird with a big fat worm all to itself."

"Oh, Aunt Marion, cut it out."

"Well, I'm sorry. I suppose I'm still upset at the things you said. You're always so sure you're right, even when you're dead wrong, and you get that look of yours—it's straight off her face." In the fading light, her eyes shifted and became distant, looking back. "I was always on my sister's side, of course. I couldn't see what she got out of that marriage, right from the start. Frank Robinson always had such a *picture* of himself—"

Marion spoke bitterly, out of years of resentment, and Betsy wondered if the picture was like hers: the Arrow collar man with the burning eyes.

"He wanted to be a great lawyer, and I think he had visions of going into politics, too. His association with Emily queered that, of course. There's always somebody who knows about these things. They always get dredged up—we all know what politics is like. He wouldn't have had a chance. But back in the old days, he saw himself as a leader of men, and he needed a quiet, domestic wife, one who'd stay in the background and keep his house upright—a politician's wife. Helen was just the thing, a quiet little mouse who worshiped him. Oh, but she was misguided, Betsy, marrying him. Look what her life became."

Helen's famous hard life: there was plenty in it, after all. "I've seen those letters, the ones you wrote her when all this was going on."

Marion looked startled, then pleased. "I knew she'd saved them, she told me she did. She said they gave her strength." She spoke with pride, as an author who touched hearts. "Lord," she went on. "It all seems far away now. Helen and her poor baby, dead and gone."

There was a pause, during which the words echoed like a bell: dead and gone, dead and gone. Betsy listened, but there was no noise from upstairs, and the baby had settled down inside her. There was no sound at all but the snow blowing crisply against the window and the furnace rumbling in the basement. It was nearly dark. Betsy and Marion sat without a light, and the kitchen looked gray and ghostly in the dusk, with only a faint glow from the streetlight outside. Dead and gone, dead and gone . . .

"How do you remember her?" Marion asked abruptly. "My sister, Helen—how do you think of her?"

Betsy welcomed the distraction. The present was painful, the future uncertain; talk of the past could do no harm, at least.

"In the kitchen," she said promptly—surprising herself, that she should recall Helen at her best. Helen in the kitchen, with her sallow cheeks red from the heat, her mousy hair frizzed, her thin lips pursed over a spoon: she came alive there. In the kitchen, unless you were in her way, she could be almost pleasant, offering samples on a long spoon, cooling hot fresh applesauce with her own breath, saving the frosting bowl for Betsy to lick. But she could turn unexpectedly mean and order Betsy out of the room for no good reason, just because she was there, and she could knead bread with fury or work her big knife through a pile of onions as if they were little girls. That was the thing about her good moods—you couldn't count on them. They didn't last, and she would do nothing to preserve them. She gave way to the least flutter of ill temper and let it take her over and sometimes would not speak a civil word for a week. The agony of the dinner table, with Violet and Frank and Betsy making stilted conversation over the noise of Helen's silences . . . No back was ever so straight as hers, no lips were ever so set and thin, no eyes so dark with scorn.

"Surprisingly, she was a good cook," Betsy said.

"Why 'surprisingly'?" asked Marion, tartly.

"Well—that she enjoyed food—enjoyed anything—and let us enjoy it."

"Don't exaggerate your grandmother's faults. She was a real person, you know, like you and me."

Betsy didn't doubt it. She was remembering the corn. Helen would have her big black kettle on the stove, boiling madly, and the butter and salt and corn-shaped spiked holders on the table, and she'd say to Frank, "Ready!" and Frank would take his knife out to the garden and sprint back with a dozen ears. The four of them would strip off the husks and silk on a newspaper, and then the corn would go into the pot. Helen would clap on a cover and wait five minutes by the clock, and then, with tongs, pluck the ears one by one from the boiling water, and they would make a meal of it, with a plate of sliced tomatoes on the side. "Corn is not worth eating if it's not fresh," Helen always said. It was a religion, though if anyone had said so she would have snapped out something about the first commandment. You couldn't even say, "It's heavenly" or "It's divine." That sweet corn, crunchy and salted and dripping butter, and the chunks of tomato sprinkled with parsley: it was late August, Betsy was ten, and out the kitchen window the sun was low and hot. . . .

There was silence again in the warm kitchen. Betsy leaned her head on her hand and almost dozed, with Helen in her mind. A witch in the kitchen mixing potions: punishment potions for her husband, good behavior potions for her granddaughter, back-to-the-Church potions for her daughter. The motto over the sink: Pray without ceasing. Who knew what awful prayers Helen had offered for her loved ones? All those prayers, all that cooking. Helen came toward her with something on a spoon, and she knew she mustn't eat it. . . .

"What I want to say, Betsy, is this." Marion broke into her reverie. "I'm here if you need me. I don't know if you *want* me, I hope we'll be closer from now on, that's all."

"Oh, I hope so, too," Betsy said, feeling weepy all of a sudden. She was tired, everything ached, and she was ashamed of her long impatience with her great-aunt—an old woman, with no one to care for but a man who had spurned her, and a dying niece, and her ungrateful self. "I'm sorry—I've been selfish lately." It was true enough, but she spoke the dutiful words with difficulty.

"It's your condition," Marion said kindly in response. "Only natural to be wrapped up in yourself." She was silent a moment, then began to cry softly again, as if the sympathetic sound of her own voice set her off.

"I'm going to sit with Mom for a while," Betsy said, getting up.

"Do that, Betsy," Marion said dolefully, but then—as Betsy hesitated, unwilling to leave her alone with her sorrows—she got up, brisk as ever—a tall, stout woman, back in control—and clicked on the light. They both squinted in the brightness. "I'll just freshen up—I must look a sight," Marion said with some of her old spirit, and Betsy started upstairs.

Violet was very still, eyes closed, but her breathing was labored.

"What's this?" Betsy asked angrily. "She's never breathed like that before. Why didn't you call me?"

Terry shook her head. She looked frightened: as if to say that there was nothing she could do, that dedication and efficiency were useless. "I called Dr. Baird, and he said—" She spread her arms out helplessly. "All we could do is call an ambulance and get her to the hospital."

"No."

"I knew you would say that. I told him—"

"You should have called me. Did she wake up? Did she say anything?"

"Just her father. She's been asking for him."

"You said you'd *call* me!"

Terry shook her head, with her hands pressed to her mouth.

Betsy knelt beside her mother. Her face was beautiful, emaciated and peaceful. Betsy's anger toward Terry subsided; what was left was directed not at the nurse but at the menace invading her mother, stretching the skin over the bones and reducing the hand, so still beside her pillow, to a bundle of blue-veined sticks. Betsy reached out and stroked her mother's hand.

"No hospital, Terry. We promised her. And they can't save her, you know—only prolong it. She didn't want that."

"I know, but—"

"It's not wrong, Terry. It's the right thing to do."

"I know, but—" Terry was sobbing softly. "Oh, I wish Mr. Robinson was here!"

"He can't save her, either," Betsy said sharply. Terry turned away and began to bustle around, sniffing and wiping her nose. Betsy knew Terry wanted her to go, but she stayed where she was beside her mother's bed. She willed herself not to cry. There had been enough tears in that house, enough sniveling women. It wasn't tears she wanted to offer Violet, but the anger that still lingered in her—great, vital transfusions of anger, to beef up the family line. She gripped Violet's limp hand, as if she could communicate this to her. Violet's hazy drift into death seemed dreadful to Betsy now. Her mother's life had been without substance, composed of memory and lies. It had been all wrong, and her death was its logical conclusion. Violet was going to meet it willingly, almost eagerly, accepting death without protest, as she had accepted her flat, circumscribed life. Betsy hung on tight to the frail hand. She would pull her back if she could, and not for her own sake, either: for Violet's sake.

"Don't die, Mother," she whispered when Terry went down the hall on her rubber-soled shoes. "You've hardly lived."

While she sat there, Violet murmured and opened her eyes. Betsy smiled at her; for a moment, it was as if Violet had heard her and was coming back. Then Violet cried out, and Betsy saw that her eyes were wide with pain. Terry returned, and Betsy heard her preparing the injection.

"Where's my father?" Violet asked in her soft, hoarse voice.

"He's not here . . . he'll come."

Violet sighed. "But I want to tell him—"

"Tell him what?"

Violet focused on Betsy in confusion. "No," she whispered, "I want to tell you, Betsy." Betsy understood what an effort it was for her to speak, and she leaned close. "I know about the baby," Violet said. "That you're going to have a baby. Why did you keep it secret from me?"

"I thought it might upset you," Betsy said. The relief was enormous. Violet had known all along.

"Do you want a baby, Betsy?"

"Yes. I want this baby."

Violet smiled and then grimaced. "Good. Good. It will be a nice baby. I think Terry had better give me something."

Terry approached with the hypodermic.

"Mother." Betsy clutched her hand again. "Mother, I need to ask you this. Have you had a good life? Really?"

Violet squeezed Betsy's hand, just a little. "Oh, yes," she said with her gentle smile. "A wonderful life." She closed her eyes, but the smile remained, and the raspy breathing. "A wonderful life, Betsy. I don't regret any of it."

Life is the great adventure, she used to say. Had she believed it? Had it, somehow, been true?

"Mother!" Betsy said again.

Violet's eyelids flickered as Terry gave her the injection. "Don't be sad, Betsy. Really. There's no need." Her voice was a whisper; she was sinking into sleep.

"There is need, Mother," Betsy said, but she doubted Violet heard her.

A few minutes later, the phone rang. Frank and Emily had had a minor accident, they had been delayed, they were at a trooper station near Albany, and they would be there soon.

CHAPTER TEN

Violet

The empty spaces in her body were beginning to fill with pain. Sometimes, coming back from sleep and feeling the pain gather in her, Violet saw it as another person inhabiting her body. This alien being's force was too much for her. It was straining to get out, pushing at her bones and beating on the inside of her head. When the invader got out, the emptiness would take over and she would die.

Violet had lain quietly in bed, day after day, but her mind raced. She thought how there was no one else on earth who remembered Will as she did. She took pleasure in the thought of him. It seemed harmless to believe she was traveling toward him; it seemed, in fact, plausible—inevitable. She saw it as a reunion of bodies, not merely of souls. There had been a look of innocent surprise on his dead face. He would show the same surprise at their reunion. "Why, Violet!" he would say, holding out his arms, and a slow smile would spread over his handsome, beloved features. It was absurd—it wouldn't be like that—she had no idea how it would be—but it would be something, of that she was positive, and she lay in bed, contented enough, while the pain slowly gathered strength.

It was only when she had one of her dreams of being abandoned that she wanted Emily. There was snow—sometimes just darkness—and she was alone, searching (sometimes for home, sometimes for a thing that had been lost—a locket once, Betsy once), and she suddenly realized that the other searchers had left her, and she was alone, not knowing where to turn for help. In the dream, the illuminating thought was always the same: Of course! My mama! Emily will help me! And she called for her. Sometimes she awoke then to hear her own voice and to see Betsy there, or Terry, in tears. She didn't like to make anyone cry, especially Betsy. It was wrong to make children cry, the way her mother had made her cry. She raised a hand to wipe away Betsy's tears, but it fell back, and there was Terry with a glass and a pill.

She listened sometimes to Betsy and Frank talking back and forth. They kept their voices low because of the nurses and because of her. It was a secret, but she knew they were talking about Emily. They argued. *Don't,* she wanted to say. It didn't seem important—only on those long rides back from sleep did she want Emily, when she was lost in the snow and the dark. It must be the pills, the needles. Awake, she didn't care. She had her father, her daughter, the comforts that remained to her, and the scenes inside her head.

"I did it for my mother's sake."

"I suppose you know everything."

"It's time someone knew!"

"That damned woman!"

The pill took hold, and she drifted away to the sounds of their voices, Will in her mind, always Will. He rose up before her, lifting a glass. When Betsy bent over her, she looked in vain for Will's large, candid features in Betsy's sharp face, just as she used to try to force memories from the child. It was no use. She wouldn't find Will in Will's daughter. But she had him, all the same, stored away for herself, and that was enough. She hugged him to her heart.

"She won't come, Grandpa."

"Because of me?"

"Partly. And she has troubles of her own."

"My God, the woman is unreasonable. It's been years. Years!"

It's all right, Violet would have said if it wasn't for the drug. But their voices were like distant music to her.

It was pleasant to lie listening to them. She liked some noise—the radio, the TV, people in the room. When she was little, it had been so deathly quiet in the house sometimes, with no sound but the rustling of her father's newspaper or the pages of the briefs he brought home with him. Her mother banging an occasional pan in the kitchen. And then, in 1931, they bought a radio, and when she was in bed they tuned in Bing Crosby. Her father put down his paper, her mother came out of the kitchen, and Violet, upstairs in her room clandestinely reading, fell asleep to the sound of the music and her parents' voices talking low—even that rare sound, their mutual laughter. It was so much better, they were all happier with the radio. Helen loved it. She used to listen in the daytime as she worked around the house. And the television—she was a great fan of the soaps. They could get to her as real people couldn't. Her mother had had a stroke a month before her death, and she spent that last month in bed in front of the TV, the remote control in her one good hand. She had died during *Search for Tomorrow,* but it was a while before they found her, and by that time her dead eyes were watching *The Edge of Night.*

When she died, the whole house brightened, and breathed easier. It was like a good spring cleaning, all Helen's anger and piety swept away. Betsy became a plumper, happier child. Violet never again had to cower in her room and cry while Helen spanked Betsy, no longer had to make it up to her daughter: all those trips to the 5 & 10 for presents, those white barrettes with the yellow flowers, the Japanese fans, the cup-and-ball trick, the cowgirl suit. After Helen's death, the presents continued, but for the joy of them, not as compensation. Violet loved any excuse for gift giving.

This Christmas had been hard for her. They put the Christmas tree in her room, but she cried because there were no presents under it from her.

"I wanted to give you something pretty," she said to Betsy. Something colorful, a scarf to wear next to her face, maybe a blouse that tied in a bow under the chin, something to soften and brighten. Violet let Betsy dab at her eyes with a lace-edged handkerchief. Betsy didn't like her tears any more than she liked Betsy's. At least my daughter has loved me, Violet thought, as Betsy's big eyes and thin nose leaned over her: Elizabeth Jane. "It's a girl," Will had whispered as she came to. A bunch of flowers, and whiskey on his breath. "It's a beautiful little girl, Violet, she looks just like you." He put his head down on the pillow beside her and whispered that he loved her.

Now the sketches came back to her, the fragments of herself that had obsessed her husband. Over and over he had drawn her—mouth and eyes, mouth and eyes, sometimes with the suggestion of the curve of her cheek or chin, sometimes with a bit of nose. She would sit and read, or they would have the radio on, and he would have his sketch pad on his knee, the black-and-silver pen moving languorously over it with a soft scraping noise. His concentrating frown looked like anger, and she would cry, with a pretended pout, "Smile or I won't let you draw me anymore," and the frown would smooth out, he would laugh and close the sketch pad, and take her in his arms.

Later she would look at what he had done and find those bombed-out fragments of her face. Sometimes the lines and curves were harsh and spare and thickly inked, sometimes all delicate detail, but the subject was always the same.

She used to study her face in the mirror. She did have a remarkable mouth, fine eyes—the face of a passionate saint, he said. She would have liked a portrait, she was always asking for one, and after Betsy was born she thought how striking a portrait of the two of them would be. Mother and child. Betsy's soft, light curls. The same eyes. The two of them on the wine-colored sofa. She could wear her black taffeta and the pearls. But he just frowned over his sketch pads, rendering the bits of her more and more harshly, raggedly—and even these less and less frequently as the years went by. The last sketches, from the summer of 1948, were crude and angular, not like her at all, and Violet destroyed them when she and Betsy moved to Syracuse.

She would ask him (she thought, lying in bed and smiling secretly), she would make him tell her, once and for all, why he had never drawn her whole face. He used to joke, say her beauty overwhelmed him, he could only take it in a little at a time. But she knew it was something in him, not in her, and now she wanted to know. In those days, back in the blessed forties, she hadn't understood him enough; she was too busy making sure he understood her. She had been twenty-seven when he died, still learning. I will be a better wife to him this time, she thought. Sometimes, in her snow dreams, it was Will she sought or Will who came to her aid, and she awoke with his name on her lips.

The Christmas tree was so beautiful, so beautiful, and the smell was like youth and health and splendor returned. She and Will had always cut down their own tree, out in someone's woods. Will probably shouldn't have, with his bad heart, but he swung the short ax strongly and had the tree down in two shakes. Little trees for their little apartment. "Infanticide," Will said, hoisting it on his back. Betsy with her bright cheeks in that hat with the yellow yarn braids. Her one doll, the well-beloved Samantha—was it Samantha? Will, stringing popcorn, put the needle right through his thumb one year after too much Christmas Eve cheer, and the blood bubbled up over his nail. His face went dead white. She grabbed the thumb herself and pulled out the needle and sucked the wound clean, and had to laugh at his astonishment. How she used to love to get her mouth on him. . . .

She didn't often rage at her fate, and she didn't for long on Christmas. She lay back and opened her presents, lazily. What did you give a woman with no earthly future? Books. A tiny TV with a screen like a snapshot. A quilted bed jacket from Marion. They hovered, hoping they pleased her. Of course they pleased her, everything did. And why not? They seemed amazed that she took the waiting so well. They had no knowledge of the bewitchment of a contracted world. I have three complaints, she said to herself, trying to order her thoughts. There is my fear that the pain will get worse and be bad for a long time before it bursts out of me. Happiness will come hard if the pain is great: waiting won't be easy. But I don't think of this often. And there is my longing for Emily—but it only comes when I dream. It's enough—almost—to know she exists and loves me. And there is my regret at leaving them, Betsy unsettled and my father so blue. How will they get on without me? But life is short, it won't be for long. There was always comfort if you looked for it. *That man,* at least was gone—that hairy man of Betsy's—gone and left them all in peace.

Peace. From her windows she could see a long, down-curving branch of the big side-yard maple, the Mannings' porch with the shutters up for winter, three trees in the line of oaks that marched down Stiles Street, gray sky over the Mannings' porch, where she used to watch the summer sunsets. In the summer the view had been full of green, with roses climbing over the trellises, the shutters down and stored, people on the porch, glasses clinking, chatter, like a play. She had grown fond of the people on the porch, and she missed them now that winter was here, but she was fond of the gray sky and the snow, too. Peace on earth. After a storm, when all the branches were outlined and weighed down with snow, her heart leapt with excitement. It seemed years ago that she had gone downstairs or to the hospital or outside. She had missed those things, too, at first; now the window and her pretty room were enough, more than enough.

She used to tell lies to spruce up her life. It was a flat one after Will died, even a lonely one. There had been a couple of men-friends. Jack Denslow at work had been the last. What a disaster he had been, with his wham-bam lovemaking and football talk. And then she had stayed at home, keeping house for her father and daughter, both of them gone all day and coming home with stories of school and office. She'd lied to survive, harmless fibs and exaggerations: who had telephoned, what the butcher said, the antics of the neighbors. She improved on things, changed them by running them through her own richly colored mind. Lying made her present to others; she had a horror of being a woman no one noticed.

But now there was no need to embellish. Life was so full, so concentrated, she had to close her eyes sometimes to shut it out and withdraw to the cool recesses where Will was. They thought she was asleep, and the music began.

"Grandpa, it wasn't fair!"

"It was my business."

"How *can* you? Don't you understand *anything*?"

Don't use that sharp tone to your grandfather, Betsy. We must be kind to him, kinder than ever.

"I won't have your mother grieving like this! I'll drag that woman up here!"

Violet understood from the music that Frank was somehow, miraculously, her father. He should have told me—the words paraded through her mind like words on a banner, until the pills took them away. She slept, and it was 1941.

Will came in with his mother to buy her an Easter hat. Mrs. Ruscoe had raised four boys, and they were all dead but Will—the heart condition. There was a daughter, too, but she was in California with her husband. Will was his mother's pride and happiness. This was obvious to Violet when Mrs. Ruscoe tried on hats, primping. They had decided on a crazy thing with blue roses and veiling. Will had been magnificent—just right with his mother, flattering and teasing, but no mama's boy. He hadn't been able to take his eyes off Violet; both Violet and Mrs. Ruscoe had noticed. He had come back the next day, alone, to take her out for dinner after work. He'd given her no room for saying no; he just took her. They walked down Salina Street to Lorenzo's. It was early for dinner, and she had a Coke while he drank bourbon. He dazzled her with talk, but she made sure she held her own with him and didn't just sit and gape. She told him about selling hats to get him laughing; she was still new at the job and made mistakes. She kept watching his big, handsome, pink face, wondering if he was getting drunk—she had never seen anyone drunk—but he acted no differently as the evening went on except that his compliments to her became more florid and ingenious. She wore her cream two-piece with the rose-printed blouse. They had a long, leisurely dinner, and he took her home in his old Ford. She had forgotten to call home after work. "We've been worried sick," her father said. He had been waiting at the door, looking ready to beat them both. Her mother, as usual, was in the kitchen, but she came out in her apron and said, "Who is this man?'

It was a bad beginning. It took him a while to charm the two of them, to get permission to see Violet again, but in the end he won them over, even Helen. "He can certainly tell a story," she said once, and on another occasion, "That man could charm the skin off a fish." For Helen, this was a giddily colorful remark. Violet thought Will was a good influence on her mother—he loosened her up.

Mrs. Ruscoe did her best, but she never took Violet properly to her bosom. She was always the usurped, the abandoned, and Violet knew Will's mother thought a wife and family were bad for his heart. She died, of the family curse, not long after

Betsy was born. Will began to fear, from that time on, for his own life. (Was that when the sketches turned angular and harsh?) The shocked look on his face—Violet had found him in the shop where he fell, stretched flat—couldn't have been caused by the surprise of death: he'd expected it. She believed it was caused by his vision of paradise. He had always scoffed at Violet's hope for an afterlife, as if it was in the same class with her vegetarianism or her experiments with the tarot pack—and there it was, a lovely surprise. He was waiting there for her now. But it was dark, very dark, and she stumbled, searching for him. Will! Will! The others were gone, she was all alone, afraid in the dark—when suddenly she remembered: Emily! Of course! Emily, my mama, she will help me, Emily. . . .

She slept and dreamed, and woke. There was always music now, distant singing in her head. Funny that Emily had been a singer, funny that she would never hear her sing. The snow fell steadily on the maple bough and on the Mannings' roof. Terry had French toast ready for her. She didn't feel like eating it, but she let Terry feed her a couple of bites.

"I'm getting used to your eye shadow, Terry," she said, and she was shocked when two unmistakable tears hung in Terry's eyes and spilled over. "Don't!" she said. It seemed to her that Terry was trying to wash away the blue eye shadow. "Really, Terry, I do like it." Remorsefully, she ate another bite of French toast.

Food didn't interest her anymore. It seemed strangely irrelevant, and it stuck on the way down. She would rather remember how she and Will had cooked together. She had liked making big pots of things; he had liked the finicking details. When he died, it was months before she could so much as peel an onion. Oh, the meals they had eaten together, the good times they had, beginning with that first evening at Lorenzo's. They loved to go out: first dinner, then dancing. People don't dance anymore, Betsy and Judd never went dancing. She and

Will went out all the time. He loved to have her dress up. Silky skirt, nylon stockings, brocade bag. The pearls, the rhinestone clip, the jade necklace. The hat that was nothing but a big red rose with a black veil. The time she had put on her black V-neck satin and he had knelt before her and pressed his face to her, raised the skirt, rolled down her stockings, and right there on the bedroom floor . . . Oh God, the things he used to say, the things he did, such soft skin he had, and he was strong as a bear—he could lift her up and carry her, even when she was heavy with the baby. He shouldn't have, maybe there shouldn't have been so much dancing, either. But it was so lovely, clinging together late at night, drowsy, and then going home. . . .

Her father had paid all their bills when Will died. There were more bills than she had ever imagined, and the business was further in the red than she had thought a business could go without collapsing. Frank didn't grudge any of it, just totted up what was owed and paid it. "Will never asked for a dime," he'd said with a kind of stunned admiration when he was done. "Seize the day," her mother had commented, with her mouth turned down, "and let tomorrow go to the devil." But Frank shouted at her. "The boy's gone, Helen—let him be, for Christ's sake." And then Helen had railed at Frank for the blasphemy, until Violet distracted them both with her weeping.

She had never thanked her parents adequately for taking her and Betsy in, and she wondered sometimes why Helen had let them come back. Without knowing why, she was aware that her mother didn't love her. She had been indecently glad when Violet got married and left the house, almost as glad as Violet herself. It must have been Betsy Helen wanted—not that Helen was easy on her—that was never her way or her philosophy—but Violet could see her trying to be, at least, just. She was a marginally better grandmother than she had been a mother. All the same, Betsy preferred Frank, just as

Violet had. To Violet, her mother had been a stern figure of dread—short, hard, mousy, dour, religious. She could never recall Helen's virtues. But as she lay in bed there came to her, for no reason, Helen's laugh—a loud, hoarse bellow: "*Woa ho ho*!" It was infectious, and always a shock because it was so noisy and rare, usually called up by something on television. When it sounded in her mind, Violet laughed softly and looked around for Frank, but Terry was there, and she couldn't tell her—Terry had never known Helen.

Violet let Terry wash her; Dr. Baird was coming. "It's still snowing," she said. She could just make out the big flakes falling. She had been having a blank about snow. It entered her dreams readily enough, but what it was *like* eluded her, she kept thinking it was dark, dark. . . . She hadn't wanted to ask. Maybe it was the feel of the cool washcloth on her skin, but suddenly she got it. *Snow was cold and wet.* They all came back to her, the thousand and one snow-belt winters, and she smiled happily at Terry.

"Of course!" she said. "It's winter." She didn't say any more because of the look of sorrow on Terry's face. It puzzled her, but she figured that out, too. She was going to die, and it made Terry sad.

"People die all the time," she told Terry later that day, but it was Betsy. Betsy came close to the bed and leaned down where Violet could see her. She was crying.

"Don't," said Violet. It wrinkled her face so. There was a flurry of movement, and the room was full of people blocking the light. "I can't see—" They moved away. There was snow-brightness, and she could see it wasn't Betsy. It was an old woman. Emily?

"Violet," Emily said. "My dear child."

Violet could hardly hear her for the pain. It gathered all its forces and rushed into the empty spaces.

"Will!" she said before it burst from her, and he was there with flowers.

CHAPTER ELEVEN

Emily

Telegrams were dispatched to distant relatives—Will's sister in California, and the wife (remarried) of Frank's long-dead brother, Ted. Regretful telegrams were received back. Frank's friends called up and Betsy spoke to them. Flowers were received, in spite of Violet's wishes, and were banked around the closed casket at the funeral home—Henderson's, because Frank had known Chuck Henderson for fifty years and handled both his divorces. Even Frank sent flowers, in spite of Betsy's protests—a blanket of yellow roses.

"I can't stand to have her go into that cold ground without flowers, Betsy," he said, and insisted that Violet hadn't meant it about not wanting flowers, it was only to save them trouble, it was just like her. The tears came, and Betsy gave in about the yellow roses.

"My mother detested them," she said to Emily.

"They're for him," Emily said, imagining them draped over the coffin like fancy frosting.

Emily didn't believe in funerals at all. She had once said to a group of friends, "I'd like to be put out on a hillside, and let the crows and the little animals pick me clean, like they do in Africa." As soon as she said it, she knew it wasn't true. The idea was horrible—crows pecking out her eyes! But it was well received and was considered one of Emily's charmingly cracked notions. She almost said it to Betsy but refrained, fearing Betsy would act on it at her death.

Emily didn't go to the funeral home to receive sympathizers. She could see Frank didn't want her to. He didn't say so, explicitly, but it was there in the turn of his head and the flicker of his eyes when he said, that first day at lunch, "I'm not going over there for long—Violet didn't want a fuss." Before he could propose that Emily stay home and rest—she could see it coming—she suggested it herself, for reasons of her own, and the relief that smoothed out his troubled face amused her.

"That might be best, Emily," he said. "All things considered."

"What things?" Betsy asked.

He didn't stop eating; he forked up a piece of meat. "You know what I mean."

Betsy gave Emily a look expressing mortification and anger and apology: Frank's transparency obviously embarrassed her. "I'm not sure I do," she said. "It seems to me that it's absolutely fitting for Emily to go. She's my mother's mother!"

Frank set down his fork. "Betsy—"

"You don't even have to *say* who she is, Grandpa—just say she's an old friend."

"I'm not going, so you can both forget it," Emily said firmly. "I don't want the sympathy of a pack of people who are strangers to me. And I'm too old to tell lies about who I am. I'm seventy-two years old! I like to stay home in the evenings. And it's snowing."

"But, Emily . . ." Betsy said.

Emily nodded at her grimly. I know, the nod implied, we're letting him get away with it. She pushed back her plate, no longer hungry. She was aware of something Betsy didn't see, that Frank would prefer his hugely pregnant unmarried granddaughter to stay home, too. The two fallen women, Emily thought with glum amusement. The *traviatas*.

But Betsy didn't stay home. Emily saw the two of them off, and when they were gone she turned on the television and sat before it all evening, unseeing, while the beginning of a grudge worked its way into her heart. The next night was the same, except that instead of watching television she wandered around the house, touching nothing, breathing the air of Frank's study (looking without curiosity at the shelf of photographs), Betsy's room (with its odd mixture of furniture, its melancholy Madonna, and *Your Guide to Pregnancy and Birth* on the bedside table), Violet's sickroom (where the flat smell of illness lingered), and finally the guest room, where she was installed. She snuggled up in there under a blanket with a murder mystery and her resentment, and let Betsy come looking for her when she and Frank returned—Betsy looking white and stern, Frank oblivious.

"We ought to have the casket open, Betsy," he kept saying at the dinner table. "She looked so beautiful toward the end."

"She didn't want to, Grandpa," Betsy always said patiently in return.

He seldom replied, but made a noise expressing the disappointment, bewilderment, and frustration he felt. He would have liked to gaze on his dead daughter's face each night—he would have liked to hear people say how lovely she was, how peaceful.

"She had the face of an angel," he exaggerated to Emily.

The night before the funeral, the two of them were sitting in Frank's study—Frank in the swivel chair at his desk, Emily in the wooden armchair with the orange-and-blue university seal on it. They both held themselves very straight, as if to impress each other with their physical fitness or their self-control, but, though Emily remained clear-eyed, the tears ran down Frank's cheeks as he talked.

He had been talking—always with tears—since the night Violet's body was removed. He had talked far into that night, long after Betsy had gone off to bed, and Emily—nearly dead from exhaustion (as she put it to herself)—had had to force herself to stay upright and awake. But she had done it. She had listened for hours and hours, that night and the next day and now again, to his talk, his tedious old-man ramblings—or rather, she had stopped listening after a while and, absorbed in her own thoughts, had just let him rattle on, like a television show she wasn't interested in.

Her own thoughts were not pleasant—weren't even decent, probably. She was ashamed of them, but there they were: what could she do about them? She had come all the way here in a snowstorm, risked her life in an accident—her heart banging around in her chest like a bird caught in a barn—thanks to Frank's foolish faith in his own driving. Seventy-seven years old and rash as a teenager; you couldn't tell him anything. And then a state police escort, of all things, across half New York State—so that she could arrive to find a wan, wasted woman who didn't even recognize her, who died at her approach as if she were a blight.

Emily too had wept a little at first (while Frank's voice droned on), but she wept for her baby, the little Violetta who had been snatched away while she slept. She had no tears for the dead Violet. The woman was nothing to her. The suspicion that she would feel nothing had been half of her reluctance to come; the other had been that she would feel too much. Well, she had let them push her into this grotesque family reunion, and she had faced up to her failure. And now she wished only to be rid of them all—Robinsons and Ruscoes, the gloomy rooms, the weepy nurse who kept dropping in, and that frightful old Marion Palmer. She wished for nothing more than to be back home hibernating in her snug house, with the cats curled around her, and the kettle on.

Frank talked, his face glowing and rapt with the painful pleasure of reminiscence. It was Violet he talked about, filling Emily in on their daughter's unremarkable life. She had been a sweet, vague, simple woman, Emily gathered—a loving daughter, a daughter to be mourned. Frank's mourning was garrulous. But no matter how he talked of his loss, it was only Betsy who moved her grandmother's sympathy—and that was probably (Emily admitted sternly to herself) because the girl was pregnant. Even pregnant women on the street touched her; it was only natural that her own granddaughter should inspire tenderness. The poor girl, with no man to stand by her, and her mother wasting away before her eyes. She had watched Betsy, in the two days since Violet's death, drag herself around the house, taking the phone calls and doing the cooking, her eyes red-rimmed and curiously vacant-looking, and she had longed to comfort her—to sit and talk with Betsy instead of with Frank. But Betsy, though affectionate, seemed glad to be alone with her thoughts, and seemed to relish the chance to throw her long-estranged grandparents together. Emily excused herself to Frank from time to time and went in search of Betsy; the girl had taken to sitting, down in the living room, in a hideous flowered armchair, looking out the window at nothing. Once when Emily came upon her, she was dozing, with her swollen ankles stuck straight out from her maternity slacks and her hands clasped high on her belly. Seeing her thus, Emily's heart overflowed with pity and tenderness. It was herself she saw there.

Back in the study, the cold winter light, reflected through the north windows off the blue snow, lit the room dimly. Emily turned on the desk lamp and sat back down. Frank picked up his story where he had broken off, tears polishing his face. He didn't bother to wipe them away. Perhaps he thought she would do it for him, but Emily sat stiff in her chair and made no move toward him. Let him weep, she thought, I've done my share.

"Then when Will died she came back to us, Emily. She wasn't sure we wanted her—can you imagine? It was the happiest day of my life, I think, when she moved into her own room again. And little Betsy down the hall. It was the only thing Violet could do, really—I doubt she could have cared for herself. Of course, Will left debts. I took care of everything, glad to do it. He was a charming fellow, I don't deny it —and funny! He even made Helen laugh, believe it or not. But improvident. Foolhardy. And he drank. Now, I'm not saying he was an alcoholic, but I will say that a good deal of the money that should have gone into other things went for drink. I suppose it shortened his life, too. Of course, Violet went to pieces when he passed away. She adored that man. It was her way, to throw herself into things, to invest everything . . ."

Emily looked around Frank's study—the room where, she could see, he had gathered his things about him, as old people do. It was here he had retired to, to this fancy swivel chair behind the fancy desk. Like a big tycoon, Emily thought, instead of an aging and superannuated lawyer in an insignificant provincial city. More sham, more lies. It was pathetic—*he* was pathetic. If only she had seen it sooner—years back!—before he made her pathetic, too. If only she had seen then what a fake he was, stewed so deep in hypocrisy that it was his natural element. She'd had to come here with him to see it. She'd had to listen to his confession—made almost with pride!—of his affair with Marion Palmer, and his bizarre tale of poor Helen's baby. She'd had to listen to his callous, selfish ramblings, and to see how he was ashamed of her—of *her*! after fifty-five years!—and of his granddaughter. Even his wooing of her back in East Haddam three days ago (it seemed years) had had a purpose: to get her to Violet's bedside. Well, she had come, and what had she gotten out of it? The ramblings of an old man grieving for his daughter. *Rigoletto,* Act III. She might as well have been a robot or a tape recorder, or Marion Palmer, for all he cared who listened to him. If she left the room he'd talk to himself, he'd talk to the snapshots on the wall.

She didn't leave the room, though—except to check on Betsy, to go to the bathroom, once or twice to get herself a glass of sherry from Helen's showy cut-glass decanter in the dining room, and when she did she went right back. There was a fascination, to her, in the way Frank's paternal reminiscences left her out entirely, the way he rode right over her very existence as if it hadn't been she who'd given birth to Violet in Myra Bell's back bedroom, as if she had no feelings at all. Well, maybe she didn't. I'll stick this out, she thought grimly. You're never too old to learn. She'd sit there with him and let the cozy family stories flow. But she didn't have to listen. She didn't want to hear his memories—why should she? They had nothing to do with her.

He was an old man, it seemed to her now—no matter how straight he sat in his chair. To live in the past was a sign of old age: it was not for her. And to live for the future was just as bad, she mused. She ought to know. Thanks to him, she'd put her faith in the future for those long twenty years—a future that never came. She was beyond that kind of time travel now. She'd look no further back than yesterday, no further ahead than tomorrow; after the funeral she was going straight home. He's an old man, and his life is over, she thought (listening to Frank's voice but not his words). All her carefully nurtured defenses rushed in to prevent her thinking the same of herself. On the contrary: her life could go forward, day by day, with its old comfortableness not only intact but enhanced. She could go forward, really, in triumph; she had conquered this old man, whether he was aware of it or not, and she knew (another unpretty thought, but satisfying) she would outlive him. She could scuttle back to her old life with no harm done—almost as if that poor woman's death, instead of breaking her as she had feared, had propped her up. Yes, it is wrong, it is unnatural to outlive your child—but it proves you're strong.

"It was funny, that Violet wouldn't let Betsy wear lipstick when she was sixteen. It was okay by me, I liked it, but Violet put her foot down. Usually she was so easygoing, but there were times . . . She didn't want to lose her little girl, I suppose. Didn't really want Betsy to grow up."

Everything suggested Violet to him. Over lunch, it was Violet's food preferences. The snow reminded him of Violet, as a child, on her sled—how red her fat little cheeks used to get! Emily's lavender sweater recalled the afghan Violet had crocheted the time she broke her ankle. Even his study, his desk, the mechanical bank—if all else failed, he had only to look around him for a chapter of his daughter's biography. These were the stories that had been going through his head all those long months by Violet's bedside; now they were his tribute to her, along with his tears.

An old tune from an operetta kept running through Emily's head. She had sung it—oh, years ago, and right here in Syracuse, too, at the Empire. It was one of her pagan, free-spirit, bohemian roles:

> The old times are gone now,
> The future's far away,
> So live, love, for the present hour,
> Hold fast, hold fast the day. . . .

She would have liked to sing it to Frank now, had her voice permitted. What would he do if she began, suddenly, to sing in the young, light soprano that had once moved him so? Fall on his knees before her? Repeat the insane proposal of marriage that he seemed to have forgotten all about? Abandon his grief, just for a moment, and clasp her to him in love and gratitude?

Gratitude. That was it, the missing ingredient that—of all the missing ingredients—most rankled. Where was her thanks for coming here to the house he'd shared with Helen? For risking her life—at her age!—to rush to his dying daughter's bedside? With humiliation she reflected that she had done it for him, that sitting on her sofa with him back in East Haddam she had rejoiced that the burden of anger had been lifted from her shoulders and the sweet dream had taken its place once again—light and lovely as a lace cape. . . . And what had he ever done for her? Nothing! It was Betsy, after all, who had sought her and found her. He hadn't bothered. He would have gone to his grave without ever seeing her again. He'd probably considered her an embarrassment, if he'd considered her at all, until it suited his purposes to track her down and, after twenty years, to scatter the old lies before her like birdseed.

And she had eaten from his hand—only to become an embarrassment again, too problematical an entity with which to confront his dried-up old lawyer pals. What if she took a cab over to Henderson's Funeral Home during calling hours and went around introducing herself: "Hello, I'm Emily Loftus, one of Frank's old mistresses—Violet's mother, actually." She even knew one or two of them: what was his name, that fat man they'd kept running into despite all their precautions? Corelli? Cannoli? Corleone? Nasty man with a dirty mouth, who *knew*—you could see it in his bleary alcoholic eyes; they stripped her and put her naked into Frank's bed before the introductions were over. "This is Miss Loftus," Frank had glibly lied, "an old school friend of my wife's." Was he dead of drink or would he be there? "Hello, Mr. Cannoli—remember me? Helen Robinson's school friend? You weren't taken in, were you? You knew who I was. And, as a matter of fact, I was Violet's mother, too. . . ."

Frank paid no attention to Emily's stony glares. It was doubtful he saw them. He was chuckling over Violet's flirtation with theosophy. "She used to carry this book with her everywhere, Emily. By Madame Somebody—her picture was there, a fat woman like a buddha—like a hippo! Claimed to be in direct contact with God! Well, Violet used to go on about that stuff—trying to convert me, I suppose. And then, after theosophy, it was Yoga. . . ."

They had dinner in the dining room, the three of them. Marion Palmer had packed and gone back across town to her condominium, weeping, shortly after Violet was taken away. She would see them at the funeral home. She left in a hurry, and she and Emily had not said a word to each other beyond, "Hello, Marion," and "How are you, Emily?" and then good-bye. Marion had been a shock; she had not aged gracefully. Emily wondered how far gone she had been when Frank had his fling with her. She took a grim satisfaction in imagining them in each other's arms. Betsy, she noticed, had given Marion a big hug and tried to get her to stay, but Emily was relieved when she went, lugging her cheap flowered suitcase out into the snow. Even now, half a century later, she was afraid she would fly at the woman, pull her hair out, claw the bright makeup off her face, and demand the return of her baby.

Betsy had fussed a bit over dinner: fried chicken supplied by Mrs. Manning from next door, hot rolls, wine, and a spice cake donated by the weepy nurse. Betsy got out the good china and cloth napkins and cut-glass goblets. Good for her, Emily thought fondly. She admired Betsy's strength of character; it was in the blood.

But Betsy wasn't eating much. Emily knew she suffered from terrible indigestion as well as from grief. Her hair, none too clean, was screwed back in a knot, and her face looked puffy. The baby was due soon. I should stay to see her through, Emily thought fleetingly, knowing she wouldn't. It could be a couple of weeks yet, and she'd be stuck in this ugly house or in some cold motel. . . .

I've got to get back to my own life, she apologized in silence to Betsy, watching anxiously as Betsy picked at her chicken.

"Try to eat, Betsy," she said.

"Oh, I'm eating," Betsy said cheerfully enough. "I just can't eat a lot at once."

"Your mother didn't eat enough to keep a bird alive the last few weeks, did she, Betsy?" asked Frank morosely.

He ate plenty, Emily noticed. All his talking had put new

heart into him, she thought. He'd collapsed in tears when Violet died. Of the three of them plus nurse plus Marion looming in the background, he was the first to cry out, he was the one who threw his arms around Violet's still body, cradling it and sobbing until Betsy led him away. He had gone blindly, shrunken and stooped, like an aged, aged man.

But he had perked up during these two days. The sound of his own voice was a tonic—and her own flattering, deferent silence, Emily thought wryly. Well, let him have what he wanted this one last time, let him be, she thought, and congratulated herself on her charity. The idea came to her again that he had been broken somehow, or at least weakened, by Violet's death, and he hadn't long to live. She lingered briefly on the thought before she pushed it away with distaste.

She and Betsy talked of Betsy's plans. She would bring the baby to Connecticut in the summer for a nice long visit? Betsy promised. And everything was prepared? Diapers? Receiving blankets? Warm sleepers? One of those zip-up thermal things? What a time of year to have a baby!

Frank took no part in the discussion. He sucked a chicken bone, above it all, and Emily wondered at the distance between him and his granddaughter; it had become more pronounced as Frank recovered his spirits. It was obvious that his disapproval of her pregnancy had worn away some of the fondness and trust between the two.

Betsy was not openly hostile to her grandfather. She was courteous with him, and respectful of his grief, but she seemed to have things on her mind. Sometimes during his dinner-table ramblings, she glanced at him with vexation, as if his words were at war with her thoughts. But she said nothing.

Frank had little to say to her; he did most of his talking to Emily. The sessions at the funeral home, with his pregnant granddaughter at his side, were clearly difficult for him. No doubt he considered himself to be bearing them stoically

—even heroically. Emily imagined him with his friends, neighbors, former business associates, introducing Betsy, not batting an eye but managing at the same time to convey subtle disapprobation and his consciousness that unwed motherhood was not a proper state for the granddaughter of Frank Robinson.

Emily observed all this almost with glee. His own past come back to haunt him, she thought. It's in the blood, old man! She giggled aloud and turned it into a cough. Poor Frank . . . but she caught herself, thinking: Enough! Why should I let him be? Why should he be spared again? Damn the man! She came to a decision: She wouldn't let him get away with this one. Before she left, she would reconcile Frank with Betsy. She'd make him face up to it, make him give his errant granddaughter what he never gave his mistress: generous, uncritical, free, and courageous love when she needed it. She would do it for Betsy—leave her mark on them both, for Betsy's good. And for Frank's, too.

Emily poured herself another glass of wine and smiled at Frank and Betsy. "It's good to have you here, Emily," said Betsy warmly, and Frank looked up from his plate with an absentminded nod of agreement.

After dinner she sat on the living room sofa. No more holing up alone with him, no more biography, no more pampering. She'd given him her presence—an ear—shared her strength with him. He looked fine, she thought, watching him poke at the fire—except that he looked so old. He'd get over his daughter's dying. Oh, he'd weep some more at the funeral, he'd be blue for a while, but he'd bounce back. That was death, after all: the shock of the blow, then the comforting memories, then the dull ache, and somewhere toward the end of it all life resumed—business as usual. Frank was no different from anyone else—except that he was old. He'd become old suddenly or else she hadn't seen it before—old, old and failing. All the more reason to reconcile him to the baby.

She patted the sofa next to her. "Sit by me," she said to Betsy—before Frank could park there and start up his reminiscences again. She smiled at her granddaughter. "Now. Why didn't you tell me how much Frank disapproved of your pregnancy?"

Frank's fire poking stopped for a second, then went on. Betsy frowned, but whether it was at Emily's words or at Frank's disapproval, Emily didn't know.

"What about it, Frank?" she said loudly. "Do you have something against fallen women?"

He turned around at that, with the old familiar hurt face. "That's enough, Emily."

"I don't think so," she said. And then to Betsy: "It hasn't helped any, has it? To have your grandfather turn away from you at a time like this?"

"It has hurt me very much," Betsy said softly after a moment.

"Betsy!"

They both looked up at him, there was so much anguish in the cry—but the anguish was all for himself, Emily saw. And so did Betsy, apparently. She went on in her clear voice: "It has, Grandpa. And your not telling me about my mother. I'm sorry. I know quarreling is painful for us both. But you know how I feel."

He turned back to the fire, grasping the mantel with both hands and bowing his head, like a man in a movie. There was a painting over the mantel, of washed-out-looking flowers in a pink transparent vase. Helen's taste, thought Emily.

"It's been hard for me, Betsy," Frank said.

"Hard for you!" Emily flared up. "What about Betsy? Hard for you? You're not pregnant and alone. You don't get stared at and asked insulting questions and called names. You don't cry yourself to sleep from loneliness."

"Shh, Emily," Betsy said. "It's not like that."

"Don't shush me! I know what it's like. And I haven't yelled at him properly in twenty years."

"I'm not listening," Frank said with his back turned.

"Oh, yes you are, Frank. I've listened to you for two days straight and you can just listen to me now for a minute. This granddaughter of yours is the only one of your women left who's worth anything and who still loves you. Now you just do your duty by her before you die. You accept her baby and accept it cheerfully and gratefully, and forget about yourself for once."

He pushed himself away from the mantel and faced her. "Dramatizing as usual, Emily. Leave me alone." His voice was shaky, and it rose—Emily thought—unbecomingly. "I *accept* the baby, as you put it. Of course I disapprove—so would you, if you weren't always posing and acting, playing the liberated female. I disapprove for her sake—it's got nothing to do with what happened years ago. It's her career that concerns me, and the baby's future."

"Come off it," Emily said, sitting back on the sofa. She was prepared to go on, but Frank left the room without another look at her. "Hypocrite!" she called after him, and heard him stump up the stairs.

"The old humbug," she said to Betsy.

"Emily, please," Betsy said in a voice full of fatigue. "He means well."

Her mildness infuriated Emily. "You can't believe that! He means well to Frank Robinson, my girl, but not to anyone else if it's going to inconvenience his precious self. I know all about him! He doesn't fool me with that saintly preacher face."

Betsy was silent for a moment, and Emily watched her with some anxiety. She was angry with Frank and impatient with Betsy—she could have swatted her for her meekness—but she didn't want to quarrel with her granddaughter. The sweet dream was dead. She'd awakened from it at last. She would gladly leave Frank Robinson behind—as he'd left her twenty years ago, without a backward glance—but she wanted this dear, awkward girl and her baby. She wanted some stab at the kind of family life Frank had been yakking about for the last two days. My little family, she thought: I haven't had any family in—how long? how long? And he'd had so much.

She squeezed Betsy's fingers gently. "Am I right? Am I?"

Betsy sighed. "Of course you're right, Emily. But you have no idea how hard this is for me. I've been thinking and thinking, these past few days. I've been thinking about my mother—not about her death, but about her life. What a *nothing* it was. And she was happy! That's the ugliness of it." She stopped and pressed one hand to her forehead. "No—not ugliness. Nothing about my mother was ugly. She was entitled to her life—to that kind of life, if she wanted it. She told me she'd had a wonderful life, and I believe her. But I see it ahead for *me,* Emily, and I don't want it. Living for the past, or for dreams, or for other people's comforts. *Only* for that!"

She stood up and walked to the fire with her odd pregnant walk, hands on belly.

"And you, Emily," she went on.

Emily put her hand to her heart, but she wanted to hear it, whatever it was. "What about me?" It was like a play, exactly.

"Waiting for him all those years. As if that was all there was to life. You! With your gifts! I don't—oh, God, Emily!" She twisted her hands together. "I don't want to inherit that."

"I was a fool, Betsy," Emily said readily. "When I *think* what a fool I was! It's taken me a long time to see it clearly. And he almost made a fool of me again—would you believe it?" The memories came, unbidden and irrational, of Frank in her bed in East Haddam, of Frank sitting with her at the breakfast table, of Frank kneeling before her and confessing his long love. . . . She washed the pictures, like dirt, from her mind.

"You two aren't going to go off into the sunset together, then?" Betsy asked, with the hint of a smile that Emily perceived as partly wishful.

"No, thanks. I'll stay the way I am." Emily patted the seat beside her, and Betsy sat down again. Emily took her granddaughter's hand. "I'll tell you something, Betsy. I'm never unhappy, and I'm never what you'd call happy, either —not that kind of happiness that comes when you're always expecting something good to happen. No, I don't want commiseration," she said quickly, seeing Betsy's melancholy look. "There are better things than happiness, Betsy. I'm contented. My life goes along, day to day, just as I want it to. I like it. I wouldn't change a thing. Oh, I'd take my voice back," she said with a shallow laugh. "But I wouldn't have the rest of it for anything. No thanks," she repeated firmly. "And that includes *him*." She jerked a thumb upward to the ceiling. "I'll leave him to his lies and his memories."

They were silent again, sitting with clasped hands. "I'm not good at this, Emily," Betsy said at last. "I find the whole thing very depressing."

"What? That your whole life has been an evasion?"

At this, Betsy laughed outright. "It doesn't help when you put it like that."

"Be glad you hooked on to it while you're still young," Emily said bitterly, but then she smiled at the girl and gave her swollen fingers a little squeeze.

Betsy didn't answer. She had drifted into her bovine state, her eyes vacant and her mouth gone slack, so that she looked (Emily thought) almost dim-witted.

"Emily," she said at last, with the abrupt, shy determination Emily found so appealing, "I want to tell you about this dream I had. I'd like your opinion. It seemed to me like a good dream—almost a good omen, and I feel I need good omens just now. I had it the night Mom died, and it's been on my mind ever since. I keep wondering if it's just sick and morbid, or—"

"Tell me, for heaven's sake!"

"Well. In the dream I was in a park with my baby, and there was a wall, and on the other side of the wall was a sheer precipice—bottomless. I was taking pictures of the scenery, it was a very pretty park, and I thought it would be nice to have a picture of the baby sitting up on the wall. So I spotted a man coming down the path, and I asked him to sit up on the wall with the baby while I took their picture, and he did, and as I was taking the picture it occurred to me, what if this man was a homicidal maniac who would throw my baby over the side of the precipice? And just as I thought it, he did—the baby disappeared over the side. I began to run around and around this park, thinking, My baby is dead, my baby is dead. And then it occurred to me that I should commit suicide, to be reunited with my child—and the next minute I thought, But what if death is the end, what if there will be no reunion?"

She was silent, and Emily prodded, with a gasping little laugh, "Was that all?"

Betsy looked at her, smiling. "No. I put my faith in death. I leaped over the precipice. And I was reunited with my baby."

She waited for Emily's reaction, but for a moment Emily couldn't speak. The flames in the fireplace, the insipid painting over the mantel, a drooping begonia plant in the window, Betsy's large, soft bulk—they all came together and whirled in Emily's head with a sensation that was part déjà vu, part miserable memory, with an undercurrent of exhilaration that puzzled her. Back home, thinking it over in solitude, she would identify it as *release*. But now she sat with her hands pressed to her heart, shaking her head from side to side as if politely refusing something. "Oh, my dear Betsy," she said.

"I've had that dream—dreams like it—so many, many times."

Betsy looked stricken. "Emily, I'm sorry—"

"No need," Emily said. She took a deep breath and then exhaled slowly. She looked tenderly at her granddaughter. "Maybe I won't have them anymore. For you, it's a good dream, Betsy. For me—" She made a comical face and lifted her forefinger in the air. "Listen," she said. "Let me sing you something. It's been running through my head all day—my philosophy of life! Now don't mind my screechy old voice, I want you to hear this."

Softly, in her flat cracked alto she began to sing:

> The old times are gone now,
> The future's far away—

She had gotten that far when Frank came in. Emily blushed for her voice, but Frank didn't appear to notice it. He was frowning.

"Betsy, I'd like to talk to Emily for a minute alone."

Betsy began to get up, but Emily stopped her. "You stay, Betsy. In your condition you don't need to be jumping up and down at every whim of your grandfather's."

"No—I'll go," Betsy said.

Frank waved his hand wearily. "Forget it. You might as well hear this. I just want to say one thing, Emily. I don't want you in my house. I don't want you at my daughter's funeral tomorrow. You're a troublemaker and a bitch, just like you always were. In fifty-five years you haven't changed. I must have been crazy to bring you here." He looked not at Emily but at Betsy—defiantly. "There," he said.

Emily stood up and went over to him. She was trembling all over, but she reached up and slapped him, hard, in the face. It steadied her.

With her head high, she left the room—as she might have walked regally offstage after a show-stopping solo. This, after all, was what she had come for.

CHAPTER TWELVE

Betsy

Violet's funeral was very short and somewhat strange, an attempt at a compromise between her dying wishes and Frank's sense of what was fitting.

It was held in the university chapel—late in the afternoon (Violet had wanted an evening funeral, but that was impractical) and without music. It was presided over—what there was of it—by Dr. Wilder, the retired chaplain and Frank's old friend. There was a contingent present from the university—the crowd at the baby shower distilled into, perhaps, five or six faculty members and a graduate student or two. And there were Frank's friends—aging men in hats and tweed overcoats with their fur-coated wives—and a few neighbors Violet had been close to, but not many. It was odd, Betsy thought, as she often had, how few friends her mother had. Or rather, it wasn't odd (she reflected, with her new insight), it was perfectly natural. Violet had given up friendship along with all the rest of the components of a real life.

The service was almost entirely silent. Dr. Wilder asked everyone to bow their heads in a long meditation, and then he read from the Bible ("Thou hast turned for me my mourning into dancing: thou hast put off my sackcloth . . . "—Violet's choice) and from John Donne ("Death, be not proud," chosen by Frank—it was one of the two poems he was acquainted with, the other being Shakespeare's eighteenth sonnet). The procession of cars up Comstock Avenue to Oakwood Cemetery was short; the day was bitterly cold and smelled of snow, and Dr. Wilder's exhortations to the mourners to remember that they were dust were carried away by a sharp wind.

Frank stood between Betsy and Marion, the ends of his muffler whipping out behind him. His nose was red, his face was bone white, and he leaned unashamedly on the two women. Betsy, seeing the tears on his cheeks, wondered why they didn't turn to ice. She had wept in the chapel—the Donne poem had moved her greatly—but out in the open all she could think of was the cold, the wind, the way the weight of her belly pulled at her—and Judd.

Judd was at the funeral, and he was one of the few who ventured out to the cemetery as well. He stood alone and apart, wrapped in his black cloak—the twin to hers—like a Heathcliff, or a Manfred (she thought, with a peculiar, restful detachment that she didn't expect), or like a raven against the snow—some solitary, brooding figure. He didn't look at Betsy. His face, as he watched the coffin lowered into the ground, was expressionless, and before anyone else he turned and walked away without a word to her.

Her great-aunt nudged her behind her grandfather's back and gave her a look. Betsy nodded serenely. There he was—he had come—and she knew they would meet again. Why else had he come to the funeral unless he wished to see her again? She experienced the same kind of certainty about that as she had about the safe return of Frank and Emily, but she didn't know what to think of it. She thought instead of how striking he was, how vivid, striding off over the snow with his cape flapping. Seeing him, after all these months and at a distance, it seemed weird and miraculous that the two of them had once been together.

Judd disappeared swiftly down the hill, and Betsy took her grandfather's arm and guided him over the hard snow to the car. Her mother's death, like her parting with Judd, seemed to have occurred a long time ago. There was an immense distance between Betsy and her mother's last fevered whispers, and the coming of Emily, and her grandfather's anguished cry. Some of the furious revulsion Betsy had felt at Violet's bedside had left her. It was impossible to begrudge death when it was so easy, and so obviously a release. The proper emotion for it seemed to be affectionate regret—a kind of peaceful, generalized mourning for the fact of death itself, not Violet's gentle participation in it. And it was partly eclipsed by Emily's dramatic departure in a taxi late the night before, to catch the last train.

"Where is she?" Marion had asked her at the chapel that afternoon.

"Gone," Betsy said, adding, "Don't mention her to Grandpa. She told him off, and it just about killed him."

She said no more, leaving Marion wide-eyed. She kept to herself the tale of Frank's rage against Emily, the slammed doors and the cursing, and the difficulty with which she had kept her own silence.

"Ah, I'm an old man, Betsy," he had said to her before she went up to bed. "It's true what she said—you're all I've got, and I'm damned lucky to have you." He looked old and frail, his head seemed to tremble on his thin neck. That was true, too: Emily's observation that he had become an old, old man. Betsy said nothing to him, merely kissed him good night and went upstairs.

After the funeral, back at the house, Betsy left Frank with her attentive Aunt Marion and a contingent of friends, and, on impulse, went upstairs to the quiet of her mother's room. The weather had been too cold to air it out properly, and the room smelled vaguely of rubbing alcohol. Betsy smoothed the bed where Violet had lain for so long and then sat down on it, leaning back against the pillows. The old silver dinner bell, the one her mother had used for calling the nurses, was still on the table. And the little pile of books was there—*The Thurber Carnival, Carry on Jeeves, Three Men in a Boat.* Futile, to attack death with laughter. Violet had chosen, in the end, to accept rather than attack, and she had carried the secret of how to do it away with her.

Snow had begun to fall again outside the windows. From downstairs came the tinkle of glasses as drinks were fixed, and the sound of her grandfather's laughter. He and his old friend Ed Scott were reminiscing about their law-school days. Betsy heard Marion's loud hoots. But up in Violet's room, where death needn't be denied, all was peaceful. Betsy thought of her mother, tucked forever into the frozen earth. She would miss her most, she suspected, in the years to come, and as if to underscore the thought the baby kicked her, hard. Betsy smiled and, with effort, got to her feet, but before she went downstairs she put the silver bell in her pocket.

Frank urged her to go out to dinner with them—he and Marion and the Scotts were going to venture through the snow to a steak house. The invitation was clearly an overture, but she couldn't accept it. She was exhausted, and she wanted to go home. She had been in her grandfather's house for weeks, sleeping in her old room under the eyes of the long-suffering Madonna on the wall, and it was time to go.

"Forgive me, Grandpa," she said to Frank. "I'm tired. What I really want to do is go home and take a hot bath and go to sleep for twelve hours."

His face fell, and then Ed Scott called across the room, "Let her go, Frank—she's too young. Our conversation won't be fit for her tender ears." Frank guffawed and returned to his drink, but he looked quickly at Betsy with a touch of his old resentment.

Agnes Scott came over to her. "When are you due, honey?" she asked, with an air of getting it out in the open.

Ed, embarrassed at his wife's forthrightness, looked down into his glass and stirred the ice cubes with his finger. Her grandfather, Betsy noticed, had become very still, with his face turned away.

"Any day," Betsy replied.

Mrs. Scott smiled. "Isn't it funny," she said. "After all these years I can still remember the births of my three as clearly as anything—every pain!" She laughed the conspiratorial laugh of a Pregnancy Club member. "Why, I remember with Mary Patricia—"

"Yes, sir!" Frank broke in suddenly. "I'm going to be a great-grandfather! I'll tell you, Agnes, I can hardly wait! I think these modern women are terrific!"

There was a short pause after this speech, and his eyes met Betsy's with a sheepish look. She forced a smile, wondering why she kept being so grudging with him. He was doing his best.

"Don't let your grandfather spoil the baby," Agnes Scott said, unfazed by the interruption. "I see it coming on."

Marion sat in the chintz-covered armchair sipping at her Scotch and soda. "He spoils everyone, Agnes," she said. In the kitchen, after the funeral, she had taken Betsy aside and said, "I think he really needs me, Betsy. I think I can be a real comfort to him." Her eyes had sparkled and her cheeks glowed with a flush that wasn't rouge. "He's just an old pussycat," she said to the Scotts, beaming at Frank over the top of her glass.

The older people would drop Betsy off on their way to dinner. They were noisily high-spirited on the way. The grown-ups had behaved that way after Helen's funeral, too, she recalled, and Betsy—a prim teenager—had thought it shocking—the dirty jokes and the amount of alcohol consumed. Now she laughed with them, even when the jokes were about Frank's imminent great-grandfatherhood (her part in the phenomenon was delicately glossed over) and what that implied about Frank's age and capabilities.

"I never heard of any great-grandfather who could still cut the mustard, Frank," Ed Scott said a couple of times.

"But he's *young* to be a great-grandfather!" Marion insisted. She reached forward from the back seat and patted Frank possessively on the shoulder.

As they approached the east side of town, her grandfather became silent, and Betsy, sitting beside him, wondered if he was grieving. They reached Oakwood Cemetery, and the jokes from the back seat became louder as they passed, but Frank didn't laugh. When they reached her apartment, he insisted on walking her up to the door. Betsy didn't object, knowing there was something he wanted to say.

"We're looking forward to that baby!" Agnes called as Betsy got out of the car.

"So am I," she replied, and shut the door on their boozy, comfortable laughter.

Frank guided her with exaggerated care up the Brodskys' immaculately shoveled walk. The porch was lit in anticipation of her return. When he had piloted her safely to its light, Frank said abruptly, "Your young man was at the funeral."

His formal diction made her laugh. "He's not my young man, Grandpa. Not anymore."

"Then why did he come?"

It was, of course, exactly as she had put it to herself, but her answer to him was different. "Simply as a friend of the family. He always liked Mom and you."

"And you, I hope."

"But that's over, Grandpa. His coming today didn't mean anything. Please don't start fantasizing about a last-minute wedding to legitimize everything."

Betsy spoke sharply and his face showed he was hurt, but he persisted. "Would you take him back?"

She was contrite and took the question seriously, but, "I don't know, Grandpa," was all she could say.

He looked at her with a sly smile. "Damn the old lady, she

probably hit the nail on the head. I'm a selfish bastard. But sometimes it seems to me, Betsy, that if you and Judd got married everything would be all right."

"I don't see that."

"What? That I'm a selfish bastard?" His smile widened, and he shrugged. "That's what she said!"

She didn't return his smile. "Is that what Emily is to be, then? Just a wacky, eccentric old lady? Is that all the effect you'll admit she had on you, that you can pigeonhole her that way and forget about her?"

His smile disappeared. "She's not just wacky and eccentric, Betsy," he snapped. "She's unbalanced! You heard what she said!"

"I did hear her, and I agreed with most of the things she said. At any rate, I think she had a right to say them."

"Oh, for Christ's sake," he said, and started to go back down the steps. "Then I *am* a selfish bastard. That's what you think of your grandfather."

She caught his arm. "It doesn't matter what I think, Grandpa. But I want to say something—not about Emily, but about Mom."

He turned, curious but impatient. "It's cold out here," he said irritably.

"I just want to say this one thing. Before you came, she was asking for you—"

"I know that!" he cried out. "You told me that, everyone's told me that. Are you going to reproach me for not being with her before she died? Christ! Why do you think I wasn't? Who do you think I went all the way to East Jesus, Connecticut, to get that damned woman *for*?"

"That's not what I was going to say," Betsy replied calmly. "I don't blame you for that—I'm grateful. But just before she died it seemed to me that her whole miserable life rose up from her body and went whirling around the room, and I saw it for the first time. All those rotten years with you and

Grandma, all the lies and secrets, and that sick meanness she had to grow up with, when she had to take the brunt of all the rage and misery Grandma had stored up because of you and your crummy little affair—"

"Betsy!"

"And then she gave up any chance for a life of her own—she did the good-daughterly thing and came back home. What else did she know how to do? She was like some Victorian maiden aunt, with all the life squeezed out of her by—by corsets and convention and all the comforts—"

"*You—are—exaggerating!*" her grandfather said, with an attempt at thundering, but his face was bloodless.

Betsy laughed shakily. "You say that word as if it's a sin—the way Grandma would have said 'fornicating'! Of course I'm exaggerating. It's time I exaggerated—time someone did something that's not hopelessly genteel."

"You took care of that already—about nine months ago," he said, turning again to go down the steps.

"*You* can say that—*you*! After knocking up a seventeen-year-old girl and refusing to take the consequences."

"That's none of your business."

"It *is* my business. I'm the product of this family—I'm the end result of the lies and evasions, all the smiles that have been smiled in this family to cover up the awful truth. All except Grandma. *She* never smiled, and she was absolutely right!"

She let the words pour out though she could see how they wounded him, though his face was unhealthily white and waxy-looking, though some of the words almost strangled her with their violence.

"I'm not used to talking like this, Grandpa, but I have a little more to say." She took his coat sleeve. "I never understood Grandma. I always thought she was the mad beast you let everyone assume she was, but I've got to admire her. She may not have told the truth either, but at least she didn't pretend the lies were pleasant. Poor Grandma, all she loved was the church and the television and the stove—and why not? They never let her down, they never deserted her. God, when I think of the waste of her life, and my mother's—"

Marion had gotten out of the car and was coming up the steps, holding her coat around her. "Frank, it's freezing out here, and whatever you two are talking about can wait." Her voice was shrill: she had heard.

"I don't think it can!" said Betsy, realizing she had become loud and angry but unable to tone down. Her teeth were chattering, with frustration as much as cold.

"The Brodskys will hear you," Marion hissed, coming over to her. "You'd better get up to bed. Your condition is making you hysterical, and you're upsetting your grandfather."

"Listen to her," Betsy said with conscious rudeness. "Listen to the bohemian—the free spirit."

"Don't speak to your aunt that way," Frank said. "I don't care what you say to me, Betsy. I know you're all wrought up. But—"

"Oh, stop it!" she cried. "Stop *doing* it!" She fumbled in her bag for her door key, found it, and turned to go in. "Listen," she said more quietly. "Why don't you go down to Florida or someplace, Grandpa? Take a vacation—take Aunt Marion. But go away and leave me alone, let me have my baby in peace."

Marion had her arm through Frank's, and she said, "*I* think that's an excellent idea, Frank, as a matter of fact."

"No," he interrupted, "I'm not going to desert her at a time like this. She's upset, God knows we're all upset, we have a right to be, but we'll stick together." He put out his hand and touched Betsy's arm. "You get some sleep, Betsy. You'll feel differently about all this in the morning."

She took a deep breath. "I will not feel any differently, Grandpa." She meant to go on, but he was already on his way down the steps, with Marion on his arm. Betsy went inside and slammed the door as hard as she could.

Her apartment was warm, and got warmer as she drew a bath. The Brodskys had pushed the thermostat up high for her return, hanging the expense for the sake of perpetuating the race.

She took the hot bath she'd been looking forward to all day and lay in the water a long time. She put her grandfather from her mind. Deliberately, she thought of nothing, registering the baby's kicks and admiring her big pink belly with its flattened-out navel. She had just dried off and was in her nightgown and bathrobe when the doorbell rang: Judd. She had forgotten him.

She rubbed some blusher into her cheeks and ran a comb through her hair before she went to the door. It was Mr. and Mrs. Brodsky, with a covered pot and Betsy's accumulated mail.

"Betsy dear, we brought you some hot soup."

Betsy laughed weakly—with relief or with chagrin? she'd figure it out later—and took the pot. "Come in—please."

"No, no," they demurred together. They were quiet, hushed with sympathy. *Poor thing,* she saw in their sad eyes. *Such a tragedy, and in her condition.* And how much had they heard of the row on the porch?

"Go in and eat the soup," Mrs. Brodsky said gently. "Think of the baby."

"Oh, I do," Betsy assured her. "All the time."

"Good. Good. Life goes on. Anything you need, just ask."

When they were gone, she looked quickly at herself in the mirror again. It hadn't been Judd at the door, but it could have been. Her hot cheeks were flaming, from the expectation as well as the blusher, and she rubbed at them until the makeup came off. What did a bit of makeup matter? She was nine months pregnant, more or less. There were blue circles under her eyes from lack of sleep. Her fingers and legs were swollen. Her heavy hair was held back in clumps with bobby pins because she was too tired to fuss with it. And the only clothes that fit her comfortably were a pair of maternity slacks, a huge, pocketed calico blouse with a dingy white collar, and the robe and nightgown she was wearing. She made a face of despair at her mirror image, then she smiled at it. She felt unreasonably happy.

There were sympathy cards in the mail, and a postcard from Caroline DeVoto, back from Paris. She was in New York and hoped to see Betsy soon. Betsy was pleased; it was what she had needed badly all along: a friend. She sat down to her dinner. The sound of the Brodskys' television, which used to annoy her, was soothing, and so was the soup. It was hot and delicious, with rice and beans in it, and it reminded her of Violet.

With an effort, she stayed up for another hour, sipping sherry. She got out her Boswell and tried to take notes, but she couldn't keep her mind on Boswell's world. Complex though he made his life in certain areas, there was a simple inevitability about it that held her off, and she kept closing the book and roaming around her apartment. She felt restless, ready for anything.

Judd didn't come, though she continued to expect him—the ring at the door, and the snow glistening on his cloak, and his arms around her. Finally, she went to bed, strangely unperturbed, her confidence unshaken and her feelings still a bewilderment. She slept heavily, and woke only once in the night, thinking, "My mother is dead," and cried herself back to sleep.

He didn't come the next day, either. The doorbell rang once: a deliveryman with a package for her. Inside was a huge and expensive teddy bear. Irrationally, she thought of Judd again, until she saw the card. It was a gift from her grandfather, a token of peace. She knew she should call him and thank him, but she put it off. The call could only lead to the reestablishment of all the old lies. She knew it was entirely possible for her grandfather, and her great-aunt, too, to proceed as if nothing had happened, nothing been said. She knew, in fact, that this was exactly how things would go. She marveled at the durability of their protective insulation—until she reflected that she'd worn it herself, all these years. It was the family armor.

Betsy smiled at the bear and herself. Judd, indeed. Teddy bears were not his line. What was? She tried to focus on him; she was unable to. Her mind wandered when she tried to pin him down. Alien though Boswell had become to her, the eighteenth-century gentleman chronicler, with his peruke and his brougham, was more immediate to her than Judd.

In the evening, Crawford Divine called up. "I wondered if I might just pop over for a drink. I have a piece or two of news."

Betsy said she would be glad to see him. He had been at the funeral, and she was grateful. It would be nice to have company, even Crawford, so long as he didn't propose again. She didn't think he would, after being drowned in her floods of tears last time, but his chuckly voice made her apprehensive. The darnedest things amused Crawford.

She was setting out glasses and the sherry decanter when he rang the bell loud and long and then bounded up the stairs as if he couldn't wait. But when they were seated across from each other, sipping, and he had expressed his condolences, he was silent, looking appreciatively around the room as he had last time. Judd had met Crawford once and said he looked like Arthur Godfrey crossed with a toad—something in the wide mouth, the pouchy cheeks overlaid with freckles. He kept his eyes averted from her middle, blinking at the bookcases.

"What's your news, Crawford?" Betsy asked, and then, fearing she sounded abrupt, as if it was gossip she wanted and not his company, she appended, "How's everything going this semester?"

"All right. Feels good to be out of it, I suppose," he said, gazing at a lamp and then at her.

"Yes," she said, though she suspected it wouldn't be true

much longer, and she would begin to miss the bustle of classes and meetings. The forgotten fear that her job was in jeopardy came back to her. She was being fired. That was the source of Crawford's nameless glee: revenge.

"You look like a rabbit at bay," said Crawford. "Are you all right? Or has everything got you down?"

"I'm okay. I'm still worried about my status at school." He looked puzzled. "My job," she said. "That I might not have one to go back to in the fall. After the fuss last semester."

"Who put that flea in your ear? You mean you actually feared that you'd get canned for having a baby?"

"Crawford, it was you who said—"

"Bosh!" He dismissed the whole thing.

"And John Alderman is after all my best courses—"

"My dear," Crawford said with the air of a man about to say something quotable, "John Alderman could go after your courses with the Third Armored Division and he wouldn't get them." He guffawed and even slapped his plump knee. "Sweet Jesus, were you honestly worried about that? Don't you know you're a catch?" He had a funny, wheezy laugh, usually repressed in favor of amused archness. "In fact," he went on when it subsided, "one of my bits of news is that your students miss you—and vocally. Hordes of them have come down like a wolf on the fold to communicate to me their outrage. They don't want John, you see—they want you." He lit a cigarette and threw the match on the floor, then picked it up with a shamefaced smile, and sat holding it. "Actually, one of the reasons I called was that Rachel Grace telephoned me. She couldn't get in touch with you and was worried—afraid you'd—" He grimaced. "Who knows? What are the suicidal fancies of the young? Afraid you'd overdosed on some bizarre chemical? Put your head in the oven à la Sylvia P.? Jumped into the river with a pocket full of rocks like you-know-who? That sort of thing. But I see you're well?" He ended on a note of inquiry, stroking his little moustache.

"Yes, I'm well. Suicide is one alternative I never think of."

"Hmm," he said, stroking. "An interesting case. Have you seen anyone about this?" His eyes twinkled benignly, impersonally, as if he had never laid his heart at her feet. It occurred to Betsy that he might not remember having done so.

Betsy propped her hands on her belly, which felt tender and bruised. It seemed to have dropped, it was a heavy load of fruit in a sling, pulling her down. Perfectly natural, the doctor had said last time, the baby is getting into position. How clever of it, like a racing-car driver at the starting gate. . . .

"I suppose you've heard about the Blakes?" Crawford asked.

"I haven't heard about anything. I haven't seen a soul in weeks."

"Well, they're splitting up. Roger and Karen."

"Oh, *no*!" It was all wrong—the warm and welcoming house, the parties, the kids, all for nothing. "That's terrible, Crawford. It's crazy!" She remembered kissing Roger and put her hand to her lips.

"Apparently, it's been coming on for years." Crawford shrugged.

"Oh, but it's such a damned shame!" Betsy felt close to tears; there was a dreary predictability to the breakup that depressed her utterly.

"Roger says he's had it up to here," said Crawford. "Wherever that is. Of course, that's just what Roger *would* say—always ready with the inexpressive cliché. I'd like to hear Karen on the subject, personally. But she's gone to her parents in Detroit. With the kids, I understand."

"Oh God."

"He does indeed move in mysterious ways, his wonders to perform." Crawford paused and checked out the bookcases again. "Now for the rest of my news." He halted, smirking. The pause was meant to tantalize; clearly, this was something bigger than the Blakes' separation or distraught and devoted students.

"Tell me, Crawford," she said, with apprehension.

"Well—" He took another cigarette. "I—" He lit it, puffing through smiles. "—am getting married," he finished, shaking out the match and beaming at her.

"Crawford!" She felt huge relief. His words were a happy counterpoint to his other news. Part of her relief was a form of deliverance, that a man she'd rejected had been taken in hand by another woman. "That's wonderful!" She spoke from her soul.

"I'm quite thrilled," he said, dropping the burnt match on the floor this time and leaving it there, oblivious to earthly concerns. He looked dreamily toward the window. "Her name is Deanna, she's a little younger than I am, and after we're married she's going back to school for her Master's, possibly in library science." He cleared his throat. "At the moment, she's working as a cocktail waitress, which is how I met her. Down at the Holiday Inn." He looked fixedly at the window as if he could see her there, carrying drinks on a tray. "She's divorced, and she has a small son to support." He let his gaze wander slowly back to Betsy. "She's also a published poet," he said with solemn joy. "She's working on a very innovative sonnet sequence. Her son's name is Darius, age four. My children are enchanted with him, and with Deanna. She's very beautiful. She'll make me a good wife."

He had finished, and showed it by picking up his glass and settling back, sighing. Betsy said, "It's wonderful, Crawford—wonderful. I hope you'll be happy. You deserve to be." She searched for something else. "She sounds great."

Crawford smoked peacefully. He looked as if he might stay there a long time, musing happily on his future wife. "The wedding will be soon—in March—and we'll be going to Greece on the spring break. Deanna has always wanted to visit Greece." It was a noble virtue, wanting to visit Greece. "Deanna also paints and has an uncommon flair for seascapes. She's eager to do some work there."

"I hope I'll get to meet her soon. She sounds remarkable."

"That's just what she is," Crawford said approvingly. "A remarkable woman."

He stayed for three glasses of sherry and then, suddenly agitated, left to pick Deanna up at work, checking his watch several times at the door. "I have a feeling this will create as much sensation, in its way, as your event," he said. "Don't think I'm too bemused to be aware that there's something shocking—something downright spicy—about someone like me marrying a cocktail waitress. But no matter what anyone says, I'm very happy, Betsy." She saw that he was; his eyes were glazed with happiness. He rushed out, with another look at his watch.

Betsy drank another glass of wine. She refused to think about the Blakes—the Blakes wouldn't bear thinking about. She cradled her belly and hummed tunelessly, looking around the room. She would have to buy a new coffee table, something with harmless blunt corners, and she meditated on this peacefully, blankly.

She sat drinking wine and waiting, and she realized that she was no longer waiting for Judd's ring at the door but for a good, hard pain. It was the baby's birth she longed for. Everything was ready—a sheet on the crib, the diaper service on the alert, books on their shelves with her grandfather's stuffed bear, and the driver at the wheel, ready to take off. She went to bed and slept fitfully, hoping all night for the start of the race—for nothing else but that.

Her grandfather called the next morning, asking facetiously if she was feeling better.

"I feel fine," she said. "Thanks for the bear."

He chuckled. "Reminded me of you—ferocious." Oh God, she thought: big joke. He went right on. "You know, I just might take you up on your suggestion and go south for a month."

It was, in fact, all settled. He had rented a condominium on the east coast of Florida and he was leaving in two days.

"I was lucky to get it. I had to have Ed pull a few strings for me. Oh—" He hesitated. "I thought Marion might as well go down there with me. She could use a vacation. She had that bronchial thing last winter, it'll do her good to get away. If you really think you can get along without us."

"It'll do us all good," Betsy commented.

"Well—I have to agree," her grandfather said unexpectedly. "It might be best for you and me to get away from each other. I know you're mad as hell at me, Betsy—I'm still not sure why, but maybe you've had too much family lately."

It was as close as he'd get to any kind of concession, but for Frank the words were remarkable, and Betsy felt a rush of love for him.

The delivery of the bear was followed by an elaborate English pram, which he carted over himself and set up for her, showing off all its tricks and conveniences, and wheeling it back and forth in her tiny hall, where the Blakes' battered old carriage sat.

"Now you can get rid of that thing," he remarked, giving it a delicate kick: only the best for his great-grandchild.

Emily called her, too, with inquiries about her condition. "I want to be *in on* this, Betsy," she said. "I want this baby to be *my* great-grandchild, too!" It was the only reference she made, even obliquely, to Frank.

"He's come around," Betsy felt impelled to say. "He's being very, very nice about the baby now. You did him a lot of good, Emily."

Over the phone, she heard Emily set her teacup down with a clank. "Well, that's something!" Her voice was pleased and gratified, even amused, but that was all she said, and she changed the subject quickly.

Two weeks after the Great Blizzard, the weather turned unexpectedly springlike, and snow dripped off the roof and down the windows. Betsy began taking a walk each day. She walked up Westcott Street to the supermarket, and to the university to check her mailbox. When Mrs. Brodsky told her about nipple shields (she had taken to sharing Pregnancy Club gossip with her landlady), she walked all the way to a drugstore on Genesee Street to get some.

She even went on foot down University Avenue for her weekly trip to the obstetrician—hoping all the walking would speed things up. She was officially overdue, though Dr. Levine assured her that everything was fine, everything was perfectly normal.

"I think you'd tell me that if I was pregnant with an alligator!" she said in exasperation.

He stripped off his rubber glove and smiled at her. That was normal, too: overwrought, overdue women.

Betsy walked slowly home, longing for her child—for the company the child would be. She was lonely. Her life seemed empty without her mother, without her grandfather—most of all without her students, she was beginning to realize. She did miss teaching, as she knew she eventually would: the daily bouncing off of ideas, the purposeful reading, the academic politics—even her grungy, cluttered office with its stained coffee mug and all her favorite books. Crawford had told her, in passing, about the proposed renovation of the Hall of Languages. She felt left out; she wanted to be in on the bitching and grousing at the inconvenience.

But she was not unhappy. Expectation filled her, and she was proud of her patience. If she could wait this out without going crazy, she could put up with anything in the future. Pregnancy was a better discipline than studying for language exams.

When Judd did, finally, ring her doorbell, she had ceased to expect him. She thought it might be Caroline at the door;

Betsy had invited her for dinner. But it was still light when the bell rang, and it was Judd.

He wasn't wearing the cape: that was her first thought. He had a new jacket—brown leather lined with sheepskin. He threw it on a chair back, and she picked it up and hung it in the closet—like old times.

"I'm sorry about your mother," he said, sitting down.

She sat beside him on the sofa, but at a distance. He looked different—was his hair longer?—and then he looked just the same, so familiar she could, just looking at him, remember precisely the feel of his rough cheek on hers.

"I appreciate your going to the funeral, Judd."

"Well, I liked her." Silence. The baby gave a kick. "How's your grandfather?"

"He's taking it pretty well." Betsy smiled. "He's gone to Florida with my Aunt Marion."

"Oh, *really?*" he asked, raising his eyebrows and inclining his head—a gesture she remembered with affection—and they both laughed.

It seemed to release some constraint in him. He moved closer to her and began to talk. He never used to talk much; now his face contorted with the necessity of it, and the words poured out. His work had suffered since they split up, he had found himself getting sick a lot, a series of colds, then flu, he thought he might be getting an ulcer. . . .

"You aren't very good at living alone, are you?" She meant it as a mild joke—knowing as she did that he probably hadn't been alone much—but he regarded her soberly.

"No, I'm not."

When she said no more—merely sat, staring down at the books on the coffee table—he continued. He had missed her so much, they had had something so good going. . . .

He said nothing about Joan Arletta, and Betsy didn't either, afraid he'd tell her some shabby lie. And he didn't mention the baby; it was as if the huge belly under the maternity top didn't exist. More sham! More evasion! She had tricked him—yes. But all the cards were his, nevertheless.

She understood fully what she had dimly sensed last spring: that between them there would never be anything but the narrowest, shakiest bridge—one that would not hold her new weight.

His feverish words ran on, and it became almost visible to her as he talked—the bridge like a spider web, so vivid that she moved her hand, to destroy the fragile thing. He caught her hand and held it tight, and at his touch her detachment almost deserted her. He rubbed her hand slowly between both of his; she was ashamed of her swollen fingers, and of the small flame of desire he was bringing to life. "I'm never unhappy and never happy, but I don't want it back," Emily had said. But I do, Betsy thought—a loud, insistent thought. I *do* want it back.

She knew, though, that if the shaky bridge held, it would be only because she put her back under it, gave all her strength to its preservation. She would be the waiter, the watcher, would spend all her life—or however long he gave her—spying out his moods and shaping herself to them. And then what? Emily in her lonely house, Marion perpetually rouging her cheeks—and her mother, with her gentle, out-of-it, accepting smile.

"I want us to get back together, Betsy."

"How? How together?"

He smiled briefly. "This time, let's be honest with each other," he said, looking at her straight. She took the words, meekly, as a rebuke, and nodded. "I'm still not the marrying kind," he went on. "I still don't mean that. Not yet, anyway."

"Have you noticed I'm going to have a baby any minute?"

He looked down at her stomach, then at their linked hands. "We can work things out," he said vaguely. "I just want you in my life—somehow. If you don't feel the same way—" He raised his pale eyes to her face. "Then I guess I'll go back to

Texas. For a while, anyway. There's nothing keeping me here but you."

"Back to Texas? To do what?"

"There's a lot more I want to photograph." The glitter of excitement in the pale eyes was brief, but it made Betsy wonder. Would he really give it up for me? or does he know I'll refuse him? There was no telling; there never was, with him. There was just the impetuous outstretched hand followed by the turning of the Lincoln profile toward the future. And, for her, the old, silent struggle, the familiar headaches, the tears ready to slop over.

"You go back to Texas, Judd," she said unsteadily, and then didn't know how to take it when he bent his head over her palm and kissed it. Was it gratitude? anguish? remorse?

"I'm glad we saw each other again," she said, and when he let her hand go she stood up and got his jacket from the closet.

When he was gone, she wandered into the baby's room. The last bit of sun lit a patch on the rug; Betsy stood in it, and it warmed her bare feet. She stretched out her hand and moved a toy train, idly, back and forth on the shelf.

Ah, what will become of us? she asked the imaginary baby. But of course the baby didn't answer. She was closing her eyes, nodding off, her tiny pink fingers clenching and unclenching, a dribble of milk down her chin. In her mental picture, Betsy wiped the milk away, knowing herself to be rescued by such acts.

And, in fact, in years to come, when life was easier, there were times when Betsy would look on her daughter as her saving grace, as if it really were that simple.

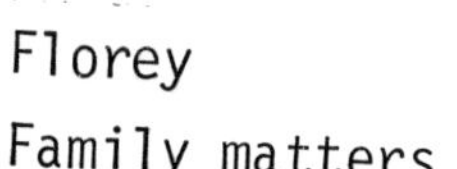

Florey

Family matters